COMET HALLEY

COMET HALLEY

a novel in two parts by

FRED HOYLE

ST MARTINS PRESS – NEW YORK

To Geoffrey and Evelyn Jackson

PART ONE

First Contact

Chapter 1

Frances Margaret Haroldsen parked her bicycle in a rack outside the new Cavendish and walked with quick athletic steps towards the main door of the Laboratory. A physicist in her mid-twenties with a junior position as demonstrator, she was the sort of girl men look at once, twice, and then go on looking at.

Her office was along one of the downstairs corridors, an interior corridor that was dark because it was Saturday afternoon and only a minimum of artificial lighting was switched on. Why was it, she wondered, that buildings which seem quite normal when they are fully occupied on weekdays seem all passages and spaces when they are empty at weekends? It was a Saturday afternoon in late October, one of those unforgettable Cambridge afternoons with a cloudless sky that make you feel there should be a smell of wood-smoke over the whole town. The undergraduates were 'up' for a brand new academic year, undergraduates young enough to feel the whole world opening out before them. It was an afternoon with sounds travelling in the crisp air, so that even as far away as the Cavendish Laboratory you could hear sporadic roars from the large crowd assembled at the University rugby ground in Grange Road.

Frances Margaret had not quite reached her office when there was the bang of a violently slammed door from farther along the corridor. A slim man about six feet tall erupted from another of the offices. From the silhouette appearing darkly in the ill-lit corridor, Frances Margaret recognised the man, Mike Howarth, also a junior member of the Laboratory staff.

'Hello, Mike, anything the matter?' the girl called as the figure approached.

'This,' Howarth replied tersely, holding out an envelope which he pulled angrily from an inner pocket of a fur-lined jacket.

Once they were inside Frances Margaret's office, it could be seen that the envelope bore the crest and initials of the large Government-operated research council CERC. Howarth put a case he had been carrying on a chair while the girl read the letter.

'They've cancelled my contract,' Howarth burst out.

'So I see. It's a pity,' Frances Margaret replied with a sympathetic nod.

'It's more than a pity. It's a disaster.'

'I'd say it's pretty appalling, Mike, but I wouldn't think of it as a disaster. CERC hasn't stuck you with a knife or bashed you over the head with a crowbar.'

'Oh, haven't they though!' Howarth exclaimed.

'We'll have to think what to do,' Frances Margaret offered, as helpfully as she could. 'The trouble is that people are likely to say you were on a risky course.'

'How else could I have got the results?'

'That's why it isn't a complete disaster,' Frances Margaret continued, again as encouragingly as she could. 'You have some results. CERC can't cancel what you've got already.'

'I've enough to convince myself. Enough to convince you and perhaps a few others. But not enough to come out into the open about it. I had to get more signals from Comet Halley. Otherwise people will just laugh. You can hear them laughing, can't you?'

'We can appeal against the decision.'

'Some hope. You know that.'

Frances Margaret sighed and then nodded.

'It would help if we had a Professor who could throw his weight around a bit.'

'They've been fiddling around with the job for a year now,' grunted Howarth as he retrieved the letter and slipped it back into his jacket pocket. 'Imagine it, fiddling around with the Cavendish Professorship. God knows what we're coming to. But I'm going to fight it. Somehow.'

'The question we have to think about is *how*.'

'God knows about that, too. The thing's moribund. Have you ever thought of getting out, Frances Margaret?'

'I keep turning it over in my mind. I thought of applying for a job at CERN.'

Howarth retrieved his case as he prepared to leave, saying, 'Particle physics. That's more your line than mine.'

Signals from comets, Frances Margaret reflected as the office door closed. Preposterous. And yet there was something distinctly curious in Mike Howarth's data, sketchy as it might be. Besides which, there were one or two curious points she'd noticed herself. She'd intended to tell Mike about them, but he'd been so turned-in on himself that she'd thought it best to wait until after the weekend. Then, on a sudden impulse, Frances Margaret decided that letting Mike go off without telling him what she'd discovered wasn't right. Deciding she should call him back, Frances Margaret dashed out of the office into the corridor.

There had been enough time for Mike Howarth almost to reach the outer doors of the Laboratory. As she hurried along the corridor Frances Margaret noticed a diffused light appearing from around the corner which led to the main lobby. With the thought that Mike might have switched on the lights in the lobby, she continued quickly. But the light wasn't right: it was too red in colour to be the fluorescent lighting used in the Laboratory. The light was brighter as she turned the corner, but by the time she reached the main lobby it was suddenly gone, and so was Mike Howarth. A quick check showed that the fluorescent circuit had not been switched on.

Frances Margaret retrieved her bicycle and rode slowly along the lane which leads from the new Cavendish Laboratory to Madingley Road. She tried to persuade herself that the business of the light really hadn't been as scary as it had seemed. She'd forced herself to return along the corridor to her office. After collecting a file of papers, she'd then quit the deserted Laboratory in short order, if not literally at a run. As events unfolded, Frances Margaret came to believe that she understood what the light had been; for she was to see it again.

Chapter 2

Two days later, on the Monday morning, it was just on 10.00 a.m. when a car bearing diplomatic number plates drew up outside the main gate of CERN, the Conseil Européen pour la Recherche Nucléaire on the outskirts of Geneva, Switzerland. A man of Pickwickian appearance with an alarmingly high colour showed papers to a guard at the gate, and the car was then waved on into the CERN complex.

An hour before, two men had met in an office in the administrative block of CERN. Both were in their middle thirties and both were physicists, the one from Hamburg, West Germany, the other from Cambridge, England – although from a slight accent it was clear that the Englishman, who was noticeably tall, must have had his origins not in East Anglia but in the south-west. He and the German were examining bubble-chamber photographs strewn across a long table.

'Well, Kurt,' the Englishman remarked at last with a quizzical expression, 'it certainly *looks* like top quark. At last.'

The German had a broad forehead and a quiff of hair that tended to stand up, causing him to push it back into place from time to time, which he did now.

'*Ja*, it *acts* like top quark. Pettini wants to publish.'

'Pettini is an impetuous Italian.'

A slow smile appeared on the German's face.

'It wouldn't be good to tell him that, I think.'

'And it wouldn't be good to publish and then find we're wrong.'

'There is pressure from the Italian Government.'

'There's always pressure. In my thirteen years here at CERN I've never known a time when there wasn't pressure. I'm getting plenty myself. The British Government would love to save all the millions we're spending on top quark.'

Once again the German brushed back the quiff of hair.

'It won't seem so good if the Americans claim it first.'

The Englishman nodded.

'I'm aware of that. As much as Pettini is aware of it.'

'So, Isaac, what do we do?'

'We consult our conscience, Kurt.'

'I'd be glad to learn how to do that.'

'Are you convinced yourself? About this really being top quark. Are you *really* convinced?'

Kurt Waldheim shuffled uneasily among the photographs. He picked up one of them and studied it for a while. At last he shook his head regretfully.

'I *think* it is, but I am not certain.'

'You'd like another run at it?'

'*Ja*, I'd like another run. But you will have Pettini speaking very loudly down your neck, I'm afraid.'

'It won't be the only thing I've got down my neck just now.'

Kurt Waldheim moved away from the table, dismissing the photographs from his mind.

'*Ja*, I've thought for a little while that you have a worried look, Isaac. Is it anything I should know?'

'Cambridge has asked me to take the Cavendish Professorship.'

Kurt Waldheim pondered this news and then shrugged expressively.

'Well? It would be a very distinguished appointment – and a return home for you. Sometimes it is nice to return home.'

'We always try to remember the Cavendish the way it was in Rutherford's day. Unfortunately this isn't Rutherford's day.'

'You could make much of it, Isaac.'

The Englishman shook his head doubtfully.

'If big money hadn't ruined things, perhaps. You don't know the way it is with the British research councils, I'm afraid.'

'I know it from Germany, I think.'

'I doubt that Germany is quite as bad.'

The slow smile appeared again on Waldheim's face.

'It's like somebody else's canteen,' he said. 'The food always seems better than in your own canteen.'

'The problem is that if I refuse it certainly won't help the British grant to CERN.'

'I see it is a problem. But I thought there might be something else.'

'Something else?'

Kurt Waldheim persisted.

'Yes, I thought there might be.'

There was a long pause before the Englishman replied.

'We've known each other for a long time, Kurt. If I were to talk to anybody it would be to you.'

'Can I help?'

'It's a confidential thing, I'm afraid. Hopefully, it won't last. Then I'll be able to concentrate on top quark again.'

'Which will be good for top quark, I think.'

The Englishman returned somewhat wearily from the table with its bubble-chamber photographs to his desk, saying, 'Break the news gently to Pettini.'

When Kurt Waldheim had left the office, the tall man walked to a window from which he could see snow-covered mountains across the Swiss-French border. He was lost in thought when a secretary came in with the announcement:

'Your visitor has arrived, Dr Newton.' She pronounced his name New*ton* in the French manner.

The man with the florid face and Pickwickian stature followed immediately behind the secretary. He came forward effusively with outstretched hand.

'Dr Newton, I'm John Jamesborough – Foreign Office.'

'I had your message.'

'Yes, well, I thought we should make contact.'

'Why, if I may ask?'

'I'm under instructions to offer you any assistance you may need.'

Isaac Newton had no liking for the direction in which he suspected the conversation was leading.

'Frankly, I wasn't looking for any assistance. You see, Mr Jamesborough, I've lived for thirteen years in Geneva, so I know my way around the town reasonably well by now.'

'We weren't thinking about that, of course.'

'It might help if I knew what you *were* thinking about.'

'Your report, Dr Newton. About conveying it to the Prime Minister.'

'It isn't ready yet.'

'When it is, the report should go through the diplomatic bag. From the moment you set words on paper, Dr Newton, those words will have a high security status. Obviously.'

A wry expression flitted briefly across Isaac Newton's face.

'Obviously,' he acknowledged.

'Many people will be curious about them.'

'Including the Foreign Office, no doubt.'

'I would hope, Dr Newton, you will copy your report to us – as a matter of courtesy, obviously.'

It was an advantage of Jamesborough's very high colour that you couldn't tell if he blushed as he made this request. The wry expression returned as Isaac Newton replied immediately:

'I can set your mind firmly at rest there, Mr Jamesborough. My remit is to report directly to the Prime Minister. Whether the Prime Minister decides to copy the report to you is not for me to decide.'

'The situation is *very* irregular.'

The conversation was evidently leading nowhere, with Isaac Newton finding it increasingly difficult to hide his mounting irritation at being asked to divulge what, honourably, he could not divulge.

'The trouble, Mr Jamesborough,' he began in some distaste, 'is that nuclear warheads are also *very* irregular. I'm sorry if this sounds inhospitable, but nuclear warheads aren't very hospitable either. My promise to the Prime Minister requires me to attend today's session – for my sins.'

'Is anything special expected?'

'I trust not. If anything special ever happened at disarmament talks we'd have people in shock all over the place.'

'That's rather cynical, isn't it?' Jamesborough asked with a disapproving frown, seeking to gain a small point. Disregarding the frown, Isaac Newton glanced at his watch to indicate that he was required elsewhere.

'You may count yourself lucky, Mr Jamesborough, that you haven't had to listen to these superpower talks for weeks on end the way I have. Otherwise the worm of cynicism would long ago have hatched itself inside your bosom.'

It had been on the tip of Isaac Newton's tongue to say 'ample bosom', but somehow he managed to bite back the temptation.

'Can I give you a lift into town?' Jamesborough asked.

'Thanks, but I go, I come back, as they say. I'd prefer my own car, if you don't mind.'

Realising that nothing substantial could be won, Jamesborough moved towards the office door, saying as a last small manoeuvre, 'You will remember the security aspect? If anything came out it would be exceedingly embarrassing.'

The wry expression flitted once more across Isaac Newton's face.

'Yes,' he nodded. 'You have my solemn word. I'll remember security. I rarely forget it.'

Isaac Newton parked his car, a large Mercedes, and walked into the Geneva disarmament centre, which had a record for nil results dating from the pre-1939 days of the League of Nations. After showing his badge and identification card he was conducted to the conference hall by a girl of more pleasant aspect than the place itself. As Isaac Newton took his seat in an area reserved for diplomatically-accredited observers, the delegates of the superpowers came to order, facing each other in rows – like two ancient armies of the classical age, except that each delegate had a name placard, which courtesy had not been accorded to ancient fighters in their long-since-forgotten causes.

A senior Russian delegate began speaking and, as a formal gesture, the Americans put on headphones, ostensibly to hear an immediate translation of the Russian, but actually to daydream. Without enthusiasm Isaac Newton also put on headphones. His remit was to make a report, technical and otherwise, on how the British nuclear deterrent related to the talks. Although this was a matter on which the Russians made trouble whenever it suited their purpose to do so, it lay strictly outside the immediate proceedings, and this had permitted the Prime Minister to ask for a technical report rather than a diplomatic one. The Foreign Office had no liking for this procedure, especially with the report coming from an outsider like himself, instead of from an insider who could be relied upon not to disturb the status quo.

After the Russian had been speaking for an hour and a quarter, Isaac Newton decided that enough was enough – he could always read the translation, which he would have to do anyway, just as the Americans did. By now he knew his way out of the building more or less like the proverbial back of his hand. He had moved quietly from the conference hall and was just on the point of punching a lift button when a man he half-recognised stepped into the cage beside him. The half-recognised man had not used headphones back there in the conference hall, so that it was apparent he belonged to the 'other side'.

'Is a breakthrough near?' Isaac Newton asked as the lift moved.

'A breakthrough is always near,' the man replied.

'It must keep you busy.'

'In Russia we are always busy.'

'I imagine it makes for a happy life,' Isaac Newton continued, doing his best.

'A very happy life,' was the gutteral response.

The lift stopped and both men got out. Isaac Newton nodded, smiled, and said:

'Well, I'm glad to have met you, sir. It's always nice to meet cheerful people.'

Somehow this little conversation epitomised the situation. Whatever technicalities he decided to report to the Prime Minister, Isaac Newton was convinced of the broad proposition that little positive would happen on the superpower front without some drastically new approach being made. It would have astonished him to have learned how close such an approach might be, and how deeply he would be involved in it himself.

Chapter 3

Two months later, Isaac Newton travelled from Geneva to London by an early morning flight. Because he was tall and had a long stride he outdistanced other passengers to the immigration desk, and so was first into the Heathrow customs area. He'd brought no baggage beyond a briefcase, which he'd carried with him on the plane, so he walked immediately towards the 'Nothing to Declare' exit. Here, however, he was stopped by a zealous customs officer who viewed fast-moving passengers with suspicion.

'Are you resident in this country, sir?' the man asked.

'No, in Switzerland.'

'Would you open your briefcase, please?'

Isaac Newton complied and explained:

'Business papers.'

The official ran his hands around the interior of the briefcase, obviously on the lookout for drugs, and missed Isaac Newton's report, the report which the Foreign Office would have been so glad to get its hands on. The official eventually stepped back from his bench with a nod. Walking quickly to the taxi rank, Isaac Newton disregarded the advice of Sherlock Holmes always to take the third taxi, and took the first instead.

'Where to, sir?' the driver asked.

'10 Downing Street.'

When the taxi driver reached the heavy traffic of central London, Isaac Newton found himself watching the manoeuvrings of nearby cars, at first idly and then with some attention. There was the usual sprinkling of people waiting outside 10 Downing Street. Waiting for what? For the skies to fall in, presumably. There was a man with a walkie-talkie radio set who suddenly moved away into Whitehall. Media personnel? Perhaps, perhaps not.

The policeman on duty outside Number 10 had been told to expect him and Isaac Newton was quickly admitted into the Prime Minister's residence, where he was greeted by a slim young man with lank fair hair.

'I'm Pingo Warwick, the PM's PPS. The PM's waiting.'

'I'm sorry I'm a bit late. The traffic was heavy. I suppose I should have stayed in London overnight,' Isaac Newton apologised, shaking hands with Pingo Warwick.

'That's all right. Before I show you up I should mention about lunch. There's a delegation from Qatar, but you're welcome to stay...'

'I'd like to catch the afternoon flight back to Geneva.'

Pingo Warwick nodded.

'From your message that's rather what I thought.' Then he led the way upstairs to the Prime Minister's home office.

'You had a good journey?' the Prime Minister asked as a formality.

'Except for a customs chap who almost impounded my briefcase.'

'Didn't you use your diplomatic passport?'

'I kept it in reserve. You have the papers, Prime Minister?'

'No. Should I?'

'They were sent in the diplomatic bag.'

'When?'

'Two days ago. Which isn't a long time I suppose, the way Whitehall sees time.'

This remark almost succeeded in its aim of provoking an explosion from the Prime Minister.

'Not a long time!'

The voice was sharp. Affecting not to notice, Isaac Newton held out a slim blue file.

'I've prepared a short summary of my main report. You can skim through it in a few moments. My taxi from Heathrow was followed, by the way.'

'Are you sure?' the Prime Minister asked with raised eyebrows.

'I've grown pretty watchful these past three months. I had the idea, Prime Minister, that quite a lot of people would have been happy to stop these papers from reaching you.'

'Then perhaps I'd better get on and read them,' the Prime Minister said, opening the file energetically, an edge still in the voice.

John Jamesborough was not enjoying his meeting with Sir Arthur, partly because there was a feeling in the air that he'd bungled the job, and partly because he hated having the riot act read to him in front of Smithfield. In contrast to Jamesborough's own high colouring, Smithfield always had a drained look about him, drained like the meat carcasses in the market of his name.

An imaginary observer would have noticed that the document in a blue file lying on a polished mahogany table in front of Sir Arthur was identical to the one which had just been handed to the Prime Minister. As a non-imaginary observer, John Jamesborough noticed with distaste that ash from Smithfield's cigarette had tumbled onto the table. Particles of the ash were dancing on the dark smooth surface, dancing to a tune called by a draught from a large ceiling fan, which Sir Arthur, an old India man, had insisted on installing in his office in memory of former salad days.

Smithfield scanned the blue file, took a pull on his cigarette, and said in his flat way:

'Clever bastard, if you ask me. Travelled Swissair, Geneva-London, internal booking by CERN travel office, no name given. Used ordinary passport at Heathrow, not diplomatic, but was spotted because of distinctive appearance. He was among the first at the immigration desk and went straight through customs. No baggage, see? We picked him up near White City, making straight for Downing Street. He sent this blue report two days ago in the diplomatic pouch. Why would he do that if he was going to bring it over from Switzerland himself?'

'Perhaps he had afterthoughts,' Jamesborough suggested.

'Afterthoughts, my keister! He did it to find out. He'll know by now that it didn't reach the PM. And the PM will know, and all the fat in hell will be in the fire. See?'

Smithfield took another pull, blew out the smoke, and only just stopped himself from stubbing out his cigarette on the mahogany table itself. Sir Arthur, he remembered, was very proud of the mahogany table, not that there was likely to be much of Sir Arthur left once all that fat started to sizzle.

'Have you an ash-tray?' he asked belatedly.

Sir Arthur picked up the blue file.

'Yes, well, it will be easy enough to send this along, after copying it, of course.'

'Of course,' nodded Jamesborough, relieved that the meeting was coming to a close.

'Two days late! If the PM swallows that eternity then all I can say is God help the country,' Smithfield remarked, in a voice which Jamesborough had always disliked.

The Prime Minister put down the slim blue file, was silent for a moment longer, and then said:

'You put it very clearly, very decisively – just what I wanted.'

'I'd say that's rather overgenerous, Prime Minister,' Isaac Newton demurred.

'I think you hardly appreciate one of the big problems in Government. To obtain *unbiased* information, I mean.'

'I can appreciate that.'

'It's impossible, you see, to do any better than the quality of the information one receives. Will you have a sherry?'

'I believe you have a special lunch coming up.'

'Qatar. Islam. No alcohol.'

'Then a dry sherry please.'

The Prime Minister went to a small cabinet and poured out two glasses, saying, 'They have more than a quarter of all the natural gas in the world.'

'Who, Qatar?'

The Prime Minister brought the glasses.

'Amazing, isn't it. More than a quarter of all the natural gas in a tiny place like Qatar.'

'How are they going to get it out?'

'The best way would be a pipeline into the Med. Then into Europe. It would keep European industries running for a very long time, without any Eastern bloc interference – which connects quite clearly with your report, doesn't it?'

'How's that, Prime Minister?' Isaac Newton asked, sipping the sherry.

'Well, if we and the French give up our nuclear deterrents in the extremis of the superpower struggle there'll be nothing to stop all Europe from being held to blackmail. Not from the superpowers in this case, but from any little pipsqueak with a pretension to nuclear technology. Frankly, I hate pipsqueaks.'

As if a switch had been pressed, the Prime Minister suddenly rushed back to the cabinet, seized a canister and began spraying its contents into the air so liberally that Isaac Newton instinctively covered the mouth of his glass with a hand.

'Ha!' the Prime Minister almost shouted, 'A fly. I hate flies. They come in from somewhere. Horse Guards Parade, I expect. You were saying?'

'I wasn't. It was you who were saying. About Qatar.'

'Oh yes, about Qatar,' the Prime Minister acknowledged, taking the canister to the cabinet and returning with a sherry decanter. 'But to change the subject: I believe you've had what is known as an approach from Cambridge.'

'Yes, I've had an approach about the Cavendish Professorship,' Isaac Newton replied noncommittally.

'I hope you will accept.'

'Frankly, Prime Minister, I wasn't thinking of doing so.'

The Prime Minister came forward with the decanter and recharged Isaac Newton's glass, saying with a suggestion of a frown, 'A pity. Since you're being frank, can I express a frank opinion?'

'Of course.'

'I understand CERN offers the best opportunity in your field – a very expensive field . . .'

'Top quark *is* expensive, admittedly.'

'Top quark?'

'The particle everybody is looking for at the moment.'

'I see. Yes, well, your success at CERN is what we all hoped for when things were started more than thirty years ago. Even so, one has to remember that it is contributing nations like Britain which keep CERN going.'

Isaac Newton smiled a little ruefully.

'Meaning people at CERN like me should do something in return? Like accepting professorships when they're offered?'

'An investor expects some return for the capital he invests.'

Taking the bull by the horns, Isaac Newton pointed towards the slim blue file and said with a smile:

'Could I suggest that my report . . .'

'Is something of a return. You could suggest it and I would agree with you. Privately. What I can't do is acknowledge your report publicly.'

'Why not, Prime Minister?'

'Because no official channel of communication exists between us,' was the Prime Minister's unexpected reply.

'Then how are you supposed to obtain information? About anything, I mean?' Isaac Newton asked, showing his surprise.

The Prime Minister grinned without humour.

'Through the Civil Service, or through officially constituted committees of enquiry appointed with the knowledge of Parliament.'

'To be fair, I can see some sense in that.'

'Yes, it keeps out quacks and soothsayers. Of course, I'm not suggesting . . .'

Congratulating himself that the topic of the Cambridge Professorship seemed safely out of the way, Isaac Newton continued quickly:

'I understand that too. But doesn't it mean that you're subject to manipulation? I'm sorry to put it so bluntly.'

At this the Prime Minister reared up.

'Put it as bluntly as you like. I *am* subject to manipulation. Every Prime Minister is subject to manipulation. That's why the manipulators scream to high heaven when I step outside the pattern. That's why the FO is screaming about your report. In their view, it's an improper document. Why did you send it in the diplomatic pouch by the way?'

'So they wouldn't think I was coming to London myself.'

'Good heavens! You're as suspicious as I am myself. The maddening thing is that they have it so tied up that it's hard to do anything. A bit of lopping here and a bit of chopping there, but you can never go at it like a gardener, giving the whole thing a thorough pruning. So I take it out on the flies. Flies don't affect the opinion polls, not yet at any rate. But to come back to Cambridge – you wriggled away from that subject quite cleverly – I need something to justify the position at CERN. Something firm I can argue. Something like your return to Cambridge.'

Isaac Newton realised that it was now or never, that he must dig his toes in if he was not to be outmanoeuvred.

'I still feel,' he said, 'that it would be a little like paying you twice for the same article: once the report; twice the return to Cambridge.'

'Then you'd have a credit balance, wouldn't you?' the Prime Minister replied in a flash. After a moment's pause Isaac Newton continued as best he could:

'It may seem mercenary, Prime Minister, but would you care to spell that out?'

It was now the turn of the Prime Minister to pause. Whatever might have been said was interrupted by a light tap on the door, giving the Prime Minister an easy exit.

'Ah, that must be Pingo. My goodness, how time has flown. Qatar is upon us.'

The tap was repeated. When nobody entered at a call from the Prime Minister, Isaac Newton went to the door and opened it, appearing, to the Prime Minister, to stumble for a brief moment. It was indeed Pingo who was there outside. He caught Isaac Newton by the arm, and asked with anxiety in his voice:

'Is anything the matter, Dr Newton?'

'No,' Isaac Newton replied, squaring himself up. 'I think I must have stumbled, that's all.'

'There's a bit of a step in the doorway,' the Prime Minister called out from behind. 'It's a nuisance, but there's no changing it. The step you stumble over in the Prime Minister's doorway has become quite a tradition, you know.'

Pingo Warwick was less certain.

'I have a car waiting. Dr Newton, are you sure you're all right?'

Once again the Prime Minister called out from behind:

'Of course he's all right. Why wouldn't he be all right? How much time do I have before lunch, Pingo?'

'About half an hour.'

'Good heavens, I must rush.'

The Prime Minister joined Isaac Newton and Pingo Warwick outside the office. After shaking hands, the Prime Minister smiled and said:

'Well, many thanks, Dr Newton. I hope it will be Professor Newton the next time we meet. Professor Isaac Newton. Pity it isn't the same Chair as your great predecessor's.'

'That was the Lucasian.'

The Prime Minister smiled again.

'I see you haven't forgotten your Cambridge lore. Well, *bon voyage* and thanks again for the report. It's just what I wanted.'

Ten days later, Isaac Newton was sitting in late-afternoon sunshine on the verandah of the Waldheim chalet in Wengen, overlooking the immense Lauterbrunnen Valley. The high mountains of the Oberland were already gleaming white with the first snows of winter. On a table were glasses and a half-full bottle of wine. Kurt Waldheim's wife, Rosie, was preparing the evening meal. Kurt Waldheim himself picked up a glass.

'The wine tastes good at the end of the day.'

'Yes,' Isaac Newton responded, taking up his own glass. 'I'm afraid, Kurt, that I haven't been in very good form lately.'

'You have been a little withdrawn, I think.'

Isaac Newton stared into his glass for a while and eventually said abruptly:

'I've accepted the Cambridge appointment.'

Kurt Waldheim looked up towards the mountains and at last replied quietly:

'I was wondering.'

'The wine is threatening to loosen my tongue. You see, Kurt, it was my intention to refuse. Then all in a moment my mind was changed.'

'How do you mean your mind was changed?'

'I mean it was changed without my having any control over the decision. Or so it seemed.'

Kurt Waldheim's face wrinkled and he brushed back the quiff of hair that was, as always, threatening to fall over his forehead.

'It doesn't sound like you, Isaac. I always thought you had control over everything.'

'So did I.' Isaac Newton sipped again from his glass. 'I'd like to ask an absurd question, Kurt. It embarrasses me to ask it, but since I've mentioned this thing I'd better . . .'

'Better what?'

'Ask if you believe in ghosts.'

Kurt Waldheim was taken so much off guard that he was reduced to biting his lip in amazement.

'Geister!' he said.

'I see you don't believe in ghosts. Even after consuming a bottle of excellent wine.'

'Frankly, no.'

'Neither do I,' Isaac Newton concurred. 'Yet I saw this huge thing. It wasn't pale and wan like story-book ghosts. It was bright and glowing orange-red. You'd have needed to be blind to have missed it.'

'Isaac, have you seen a doctor?'

'No, I haven't.'

'Perhaps you should.'

'I haven't, partly because I'm embarrassed.'

'Not worried?'

'I'm more puzzled than worried. You see, it was just in the moment when I saw this thing that my decision about the Cambridge job went through a sort of quantum jump.'

Kurt Waldheim frowned heavily.

'There must be other explanations.'

'Like *déjà vu*? Induced by the stress of the moment? Frankly, Kurt, I can think of easy stuff like that for myself.'

'It must have been some sort of storm. A storm, I think, in which you decided to do what you really wanted to do.'

It was Isaac Newton's turn to look away towards the mountains. He lifted his eyes and then shook his head, saying, 'What I can't understand is why any sort of brainstorm should have produced the thing I saw. Or the thing I thought I saw.'

'Why not, Isaac?'

'It was the face. Even in my wildest dreams I don't think I could have imagined such a face.'

'What sort of face?'

'I can't really describe it. But if I have to put a name to it, I'd say this enormous, glowing, orange-red thing had a face like the Greek mask of Tragedy.'

Chapter 4

Isaac Newton swung his car into a vacant space in the parking area of the New Cavendish Laboratory with its buildings in Madingley Road, Cambridge. It happened that the car was facing the Laboratory, so he could see the buildings through the windscreen as he switched off the engine. He remembered them from his student days as being enormous. Yet after a decade at CERN they seemed rather small.

A return of youthful shyness had caused him to arrive at the Laboratory very early so that he could take a look around before most people arrived. It was strange the way he remembered every detail, even down to the cupboards used by the cleaners. He couldn't have described it all beforehand, but somehow everything was as familiar when he came to it now as if the past thirteen years at CERN had never been.

Inevitably his wanderings took him to the display of old equipment used in critical experiments by famous physicists early in the century, and of course to the desk used by James Clerk Maxwell, the first Cavendish Professor, the man who had made the telecommunications industry possible. Would anything of the like ever happen again, he wondered? Would the world ever again be transformed by the ideas of one man seated at his desk, or by ingenious but simple bits of equipment, like the ones in the glass cases around him? Or did the future belong entirely to mammoth projects and to mammoth organisations like CERN, and like the multi-national corporations which now dominated the field of electronics? It was hard to believe the clock could ever be turned back to the way it had been even thirty years ago. The irony of it was that the mammoth organisations which had now overwhelmed every university in the world had really been created by the universities themselves. As the need grew for larger and more expensive equipment, it had seemed sensible for Governments to concentrate resources into national centres – administrated centrally on behalf of the universities, not on behalf of the central organisations themselves. This had been the clear initial presumption. But as the system had evolved down the years, the central organisations had arrogated more and more power to themselves, eventually leaving the universities pretty much in the condition of a school of beached whales.

Nor was this the worst of it. The needs had then outgrown even the capacity of individual nations, so that it had seemed sensible to amalgamate the resources of many nations, exactly as had been done at CERN, with consequences that, predictably, were the same. The international agencies had grown more and more into autonomous bodies, with universities pushed ever towards the sidelines of research. In theory, the participating nations could exercise control over the international agencies by withdrawing or reducing their financial contributions. But while noises were sometimes made in that direction, nothing ever happened. This was because the participating nations were never unanimous among themselves. No Government was prepared to accept the disapproval of the others by withdrawal. Indeed, the international organisations had grown so powerful that they persistently squeezed out even the national centres, while the universities had been ejected like cherry stones pinched contemptuously between the thumb and first finger.

Isaac Newton was acutely conscious, sadly and belatedly, that he was a quixotic madman to put himself in a position where he must fight such a situation. In effect, this was what his return to Cambridge implied. The world had evolved implacably from small to big, with the little fellow going inevitably to the wall.

These were the thoughts in Isaac Newton's mind as he descended the steps past the main lecture theatre. They were interrupted by a distant shout from the far end of one of the diverging corridors. Isaac Newton recognised the silhouette along the corridor seconds before he could discern the features of the man who came hurrying towards him.

'Well, if it isn't old Scrooge,' he exclaimed as they shook hands.

'Young Isaac Newton! You haven't changed a bit, sir. The Professor now! Who would have thought it when you came here first. How long ago would that be?'

'Nineteen years, I think.'

'Nineteen years makes a change, doesn't it, sir?'

Scrooge was the assistant, who from time immemorial had been keeper of the Laboratory stores. He had a long-standing reputation for being niggardly with the stores – hence the name – a reputation which extended to the staff, the Professor himself even. Isaac Newton had liked Scrooge ever since the time nineteen years ago when he had first come to Cambridge, a diffident schoolboy 'up' for the scholarship examination. In the physics practical he'd been issued with a dud galvanometer which Scrooge had ungrudgingly replaced. And he'd always liked Scrooge for his use of the adjective 'young', *young* Isaac Newton, not the derogatory adjectives he'd mostly had to suffer. Scrooge had aged over the intervening years. While the buildings were the same, the lines on Scrooge's face made Isaac Newton conscious of the jump in time. As if the thought had been read, Scrooge said:

'I'll be retiring in two years. But don't worry, sir, I'll see you through before I leave.'

'When did you first come here?'

'It was before the last war.'

'In Rutherford's time?'

'In the last year before he died. I was just out of school. My first job. My only job.'

'It must have been an exciting place in those days.'

'It was. It hasn't really been the same since,' Scrooge acknowledged, and then added hastily:

'But it will be, now that you're back again, sir.'

'We'll do our best.'

'Well, sir, we're not likely to do our best chattering here all day. I've got some stock-taking to do, and you'll be wanting to see the Dragon. She'll be in her office. She comes in early, like me.'

The Dragon was the time-honoured name for the Professor's secretary. Isaac Newton had spoken with the Dragon over the telephone; she was a lady with a firm Scottish accent whom he'd visualised as of solid build and fifty-five years old, guesses which turned out to be almost exactly correct. No sooner was he in his office than the Dragon came in, large, powerful-looking notebook in hand.

'Ah, Mrs Gunter, we both appear to be early.'

'I am always early, I'm glad to say, Professor,' the Dragon remarked as they shook hands. It struck Isaac Newton that although he knew the Dragon's name, and she a woman he'd never seen before, he hadn't the slightest idea of Scrooge's real name. This had to mean something, although he couldn't quite think what. Not that the Dragon gave him much time to think. With a decisive flourish of the big notebook she said:

'We might go through the appointments and committees, Professor, so that you can see how things stand.' The Dragon was evidently one of those secretaries who believed in managing their bosses.

'I haven't made any appointments, Mrs Gunter, and I'm not a member of any committees,' Isaac Newton replied, thinking it would be as well to get things in the usual order of command right from the start.

'Oh yes you are, Professor, if you don't mind my saying so. There's a meeting this afternoon of the Faculty Board. You're a member of that, *ex officio*; and there's a meeting on Wednesday of the McFarlane Committee. You're also a member of that, *ex officio*. Professor Boulton wants to see you, urgently he says. He's the Professor at Geostrophics, on the other side of the road. One of your staff, Michael Howarth, wants to see you. He also says it's urgent, and that may well be true because he's involved in a scandal, which I would prefer you to hear from other lips than my own. Mr Clamperdown from CERC is coming to discuss the same scandal, and no doubt you will hear a good deal about it from him. Mr Clamperdown says that it would be convenient for him to come tomorrow afternoon, but that I am to confirm the time after discussing it with you.'

'Thank you, Mrs Gunter, and thank Mr Clamperdown for troubling to confirm his appointment. I wonder if you can let me have a list of these formidable and amazing arrangements?'

This remark caused the Dragon to observe, later in the morning over elevenses, to her friend the secretary to the Professor of Crystallography that the new Professor looked as though he was going to be a 'bit difficult'.

The Dragon had no difficulty in coping herself.

'I have the list here already,' she said, conjuring a sheet of paper from her notebook. 'I should explain that there is one important item I have not included on the list, Professor. Any day now we are expecting a visit from the Geister.'

'The *what*, Mrs Gunter?'

'The Geister. We call him that, Professor, because we never know what day, or what time of day, he might appear.'

'And who, may I ask, is the Geister?'

'I would prefer you to learn for yourself, Professor, when the time comes.'

'For him to appear?'

'Yes, Professor.'

'And am I supposed to sit around twiddling my thumbs, waiting for this apparition to show itself?'

'You're not required to twiddle your thumbs, Professor, but it would be advisable to sit around. The other heads of departments do.'

Finding himself beggared for further effective comment, Isaac Newton contented himself with saying, 'You may inform Mr Clamperdown that it will be convenient for him to come tomorrow, dragging his tale of scandal behind him. Although what would happen if the Geister or the Cheshire Cat were to appear during his visit is almost too hideous to contemplate.'

The Dragon sniffed audibly at what she took to be a lack of a proper sense of responsibility. 'Frankly,' she said darkly to her friend the secretary to the Professor of Crystallography later in the morning, 'I don't give him long for the job,' a sentiment that Isaac Newton was rapidly coming to share himself.

'Do you take dictation, Mrs Gunter?'

'Of course, Professor.'

'I have a few letters to attend to, shall we say in an hour's time?'

'Very good, Professor, if you are not ready now,' the Dragon replied, drawing herself up squarely. In this posture, she delivered her final and what she evidently hoped to be her decisive broadside.

'And if I may offer you a piece of advice, Professor?'

'What would that be, Mrs Gunter?'

'There is a young lady in your department, Professor, who should be avoided. She spells trouble for one and all.'

'That is very interesting news – I mean grave news, Mrs Gunter. Who may this young lady be?'

'Her name is Frances Haroldsen. She is reputed to be attractive, although whether she is really as pretty as the men seem to think, some of us have our doubts.'

'Is the young lady one of the secretaries?'

'Not she!' the Dragon almost shouted in an offended voice. 'Miss Haroldsen is one of the demonstrators. Although just what she demonstrates, I wouldn't like to say.'

'You'd advise me to give the young lady a wide berth?'

'I'd advise more than that. If I was in your shoes, I'd march her straight to the front door and say "Out!"'

The Dragon clapped her hands together in a gesture that seemed to imply contempt, contriving to do so without dropping the large notebook, which remained in position as if it were attached magnetically to her arm.

'Otherwise you'll find *yourself* embroiled, mark my words, Professor.'

The beginning of the fourth movement of Beethoven's Pastoral Symphony flooded into Isaac Newton's head as the Dragon quitted the office, a hymn of thanksgiving after the storm. He thought about escaping from the office for another talk with Scrooge, and then decided to make a call to Kurt Waldheim at CERN, using a credit card so that nobody could tell him international calls were forbidden by the rules of the McFarlane Committee. And to avoid the possibility that the Geister might be tapping the line he spoke in French, ending by saying, 'Expect me back at the end of the week. I've run here into some kind of a lunatic asylum.'

Chapter 5

A man in his fifties erupted into Isaac Newton's office in a passable imitation of bird-like flight.

'Boulton, from Geostrophics,' he said. 'Sorry to use the wrong door, but your secretary, Mrs Gunter, gives me the creeps. I'd get rid of her if I were you.'

'Would you, indeed?' replied Isaac Newton after they'd shaken hands.

'The trouble is that there's been no proper head of this department for more than a year now. When the cat's away the mice come out to play. It's lucky you managed to come so quickly. Before you had the offer of the Chair we hawked it around for quite a time.'

Aware that Boulton had been a member of the electoral board for the Chair, Isaac Newton asked:

'Would it be out of place for me to thank you for the job?'

'Frankly, I thought you were a bit off-centre to take it. I wouldn't have done. Of course, I know all about the problems here. Besides we don't have international agencies in the earth sciences. I get by because I have a contract with the University of California – for the summer quarter each year. I'll be out there a couple of weeks from now. I was supposed to be having a sabbatical this term, you see, but I've been delayed by admin. A NERC meeting which affected the Geostrophics grant. This is why I came over to see you now. Would you like my house?'

'I'm not in the market really.'

'Oh, I wasn't meaning to buy. I mean while I'm away. It's quite a nice little place in Adams Road. The rent would be nominal. What I really want is to have the house occupied, otherwise it's pretty certain to be burgled. I'd like someone who won't ruin the hi-fi and that sort of thing. Where are you staying now?'

'In College.'

'That's all right for a few days, but you won't be able to stick it for long. Too cramping. By the way, if you feel like shedding a few members of your staff there's one I wouldn't mind having. She's a real smasher. Have you seen her yet?'

'Not yet.'

'Well, when you do you'll see my point about the house. Can I take it that you're interested?'

'Yes, I'd be interested. What, if I might ask, would you regard as a nominal rent?'

'I'd say three hundred a month would be fair all round. I was thinking of buying contracts for Swiss francs. What d'you think is going to happen to the franc? Over the short term, I mean?'

'I'd say the Swiss franc has a habit of doing well, so it's likely to go on doing well.'

'That's what I think, too. I suppose your salary at CERN was paid in francs. If you have property over there, I'd keep it. And of course if you have a bank account, keep that especially.'

'While you're here, I wonder if you'd fill me in on a few points of procedure,' Isaac Newton said, in the hope of deflecting the conversation.

'University procedure?'

'Yes.'

'You'll find everything in the *Statutes and Ordinances*. Everybody works from there. If you don't work from there it's easy to land yourself in trouble.'

'Would I find the McFarlane Committee there?'

'Oh, not that, of course.'

'What is the McFarlane Committee?'

'A waster of time. Thank God I'm not on it. Somebody had the idea of joining the Physics and Chemistry Faculty to the Faculty of Engineering. The idea is to save money by avoiding duplication but they'll talk around that one for ever. In any case, there's a rumour that McFarlane, he's the Chairman, has been dead for six months and the University hasn't noticed it yet. You see the Committee will need his signature if it ever comes to the Report stage, so they have to keep his corpse at the ready whether they like it or not. If they do make a Report it won't stand a chance. Regent House will kill it, of course, although I might vote for it myself. Somebody should do something about those engineers. They've got equipment down there in the town that would wreck half of Trumpington Street if it ever got loose.'

'You said you would change my secretary – if she were your secretary. How would you go about that?'

'How would I go about it? I'd give her the push, of course, straight into the pool.'

'Then I could advertise the job, I suppose.'

'No, you'd have to take someone else from out of the pool. As one goes in another comes out; or as one comes out another goes in – whichever way round you prefer to think of it.'

'What you're saying is that I can't really choose my own secretary? Are you being serious?'

The suggestion of a squeak in Isaac Newton's voice was lost on the Professor of Geostrophics.

'It's the way the Cambridge system works,' Boulton said in an unconcerned voice. 'You choose somebody, and if she's not suitable you simply hoof her back into the pool. Then try somebody else. And so on, *ad inf. Actually* there is one way you can do it – by employing her on a research contract. That's how I do it myself, except that I'm NERC and you'll be CERC. But the rules are probably the same. Anyway, about the house, shall we take that as settled? I was going to invite you to a College Feast, only by the time it comes round I'll be off on my sabbatical.'

'Perhaps I could see the house?'

'There are a few things you need to be a bit careful about – the cat for one thing. Oh, and if there happens to be a long spell of dry weather and you hear cracking noises, don't worry. It's quite common in that part of Cambridge for the foundations to shift. So let's go. We could have a cup of coffee at The Ragamuffin on the way.'

'Now?'

'Yes, now,' Boulton replied, moving energetically as if about to become airborne again.

Isaac Newton pressed a buzzer. When the Dragon came in he said:
'Ah, Mrs Gunter, I am going to be *ex officio* for an hour or so.'
Then he handed the Dragon a sheet of paper on which he'd written
a name and a Geneva telephone number.

'I've already called this gentleman about an hour ago. Would you
please call him again, telling him that I want to confirm the last part of
our previous conversation, especially my last sentence.'

'What do I say, Professor, if he asks where he can contact you?'

'Tell him to try The Ragamuffin. He'll understand perfectly.'

Chapter 6

Both men were tall and slim; both were physicists. Yet an observer
would have seen an infinity of difference in psychology between them.
At twenty-eight, Mike Howarth still had the look of a youth in his late
teens. His hair, which he wore about three inches long, stood straight
up, making him seem rather taller and less co-ordinated than he really
was. The hair and eyes were light brown, and whereas Isaac Newton
had bowed to the tradition whereby heads of department wore suits,
Mike Howarth was dressed in casual shirt and jeans. He would have
said he couldn't afford to do otherwise, not on the salary which a
grateful University paid to him, and in this respect, at least, the two
men would have agreed, since Isaac Newton's after-tax salary would
now be less than a half of what it had been at CERN. The British were
always appealing to their expatriots to return home but they certainly
took the opportunity to make the process a costly one for the
expatriots. *Noblesse oblige* they would say, of course, but that didn't
pay the butcher's bill. Isaac Newton found himself wondering if he'd
be able to afford suits any more.

'You don't think there's any chance then?' Mike Howarth asked
appealingly.

'No,' Isaac Newton replied, 'you broke the rules, civil service rules,
and for that there is no forgiveness, either in Heaven or on Earth.'

'I could appeal to the Ombudsman. I'm mad about it all, you see.'

'The Ombudsman must have an interesting life. I remember
circumstances from my earlier years rather like your position, which

always struck me as a bit unfair. There was a chap who went under the soubriquet of Brass Jack, a manager of one of the local factories. Well, Brass Jack discovered how to get more product out of the same amount of raw materials. Instead of giving the increased production to the factory owners, he gave them the same output as before from the same materials as before, and proceeded to sell the extra produce on his own account. Then he made the bad mistake of splashing the money all over the district, which was how he came to be called Brass Jack. They caught up with him, eventually, and at his trial the judge struck him down for two years. That's pretty well your own case, isn't it? Except in your case it's *these*, not money,' Isaac Newton concluded, pointing to a long table on which tapes, disks, and a score or so of large sheets of paper were scattered.

'What did they get him on, this Brass Jack?'

'Breach of contract. His contract with the factory owners wasn't written in the way he'd interpreted it. The fact that Brass Jack had been ingenious, just as you were ingenious, didn't help at all. Indeed, I think the ingenuity made it worse. All the legal mind looks at in such a situation are the details of the contract.'

'But I didn't have a contract!' Mike Howarth exclaimed. 'Except to provide exactly what I provided. Satellite telemetry with specified performance within a specified weight. I can show it to you. That's *all* it says. *Nothing* of what was to happen if I saved a margin of weight.'

'What the legal mind does then is to look at what it calls the "usual practice" employed among "reasonable people". That's what CERC is doing in your case.'

'But there isn't any usual practice. Or you might say the usual practice in satellite work is for everybody to struggle to stay within their weight limits, like jockeys before a horse race. This was unusual.'

'Nevertheless, you won't win.'

'It seems to me that CERC has set itself up as judge, jury and executioner.'

'That's exactly the way the Government wrote the CERC contract twenty years ago, and in twenty years a judge and jury rolled into one can get through a lot of executions. If you want my opinion,' Isaac Newton said, 'you're not going to get anything out of CERC unless you crawl to Canterbury in sackcloth and ashes. When the bureaucrats see a scientist squirming in front of them they might relent a bit.'

'I'm certainly not going to do that! What have I to apologise for? Making a great discovery without spending any money at all? *They* spend money by the million and what do they get out of it? Piddling stuff.'

Isaac Newton didn't like Mike Howarth's remark about a 'great' discovery. That sort of thing was crackpot. He'd never once himself referred to his own discovery of the vacuum strings as 'great'. You left such talk to other people. He minded the denigration of CERC less. CERC, he knew, had its sticky fingers in pretty well every aspect of British scientific life – most improperly, even in University appointments, subtly not overtly, of course, with a nod and a wink. He'd little doubt his own recent appointment would have been cleared with CERC, to make sure he was regarded by CERC as an OK guy, one who would therefore be in a position to secure ample research grants for the university.

The disaster of twenty years ago, when CERC had been set up by an unsubtle Government acting on the recommendations of innocent, unsubtle advisors, had by now reduced the universities to a pitiful crowd of whining beggars, a situation which had been triumphantly avoided at CERN, and which would simply have to be reversed in Britain if the physical sciences were ever to amount again to as much as a row of beans.

'You have to take situations from where they actually are, not from where you'd like them to be,' Isaac Newton told the unstable Mike Howarth, who was sitting sprawled and dejected beside the strewn table.

'Without more observations there's nowhere for me to go. With Halley's Comet coming next year it was ideal. You see, I was gearing up for Halley's. Then Comet Boswell happened to come along, and it seemed sensible to try a dry run. It was bad luck that someone happened to notice I'd put an extra channel in the telemetry.'

'Someone at CERC?'

'Unlikely. I think it was one of the University groups who shopped on me. Some of them would do anything to curry favour with CERC.'

'Well, let's start from square one, to make sure I've got the story right. Your illicit equipment, which made up the weight you'd saved on your telemetry contract from CERC, was designed to receive signals at a very long wavelength, well out beyond the ionospheric cut-off.'

'Right.'

'Therefore all man-made transmissions at ground level at your wavelength must have remained trapped below the ionosphere, and so could not have reached your satellite.'

'Right.'

'Therefore if the signals you received were man-made they had to come from some other satellite.'

'Right.'

'Well, why not? There are scores of satellites going around the Earth, many we don't know about – military satellites, for instance. Why shouldn't the signals you received have come from one of them?'

Mike Howarth picked up a sheet from the table.

'You can see for yourself. The signals are a sequence of dots and dashes – like Morse code, only it doesn't seem to be Morse code as far as I can tell. Nobody uses that kind of transmission these days. It's wasteful of capacity.'

'The military might be doing so. They wouldn't worry much about a bit of waste.'

'It needs very bulky equipment to transmit at such a long wavelength.'

'There might be some new technology you know nothing about.'

'Every time around its orbit the satellite came into the Earth's shadow.'

'Of the Sun or of the Comet?'

'Of the Comet. Whenever the line to it was cut off by the Earth, there were no signals. So a military satellite, if there was one, would have had to move in an orbit that somehow contrived to imitate the Comet.'

'Which doesn't seem very likely,' agreed Isaac Newton thoughtfully, then adding, 'but of course extremely unlikely things do happen in the world from time to time.'

'If I could get a shot at Halley's, I think I could settle it,' Mike Howarth exclaimed eagerly.

'I doubt it,' Isaac Newton replied shortly, dashing Mike Howarth's momentary flicker of hope. 'There's never any way to be completely certain in this kind of circumstantial argument. What you have to do is to establish something explicit, calculate something precisely, or, of course, actually decode these dots and dashes. Have you tried that?'

'I had a look at it, but I didn't get very far. One trouble is that the amount of really good data is small. The signal was weak for a lot of the time. Although there are certainly regular signal pulses, it isn't easy to say which are dots and which are dashes – it's a bit like a blurred message in Morse code.'

'Have you a print-out of the more typical stuff?'

'Yes, I've got a fairly typical bit of the record somewhere.'

Mike Howarth searched among the scattered papers with quick, nervous gestures, eventually selecting a sheet which he handed to Isaac Newton, together with a sheet of good data, saying, 'You can see there's quite a difference.'

Instead of simply glancing at the sheets, Isaac Newton took a magnifying glass from his desk and proceeded to study the records for what seemed an unconscionable length of time. At last he leaned back in his chair and said in a positive tone:

'This data could be improved a lot by applying a proper computer technique to it. With the sort of programme we use at CERN, the computer starts with the good stuff. It learns the lengths and shapes of the pulses. Then it passes to the somewhat less good data, which it updates in the light of its experience so far. Then on to poorer data, and so on, learning and updating all the time. You know the sort of thing I mean. Have you tried it?'

'It would need a bigger cruncher than we have here in Cambridge, and if I applied for a grant to do it somewhere else – well, there'd be a long delay and I can guess what the answer to a grant application to CERC would be. Besides, I'd probably have to turn over the data, and that's just what I'm not going to do. If I'm forced to suffer for it, I'm going to keep it.'

'I could get it done at CERN. Would you turn it over to me?'

Mike Howarth thought for a while and then said seriously:

'Yes, I think I would. Mostly because you've done something important in physics yourself. But I'd ask you not to tell anybody what it means.'

Isaac Newton nodded and asked:

'Are all the disks here?'

When Mike Howarth nodded in turn, Isaac Newton went on:

'I have to go to Geneva later this week. I'll take them with me and get it started. I'm still tying up loose ends at CERN, so I'll be making quite a few trips there. I'll make certain the job is done in good time. Sort out the right disks, label them carefully, and I'll lock them away in the desk here.'

Isaac Newton was sensitive to Mike Howarth's reluctance to part with his data, but he was unprepared for Howarth's reply.

'I'd rather not leave the disks here, if you don't mind. I'll keep them and bring them if you tell me when you expect to be leaving for Switzerland.'

'Don't you have copies?'

'Yes, but it isn't that.'

'Are you worried they wouldn't be safe?'

'They wouldn't. This office has been used by all sorts of people over the past eighteen months. I've no idea how many people might have keys to your desk.'

Curious at what he took to be Howarth's paranoid state of mind,

Isaac Newton leant forward in his chair.

'But why, then, do you leave them in the Laboratory at all?'

'I don't. I wouldn't dream of it. I brought my material in specially to show you.'

'I don't understand why anybody would want to steal them.'

'Ah!' cried Mike Howarth. 'That's because you think it's all a lot of nonsense, because you're humouring me. But if you once admit that I'm *right*, then you can see why plenty of people would want to steal the disks. People at CERC for one thing. Civil servants never like leaving the evidence around, do they? Sensitive matters are dealt with over the telephone, not by letter, aren't they? Then, when the disaster happens, there's nothing definite on paper, except perhaps a few ambiguous sentences which were understood to mean something, but which don't when you look at them carefully. I'm sure you know it all better than I can tell you.'

'I suppose it would be awkward for them, if you do turn out to be right, I mean,' laughed Isaac Newton. 'I hope it comes out that way, but we'll see. What I can't see is how CERC could contrive to burgle the Cavendish Laboratory.'

'They wouldn't. It would be done from inside, of course. I said before there's lots of people wanting to curry favour with CERC.'

'Is there no one here you trust, then?'

'Well, I'm trusting you, and there are others of course. Frances Haroldsen for one.'

Isaac Newton felt a sudden lurch back to his conversation with Boulton and with the Dragon, realising that the technicalities of his discussion with Howarth had momentarily calmed his suspicion that the financial stringencies of the past thirteen years had somehow pushed the University into a state of mass insanity. Determined to have no more nonsense, he said sharply:

'I suppose you have a bank account?'

'Yes, of course.'

'Where?'

'Barclays.'

'Which branch?'

'The main branch at Bene't Street. But why?'

'Because we're going down there right now to see the manager, and you're going to ask him to put these disks in his safe. And furthermore, you're going to tell the manager that the only person who is to be allowed to take the disks away is myself. Is that clear? Otherwise you can forget the whole thing.'

Chapter 7

Isaac Newton hadn't been long returned from his visit to Barclays Bank when the Dragon appeared in the doorway, and as if discharging an arrow into his office, announced:

'The *Geister* has arrived!'

A small man with spectacles and a rather large head came in, saying, 'Professor Newton, we haven't met before. I am John Jocelyn Scuby, Secretary of the Faculties.'

By long-standing tradition a capacious black leather armchair was strictly reserved for the Professor's special visitors. Jocelyn Scuby sank into the armchair with a momentary sigh of pleasure. Then instantly he hitched himself awkwardly to the edge of the chair, as if its soft comfort had made him suddenly uncomfortable.

'I must explain,' Scuby began in a hushed, almost breathless voice, 'that in happier days the General Board left individual departments to make up their own accounts.'

The one thing that was not straightforward in this statement was that Scuby, like many people in Cambridge, pronounced 'General Board' as if the vowel 'o' in Board were absent, an oddity which had Isaac Newton momentarily confused.

'The accounts were, of course, scrutinised by the University's auditors, but frankly speaking and without any explicit criticism intended, that was never a very satisfactory procedure,' Scuby continued.

'I know what you mean. When is an auditor not an auditor, and that sort of thing.'

'Exactly so. I'm glad you understand what I mean – with a minimum of explanation on my part. The matter, when it reached the Discussion stage, took up a great deal of the General Board's time.'

'I can imagine it would.'

'Well now, the upshot was that I myself make the rounds of the departments. Before the accounts are made up, that is to say. I do this partly to verify that everything is in good order, and I also find it possible to make suggestions as to where little economies might be made. I hope you understand all this too, Professor Newton.'

'As a matter of precise fact, I understand it very well,' replied Isaac Newton. 'You see, Mr Scuby, my first administrative experience at CERN – that's the Conseil Européen pour la Recherche Nucléaire – I don't like acronyms myself, but otherwise it's rather a mouthful – came when I was put on the laboratory's committee for small items, the *Conseil pour quelque chose restraint* as we called it. I was twenty-five at the time, recently down from Cambridge, and therefore pretty raw. It was our job to stop unnecessary waste around the laboratory. It was quite an eye-opener to me to find out just how much waste there really was – things that otherwise I'd never have noticed.'

John Jocelyn Scuby clapped his hands lightly and hitched himself still further forward in the armchair.

'You mean you were self-policing?' Isaac Newton nodded, and Scuby went on: 'Well, that's a bit of news. I've never known scientists show much discipline before. I've never known any department show much discipline, for that matter.'

'It's partly a question of scale. When things get big like CERN, either you're disciplined or you go out of business. In our case we had a lot of motivation. So long as we kept in budget – inside the internationally-agreed estimates – we were kings of our own castle. No outside interference. But if we went outside budget, all sorts of questions were asked by the various bureaucracies. Once you've experienced that kind of intervention you take a lot of trouble to avoid it ever happening again. Besides which, this early experience with the committee on small items was of great use to me when I came later to be a big spender myself.'

While Jocelyn Scuby was plainly delighted by the trend of the conversation, he shied visibly at Isaac Newton's mention of himself as a big spender.

'Well now, Professor Newton, in view of your experience, perhaps I should come to the bad news immediately, leaving the good news for later.'

'Yes, I'd like the bad news immediately. The more bad news I have immediately the better,' Isaac Newton replied with a straight face.

Jocelyn Scuby suppressed a smile of approval, telling himself that it would be wrong to announce bad news with a smile. In the same hushed voice he said:

'I'm almost afraid to tell you, Professor Newton, but this department is ten thousand pounds overdrawn.'

For answer, Isaac Newton fished in his pocket and took out a 10 pence coin, which he placed on the desk in front of him.

'To remind me,' he said, forbearing to tell Jocelyn Scuby that the discovery of the vacuum strings had cost thirty million sterling and had been declared cheap at the price by a delighted world.

'Ah, yes,' Scuby nodded, 'to remind you, like a knot in your handkerchief. A very good idea.'

'Can you fill me in on a few points, Mr Scuby? What would you say is the University's overhead as a percentage of the total budget?' Isaac Newton asked.

'I *can* tell you, because it is something I bear constantly in mind. Of course, the question is really very complex, because of the diversity of the departments and faculties. The overheads aren't the same for the science departments as they are for the humanities departments, naturally. But if I take a broad average, I would say our overhead is about half our gross. By trying hard and being very watchful, I manage to keep it there. I don't quite know why it should be, but that's the way it always seems to work out.'

'Calculating the overheads above what?'

'Salaries.'

'Including the salaries of secretaries and technical assistants?'

'No, academic salaries only.'

'Does the University pay rates?'

'I should say it *does*. The town treats us like a milch cow. What d'you think? I mean, would you expect us to do better than that?'

'I'm still not clear just what your overheads include?'

'Well, town rates, as you've just mentioned, lighting, heating, libraries, upkeep of buildings and grounds, telephones.'

'Laboratory equipment?'

'Not research equipment, on the whole. That comes from outside grants, from NERC, CERC, the MRC and a little from industrial sources. But equipment for teaching purposes, yes.'

'Computing?'

'Yes, computing also. You know, Professor Newton, when you use the word "overheads" to an uninformed person it sounds like a collection of doubtful luxuries. But really it is a collection of essential things without which the University could not operate at all.'

'I'd say, Mr Scuby, that you're really doing quite well. I'd say, keep it up.'

'Would you now!' exclaimed Jocelyn Scuby, vaguely conscious that in their discussion the tables had somehow been turned from their usual position in his dealings with the heads of the science departments – in his dealings with Boulton of Geostrophics, for instance, a man whose accounts were a veritable and perennial quagmire.

'And now,' said Scuby with another delicate clap of his hands, 'to come to the good news. There is a certain member of your staff, a young lady, a Miss Haroldsen, who apparently has something of a gift for causing trouble. There have been several recommendations to the General Board that she be dismissed. As you're doubtless aware, there have been several temporary heads of this department in the recent past, rotating heads as they are known, and in each case the General Board received the same recommendation.'

'For Miss Haroldsen's dismissal?'

'Indeed.'

'Does she have tenure? I'm afraid I haven't had time to learn the status of my own staff, or even to meet most of them yet.'

'No, Miss Haroldsen does *not* have tenure, but as you probably know things have changed very greatly in respect of dismissals over the past fifteen years – changes that are almost unbelievable, I might say, to anyone who knew Cambridge thirty years ago. In the more distant past, temporary appointments were elevated to tenure appointments on the grounds of positive merit. The person in question had to demonstrate outstanding qualities to the satisfaction of their more senior colleagues. But nowadays the University is required to demonstrate reasons why a person in a temporary position should *not* be accorded promotion. In other words, the cart and the horse have become reversed, changing what used to be normal terminations of temporary appointments into cases of contested dismissals.'

'Making dismissals an unpleasant business, I would think.'

'Especially if they reach the stage of litigation,' nodded Scuby, worries so creasing his face that for a moment Isaac Newton thought he was going to cry.

'With the biggest troublemakers naturally causing the most trouble.'

'Precisely so, Professor Newton. So it will be easy for you to imagine the General Board's reluctance to become involved in the case of Miss Haroldsen, a young lady who has the reputation of being a troublemaker of uncommon proportions.'

'Rather comely proportions, I suppose, Mr Scuby?'

'Oh, ah, yes. Well possibly, although I rather gather it's the young lady's tongue that's the real problem. I believe it was William Congreve who said:

> But soon as e'er the beauteous maiden spoke
> Forth from her coral lips such folly broke...

'You will be glad to know, Professor Newton, that as a gesture of good will towards yourself the General Board had decided to go ahead with the recommendations. In this case we will grasp the nettle on your behalf no matter what the consequences may be.'

Isaac Newton felt a desperate urge to shake himself in the fashion of a dog newly-emerged from a deep pool. First, they wouldn't let him choose his own secretary; now they were actively engaged in the dismissal of his staff. Next there would be something still more devastating, like a hammering of the Laboratory with water cannon.

'I can imagine only one reason why I would feel it necessary to recommend the dismissal of any member of my staff, Mr Scuby, and that would be gross incompetence.'

Making a mental note to replace the ridiculous thing by a proper intercom system, Isaac Newton stabbed the buzzer on his desk. The instant the Dragon appeared in the doorway he called out:

'Mrs Gunter, will you please bring me the file on Miss Haroldsen.'

'I'd be more than glad to do so, Professor,' the Dragon replied, with more than a hint of a broad smile as she remembered the sizzling reports on the Haroldsen girl which it had been her good fortune to type and to send on to the General Board.

The sizzling reports were there all right, towards the front of a bulky file. Ignoring them, Isaac Newton ran quickly through the rest of the papers, coming eventually to what he wanted – the *curriculum vitae* on Frances Margaret Haroldsen. It took only a few seconds to find what he was looking for. Glancing up towards John Jocelyn Scuby he said:

'A first in the Natural Science Tripos Part I, a first in Physics Part II, and a Ph.D. here at the Cavendish. Precisely my own record, Mr Scuby, and I always thought I did rather well.'

Jocelyn Scuby struggled out of the armchair, saying, 'Well, of course, if you're happy with the existing situation, the General Board will be happy with it too. We only wanted to help. And now I think it's time I got down to work. Your secretary can show me the details, but I'll be coming back for another talk, shall we say an hour and a half from now?'

Then, pointing towards the 10 pence coin lying on the desk, Scuby added:

'We have some hard thinking to do.'

Chapter 8

If Isaac Newton thought his first day in the Laboratory had been turbulent, worse was to follow. The storm didn't threaten to break until the afternoon of the next day, however, the morning being calm, as one expects before a storm.

In the morning, Isaac Newton called Boulton in Geostrophics, to say he would rent the house in Adams Road. At the end of the daily uproar in the Laboratory he'd need some corner to which he could retreat like a wounded animal to its lair. Dinner in College every evening, in a turmoil of fifty to a hundred other dons, would be too hectic, he'd decided.

Boulton was around to his office in what seemed but a trice, come to collect the rent.

'Would you like it in cash, or will a cheque do?' Isaac Newton asked.

'A cheque will do. You see, I'm going to convert it into dollars. So cash really wouldn't help. I hear Scuby was around yesterday.'

'How did you know that, now?'

'Oh, we have what's called a Scuby watch. Some people make a book on it. His movements are plotted hour by hour so that nobody is surprised by his visits, although I bet you were. Ha! Ha!'

'I *was* surprised rather.'

'Well I can tell you how to avoid a lot of trouble for yourself in the future.'

'How would that be?'

'You just get your secretary to book everything – everything in and everything out. Get it all typed into the University computer. Include the cost of every last stamp. The more detail the better, because it chokes the computer and confuses the picture, besides which, they can't say you're concealing anything. Then, when the heat is on, you just go away – on sabbatical, if you can, but away somewhere. *You* could be off to CERN. You keep in contact with your secretary. They can't take for ever on your accounts. Then, when the heat's off, you simply come back.'

'Should I pay you monthly, or would you like the cheque made out for the whole period?'

'The whole period, if you don't mind. You see, I'm thinking of joining a drilling partnership.'

'I hope the well doesn't turn out to be dry.'

'Oh, you don't put your money into one hole. You buy yourself bits of a lot of holes. I'll tell you about it when I get back.'

'Just a word about the house. If the cracking gets bad d'you want me to have the foundations grouted?'

'Wouldn't do any good. You see, it's the ground that moves. It swells when it rains and shrinks when it's dry. Concrete gets cracked. In fact it's best to build on rubble in that part of Cambridge. If it gets bad just think you're in a ship at sea.'

Boulton exited, as they say in movie scripts, but then almost immediately poked his head back through the doorway, saying, 'Oh, and if the cat gets on your nerves just take it along to the Small Animal Hospital. That's at the Vet School. Say it's badly ill with the shivers and they'll look after it.'

It was coming up to 2.15 p.m. when the Dragon discharged another of her arrows.

'Mr Clamperdown from CERC,' she announced.

Clamperdown seated himself in the big black armchair, sinking well into it with a confidence borne of previous visits, and with an air of proprietorship that would hardly have been possible in Rutherford's day. He curled up his right leg so that the foot rested over the left knee.

'I don't suppose you remember, but we've met before,' he said, as if to suggest that Isaac Newton lived in a mental fog.

'Oh, yes, I do,' Isaac Newton replied, quickly trumping that particular trick. 'It was on the occasion of the visit of a British Government delegation to CERN. We met at a restaurant called *L'Oiseau de Feu*, on a hillside on the French side of the frontier. You drank *orangesaft*, while the rest of us, in conformity with the traditions of the house, drank cocktails.'

'I admire your memory,' Clamperdown acknowledged, retreating further into the chair. Clamperdown's voice was rich, too rich to be natural, as if a student of elocution were seeking to attenuate a socially undesirable accent.

'Yes, well, now,' Clamperdown continued, 'I thought it would be a good idea to call at the earliest possible moment to discuss the status of CERC grants to the Cavendish Laboratory.'

Remembering he'd found an empty cigar box in his desk, Isaac Newton held up an arm in the fashion of a traffic policeman.

'Would you like a cigar by the way? I should have asked before.'

'That would be very nice.'

Isaac Newton took out the cigar box and walked over to the armchair, where he opened the box with a flourish under Clamperdown's nose.

'Gracious me, now,' he exclaimed, 'the Laboratory seems to have fallen on hard times, doesn't it? You were saying about the CERC grants?'

'Yes, well, ah, there's one particular contract I'd like to discuss. I don't know if you've heard about it yet. But if you haven't I'd be glad to fill you in.'

'On it?'

'You haven't, have you?'

'As a matter of fact I think I may.'

'I'm referring to a grant for satellite telemetry.'

'I thought you might be.'

'To Michael Howarth.'

'Yes?'

Isaac Newton waited while Clamperdown adjusted his neck inside his collar as a prelude to bursting out:

'The situation is impossible.'

'I don't see the situation as impossible at all. The situation would have been awkward, I'll grant you, if Howarth's playing around with the telemetry had caused the satellite to fail. But it didn't. The telemetry worked and everything's fine.'

'But if we were to go on like this, with everybody making unauthorised changes to satellite packages, how long would it be before we had a complete disaster on our hands?'

'Not very long, I'd imagine. Something must obviously be done to make sure it doesn't happen again.'

'I suppose you're aware we've already taken steps to make sure it won't happen again.'

'Mike Howarth tells me you've cancelled his contract.'

'There wasn't anything else to do.'

'I can think of half-a-dozen other things that might have been done. Terminating the contract seems to me like curing an attack of dermatitis on the hand by chopping off the arm. Howarth may be on the verge of an important discovery.'

'Nobody seems to think so.'

'Ah, we're coming to it now,' Isaac Newton frowned. 'If everybody thought Howarth was onto something big, you'd simply have come in here with the mild suggestion that I keep a watchful eye on him in the future. It's really a matter of setting yourself up as an umpire in the science race. Isn't that so, Mr Clamperdown?'

'We've taken a great deal of trouble, Professor Newton. The case has been before three of our committees, and nobody thinks Howarth's ideas are anything but total nonsense.'

'I have to admit that I haven't had much time on the matter, Mr Clamperdown. But I have at least begun to think rather seriously about it, and *I* wouldn't call it total nonsense.'

'Surely *you* don't believe it.'

'I don't believe it and I don't disbelieve it. My position is that *I don't know.*'

'But it's outrageous. Comets alive! If the Cavendish Laboratory is coming down to that sort of thing, where are we then, by God!'

Isaac Newton felt himself to be slowly losing an internal battle to control his temper.

'If I were required to put a number to the chance of Howarth being right, I'd say roughly a hundred-to-one against, but that isn't the same as *total* nonsense,' he tried mildly. But, crashing ahead like a bull in a china shop, Clamperdown spurned the olive branch.

'We're not interested at CERC in poor odds like that,' he said shortly.

'You should be,' Isaac Newton continued, still holding himself down. 'When there's a chance of something big coming from a rather modest expenditure, you should bet, because sooner or later one of your bets will pay off.'

'We have the Public Accounts Committee to consider, Professor Newton. Your kind of thinking isn't their kind of thinking.'

'Which is why the public funding of sciences is an unmitigated disaster,' Isaac Newton replied, opening the throttle a little, 'the way it would be if exploration for oil were financed with public money. Because nine wells out of ten turn out to be dry, you fellows would never drill at all.'

'Most people wouldn't agree with you, I think,' said Clamperdown still more shortly, heaving himself out of the armchair. 'I hope you're not going to press this matter.'

'Does CERC give me no right of appeal?'

'You could appeal, of course, but after the time that's been spent on the case already I doubt the appeal would be successful. I wasn't thinking of CERC, but I *was* thinking of the wider interests of your Laboratory as a whole.'

Isaac Newton tapped the desk hard with a pencil.

'The notion in your mind, I suppose, is that I happen to have connections going somewhat outside normal channels. Well, you may rest easy on that one. I don't gamble when the odds are a hundred-to-one against me.'

'That's very sensible.'

'But if the odds should shorten, as they may, my point of view might change. And as regards your implied suggestion of blackmail on this Laboratory, let me tell you very plainly that future grant applications from this Laboratory will be well-thought-out, well-documented, and well-costed. If the applications should receive adversely biased treatment from CERC, I would have little hesitation in pulling out all the stops that lie within my reach. But because you understand this very well, Mr Clamperdown, there will be no such biased treatment – rather the reverse. Because survival, not science, is your primary motivation, you will undoubtedly take good care to lean over backwards where grant applications from this Laboratory are concerned.

'That, I think, is much the most useful part of our discussion. Perhaps we shall meet again, Mr Clamperdown, under happier circumstances in the future, over a glass of *orangesaft*.'

Chapter 9

To get the encounter with Clamperdown of CERC out of his system, Isaac Newton felt a compelling need for a breath of fresh air. He thought of exploring the buildings on the far side of Madingley Road where he knew the Astronomy Department was housed. It might be a good idea to borrow a book or two on comets while he was about it. So he headed towards the road and had just about reached it when there was a shout in his direction.

'Heh, mister! Will you give us a heave?'

Three youths were attempting to manhandle a van against the slight gradient of the road, causing passing traffic to give them a wide berth. Since it would have seemed churlish to refuse, Isaac Newton joined one of the youths who was pushing at the back, the other two being on each side at the front.

'How far are you going? St Neots?' he asked.

'Not likely,' grimaced the youth by his side, 'only a few hundred yards, but far enough. I'm streaked out, man.'

As Isaac Newton began to push with his body at an angle to the vertical, he became aware of a grisly noise emerging from inside the closed van, a noise he couldn't place at all – a growling which at first he thought must be a big dog but which he soon realised wasn't. A point came when they had to swing across the road against the traffic. They entered a concreted lane on the same side of the main road as the Lab, and all the time the growling continued. Isaac Newton was just thinking of asking for a pause in their labours when there came an immensely loud roar from the interior of the van, followed by a violent bang on the rear door immediately above his head.

'Susie's getting stroppy,' explained the youth by his side.

'*Who* is Susie?' Isaac Newton managed to mutter.

'Susie is our lion,' the youth explained. 'She's going to have her teeth fixed, man.'

Then Isaac Newton realised that of course the concreted lane led to the Veterinary School.

They were joined now by several other youths and girls, so that quite suddenly the pushing became light work, permitting Isaac Newton to take note of a signboard which read TO THE LARGE ANIMAL HOSPITAL.

A crowd assembled in front of the school and a man who was evidently the boss appeared. He had a broad smile with turned-up corners to his mouth and clear blue eyes. Noticing Isaac Newton standing out from the crowd, he came across and said:

'I'm Featherstone, Professor of Vet Science.'

'I'm Newton, I've just arrived at the Cavendish.'

'Of course, I've seen your picture,' the blue-eyed man nodded. He then shouted: 'Now everybody stand back, well back.'

The rear doors of the van opened. Isaac Newton expected the lion to spring out instantly, but it hesitated momentarily and in that moment there were several soft phuts. He was amazed at how very quickly the tranquillizers took effect. Susie slumped, and in a moment they had the creature rolled onto a stretcher and into the building.

'We have to work quickly,' Featherstone explained, 'otherwise there would be unlimited mayhem.'

'I didn't know you had such creatures here.'

'Oh, we see everything. Elephants, giraffes, llamas. You name it, we get it. A real menagerie.'

'It's rather the same at the Cavendish. Could you tell me, by the way, where I could lay my hands on one of those tranquillizer things? It would come in handy.'

'I'll bet it would,' laughed Featherstone, 'but the authorities are as keen as mustard on controlling tranquillizers. It's quite a bit harder to get them than normal firearms. But with our work they're essential.'

'I'd be glad to swop you two or three large bombs for one of them.'

'Better give me your hit list and we'll see what can be done about it,' Featherstone grinned. 'Maybe I'll look in on you one of these days.'

They shook hands and everybody except Isaac Newton was suddenly away into the building. Not wishing to attend Susie's appointment with the animal dentist, even though the thought of it conjured up intriguing visions, Isaac Newton took the shorter field path back to the Laboratory. Passing the signboard on the way he studied it for a while and thought that he would have Scrooge erect a similar signboard outside the Laboratory, reading TO THE STILL LARGER ANIMAL HOSPITAL.

He ran up the stairs back to his office, conscious that from the moment he'd begun to push the van he'd completely forgotten Clamperdown from CERC. A girl was waiting there for him, a girl with the agreeable proportions perciently foreseen by Jocelyn Scuby. So this must be Miss Haroldsen, Isaac Newton instantly decided. Also instantly he disposed of the baffling problem of how a latterday Mata Hari could have compiled Frances Haroldsen's academic record, for there was nothing at all slinky or sidelong here.

Frances Haroldsen was what transatlantically would be called an all-American girl, which is to say there was the instant suggestion of 'Anyone for tennis?' about her. The fair hair was worn shoulder-length and straight, in a 'nothing-disturbs-me' style. But the trouble, Isaac Newton also saw immediately, were the deep-violet eyes. He knew they were deep-violet because they were quite a bit darker than Featherstone's blue eyes, rivetingly so, he found.

'Are you quite satisfied?' asked Frances Haroldsen coolly. 'How would you like it if you had to work in a women's dress shop and all the women were looking at you all the time?'

'I'm sorry. I promise not to look at you all the time.'

'Actually, I came for three things. First, to thank you. Second, to strike a bargain. Third, to set you right on one or two points.'

'I'm always glad to be set right on one or two points, but I can't think what I've done to deserve your thanks, Miss Haroldsen.'

'Everybody here calls me Frances Margaret. You know I wish I could get hold of that little Scuby fellow. I'd like to wring his neck,' she said, apparently ignoring Isaac Newton's question.

'So, I gather, would many others. But what is Jocelyn Scuby to you, Frances Margaret?'

' "A fellow of infinite tongue who seeks to rhyme himself into favour, but reasons himself out." Shakespeare, and Shakespeare was a better poet than Congreve. But what I wanted to thank you for was what you said about my academic record. When people see it they usually say "Of course, she *must* have slept around with the examiners." Frances Margaret seated herself on the corner of the desk and added: 'Which is both mean and stupid, because if it was as easy as that there'd be a lot more first classes, wouldn't there?'

Isaac Newton opened his mouth and then forgot what he'd intended to say. Instead he asked in a suddenly raised voice:

'But how do you *know* all this?'

For answer, Frances Haroldsen took a small bright metal object from a pocket of her slacks. A dark piece of strong thread was attached to the object.

'This office is bugged, of course,' she said.

'It is *what?*'

'Bugged. Everybody in the Lab knows just what's going on. I wanted to know about Clamperdown especially. You see, I don't happen to like that CERC business.'

'Frances Margaret, you will turn your eavesdropping tape over to me forthwith.'

'You can have a copy of it, of course. I liked the bit about *orangesaft* by the way. It showed you can stand up for yourself.'

It was becoming more than clear to Isaac Newton why the activities of Miss Frances Haroldsen had attracted recommendations for dismissal. As if reading his thoughts, she continued from her perch on the corner of his desk:

'Those recommendations for dismissal now. It was sweet of you to take no notice of them. But you *are* sweet, aren't you?'

'I hadn't noticed it,' grunted Isaac Newton.

'Well, you are. Rather. But really it's a bit late. You being sweet, I mean. You see, I'm pretty sick of it all, which is why I'm willing to strike a bargain. If you'll put in a recommendation for me at CERN, I'll go quietly.'

'I'm not following you, Frances Margaret.'

'It's a fair cop, guv'ner. I'll go quietly. That sort of thing. If I stay and fight the General Bard, the struggle will become unbelievably bloody. I'm a good fighter, you see. I'll promise not to let you down at CERN. My qualifications are quite good – you said so yourself.'

'But I'm not recommending your dismissal,' Isaac Newton roared.

'No, but you will. Everybody does sooner or later.'

'Then why should you want to start it all over again at CERN?'

'I think it would be different there. CERN doesn't have the same long-standing tradition against women. Besides, it's bigger than the Lab here, and I think I could melt in more easily.'

'I'm sure you could,' nodded Isaac Newton, forbearing to mention Scuby's opinion of his visitor's unusual proportions. 'There will be no such infamous bargain,' he went on. 'As soon as I've had a chance to assess your work, if it's as good as I expect it to be, then of course I'll give you a recommendation. If you still want to leave, that is. Now, what was your third point? Advice, wasn't it?'

'Yes, I think I ought to tell you a few things which Mike Howarth didn't. I'm not breaking any confidences, because he's always telling people about them. It's just that he's got his head full of CERC these days, instead of concentrating on what really matters. You said the odds against him being right are a hundred-to-one. On what he showed you yesterday that might seem reasonable, but if you knew all I could tell you with these coral lips – it *was* coral lips wasn't it?   you'd see that a hundred-to-one is too high.'

Frances Haroldsen paused for a while. 'Well, go on,' said Isaac Newton impatiently.

'It's just that it's a big subject and it's now getting late in the afternoon, and I thought that if you'd like to take me out to dinner this evening it would be an excellent topic for an intimate *tête-à-tête*. Nice and technical with nothing personal, if you don't mind.'

Chapter 10

Isaac Newton drove to the multi-storey car park in Jesus Lane, and walked from there past St John's to Trinity. The sweep of Great Square opened up as he entered the College. Over the past thirteen years he'd forgotten the full impact of its spacious magnificence. It had been much the way it was now in the days of the great Isaac, whose rooms had been just to the right of the main gate.

Sundry people were walking across the square, moving in zig-zag patterns as they avoided the patches of mown lawn. As always, the people seemed dwarfed into the dimensions of ants by the scale of it all. *Plus ça change, plus c'est la même chose.*

Isaac Newton had dined in College the previous evening. The Fellows had assembled beforehand in the Combination Room, swathed in their black gowns. There were the small glasses of sherry and the conversation ran exactly as he remembered it. Then they had mounted up to the dining hall. In deference to his appointment in the steps of J. J. Thompson and Ernest Rutherford, and in view of his status as a returning prodigal, he had been moved up close to the Master, instead of joining the rough end of the younger Fellows at the bottom of the table, as had been his lot in earlier years. It was easy to make the accepted form of conversation, at the same time thinking of something else or listening to what other people at various places removed along the table were saying.

'I'd had the idea, you see, of examining the sixteenth-century records of colliers out of Newcastle.'

'Schubert? Oh! Those boring, boring woodwinds!'

'What kind of tie is that?'

'He said they went to Majorca, but I don't believe it. Who would?'

The man with the colliers' records out of Newcastle was an aging Professor of History who champed bread rolls throughout the meal. As soon as he finished one roll a waiter brought him another. He was among the dozen or so Fellows whom Isaac Newton remembered clearly. Watching the waiters walking backwards and forwards along the aisles, to and fro between the Hall and the kitchens, watching them with stacked plates on their arms, there was a kind of inside-out similarity, he thought, to the old story of Sleeping Beauty. A bustling scene where time suddenly stops and everything halts in mid-stride, held in suspension down to the last detail. Except that in the old story nobody aged while time stood still. Here it was the opposite, with everybody aging but nothing ever happening. In olden times, in the days of the great Isaac, it had been life in College which had seemed sharp and snappy in contrast to the bucolic world outside, but now it was the outside world where things proceeded apace, where things happened, like vacuum strings, or like comets alive.

At this point in his reflections Isaac Newton had decided to rent the house in Adams Road, for even a cat with the shivers would be *something*. What was it Achilles in Hades had said in the *Odyssey?*

Spare me your praise of Death, Lord Odysseus. Put me on Earth again, and I would rather be a serf in the house of some landless man than king of all these dead men that have done with life.

Dinner tonight with Frances Haroldsen would be different, no doubt, Isaac Newton thought, as he crossed Great Square to the steps which led him up to the Hall. After walking quickly through the short passage between the Hall and the kitchens, he descended the steps to the cloisters which ran towards the Wren Library. Towards the end of the cloisters he reached the staircase where the Old Guest Room was.

Once again the situation was inside-out. His apartment in Geneva had been small but with the most modern and efficient fittings. Here the situation was, as ever, spacious, but with fittings which made him wonder how, in any age or any place, anybody could ever have thought them a good idea. It would be an excellent Ph.D. topic, 'Plumbing in Cambridge', for some student in the humanities. Indeed, if suitably padded out and presented it would be a well-nigh perfect project for securing a grant from the Ford Foundation, a body with an amazing penchant for supporting the irrelevant.

For all his height, Isaac Newton had a half-drowned feeling as he emerged from the bath, a vat-like affair which amply deserved the American word 'tub'. In the bedroom there was a large four-poster bed and an immense, heavy wardrobe which would have knackered a party of strong men to have moved. In these uncertain times, the College was evidently taking no chances with its furniture, a point on which Isaac Newton made a mental note to congratulate the Bursar.

There was another hour before he was due to meet Frances Margaret Haroldsen at the main gate of the College. After dressing, he spent the first forty minutes of the hour sitting in a kind of stupor. What the devil, he asked himself seriously, had he got into? A question with an icy finger of fear in it: was the world around him really as peculiar – to put it mildly – as it seemed, or was he, in some strange way, projecting on to it a streak of madness within himself? Recalling the apparition with a face like the Greek mask of Tragedy, it almost seemed so. Forcing such disturbing thoughts out of his mind, he jumped to his feet and stepped onto the landing immediately outside the Old Guest Room, running quickly down the staircase into the cloisters.

The clock on the Edward III Tower was striking 6.45 p.m. as he re-crossed Great Square. It still wanted fifteen minutes more before his appointment outside the main gate. His route took him to the College Chapel, immediately beside the Edward III Tower. It wasn't the interior of the Chapel itself he wanted, but the large flagged antechapel where the statue of his namesake stood, the great Isaac who had exceeded all others in his genius, as the Latin inscription said: *Qui genus humanum ingenio superavit*.

There were other statues in the antechapel. He glanced briefly at those of the Victorian grandees, Tennyson and Macaulay, men with uninteresting faces, symbolising the coming decline of a once-great nation, symbolising the eventual collapse into the inverted Sleeping-Beauty state in which everybody aged without anything ever happening.

The statue on the raised pedestal was a universe apart from the others, and also unlike the formal portraits of the great Isaac Newton himself in his later, trivial days as Master of the Mint. Here was a youngish man of about his own age, the face alive and the body in motion as it walked the street, the countryside, the Great Square itself. Life burst out of the stone with a magic urgency. William Wordsworth had been a student in nearby St John's. He had occupied rooms high in an almost adjacent St John's building from which, on a moonlit night, he could look down into the Trinity antechapel, down onto the statue of the man who had exceeded all others in his genius. Wordsworth had seen the magic of it when he had written:

The marble index of his mind
Voyaging strange seas of thought, alone.

Strange seas of thought – the essence of science. Not the know-it-all attitude of the little men, whose knowledge was actually but an island of small proportion set in a vast ocean whose very existence their imaginations failed to conceive.

Chapter 11

Seven o'clock in the evening is a busy time of day at the front gate of any College, with both students and dons coming and going as the dinner hour approaches. Of all the Cambridge Colleges the front gate of Trinity is perhaps the busiest.

It occurred to Isaac Newton as he came out through the gate himself that if he'd wanted to advertise his evening engagement with Frances Haroldsen there could have been no better way of doing so. It scarcely needed a genius rising above the common ruck of humanity to guess that she would arrive to pick him up in a car well-designed to be noticed.

An open red sports car it proved to be, a sports car clearly dating from yesteryear that not only advertised itself by a bohemian appearance, but which heralded its arrival throatily as it sped towards him from St John's. Tall men usually have a bit of trouble in tucking themselves into a small sports car, and Isaac Newton was no exception. If his Houdini-like contortions weren't sufficient to advertise the arrangement to a number of Senior Fellows of the College – the bread-eating Professor of History among them, who by ill-luck arrived at this very moment – the sharp backfire which the machine delivered contemptuously in the faces of bystanders as it accelerated towards Caius just about cooked the situation. In Isaac Newton's judgement, at any rate.

'How did you happen to acquire this most attractive car, Frances Margaret?' he asked as they stopped for a moment at the Chesterton Lane traffic lights before turning left for the Backs.

'Bought it for ten pounds from a wrecker who had it from the gypsies. They couldn't do anything with it because the cylinder block was all cracked and the crankcase was in ruins. Gypsies are better with horses, you see.'

'But how does it now come to be in such excellent running order?' Isaac Newton persisted grimly. 'It seems to be just the job, as they say in the trade,' he shouted above the rush of air as they sped along the Backs.

'Welded up the cylinder block and bored it out. Got pistons and conrods from another wrecker. In fact, everything around you is from one wrecker or another,' Frances Margaret shouted in reply, her hair streaming attractively in the wind.

Their route took them by way of Fen Causeway, Trumpington Road and Long Road, out to beyond the hospital and towards the Gogs. At the Gogs their rate of progress slowed dramatically, causing Frances Haroldsen to remark:

'This damned car's a real clunker, isn't it? I told Maisie it would never get us up the Gogs.'

'*Who* is Maisie?'

'My room-mate in King's. Actually, I was having you on. This car belongs to Maisie. She's a demonstrator in engineering – very good at welding and that sort of thing, you see. I'm in bubble-chamber analysis myself.'

The car crawled at last over the summit ahead and Frances Margaret called out as she began speeding down the far side, 'Now hang on like grim death.' A broad smile on the girl's animated countenance revealed a perfect set of teeth as she stamped the accelerator flat on the floorboard.

'I'm getting breathless,' grunted Isaac Newton. 'Do you think you could ease up a bit? Where, by the way, might we be going?'

'I thought we might start at The Old Mitre in Babraham.'

The car park of The Old Mitre was full of large and expensive automobiles.

'Poor impoverished farmers ground down by the EEC,' Frances Margaret said as she manoeuvred the decrepit red sports car into a small space which had been rejected by the opulent earlier arrivals. As Isaac Newton slowly uncoiled himself from the car, the girl added:

'I seem to have misjudged things a bit. I expected it to be nice and quiet, but I *did* think to book a table.'

The noise from the bar filled every nook and cranny of the pub, and it was in the bar where they were told to wait until their table was ready.

'They've had all day to get tables ready. Thank you, yes, I'll have a tomato juice – with plenty of Worcester sauce to pepper me up,' Frances Margaret said with an expression that boded ill for the bar loungers who were twisting around on their stools to stare pointedly at her. Turning to Isaac Newton in an apparently confidential manner, but with a delivery that could have been heard at the far end of the village if need be, she continued:

'Drinking with a *meal* is good for preventing *coronaries*, you know. But drinking at the *bar-stool* is *deadly*. *Blood-clotting* and the *bar-stool* go hand in hand, *doctors* say – especially in *men*, and especially when they get *overweight*. *Blood-clotting* does its *deadly* work in *every* part of the *body*. There are *scores* of cases *every* hour. These places all have *stretchers*, ready to *catch* them as they *drop off* their bar-stools, just like *flies* . . .'

To Isaac Newton's dazed mind it seemed that a waiter and the barman simply lifted them with a single movement into the dining room.

'Good,' nodded Frances Margaret, 'that was very satisfactory, and I'll bet they serve us quickly, too.'

'Did you have to go on like that?'

'The most powerful weapon in life is *un*concern. I discovered long ago that if you don't care a bit what people think, then you're the boss,' Frances Margaret replied, crunching a bread roll *allegro con forza*.

As the dining room gradually filled up, the covert glances towards them became more and more frequent, to the point where Isaac Newton felt that something had to give again. Contriving to impart a strangely intimate quality to her voice, which otherwise remained as easily audible as before, Frances Margaret suddenly asked:

'Imagine you had an *egg*. Out in *space*.'

'A boiled *egg* you mean?' Isaac Newton replied as best he could.

'No, a fresh *egg*, straight from the *hen*. Would it *go cold*, d'you think?'

'Very likely it would,' Isaac Newton replied again, conscious of a total collapse of the conversation around them. Silence or no, Frances Margaret continued in the same clearly audible tones as before:

'*Hard* as a *stone*, would you think?'

'Or harder.'

'Quite. That's *very* important. Couldn't be *more* important, you know.'

Isaac Newton had realised by now that seemingly preposterous statements from Miss Frances Haroldsen had an undercurrent of logic and meaning to them, but try as he might through the rest of the dinner he could see no reason why an egg straight from the hen going harder than a stone in space was important. Shrugging to himself as they came to the coffee, he gave up the puzzle, wishing it could have been dumped in the lap of the great Isaac Newton, whose genius, one supposes, would have soared above it.

On their return to Cambridge, Frances Haroldsen swung the red sports car through the gap between concrete posts in front of Trinity. After Isaac Newton had extricated himself again, she quickly put up the hood and locked the car doors.

'We'll leave it here,' she said.

'We will *not* leave it here. The porters will put wheel clamps on it.'

'Let them,' nodded Frances Margaret. 'This is part of a carefully-laid plan, I might tell you. Come on now, we still have much to discuss, about eggs in space, about cabbages and kings, and why the eggs remain boiling hot and whether comets have wings.'

'But the darned car is an obvious advertisement.'

'It's intended to be, of course. Look, if you keep on arguing like this everybody will notice, and then the fat really will be in the fire. Come on, remember it's Maisie's car, not mine. She'll be glad to argue with the porters.'

'Will she?' Isaac Newton asked grumpily as they walked across Great Square.

'It's all very simple,' Frances Haroldsen told him. 'You see, Maisie is entertaining in King's tonight. But with her car parked outside Trinity nobody will suspect, because everybody in Cambridge connects Maisie with the car. So it will be thought by one and all that she's here in Trinity, right?'

'The snag with that simplistic point of view is that one and all will connect *me* with Maisie's car.'

'So people will think Maisie is being entertained by the new

Cavendish Professor, off to a very fast start. But that isn't true at all, and since truth will out, as people say, everybody will be disappointed in their unworthy thoughts.'

By this time they had reached the cloisters. 'It's here, isn't it?' Frances Haroldsen asked, scarcely checking her stride as she led the way up to the Old Guest Room. Isaac Newton followed behind as in a dream. When they were inside the door to the drawing-room, Frances Margaret shut it, but only after first slamming the outer oak with a bang that seemed designed to be detected by the distant seismographs of the Geophysics Department at Madingley Rise.

'That's just to stop somebody coming along asking for a tea-bag or a bottle of milk or something,' she explained.

A quick reconnaissance by Frances Margaret soon revealed the four-poster bed.

'Oh!' she cried. 'I've always wanted to sleep in a four-poster.'

Then she bounced herself two or three times on the mattress and added:

'This is *just* right, said Goldilocks when she saw the little bear's bed. You don't mind, do you? I mean you wouldn't want to turn me out into the bitter cold, into the snow drifts, would you? That would be a desperately cruel thing to do, which one and all would sternly condemn. Of course you can sleep on that uncomfortable-looking couch in the drawing-room if you're determined about it.'

'I am *not* going to be summarily ejected from my own bed,' Isaac Newton replied huffily.

'I can sympathise with you there, because I wouldn't want to be either, not if I were in your position – with all its attendant problems and difficulties. You wouldn't have a spare toothbrush, would you?'

Isaac Newton stalked with his pyjamas into the drawing-room and told her:

'You'll find one in the small cupboard in the bathroom.'

He took some time undressing and putting on the pyjamas, feeling that the situation merited thought. When he returned to the bedroom, he found Frances Margaret already installed in the four-poster.

'I've taken the left side,' she explained, 'because I punch with my left fist. I can also kick hard with both legs, which from a masculine point of view can be very dangerous, as doubtless you are aware. Just in case you get any wrong ideas.'

'What then, if I may be permitted to ask, have you in mind, if anything?'

'There's no need to be nasty, not when I'm doing so much to help. I thought we could talk here.'

'Keep going then.'

'Are you comfortable now? Once the aches and pains of the day begin to die down you'll feel a little less nasty. Hopefully. Although with you not being me you can never tell, can you?'

'I am *quite* comfortable, thank you. Is there *anybody* called Maisie, by the way?'

'Oh, *yes*. Maisie is real enough, just like her car.'

Isaac Newton allowed his thoughts to play momentarily on the horror of a red sports car illegally parked outside the front gate of Trinity, illegally parked for one and all to see.

'Imagine you are on an infinite sunless plane,' Frances Margaret drawled as she put out the light. 'A sunless plane where the temperature is not much above absolute zero. Imagine ice cubes dotted over the plane.'

'You did say ice cubes?'

'Yes, I did, and watch out when you touch them that you don't get severe frostbite, because the ice cubes are very cold and very hard. Some of them are of the size you find in a refrigerator. Some are much bigger, a metre in size. Some are even ten metres in size. Some are a hundred metres in size, some...are...ten...thousand...' Frances Haroldsen's voice trailed off in a manner that reminded Isaac Newton of the dormouse in *Alice in Wonderland*.

'That's impossible,' he forced himself to say. 'You couldn't have an ice cube ten thousand metres in size. It would collapse.'

'For that, Professor, you get three marks. Now, how big an ice cube would *not* collapse? That's the question, Horatio.'

'I suppose it would be a question of plastic flow.'

'Put plastic flow right out of your head, Horatio. We'll not have that there 'ere. Put it this way. Suppose I have an enormous bulldozer, and suppose the dozer is equipped with enormous claws. How big an ice cube can I pick up? Without its bottom dropping off, I mean.'

It wasn't so much the last question itself that baffled Isaac Newton as the infuriating mystery of what Frances Margaret was getting at. They were supposed to be talking about comets, not dozers with enormous claws.

'More than ten metres, I would think,' he replied.

'More than a hundred metres?'

'I don't know, possibly.'

'More than a kilometre?'

'No, glaciers begin to collapse when they get as thick as that. But what has all this to do with comets?'

'A great deal, as you will discover, Professor, once the fog clears from your mind. Actually you get an A-minus for that answer, although you have gotten it by sleeping with the examiner. Actually, the correct answer is that you could just about pick up an ice cube that was three hundred metres in size. Anything bigger would collapse.'

Frances Haroldsen gave a big yawn, saying as she did so, 'The excitement of the day is beginning to catch up with me.'

'How did you discover these amazing facts about ice cubes, Frances Margaret?'

'Measurements,' the girl continued yawningly, 'by the South... Manchurian...Ice...Company...in 1908...when the comet fell... in Siberia.'

'*What* is the connection with comets?'

There was no reply. Miss Frances Haroldsen had at last talked herself to sleep. Isaac Newton listened to her regular breathing. The evening had done little to allay his now clearly-formed suspicion that things in Cambridge were not the way they used to be.

Chapter 12

Moonlight shone brightly down into the Trinity antechapel, causing a gentle radiance to appear around the statue of the great Isaac Newton. The clock on the Edward III Tower began to strike. It was 1.00 a.m. A soft sound of people stirring in slow motion could be heard from the interior of the chapel itself, and a mournful dirge like the winter wind sobbing in the trees accompanied their movement. A cowled figure appeared in the open archway that separates the antechapel from the Chapel proper. It stepped into the antechapel carrying a bell and a book. Other hooded figures, each carrying one large lit candle, followed through the archway, so that a slow-moving procession of dark figures walked two abreast across the flagged floor of the antechapel. Their leader reached the outer door which gives onto Great Square. Stepping into the open air the leader began to ring the bell. A shaft of moonlight fell so as to penetrate his cowl, revealing the features momentarily. It was the Master of Trinity.

Two-by-two the figures followed the Master into the open air, singing their dirge monotonously all the while. It was a procession of the Fellows, a procession with bell, book and candle, following the Master with slow, deliberate, inexorable steps across the paths and lawns of Great Square, to the short passage between the kitchens and the Hall. Two-by-two the cowled Fellows of Trinity moved with their candles through the passage. Their dirge was blown away for a while by a breeze that swept through the opening, only to return to its former sombre volume when the cloisters were reached.

The Master continued ringing the bell until he reached the staircase to the Old Guest Room. Then, after pausing for a while to allow the last of the hooded figures to reach the cloisters, he began, with infinite deliberation, to ascend the staircase itself. Arriving at the Old Guest Room he lifted the arm which carried the book and hit the sported oak a seemingly gentle blow. A noise like rolling thunder filled the air. The pairs of figures who had mounted the stairs behind the Master moved one to each side to permit others carrying a stout log about twenty feet long to pass between them. The log hit the sported oak, and the rolling thunder was ridden over by a sound like the clashing symbols of the Devil's own orchestra, or so it seemed to Frances Haroldsen as she awoke from her nightmare.

There *was* a loud knocking on the sported oak of the outer door of the Old Guest Room, a determined persistent knocking. Overwhelmed by the sheer horror of it, Frances Margaret reached over and gripped Isaac Newton so tightly that he awoke with a shout.

'They're here,' half-screamed the girl.

'*Who* is here?' Isaac Newton growled, wishing Frances Margaret would shut up and go to sleep again.

'It's the Master, with bell, book and candle. And the other Fellows dressed in cowls. They're hitting the oak with a battering ram,' was her desperate reply.

'A likely story,' growled Isaac Newton again. 'Couldn't your astonishing talent for invention have waited until morning?'

The knocking continued persistently.

'It's someone come to borrow a tea-bag or a bottle of milk or something,' Isaac Newton said in resigned fashion, slipping on a dressing-gown and making his way to the light switches. He noticed, as he made for the drawing-room door, that it was just coming up to 1.45 a.m. He yawned as he opened the outer door.

It was indeed a strange sight which met his eyes, as Frances had in principle predicted. But in place of the cowled phantoms of her nightmare there were two men, one in a top hat, the other in a bowler hat. There was indeed a Fellow of the College, none other than the Dean, whose primary concern was with the morals of members of the

College. The bowler-hatted figure Isaac Newton recognised as the night porter, the top-hatted figure he hadn't seen before. The fourth figure was a uniformed sergeant of police.

'I'm sorry to disturb you, sir,' said the sergeant, 'but a serious matter has arisen.'

As the visitors pressed forward into the drawing-room, Isaac Newton noticed a most awkward detail. Frances Margaret had left her handbag on the settee, in exactly the place where he might be expected to invite the Dean to sit down.

The door to the landing outside remained open and another policeman arrived, followed by a youngish man in a clerical collar. Isaac Newton tried to decide whether to remove the offending handbag, passing it off with some well-judged remark such as, 'Oh, my aunt left this behind when she visited me last week,' or just to pretend it didn't exist. Being undecided he simply said:

'It *must* be serious.'

The sergeant nodded and announced gravely:

'We've got a dead man on our hands.'

Isaac Newton bit back the impulse to say, 'Well, what's that to do with me?' and waited for the sergeant to explain.

'We think he might be a member of your staff, sir.'

Then the unfamiliar top-hatted man said:

'I'm the night porter from St John's, sir. The dead man seems to be one of our Fellows, although why he should be here in Trinity is a mystery.'

'Who might this unfortunate person be?' Isaac Newton asked.

'Dr Michael Howarth.'

'The funny thing, Newton,' the Dean said in a puzzled tone, 'is that he was found dead in *our* Chapel. Because I understand that he is one of your men, I thought it right to come along and enlist your aid.'

'To identify the body?'

'Well, yes . . .'

'It would be easier in the morning, in the light.'

'I understand that,' the sergeant came in, 'but frankly speaking, sir, I'd like you to see the body for yourself – as a witness – because it's very queer.'

Meanwhile Frances Margaret had dressed herself. She was aware of the drawing-room filling with people to the point where someone might easily spill over into the bedroom. There were two obvious places where she could hide – under the bed, or inside an enormous wardrobe. Deciding that she definitely drew the line at hiding under the bed, she examined the wardrobe. Finding the interior smelled

musty, she decided to draw the line at that too. Besides which, being
.discovered hiding in a wardrobe would make the story of her supposed
liaison with Isaac Newton so ridiculous that it would become a
permanent part of Cambridge lore, never to be forgotten as the years
rolled on. Parties of American tourists would be told that, whereas the
older Isaac Newton had first measured the speed of sound in the
cloisters downstairs, the younger Isaac Newton had kept his mistress in
a wardrobe upstairs. Frances Haroldsen was also gifted with the sure
instinct that, whatever the situation, the best policy is always to
command the court, which meant she must simply walk out with total
unconcern and join what, according to the snatches of conversation she
had managed to overhear, appeared to be a strange business.

'And *what* is so very queer about it?' she asked clearly and
penetratingly as she came in from the bedroom, so jumping instantly
centre-stage.

The sergeant was momentarily taken aback by the girl's assurance in
what seemed a compromising situation. Then rallying himself he
explained:

'Well, Mr Kent, the night porter here, was making his rounds when
he heard a strange noise.'

'A thin wailing noise,' the bowler-hatted figure whom Isaac Newton
had recognised broke in. 'It was coming from the Chapel. So I went in
and found him there, sitting at the organ.'

'What time would that be?' Isaac Newton asked.

'I know it exactly, sir, because the clock had just struck one a.m.'

'Was the wailing noise coming from the organ?' Isaac Newton asked
in an incredulous voice.

'That's just it, sir,' the sergeant nodded.

'The problem, Newton, is to understand how a deal Fellow of a
neighbouring college came to be in our Chapel at one in the
morning, with a finger depressed upon an organ key, the organ itself
being in a live condition,' explained the Dean succinctly.

'Why wasn't the wailing noise heard before?'

'There was some wind,' the porter explained, 'and the noise was
piano, or whatever they call it, sir.'

'It was probably the traffic noise dying down which made it stand
out.'

'That's it, sir!' exclaimed the porter, glad of a rational explanation of
why nobody had heard the organ earlier.

The organ had by now been switched off. 'Gave you the collywobbles
when it was going,' the porter said as the party entered the antechapel.

They walked in the gloom across the flagged floor, the police making a disturbingly loud sound with their leather-soled shoes. A third policeman was on guard immediately inside the archway leading into the Chapel, a young fellow glad to see his colleagues back after being alone there for half an hour.

Frances Haroldsen was at the rear of the party. She had known Mike Howarth too well to have any wish to see his body sprawled in death, under what appeared to be outrageous and mysterious circumstances, so she held back in the antechapel when the others moved forward into the Chapel proper. She turned and looked back the length of the antechapel towards the statue of the first Isaac Newton. The statue was at first in shadow. Then it brightened as a shaft of moonlight illuminated the plinth. Frances Margaret continued to watch with a weird sense of anticipation. Almost as if fulfilling her expectations, the statue brightened unnaturally. Suddenly it was glowing and flaming orange-red, ten feet tall, with a face like the Greek mask of Tragedy. Giving a muffled scream, Frances Haroldsen rushed towards the outer door which gives onto Great Square and immediately collapsed on the threshold there.

Meanwhile, inside the Chapel proper, the policeman who had been left on guard told the sergeant:

'The body rolled over while you were away. For a second or two I thought it was coming alive again.'

The corpse was slumped right across the organ console.

'Can you shift it back to where it was before?' Isaac Newton asked.

'No, sir, not now. Perhaps later when we've taken photographs,' the sergeant replied. 'Is it the man? Dr Howarth, I mean, sir.'

'It appears to be Howarth, but it's hard to get a good sight of him. I said it would be better in the morning. Has the body gone stiff?' Isaac Newton asked again.

'It must have been stiff from the beginning.'

'As if he died in some kind of spasm?'

'Looks that way, sir. But we'll find out at the autopsy.'

'When will that be?'

'Today, very likely. Have you any reason to think . . .'

'That he'd commit suicide? He had reason to be worried, but hardly to that extent.'

'Well perhaps we should leave questions of motive for later.'

'Have you called a doctor?'

'Yes, but he's dead all right,' asserted the sergeant with total confidence in his own judgement.

The Dean came up, together with the so-far unidentified man in the clerical collar.

'I must apologise for not introducing the Chaplain of St John's.'

'There doesn't seem to be much we can do,' Isaac Newton said as he shook hands briefly with the Chaplain. 'But I think *you* should make the definite identification. I only met Howarth once.'

Isaac Newton was conscious in the gloom of the Chapel that the sergeant had made a note of his last remark. Frances Margaret was sitting on the outer doorstep of the antechapel.

'I needed air,' she explained briefly to Isaac Newton. 'I felt quite faint.'

Isaac Newton went back to the sergeant and said:

'The young lady isn't feeling too well. Is there anything else you want from me?'

'Well, sir, not now but later. As I said before, I thought you might want to see it for yourself. Frankly, I've never seen anything quite like it myself. That statue at the end, over there, sir, it has the same name as you, doesn't it?'

'Yes, it has.'

'And that's very queer as well, sir, isn't it? As if it was the statue that struck him down.'

Chapter 13

Back in the Old Guest Room Frances Haroldsen decided she wasn't going to make a fool of herself by talking about what reason told her she couldn't have seen, especially in front of Isaac Newton. Nevertheless, it was in a strained voice that she burst out:

'Why did he have to *do* it?'

'You don't think it was something I did?'

'How could it be? You offered to help him by taking his satellite records to CERN, didn't you? And you did what you could about his contract – to the point of having a dreadful row with that frightful fellow from CERC.'

'I thought I tried.'

'So why did he do it? Right under the nose of the statue of Isaac Newton. It involves you up to the neck.'

'The sergeant said just now that it looked as if the statue had struck him down.'

'Substitute *you* for the statue and that's what people are going to think.'

'There are too many things we don't know yet for judgements to be sensible at this point,' Isaac Newton said as calmly as he could, and with more accuracy than he realised. 'There are all sorts of things which might happen, but there's no point in crossing our bridges before we get to them. We mustn't miss the right moves by getting too emotional. The police are likely to get hold of everything of Mike Howarth's they can lay their hands on, which means that his papers may get frozen. On the plus side I already have the satellite disks with the dot-dash signals. But we need access to his other data files. It seems doubtful they'll be at the Lab, because he didn't seem to trust anybody there.'

'I think I know where they might be.' From her voice it might have been judged that Frances Haroldsen had recovered her poise.

'In St John's?'

'Very unlikely. Mike really was extremely secretive about his data, and Colleges are very open places, with so many people milling around all the time. A determined thief wouldn't have too much trouble in snitching things, because every day the porters and the bedders walk round with the keys to every set of rooms on every staircase.'

'As far as I could tell, the idea of depositing material with a bank was new to him.'

'He had a place of his own, miles out in the country – a cottage. It was willed to him a few years ago, by an uncle, I think. That's where his papers will be, the ones he valued most. I've been there once or twice, with walking parties on the Roman road. It's not too far from the Linton water tower. We could go out to Linton in the morning.'

'Much as it grieves me to say it, tomorrow morning will be too late. By then the police may be everywhere. Besides which, I can't go out of Cambridge tomorrow. It would simply invite enquiry. If we're to go, we must go now. Could you find this cottage in the dark?'

'I could try. But what if the sergeant or the Dean comes back here?'

'Then I will be away, escorting you back to your domicile.'

After leaving the cloisters, Isaac Newton and Frances Haroldsen were quickly over Trinity Bridge and along the avenue which leads to the locked back gate of the College. It was the work of a moment for Isaac Newton to use his special Fellow's key to let them through the gate. They walked at a brisk pace, first past the back of John's to Chesterton Lane. Continuing for about a third of a mile towards

Chesterton they reached a footbridge to the right which took them across the River Cam. A short walk over the edge of Jesus Green brought them to the all-night multi-storey park where nine hours earlier Isaac Newton had left his car. It was certainly a circuitous route from Trinity, but a route along which they had been reasonably safe from interception by any suspicious police officer.

The route out of Cambridge along Hills Road past the hospital was the same as the one they had taken earlier, but the Mercedes which Isaac Newton had brought back from Switzerland cleared the Gogs without any noticeable check in its speed. Instead of turning into Babraham they continued across the London-Newmarket main road, and so on to Linton.

'Keep down to the bottom past the Swan,' instructed Frances Margaret. 'Then, as you go up through the far end of the village, watch out for a left turn. It's by the fire station.'

Ten minutes further along an unmade road through thick woods, they reached a characteristic flint and rubble cottage which had had its original thatched roof replaced by tiles.

'This is it,' announced Frances Margaret. 'There's nothing else for miles around. The magic cottage all alone in the woods.'

With the headlights playing on the cottage, Isaac Newton took out the tool-kit from the boot of the car, saying, 'A bit primitive perhaps, but we should be able to cope. Just give me a bit of extra light from this torch. Play it on the window catch – here.'

Within five minutes they had the catch of one of the ground-floor windows pushed aside. In another minute they had the lower half of the window pushed up, and then, with a heave and a pull, they were inside the cottage.

'That was hardly a case of breaking and entering as the police say. Entering, yes, breaking, no. Now where is the nearest light switch?' Isaac Newton remarked, as if to himself.

'People might see a light.'

'Cottage-dwellers sometimes get up in the night, so why should that matter?'

'It's just that with a light on people outside can see us but we can't see them,' Frances Margaret replied.

Isaac Newton flicked a switch, and the light from two shaded lamps revealed that they had climbed into the parlour of the cottage, a small but comfortably furnished room with an open fireplace with wood piled at the side and a layer of white ash in the grate. There was a sudden thump from immediately above their heads and a muffled voice cried out:

'Who's there?'

'Good God, we've got the wrong cottage,' Isaac Newton whispered. Frances Margaret gripped his arm and whispered in return:

'I'm absolutely sure it's right. You can see from the physics books over there.' The girl pointed towards a small bookcase.

A door upstairs opened and the voice again shouted, but clearly now: 'I say, who's there?'

The grip on Isaac Newton's arm tightened and the hairs on his neck prickled as he recognised the voice.

'It's Mike Howarth,' half-screamed Frances Haroldsen. 'The thing in the Chapel wasn't him at all!'

Then, as the lights went out, memories of the uncanny moment in the Chapel came back in full force and Frances Margaret let loose with a full-blooded scream. Isaac Newton lifted her fingers from his arm, took the torch, and moved out of the parlour into a small hallway, showing more boldness than he felt. Footsteps above reached an upper landing and began to descend a flight of stairs which creaked with the tread.

Yet the torch showed nobody on the stairs. Noises of movement seemed to fill the cottage. With sudden decision, Isaac Newton moved quickly to the stairs, and as he began to ascend them Frances Margaret shouted:

'Come back! I *know* there's something horrible up there.'

There was an explosion like a pistol shot followed by a loud cry, and then a silence in which Frances Haroldsen could hear a hoarse breathing sound, which instinct told her was not human. A light continued to flicker upstairs, and suddenly Isaac Newton shouted down from above:

'It's all right. You can come up.'

Almost in the same moment an owl hooted in the woods outside, sounding loudly because of the open window. Frances Margaret groped her way up the stairs and into a room where the beam of a torch flickered to and fro.

'What is it?' she gasped.

'A tape-recording, amplified to speakers in various parts of the cottage. It's an ingenious kind of burglar alarm.'

The lights came on just as suddenly as they had gone off a few moments before.

'We must have tripped the thing when we came in through the window, or somehow in the parlour. I would think he had the lights on a time switch,' Isaac Newton guessed.

Electronic equipment was scattered around the upper room, which evidently had not been used at all as a bedroom. There was also a filing cabinet about three feet high with a key in the lock at the top.

'Pound to a penny this is what we're looking for,' Isaac Newton exclaimed triumphantly. Then as he reached out towards the key Frances Haroldsen shouted with extreme urgency:

'Don't touch it! The thing's a switch. Mike Howarth would never leave a key in a lock.'

'You were right before! There *is* something horrible up here.'

'Somewhere there must be a cable.'

'I doubt we'll find it easily,' Isaac Newton replied. 'If I were wanting to electrocute someone, I'd bring the supply cable up through the floor boards, directly underneath the cabinet, so it couldn't be seen by the victim; and I'd put a two-thousand-volt transformer in the bottom drawer. Not very nice.'

'We'd better switch the power off at the mains.'

'Or cut the mains cable outside the house. If I wanted to be even nastier, I'd rig up a power line that by-passed the mains switch.'

They found a large key in the lock on the front door of the cottage. Gripping the key with a bunched handkerchief, Isaac Newton grunted:

'I wouldn't think this is necessary but there's no sense in taking any risk now. Besides, we shouldn't be too prolific in leaving our fingerprints around.'

There was a shower of sparks as he cut the power cable at some distance from the cottage on its way down from an overhead post. Replacing the rubber-handled cutters in the tool-kit of the car, and putting his arm around Frances Margaret's shoulders, Isaac Newton added:

'I hated doing that because it's certain to be noticed; and thanks for the warning by the way.'

With an instant twist the girl was in his arms, trembling and kissing him fiercely.

'There's an all-night motel on the London road. Let's go there,' she whispered, 'quickly.'

Chapter 14

'After such a torrid night, both early and late, today will be a gruelling test of character,' said Isaac Newton sleepily to Frances Margaret Haroldsen as she handed him a cup of tea, brewed in the motel room they had taken five hours before. On the table beside the ubiquitous TV set was a scattering of tapes and disks, and a stack of files a foot deep, the erstwhile contents of the filing cabinet in the upper room of Mike Howarth's cottage near the Linton water tower.

'Let's begin the test of character by taking a look at those disks,' Isaac Newton went on, propping himself against pillows heaped at the head of the bed. Frances Margaret brought them to him one by one. At the end of the examination process he finished the cup of tea and remarked:

'As far as I can tell, they're exactly like the ones at Barclays Bank. I think these must be the originals.'

'Mike Howarth would have kept the originals. That's for sure.'

'So we can afford the luxury of leaving the copies at the bank, so they can be produced at any moment to suit our convenience, just to prove to suspicious people that hanky-panky is far from our minds.'

'While all the time hanky-panky is very much to the front of our minds, I suppose.'

'As we are now going to demonstrate. To begin with, have you a valid passport, Frances Margaret?'

'Yes, but why?'

'Because *you* must take these disks to CERN. Obviously I can't, now, so you'll be at CERN much sooner than you expected. Ironic the way things fall out, isn't it?'

'You were going there at the end of the week?'

'I was, but the timetable isn't as leisurely as it appeared, I'm afraid. The sooner we get these things to Switzerland the better – which means today, without delay.'

'But the whole thing's a mess. I don't see how.'

'To begin with I want you to sort out these files. Divide them into two sets: one set technical, the other personal. In effect, the technical set belongs to the Lab, because it refers mostly to investigations through contracts written formally in the Lab's name.'

'I see, the technical material is really yours anyway, as trustee for the Lab, so we haven't really stolen it.'

'That's right. Although our conduct may have seemed peculiar, and although it nearly led us to a sticky end, it was approximately defensible so far as the disks and technical files are concerned. But the situation for Mike Howarth's personal stuff is different. That's plain theft, and so we must get rid of the personal stuff straight away. The simplest plan would be to dump it into a litter bin somewhere, but that would be a bit mean because it could be important – there could be Howarth's will, or the deeds to his house. So when you've sorted it out I want you to go into Newmarket with the car. Parcel the stuff into lots of a size you can send through the post, and despatch them to the Chaplain of St John's. Use a thick black flow pen and print the address in capitals, so that...'

'OK. I understand. And what, may I ask, are you going to do? Stay propped up like that in bed?'

'Being in an exhausted condition, that's exactly what I'm going to do, while I use the phone. And try to be back from Newmarket before eleven.'

'What am I going to carry the disks in?'

'Hand me my trousers and jacket.'

'You're *not* very active, are you?'

'Nobody in their senses would expect me to be,' Isaac Newton replied, taking the car keys from a pocket and a bundle of notes from a wallet. 'Buy one of those cases in which businessmen carry their samples, the sort you can carry with you on the plane. You'd better take these Swiss francs. And buy me a packet of disposable razors.'

It was 11.20 a.m. by the time Frances Margaret returned. With something of her old ebullience she announced as she re-entered the motel room:

'Well, it's done. But you should just try parcelling things in Newmarket. I had to hunt all over for the big envelopes, scissors, sealing tape, pen. You name it, they don't have it. But I got a very nice case for the disks.'

'Then pack them carefully, so that you know how they're arranged. If the Swiss customs ask about them, don't bluff. Say you're carrying scientific material from Cambridge to CERN. I've telephoned through to Kurt Waldheim in Geneva – he was the key theoretical physicist on the top quark team. Either he or his wife will meet your 'plane. His wife's name is Rosie, and they're both in their thirties. If you do get into a tangle with the customs, let Kurt sort it out. The 'plane is due out of Heathrow at six-ten p.m. We have to pick up the tickets in Newmarket – I thought it best to use an agent there – and I've arranged for a car to drive you to the airport. It will be at the White

Hart Hotel in Newmarket High Street at two p.m. You'll want to go first into Cambridge to put a few things together, but travel as light as you can. You can buy anything you need while the disks are being processed. I've settled the motel bill and I persuaded the front office to let me have the use of their typewriter.'

'You're quite an organizer, aren't you?'

'That's what they keep me for.'

Isaac Newton handed Frances Margaret a typed sheet of paper, adding:

'Guard this with your life. It's an instruction to my bank in Geneva, to make draft available to you.'

'*You* shouldn't be paying for this.'

'No, I shouldn't,' Isaac Newton agreed, 'but the end is going to be a lot bigger than the means by which it's achieved, I'm betting.'

Frances Margaret saw that the technical files had been neatly packed into a box.

'I got the box also from the front office,' Isaac Newton explained. 'Maybe you could lock it in the boot of the car while I shave and take a shower.'

It was 12.45 p.m. when, after collecting the air tickets, Isaac Newton parked the Mercedes at the White Hart Hotel, remarking as he switched off the engine, 'We've still got time for lunch. Amazing. I thought we'd never make it.'

There was still a quarter of an hour before the hotel dining-room filled up, so they had no difficulty in securing a table. Isaac Newton decided:

'In spite of the danger of blood-clotting, you're getting no wine with your meal on this occasion. We still need to keep clear heads. We've only an hour before you leave and you still haven't explained the importance of ice cubes and hard eggs in space. Suppose you get on with it, so far as the champing of food will allow.'

'Well,' Frances Margaret began, 'do you know what a sungrazer comet is?'

'A comet which grazes the Sun, I suppose.'

'They're unusual, with orbits that take them almost inside the Sun, but not quite. It's been found by direct observation that sungrazer comets mostly divide, quite a bit later on, into two or more pieces, as if heating by the Sun had weakened them. The largest bit after division is said to be not enormously larger than the other bits, which is important. The bits can be seen by astronomers as they separate from each other. They do so quite slowly, showing that the sungrazer hasn't been burst apart by a violent internal explosion.'

'Why does it break up then?'

'Astronomers think because of the rotation of the comet - at least that's one of the explanations.'

'Isn't there something called Roche's limit? I seem to remember it has to do with tidal break-up due to gravitation.'

Frances Haroldsen shook her head vigorously in denial:

'Not in this case. Definitely not. Roche's limit works only if you can ignore the internal strength of a body. For a body as small as a comet the internal strength is much bigger than the tidal effects, by very many orders of magnitude. Well then, to come to the first big problem. Even though rotational effects are more important than tidal effects, they still don't seem to be enough.'

'For what?'

'To exceed the tensile strength of hard-frozen ice, which is what comets are supposed to be. Rounded ice cubes, you might say. I haven't been able to see any way out of this dilemma, except to say they're not ice cubes at all. They seem to be more like an *egg*, straight from the *hen*; except that the egg is spinning. If one of them happens to move in an orbit which brings it close to the Sun, the great heat cracks the shell of the spinning egg, which then breaks up gently into a number of pieces because of the rotation. Of course, comets are normally round, not egg-shaped, although they would become pretty much like an egg while breaking up.'

'Well, what's wrong with that?'

'Because in solving one problem another rears its ugly head. You see, comets spend the overwhelming fraction of their time far away from the Sun, most of them in the far reaches of the solar system beyond the outermost planets, where they'd soon cool off.'

'I see...the egg in space going harder than a stone.'

'Yes. If you start with a comet in a liquid condition, like the egg straight from the hen, it would freeze solid in about ten thousand years. Even if it had a shell that was an excellent insulator, a skin like moon dust.'

'But why shouldn't the comet melt as it comes close in to the Sun?'

'That's easy to answer. Although there seems to be a lot of heat, there just isn't enough. You see, a sungrazer comet only spends about an hour in there tight by the Sun, and it's easy to calculate that in an hour only a surface layer about fifty to a hundred metres thick would melt and evaporate. For a comet five kilometres in diameter this obviously isn't enough. All the Sun can do is to play havoc with the surface layer, cracking the egg as it were.'

'So what's the answer? Could radioactive heat be keeping the inside of a comet warm?'

'That seems to be the inference, but it requires a tremendous amount of radioactive material, and the trouble is that there are *no* meteorites with anything like such amounts – some of the meteorites are probably of cometary origin, you see. So even this idea runs into a dead end too.'

'How much do you call a lot?'

'Well, if the radioactive material were uranium, there would have to be at least a hundred parts per million by weight, and that's an awfully high uranium concentration.'

'Calculating for the natural decay of uranium, I suppose?'

'Yes, of course.'

'How did you come to learn all these things, Frances Margaret?'

'Oh, I used to argue with Mike Howarth about it. Then I came to check the facts.'

'I can see I'll be doing just that during the next few days.'

'Don't you think it's odd? Mike Howarth used to say the only way out of all the difficulties was heat production by biological metabolism, which sounds fine until you realise that comets are more than four thousand billion years old. Keeping warm biologically for that length of time never seemed right to me.'

'It isn't,' said Isaac Newton positively. 'I'd be pretty sure the radioactive explanation is the right one – but by fission, not by natural decay.'

'A nuclear reactor!' exclaimed Francis Haroldsen. 'Surely you can only have a nuclear reactor under very *controlled* conditions?'

'Have you heard of the OKLO reactor? In Gabon, West Africa?'

'Wasn't that something which happened about two thousand million years ago? I've heard it was supposed to be a natural nuclear reactor. That's an interesting idea.'

'It is, especially as it wasn't a natural reactor.'

'Explain, boss.'

'There is no time, Frances Margaret, the sands of time have run out on our conversation, I'm afraid. But when you get to CERN ask Kurt Waldheim to show you the file on the OKLO reactor. You'll be astonished at what you find there.'

When they got up from the table with the time coming up to 1.50 p.m., Frances Margaret said:

'I hope I've helped a bit.'

Isaac Newton put his arm around her.

'Not a *bit*, a *lot*. To my mind, at any rate, you've taken a hundred-to-one shot and made it into a near certainty.'

The car and driver were waiting. They kissed before Frances Haroldsen slipped into the back of the car. Isaac Newton handed into her the case containing the disks and tapes. Then, with Frances Margaret looking back out of the window as the car moved away, he shouted:

'Don't forget your passport!'

Chapter 15

As soon as Frances Haroldsen had gone, Isaac Newton telephoned Mrs Gunter to say he would be in the Lab about three o'clock. It was actually 2.45 when he drew up the Mercedes in the Cavendish Laboratory parking lot, whereon he proceeded first to hunt down old Scrooge the storekeeper.

'Ah, Professor, they've been looking for you everywhere,' Scrooge began.

'Who has?'

'Everybody. The police inspector for one.'

'Was it an inspector or a sergeant?'

'Looked like an inspector to me. They were all over young Mike Howarth's office. By what I've heard, it was peculiarly unexpected. Or I should say unexpectedly peculiar, I suppose, Professor. Is it true *you* found him in the Trinity Chapel?'

'Is that what they're saying?'

'Something like it, Professor.'

'No, it was the Trinity night porter who found him.'

'That would make more sense, wouldn't it? I couldn't see why you should be roving around the Chapel in the middle of the night, although you used to get into plenty of scrapes in your younger days. There are a few stories I could tell, you know.'

'But you won't. I'm relying on you, Scrooge.'

'You can rely on me, Professor, like I said before.'

'Did the police take anything away from Mike Howarth's office?'

'One of the younger lads said they did, but I didn't see anything myself. They left the office all taped up and sealed.'

'I'd like to take a look.'

Scrooge led the way along the corridors until they stood in front of a door with the name tag DR M. L. HOWARTH. The sides and top of the door had been sealed with a blue-coloured bond of sticky tape.

'So they'll know if anybody goes inside,' Scrooge explained unnecessarily.

'Do you have a key?'

'No, I wouldn't have. Mrs Gunter will have one, unless they took that away.'

Isaac Newton fished in his pocket, took out his own car keys and told Scrooge:

'My car is the Mercedes outside.'

'I noticed it, Professor. I bet you can kick up the dust with that. Not like the sports car you used to have.' Scrooge broke into a laugh at the memory. 'A horrible red old thing, wasn't it?'

'A distant memory now, Scrooge. There's a box of papers in the boot. Could you collect them for me and put them in the store, well out of the way, so that nobody will notice? I want you to guard those papers with your life. Promise you won't even let the Archangel Gabriel into the store.'

'You know I would never do that, Professor. Did I ever let *anybody* go roaming around my store?'

'That's exactly the way I remember it! You haven't changed much have you, Scrooge?'

'And not likely to do. I suppose I can handle this box myself?'

'Easily,' Isaac Newton said as he handed over the car keys, adding, 'leave the keys in the glove compartment when you've opened the boot.'

'OK, I'll do it right now. There's nothing like seizing the right moment, is there, Professor?'

'Now where have *you* been?' Mrs Gunter asked accusingly as Isaac Newton came into the secretary's office.

'Up to London.'

'Well, the *police* have been here,' Mrs Gunter announced, in her best arrow-discharging style.

'I see they've been in Mike Howarth's office. Did the inspector bring a search warrant?'

'Not that I'm aware of, but he might have left it with one of the senior staff.'

'Can you enquire about it, please? And will you call Professor

Featherstone over at the Vet School. If he's available I'd like to see him this afternoon, say about four o'clock. Would you also call Professor Boulton and ask how soon I can move into his excellent house, the one in Adams Road with the collapsing foundations.'

'I doubt you'll be ready by four o'clock, Professor. You see, Mr Clamperdown and another gentleman are waiting in there. It's a pity they didn't know you were in London. It would have saved them a journey.'

'Ah, but Mrs Gunter I went up to London to see the Queen, not to see Mr Clamperdown and this other gentleman. You can tell Professor Featherstone that I'll be with him by four o'clock, if it's convenient, of course. Furthermore, should Mr Clamperdown ever appear again in this Laboratory would you please ask him to wait downstairs in the entrance hall, *not* in my office.'

'Ah, Mr Clamperdown!' Isaac Newton exclaimed with mock affability as he came into his office to find that Clamperdown had taken his accustomed seat in the big leather armchair. 'And how does it feel to have a suicide on your hands?'

Clamperdown was on his feet instantly, pointing towards a sandy-haired man of middle height wearing steel-rimmed spectacles.

'This is Mr Halifax. You won't have met before.'

Isaac Newton gripped Halifax sufficiently tightly by the hand to provoke a suggestion of a wince, smiling as he did so and enquiring, 'From the CERC legal department, Mr Halifax?'

'As a matter of fact, yes.'

'Nasty job for you. The papers are likely to give poor old Clamperdown here a hard time, I would think. CERC using public money in such a fashion as to drive one of Britain's most promising young scientists to suicide. Quite a shocker you've inherited this time.'

'This wasn't what we called about,' Clamperdown managed to say.

'I'm surprised you have time for anything else. I know I wouldn't. I'd be worried the Coroner's Court might bring in a verdict of manslaughter against CERC,' Isaac Newton said, as gloomily as he could manage.

'To put it bluntly, it's a matter of Howarth's papers and things,' Clamperdown persisted.

'*Why* is it a matter of Howarth's papers and things?'

'I don't suppose you've had time yet to read the detailed terms of CERC contracts, Professor Newton, but when you do you'll find that...'

'The papers and things belong to CERC?'

'Yes, indeed.'

'Wouldn't it be a little more accurate to say they belong to the British taxpayer?'

'Oh, come now, Newton,' Clamperdown broke in sharply, 'you know perfectly well that CERC is a properly accredited agency for the handling of public funds, which this Laboratory is not.'

'I've no wish to be obstructive, gentlemen,' said Isaac Newton with feigned politeness as he seated himself at his desk, 'but isn't there a certain contradiction in your point of view. It is now just about twenty-four hours since you sat in that same chair, Mr Clamperdown, and told me that CERC and its committees considered Mike Howarth's work to be total nonsense. Why then are you anxious to acquire his records? Is CERC now openly setting itself up as a connoisseur of total nonsense?'

'I am not concerned with scientific judgements, Professor Newton. I'm concerned with the legal situation. That's my job,' the sandy-haired man interjected.

'Well, to make your job a little easier, Mr Halifax, and to put the Laboratory on the right side of the law – assuming what you say to be correct – the simple arrangement would be to return Mike Howarth's papers and things to you, once we've taken copies of them.'

'The legal situation quite plainly is that it would be for CERC to make copies available to you, not the other way around.'

'What would be the procedure?'

'You would write to the Chairman, and Council would then consider your application,' Clamperdown replied.

'Which would be considered favourably?'

'I would imagine so.'

'But how would I know we were being sent the *whole* of Howarth's things, and not a carefully biased selection?'

'You would need to trust us.'

'Surely even you, Clamperdown, must realise the absurdity of that suggestion. I regret gentlemen that your journey has been wasted. If you want Howarth's things it will be necessary for you to prove your case in court, and then it will be interesting to see how the public reacts to your conduct in this whole matter, especially in respect of the termination of Howarth's contract.'

'We would begin of course by having a word with the Vice-Chancellor,' Clamperdown said in the fashion of a whist player leading with an ace, accompanying his remark with a discreet thump on the table.

'With the implication no doubt that other departments in the University would be made to suffer from my intransigence. Ah, Clamperdown, your ingenuity terrifies me. I capitulate gentlemen, you shall have that which you seek.'

When Mrs Gunter appeared in response to a press on the buzzer, Isaac Newton continued:

'I have excellent news, Mrs Gunter. Mr Halifax and Mr Clamperdown have just agreed that a grant application to replace this damnable buzzer by an intercom will be favourably received by CERC. In return for their generosity, I am going to turn over certain papers and things to them. Would you therefore bring me the master key to the staff offices, and would you ask one of the assistants to come with a camera to Mike Howarth's office.'

When Mrs Gunter had disappeared, Isaac Newton went on:

'You'll understand, gentlemen, that for my own peace of mind, so that I can sleep at night, I'd like a photographic record of my turning the papers and things over to you.'

Scrooge and one of the younger assistants with a camera were waiting outside Mike Howarth's office.

'You can begin by taking a picture of all that taping,' Isaac Newton instructed. 'Let's all stand in the picture so that the record is clear. Come on, Clamperdown, don't be bashful. You *want* the papers, don't you?'

The picture taken, Isaac Newton then instructed Scrooge to strip off the tape, but changing his mind stepped forward himself, saying, 'No, perhaps *I'd* better do it.'

Then he unlocked the office, and taking Clamperdown by the arm walked inside. The office was quite empty.

'Now, let's have another picture. Of all this emptiness. Come on, stay in the picture, Clamperdown. You'll need it in order to prove to your Chairman that you tried. Unfortunately, somebody else got here before you. Tough luck, old friend, the world is never nice and simple, you know.'

Chapter 16

It was a few minutes past 4.00 p.m. when Isaac Newton reached the Veterinary School.

'I'm sorry I'm a bit late. I had visitors,' he explained to Featherstone, whose blue eyes flickered as he replied:

'I gather you've been having a busy time. I'm sorry to hear about your man. It's hard luck to have that sort of thing happen right at the beginning, before you've had time to settle down.'

'Have you heard the details?'

'Only rumours, and I don't trust them very much.'

'I came over because there's a point on which I'd like your advice. I'd better begin by describing what happened – as I saw it, I mean.'

Then Isaac Newton went through the sequence of events from the moment he'd been knocked out of bed at 1.45 a.m. up to the moment of his return to the Old Guest Room about an hour later, except that he made no mention of a certain Miss Haroldsen.

'In retrospect,' he concluded, 'I made a mistake in not examining Howarth's body more carefully. But the light was poor and the whole scene was quite spooky.'

The upturning corners of Featherstone's mouth twitched slightly as he nodded agreement.

'I'd have found it spooky myself,' he said. 'But it really doesn't fit, does it?'

'There's no way a body would go rigid immediately at death, I suppose? How long would it take, the rigidity, I mean?'

'Well, I'm not a pathologist, of course. But post mortem rigidity occurs in mammals generally at an interval after death that varies from one species to another – the size of the animal being a principal factor. With humans you're talking of hours not minutes, although the interval is notoriously variable from one case to another.'

'So there's no way he could have stiffened immediately. He'd need to have stiffened like a board in order to hold down an organ key. That's what I should have realised at the time.'

'Are you sure it was only a single key? Perhaps he lurched over with a hand or an arm pressing down onto the keyboard, the way you actually saw the body yourself.'

'There were three witnesses who said otherwise, and the night porter described the sound from the organ as a soft wailing *note*. A hand or arm would have produced an obvious jarring dissonance.'

'The porter may have been scared out of his wits.'

'I can't say I'd blame him if he was, but I still don't think he was that bad a witness. After all, it wasn't like you or me discovering the body. He was on his own home ground.'

'So where does that leave you?'

'Puzzled, obviously, the way the police are. The outstanding fact is that a man died. The porter and the Chaplain from St John's both said the man was Mike Howarth, and I thought so too. Let's also take that as fact. So either Mike Howarth died a natural death, or he committed suicide, or he was murdered. If the death was natural, why did it happen in the Trinity Chapel, which would be locked at that hour to someone from outside the College? How did the organ come to be live? Why didn't Howarth collapse into one of the pews, instead of climbing into the organ loft? These questions seem so unanswerable that death from natural causes looks impossible. I saw Howarth a few hours before his death and there was no sign of his being unwell physically.'

'And mentally?'

'He was disturbed, seriously disturbed.'

'Making suicide a possibility?'

'He'd had a research council grant cancelled. He was angry about it. He thought there was a sort of vendetta against him.'

'Paranoid?'

'In a way, yes. He was convinced he'd made a great discovery – that he'd detected intelligible signals from a comet.'

'That certainly sounds pretty far gone.'

'Except that it leaves the problem of the stiff body and the depressing of the single key on the organ.'

Isaac Newton paused for a while as a new thought occurred to him.

'The penny dropped?' Featherstone eventually asked with a smile.

'In a way, yes. If you ask how a single key of the organ came to be depressed, there *is* a way. Press it and then pack the gap above it with plasticine.'

'Then the plasticine should have been there.'

'So instead of plasticine you use some frozen kind of material that gradually melts, or better still evaporates, over about an hour. I'm sure that if you combed through a handbook of chemistry you could find such a material.'

'It would need a peculiar mentality.'

'Yes, it would need a very peculiar mentality,' agreed Isaac Newton. 'But if you grant that the peculiar mentality wanted to draw the world's attention to its own demise, as I think suicidal people sometimes do, then it would be hard to find a better way. This thing is going to hit the headlines, wouldn't you say?'

Featherstone grinned awkwardly.

'I think it very likely will. Especially at the time of the inquest. When is that to be? I might go along.'

'I haven't heard yet, but I'll let you know.'

'So what about the murder possibility? I suppose you're hardly likely to know about that? I mean his private life.'

'As a matter of fact there would be a motive for murder. I came over to talk to you because I think somebody else besides myself should be aware of it, you see. Not that I want to put you in an awkward position, but it should be safe enough provided you keep it to yourself. The trouble is that I probably won't be able to keep it to myself because the thing is going to explode pretty fast from here on.'

'We're fairly well used to handling dangerous animals over here,' said Featherstone with a twinkle in his blue eyes.

'The wavelength of the signals, the ones detected by Mike Howarth, was very long, too long to penetrate through the ionosphere, which meant that if transmitted from a satellite the signals would be quite undetectable by any kind of equipment on the ground. It occurred to me as soon as Howarth told me of the wavelength that it would be great stuff from a military point of view. You could have one satellite instructing others, and the only way in which an enemy could know about it would be by satellite interception. What may have happened is that Howarth made just such an interception, by a sheer fluke. So he may have stumbled on an important military secret.'

'Planned warfare in space? I didn't know anything like that was going on.'

'It's happening, covertly, all the time. More and more of it every year.'

'But why would such an idea be a secret? I'd have thought for people in that game it would be rather obvious.'

'Very long wavelengths are hard to produce without heavy equipment, too heavy for a satellite normally. But somebody might have discovered how to transmit with lightweight equipment. It would be the existence of such equipment that would be the secret, because of course if you know something to be possible it's much easier to find it yourself...'

'...than if you don't know it to be possible? I can see that.'

'It's when you mistakenly think something to be impossible that it gets really hard,' Isaac Newton nodded. 'Well, you see, it's conceivable that Mike Howarth's reception of his supposed cometary signals really blew an important military secret. Somebody might have thought it essential to nip the thing in the bud, especially after I showed signs of giving him a bit of support.'

'And it was done to look like a grotesque suicide? But wouldn't that simply draw everybody's attention?'

'To the body at the organ. To the thin wailing note of the organ. To the Trinity Chapel. To inconsequential things.'

'Even so, wouldn't it have been better and much simpler to fake a car accident?'

'To your mentality and to mine, Featherstone, it would. But the mentality of the action squads of the world's intelligence agencies isn't the same as yours or mine. D'you remember the Bulgarian umbrella with its poisoned tip?'

Isaac Newton took the last part of his conversation with Featherstone seriously enough to feel glad that his instinct had led him to get Frances Haroldsen out of Cambridge and out of sight at the drop of a hat. He also took it seriously enough to feel that he had no wish to be jabbed by an umbrella in Trinity Street, or in Great Square, or in the Fellows' Combination Room.

Returning from the Vet School to his car at the Cavendish, he first checked that Scrooge had left the keys in the glove compartment, and that the box of files had gone from the boot. Then, being of a suspicious mind, he spent five minutes examining the car itself, just to make certain that neither Clamperdown nor anybody else had monkeyed with it.

Instead of turning right on Madingley Road towards the Colleges, he went through Coton to the M11 intersection with Barton Road. Entering the motorway in a northerly direction, he took the exit east towards Milton, driving the Mercedes at a speed he would normally have regarded as unwise, just to be sure that nobody behind him did likewise. Satisfied he wasn't being followed, at Milton he turned north again onto the Stretham-Ely road. It was just 6.15 p.m. as he parked in Ely at the Lamb Hotel, where he booked a room for the night.

Over his dinner at a small table in the corner of the dining-room of the hotel, he hoped he hadn't scared Featherstone half as much as he'd scared himself. But the urge to confide in someone had been strong, and no better suggestion than the Professor of Vet Science had presented itself. A man who could deal with lions and tigers at the point of a tranquilliser rifle could surely manage to cope with the Bulgarians, or whatever.

Isaac Newton's thoughts turned back to lunch with Frances

Haroldsen and to the last part of it, to his own mention of the OKLO reactor in Gabon. The initial discovery by French nuclear scientists of large concentrations of fission products in rocks two thousand million years old had been greeted with scepticism by experienced scientists the world over, experienced scientists like himself and Kurt Waldheim, for the reason that under natural conditions you would expect all manner of neutron poisons to prevent a critical fission situation from ever being reached, even in a rich uranium ore, and even at the U-235 concentration of two thousand million years ago. Yet the French had eventually proved their point and won the day, leaving the problem of neutron poisons unresolved.

The resolution had come when an American paleontologist had visited the site of the OKLO reactor. He noticed that particularly high concentrations of uranium were associated with fossilised bacterial colonies. Hitherto unknown to nuclear scientists, there are species of bacteria which precipitate uranium from solution in water, so as to build a shell of uranium around themselves, rather as other bacteria precipitate calcium carbonate to form the structures known as stromatolites. The two processes are similar, except that when a bacterial colony is large enough to form a big enough concentration of uranium, the thing becomes a biologically generated nuclear reactor, with the carbon content of the bacteria acting as the moderator of the reactor. A particularly striking example, discovered by the Americans, was a colony that would have needed only a change in shape to have gone critical. This discovery suggested that a bacterial reactor controls its stability simply by adjustments of its shape. Inevitably, therefore, the bacteria had to be capable of withstanding enormous doses of radiation, a prediction that was triumphantly vindicated when bacteria were found alive and well inside man-made reactors. The OKLO problem had thus been solved.

A similar solution, Isaac Newton had instantly seen at the end of his lunchtime conversation with Frances Haroldsen, would also dispose of the heating problem inside comets. Comets kept themselves warm with bacterial nuclear reactors, proving that there must be life inside comets. This, Isaac Newton had argued to himself, was a long step towards the idea that comets might even harbour intelligent life. So, in his opinion, the odds had shortened dramatically since his first pessimistic estimate of Howarth's theory.

Before he collapsed exhausted into bed that night, Isaac Newton telephoned the Waldheim apartment in Geneva. A minute later he was talking to Frances Margaret. His head swam as he listened to her enthusiastic rush of words, and his last thought before sleep brought the day to its appointed close was to wonder why he was where he was. Why wasn't he in Geneva himself, off skiing for a week-end, without a care in his head, off skiing with Frances Margaret? Instead, he'd deliberately exposed himself in the track of an impending avalanche, which any sensible person could see must come roaring down the mountainside within only a matter of hours or days, to carry him to likely disaster.

Chapter 17

After sleeping well at the Lamb Hotel and not getting down to breakfast until close on 9.00 a.m., Isaac Newton was late at the Lab. Boulton, the Professor of Geostrophics, was already waiting for him. As soon as they were in Isaac Newton's office, Boulton came instantly to the point.

'Do you think you could move into the house today?'

'I thought you said the end of the week.'

'That was before my spies told me that Scuby is on the march in my direction. I'm getting out, of course. This morning. If you were installed in the house today it would make it look plausible, you see – something I could point to if questions were asked.'

'Well, actually, I'd be glad to start moving my things over. This afternoon, perhaps?'

'I've told the woman who cleans for me to send everything to the laundry, so it'll be a bit bare until the sheets and towels come back. Do you think you could bring some from College? I don't suppose they'd mind. By the way, I notice you've got moles. I'd get onto the University about that, otherwise the district will be swamped with them.'

'I'll make a note of it.'

'Another thing. D'you think you could let me have your petty cash? Until Scuby has departed on his way. I'll give you an IOU, of course.'

'What's the trouble?'

'Well, all the departments do it. We keep the petty cash flowing so that every place he visits seems to be well topped up with it. Then, when he's gone, we move it back again.'

'Couldn't you use the cheque I gave you yesterday?'

'I've sunk it already – into German marks. They're certain to do well over the next three months.'

'On margin?'

'Not likely, if you do that you're likely to get wiped out on the roller coaster. Two or three pfennigs down and you're gone.'

'How did you manage to change your airline ticket? Don't these special APEX deals require several weeks notice?'

'Oh, you should never work it that way. I can give you a place in London where they buy tickets in big blocks. I don't know exactly how they do it, but you simply walk in with cash in one hand and the next minute you're out with the ticket to any place in the world in the other. Of course it's a bother going up to London, but I send my secretary. She meets me at the airport. Good, well, I'll be picking up your petty cash and then I'm on my way. California here I come.'

'There isn't much cash, I'm afraid.'

'Don't worry, every little bit helps. I can call in on the astronomers. They always seem to have plenty – always travelling around, I suppose. Oh, yes, I should warn you: if any chaps from the tax office start poking around the house, I'd tell them you're a foreigner, otherwise they'll slap a ball and chain on you straight away. They tend to come on Sundays when they think you'll be at home.'

'Inspector Grant and Detective-Sergeant Forsyth,' Mrs Gunter announced an hour later. Inspector Grant was in police uniform, a burly grey-haired man in his fifties. Detective-Sergeant Forsyth was in plain clothes, a thinly-built fellow of about Isaac Newton's own age.

'Inspector Grant!' Isaac Newton exclaimed, rising from his desk to shake hands, 'and Detective-Sergeant Forsyth!' Then, turning to Mrs Gunter, he asked:

'Has the search warrant I asked about yesterday turned up yet?'

'Not yet, Professor.'

'Perhaps I can clear up that point, Professor,' said the Inspector, taking a sheet of paper from a large envelope he was carrying with his notebook. 'I have it here,' he added, 'for your records.'

Isaac Newton examined the paper carefully, taking a while to do so, and then said:

'Would you put this on file, Mrs Gunter. And to complete the formalities, gentlemen, would you be good enough to show me your identifications?'

'I agree, Professor, you can't be too careful,' nodded Grant as he produced an identification card with photograph. The Detective-

Sergeant was a little longer about it, being apparently surprised by the request.

'Since we can't be too careful, would you please take photocopies of these identifications, Mrs Gunter, and put those on file together with the warrant. You gentlemen have no objection, I suppose?'

The Detective-Sergeant appeared about to speak, but then desisted.

'Professor, we called to ask if you would help us with our enquiries,' Grant began.

'Into the death of Dr Howarth?'

'Yes, that's what we're investigating, of course.'

'Before we leave the subject of the search warrant,' Isaac Newton said in a businesslike tone, 'perhaps you'll explain, Inspector, how it came about that your men entered and removed papers and articles from Dr Howarth's office without the warrant being first presented.'

'They were under instructions to deliver it to you, Professor. But you weren't here.'

'It could have been left in the keeping of some member of my staff, or with my secretary, or even on my desk here. Besides which, it seems to me the taping of the door of the office was done deliberately to prevent us from realising that materials had been abstracted illegally.'

'We're only trying to do a difficult and puzzling job, Professor,' Grant replied.

'I appreciate that *you* are, Inspector. The question is whether everybody is similarly motivated.'

'We hope you will be, Professor Newton,' the Detective-Sergeant broke in.

'First, I should tell you, Professor, that the Coroner has fixed the inquest for next Wednesday, although it is just possible that we will ask for an adjournment according to the state of our enquiries. So with your help I hope we can move along.'

'My help is limited by the fact that I only met Howarth once, when our conversation was concerned entirely with scientific matters. My help must also be limited by the fact that I've only been four days in this office.'

'So the dam broke, as you might say, just as you arrived?'

'That is unfortunately the case.'

'During your conversation with him, was there anything in Dr Howarth's manner that suggested to you that he might take his own life?'

'If you'd asked me that question immediately following my conversation with him, I'd certainly have said no.'

'But now you've changed your mind?'

'To some extent, yes.'

'Why?'

'Well, if instead of asking directly about suicide, you were to ask about mental stability, I would say he had what's often called a persecution mania. I think my opinion will probably be confirmed by people who knew him much better. But with that said, in my judgement, my *scientific* judgement, Howarth *was*, to a degree, being persecuted. Others might disagree with me there, I suppose. The trouble it seems to me, Inspector, is that when you ask about suicide you're asking an almost unanswerable question.'

'I'm not following you, sir.'

'Because you're asking my opinion of somebody else's state of mind, and obviously without actually being that other person I can't form a proper judgement. I know that if a research council were to cancel a contract of mine I'd simply do something else, unless, of course, I found an effective way of fighting the decision. I wouldn't go on and on complaining about it.'

'That's what Howarth did?'

'Apparently, yes.'

'I see. Now a few questions about yourself, if you don't mind. You're a British citizen, Professor?'

'Yes. Technically speaking I'm a British citizen resident abroad.'

'But now you're resident here.'

'It takes a little while for the change of status to be made. Not everybody is as fast off the mark as you are, Inspector.'

'I was rather fast off the mark yesterday morning, Professor. In fact, I came around to your rooms in Trinity, at about nine-fifteen a.m. it would have been. Then I tried several times to telephone you both here and in Trinity. It seems you were not available through the morning and early afternoon. Would you mind telling me what happened after you last saw my men? That would be around two-thirty a.m. yesterday.'

'Yes, I had intended returning to Switzerland this weekend – I still have a number of loose ends to tie up there – but in view of events, Inspector, it became obvious that my plan would have to be cancelled – or rather that someone else would have to go instead of me. The matters were scientific, you see, and better sent by hand with a competent physicist than simply committed to the post. Otherwise I wouldn't have contemplated making the journey in the first place.'

'Who do you contemplate sending instead?'

'One of the demonstrators here in the Laboratory.'

'And that would be?'

'I don't want to appear negative, Inspector, but your questions seem a bit irrelevant. But if you must know, the person is Miss Frances Haroldsen.'

'Have you known her long, sir?'

'Longer than my patience is likely to last, Inspector. I understood you were investigating Howarth's death, not my personal affairs.'

'Would this be the young lady who was in your rooms when my men came there yesterday morning?'

'If you mean when we were brusquely knocked out of bed, the answer is yes.'

'But you hadn't known her long?' Inspector Grant continued with the wooden persistence so necessary in his profession.

'You may write down in your notebook that it was a case of trust at first sight.'

'So what happened after you and the young lady returned to your rooms, at about two-thirty a.m., I mean?'

'We decided we'd had enough of being knocked out of bed. Are you a married man, Inspector? I'm anxious not to shock you, or Detective-Sergeant Forsyth here. By the way, how do you spell your name, Sergeant? With a y, or an i, like the Leicestershire Forsiths? I hope you understand my point, gentlemen.'

'I understand this may seem a little personal, sir, but then we're dealing with a serious matter. Or perhaps you don't think so, sir?'

'If there were any possibility of saving Howarth's life, as for instance by the Research Council reactivating his contract, it would be a serious matter. But I'm afraid it's too late for that. In other words, the actual ocurrence of death is a serious matter, but the aftermath of death is a *fait accompli*.'

Inspector Grant refused to be deflected by this philosophical reply. 'Would you explain your movements between two-thirty a.m. and nine-fifteen a.m. yesterday morning, sir? You don't have to answer if you don't want to, but it might make things easier later on.'

'In the interests of making things easier later on, the young lady and I left Trinity College. We walked for a while and then eventually decided to drive to a motel. We recovered my car from the park in Jesus Lane, and then simply did so – we drove to a motel.'

'Which motel, sir?'

'A place belonging to the Ladbroke chain on the London-Newmarket road. It's about two miles on the Newmarket side of The King's Dog in Six Mile Bottom.'

'Yes, I know the motel you mean. There are others closer to Cambridge, sir. Why did you choose that one?'

'Well, we'd had dinner earlier that evening in Babraham and I suppose we just started out of Cambridge as we'd done before. You see, Inspector, the situation with Howarth was a bit gruesome, and the young lady was quite upset by it. So we were not in a frame of mind to start calculating distances to motels. I don't know half of them myself in any case.'

'I believe Dr Howarth had a cottage out in that direction,' Grant said casually.

'You have the advantage of me there, Inspector. But of course you've had the advantage of being able to comb through his papers.'

Mrs Gunter appeared in the doorway.

'You buzzed for me, Professor?'

'Yes, I did. We've finished our chat, Mrs Gunter. Have you got the gentlemen's things? They'll need them, you know.'

'Oh, yes, I have them here.'

'Good. Well, Inspector, here are your identifications. I hope this conversation has been as informative to you as it has for me.'

'We haven't quite finished, Professor, if you don't mind.'

'As a matter of fact, I do mind. You asked for a couple of inches and you took a yard. Take care on the steps on the way down. If Detective-Sergeant Forsyth here were to fall and break his neck, that would be a serious matter.'

'There, Mrs Gunter,' said Isaac Newton after his ejection of the two visitors, 'go two unhappy men.'

'They didn't seem unhappy to me.'

'That's because you can't see into their innermost souls.'

'No, I can't and I doubt that I'd want to.'

'How much did Professor Boulton take from the petty cash box?'

'Twenty *pounds*.'

'Did he leave an IOU?'

'Yes, but it's worth about as much as a used train ticket if you ask me.'

Isaac Newton took two ten-pound notes from his wallet saying:

'You'd better make it up with these.'

'But you can't be using your own money, Professor!' exclaimed Mrs Gunter in an aghast Scottish voice.

'Mrs Gunter, I begin to warm to you. Tell me now, did you notice anything peculiar about the Detecive-Sergeant?'

'Only that he seemed to be looking around all the time. I expect that's what they're trained to do,' the secretary replied.

'The trouble is that I never found out whether he spells his name with an i or a y – or how he spells it at all for that matter. Are you a connoisseur of Sherlock Holmes, Mrs Gunter? If you are, you'll remember his advice: never take the first taxi, nor the second. But in that Holmes-Watson age of innocence, it was considered safe to take the third taxi.'

'I remember something like that, Professor.'

'Well, Mrs Gunter, I'd like to give you a bit of advice myself. When two men come into your office, one big and important, the other not so important, the one talking, the other not talking, watch that little guy. Otherwise, Mrs Gunter, you're going to end up with cider in your ear. Especially if the men claim to be from the police, which might be true or it might not be true. Or one may be from the police and the other not. Do you follow me, Mrs Gunter?'

Chapter 18

'You were right, Professor,' Mrs Gunter exclaimed the following morning, 'there *was* something wrong with those two men.'

'How do you deduce that, Mrs Gunter?'

'Because the office has been gone through during the night.'

Isaac Newton looked around the secretary's office and then around his own room.

'It looks all right,' he shrugged.

'But it isn't. I can tell. Besides, the identification has gone.'

Mrs Gunter lifted a file from her desk.

'Look, the Inspector's is here, and the search warrant, but the Detective-Sergeant's isn't here.'

'Are you sure you filed it?'

'Do you think I have the havers then?'

'That would be more than I'd ever dare to suggest, Mrs Gunter. Has anything else gone?'

'Not so far as I can tell. But the files have been moved around. Look here, Professor.'

Mrs Gunter marched to a filing cabinet indicating a particular drawer, which to Isaac Newton's casual eye appeared neat enough.

'I don't see anything,' he shrugged again.

'No, you wouldn't, because you're not used to it, and perhaps you don't have an eye for this sort of thing. But the files are disordered.'

'Is every drawer the same?'

'No, some are all right. One or two things are wrong, but except for this drawer they would be hard to notice. If I didn't remember everything the way it was.'

'What are these files?'

'CERC contracts.'

'Including Dr Howarth's?'

'Yes.'

Isaac Newton walked into his own office and began to go through his desk. It had been a thoroughly professional job, he eventually decided. Small changes of detail he would never have noticed in the ordinary way of things. Two pages in the wrong order in the middle of a calculation, the master key to the Lab offices not quite in the right position. Then he could find only one of the two sets of spare keys to the Mercedes.

'And they've been through my safe,' Mrs Gunter added.

'Is the petty cash still there?'

'Yes, it's the same as with the files. Things have been moved. They seem to have been looking for something they didn't find. Except for that identification. Why would they take the Sergeant's and not the Inspector's?'

'Because Inspector Grant was a real policeman and the other fellow was not. The *soi disant* Forsyth fellow had all the hallmarks of an intelligence type about him. I could see it from the moment I walked into the office,' Isaac Newton replied. 'You see, Mrs Gunter, we had his photograph, and that would never do, would it? The idiot chose the sort of pseudonym they always use.'

'What does it all mean, Professor?'

'Dirty work at the crossroads, Mrs Gunter, dirty work. I'm afraid the great thing was that we provoked them into it. The fellow suspected so strongly I had what he wanted that he decided to raid the office. Brutal stuff, Mrs Gunter.'

Isaac Newton refrained from adding that what they wanted was partly tucked away in some remote corner of Scrooge's storeroom, partly stored in a vault of Barclays Bank, and partly being currently processed somewhere in the vast computing laboratory at CERN in Geneva.

'The great thing,' he said, 'is that my conscience is now clear. Clear, I mean, to pull out one or two stops. Mrs Gunter, would you first make an appointment for me to see the Master of Trinity some time this morning. Say it's urgent. Would you then telephone the Prime Minister's office. Here is the number. Ask for Pingo Warwick.'

'*Pingo* did you say?'

'That's right, P-i-n-g-o. Ask him for an appointment, preferably some time after next Wednesday. I'd like to get the inquest on Mike Howarth over first.'

'Yes, Professor, after next Wednesday.' Mrs Gunter nodded with enthusiasm. 'The Master of Trinity this morning, and the Prime Minister after next Wednesday.'

'You make it sound like an execution list, Mrs Gunter.'

The clock on the Edward III Tower was striking 10.45 a.m. when Isaac Newton turned in at the Trinity main gate and walked towards the north-east corner of Great Square where the Master's Lodge lies. Unlike most other Cambridge Colleges the Master of Trinity is not elected by the Fellows of the College, but by the Crown on the Prime Minister's recommendation. This practice had several important consequences, most of which were beneficial. It avoided the body of Fellows breaking up into warring factions over the election of a new Master, such as happened all too frequently in other Colleges. It avoided particular Fellows organising their careers with a long-term view to being elected one day to the Mastership. It sometimes brought non-Fellows into the College, and because Prime Ministers had no wish to be ridiculed for making weak appointments, it effectively guaranteed the College a Master of outstanding distinction. It rang the changes effectively between the arts and the sciences, and it also avoided cabals of Fellows seeking to organize the ejection of a Master, such as happened in other places from time to time. In short, it was a system most other Colleges would have been better with, if such arrangements made general had been a practical matter, which they weren't because of the impossible strain that a widespread application would have had on Prime Ministers.

The Master was currently a famous novelist and playwright, a solidly-built man of middle height in his middle sixties with a shock of white hair and blessed with a deep, powerful, resonant voice.

'Don't tell me, don't tell me. I can see it in your eye, Newton. You are the bringer of bad news. Bad-News Newton shall henceforth be thy name,' the Master greeted Isaac Newton after he had been shown upstairs to a large room on the first floor.

'Coffee, or can you manage sherry at this hour of the day?'

'Coffee, please.'

The Master moved in a kind of gliding padding motion, as if he were wearing slippers, to a sideboard on which there was a hot-plate. He reached out for a finely chiselled bright metal pot on the stand in an absent fashion and let out an agonised yell.

'Silver!' he roared. 'Whoever would have thought of making a coffee-pot out of silver? The trouble in this College is that every damned thing is made of silver. I've sent out search parties seeking heat-resistant steel but they always return empty-handed. Very well, Newton, tell me the worst. Was it murder or was it suicide?'

'Probably suicide, but others will think murder, because to believe in suicide you have to look into the darker aspects of the human personality, but to believe in murder you have only the stuff of a spy thriller.'

'Did you say *spy*?'

'I did, deliberately, Master. Which is why I came to see you.'

'Good God, *no*. Not more *spies* in Trinity? Ah ha! I have it. This spy, this Howarth, is from St John's, from over the wall. So he comes into Trinity seeking to trade on our reputation.'

'Howarth chanced on what may have been a closely-guarded secret, a technological breakthrough in very long-wave radio transmission.'

'Why would it be important?'

'Because it would give satellite-to-satellite radio communication that was completely undetectable from ground-based stations. You probably know, Master, that current thinking among the military of both superpowers is tending towards satellite warfare. It doesn't need a genius to realise that command of space is going to become what command of the air was in the past.'

'You mean if one side wipes out the other's satellites then it would be like wiping out the other's air force?'

'Yes,' nodded Isaac Newton, sipping his coffee. 'You don't need too much imagination to build quite a case – for the murder picture, I mean,' he explained.

'I'm not liking the sound of this,' boomed the Master. 'But go on. I've got a hardy constitution.'

'Looking at it from the point of view of an investigative journalist, shall we say?'

'It's those fellows I fear most.'

'Within a short time of Howarth making his discovery, the Research Council stopped his contract.'

'How did they do that?'

'On legal grounds. They had a point, you might say, but it could have been taken care of otherwise.'

'So if you were an investigative journalist you'd argue that the

Research Council stopped the grant to prevent Howarth meddling any further. How would they know to do that?'

'They have all manner of committees – committees to the right of them, committees to the left of them, committees coming out of their ears – with all manner of scientists as members.'

'So somebody in the know hears about it and moves to put a stop to it. You can just see them storming along the corridors of power, can't you?' the Master growled with his eyes hooded, as if he were scanning the windy corridors himself. 'I can hear their voices moving the necessary motions,' he added.

'The next step involves my own position,' Isaac Newton went on. 'I'll ask you to keep this strictly confidential, but recently I was involved in a security investigation myself, on behalf of the Prime Minister's office. This was well known to the Foreign Office, and doubtless to others. So when I returned to Cambridge and began to discuss matters with Howarth, and especially when I took up the cudgels on his behalf, to some extent, it might have been seen as a storm signal. At least, an investigative journalist might see it like that.'

'I see. So Howarth was removed, and in a fashion that would throw you into . . . what should I call it?'

'A peculiar light, shall we say?'

'Is this all surmise or is there anything solid to support it?'

'The police are in contact with somebody or other, probably MI6 or whatever number they go by these days. Whether the police are happy about the situation, I don't know.'

'How d'you deduce that?'

'Howarth's office was stripped and my own office has been searched.'

'For papers?'

'Papers, disks, tapes.'

'Did they get them? More coffee?'

'Yes, please. No, they didn't get them.'

The Master padded once more to the sideboard with its hot-plate and silver coffee-pot. He did so absently again, and once more there was a yell of agony.

'You should wear oven-gloves, permanently,' Isaac Newton told him.

'It interests me very much,' the Master said, as he padded back from the sideboard carrying two cups of coffee, 'that we are still talking about our imaginary, but dreaded, investigative journalist. What else would you have in mind, Bad-News Newton? Worse I expect.'

'Howarth thought the signals were coming from a comet which

happened to be passing at the time.'

'And he went around saying as much?'

'Yes, very loudly.'

'So somebody rubbed him off the picture to stop him from continuing to draw everybody's attention to what was really a highly secret military operation. Is that the position?'

'That would be the investigative journalist's interpretation.'

'OK, Bad-News. So who would this mythical murderer be?'

'A Russian, an American, a Bulgarian, Detective-Sergeant Forsyth from British Intelligence, some Fellow of the College. You name him.'

'Stop it! I can't bear mention of the College. Just think what the press will do to us!'

'To me,' Isaac Newton continued, 'all intelligence agencies are of the same kidney, which is why their operatives find it so easy to transfer themselves from one side to another. Secrecy is their common denominator, secrecy as much about the other side as about their own.'

'I'm not with you there, Bad-News.'

'Well, the CIA would go to any lengths to prevent the American public learning something about the KGB, and the KGB would go to any lengths to prevent the Russian public learning something about the CIA. They're all in the same trade union. Master, this thing has the obvious look of an inside job.'

'Don't I know it! Don't I know it! The press will crucify us, to the delight, no doubt, of a certain neighbouring College, which planted this whole thing on us and which yet manages to keep a clean-nosed image. In public, at any rate, although God only knows what goes on internally at St John's.'

The Master of Trinity started to growl like an animal at bay. Isaac Newton sat back and listened to him for a while. Then, changing the line of his argument, he said:

'But what if Howarth were right after all? What if British Intelligence is really chasing a will o'the wisp? It wouldn't be for the first time, would it?'

'I can't bear it! Change the subject, please.'

'To be serious, Master, it sounds easy to talk about a technical breakthrough.'

'For what? These long-wave signals?'

'That's right. The newspapers and the public are conditioned to swallow spy stuff about secret devices. But in the real world it's only very rarely that the military comes up with anything unexpected, if it ever does. In every case known to me it's been a matter of the military

perfecting an idea that was already well-known in scientific circles –
like the A-bomb, which appeared in 1945 but which was seen as a
possibility by every competent nuclear physicist as early as 1939. Now
generating very long wavelengths efficiently with miniature equipment, and with very little power available, strikes me as an
extremely tall order. For very long wavelengths you need just the
opposite – plenty of power and plenty of size. You need big stuff, like a
comet. That's the first point.'

'What's the second?'

'The second is that if Howarth really committed suicide there's a
chance we might be able to prove it. He would have needed to wedge
the organ key with some substance that either melted away eventually
or sublimed away into the air. There might still be traces of it on the
keyboard. We could examine the keyboard.'

'We could ask the organist,' the Master added, immediately walking
to the telephone at the other end of the large drawing-room. A
moment later he returned to Isaac Newton.

'Young Baker will be over in a minute or two. He says he can't stay
long because he's got a choir practice in about twenty minutes. But we
could ask him a question or two *pro tem*.'

Howard Baker, the College organist, was of about the Master's
height and about thirty years old with a big beard that prevented his
features from being distinguished by even a close observer.

'I don't think you two have met before. Baker is new since your
time, Newton. A cup of coffee, Howard?'

'Thank you. I've just time to swallow half a cup.'

The Master padded once more to the sideboard with its hot-plate and
silver coffee-pot with its elegant curving spout. He took care on this
occasion to grasp the handle of the pot with a thick pad, lest it be
obvious to Isaac Newton that his howling act was a well-cultivated
party trick.

'Newton here would like to ask you a brief question or two about
the organ keyboard,' the Master explained as he padded back with the
coffee.

'I suppose the police have examined it?' Isaac Newton asked.

'They swarmed all over it. Scattering powder everywhere, damn it.'

'Looking for finger-prints?'

'That would seem to have been it. Although what good that would
do, with all the people who play the organ here, I can't imagine.'

'Have you played it yourself? Since the police moved in, I mean?'

'Once they'd finished with it, yes.'

'Was there anything odd about the keyboard? Anything a bit sticky, for instance?'

'That's hard to say, because after the police had finished their duties we had to clean up.'

'Cleaned off the powder?'

'Yes.'

'Was it stuck pretty badly in some places?'

'At one spot it was. Certainly. I cleaned it up as best I could, but even then I had to get one of the choir to go over it again.'

'Do you remember the particular key? I mean if you were to depress it, with the organ on, what would be the result?'

'The result if you had the stops the way they were when they found the body would be a thin wailing note. I noticed it and I wondered about it. So I checked with Kent – the night porter. He said it was the same. Nearly fainted when I asked him to come and listen, poor chap.'

'Did you tell the police?'

'No, they didn't ask. But it made me wonder.'

'What?'

'If the key had been wedged in some way; but I couldn't find any marks on it or any damage so I more or less dismissed it from my mind. Well, I must be off. Thanks for the coffee, Master.'

When Baker had gone, the Master lifted his eyebrows and asked:

'Did you notice?'

'What?'

'Well, you could see for yourself, couldn't you? That you have to recognise Baker from his profile. He's cultivating it to look like Brahms.'

The Master padded to a table and then returned to where Isaac Newton was sitting, carrying with him a file containing newspaper cuttings and a graph.

'I've been plotting the numbers of lines on the case which have been appearing in the press. You can see for yourself that they're soaring. The start was twenty lines in the *Cambridge Evening News*, the day it happened. The next day eighty-nine lines, also in the *News*. But then the national press picked it up and we jump to three hundred and forty-two, then nine hundred and seventy-seven lines. That's this morning's papers. You can guess for yourself where we'll be by the time the inquest takes place. Reporters from London are already to be seen around the College and the Chapel. I have the porters watching for them. How about the Cavendish?'

'Frankly, I haven't noticed. I expect they've been around, talking to Howarth's colleagues. But the Lab isn't as picturesque or as photogenic as the College.'

'There lies a grievous trouble,' nodded the Master. 'The root on't, as you might say. Our cross, our millstone. To change the metaphor, the College is a sitting duck for every sniper in the business, of which I fear there are many. Which brings me to a delicate matter that has been stirring the whole while in the back of my mind. The Dean tells me there is a certain young lady in the case. Not just any young lady, Bad-News, but a special young lady called Frances Haroldsen. Her fame goes before her, you see.'

'I'm sorry if I've been a cause of embarrassment. . . .' Isaac Newton began.

'Oh, but my dear Bad-News, you *haven't*! What was stirring in my mind was the possibility of your *emphasising* at this inquest your associations with the young lady. Naturally, you will be called to give evidence. Could I prevail upon you to make a big point of your being discovered there in the Old Guest Room in bed with the young lady? I am sorry to be a little crude, but this is, after all, a serious matter.'

'What would be the point, Master?' asked Isaac Newton, his own mind searching to understand the logic of the suggestion.

'We have here what the Americans would call a match-winning play. Because this scene – I wish I could put it on the stage, and with your permission perhaps I will – of the police breaking in on the newly-installed Cavendish Professor, who is boldly ignoring all hallowed traditions by following the dictum of the great Will Shakespeare to the effect that "young limbs and lechery cannot be separated", is a story ready-made for the Sunday tabloids; and on a more refined but still sustained note – not a wailing note – for the Sunday heavies. In short, I appeal to you, Newton, I appeal to your good sense, if not on my bended knees, to lift once and for all this dark cloud of spy scandals that afflicts your College, your *Alma Mater* who gave you suck in your years of need. Do I make myself clear, or should I repeat my plea?'

'But the young lady's point of view enters into the matter, Master. Her reputation.'

'She has the reputation of being a very tough cookie, as the Americans say – what an expressive people they are. The inspired rumour which swept Cambridge recently concerning a certain Dr Goatman, an imaginary beneficiary of King's, has, I believe, been attributed to her.'

'You place me under a conflict of loyalties, Master. Who, by the way, is this Dr Goatman?'

'He has been variously described,' replied the Master in his resonant voice, 'as an aging bibliophile, as an internationally-known satyr, and as not existing at all.'

'Rather a wide range of choices.'

'Indeed. In fact the Goatman affair is just another of those things I intend to put on stage, if I ever get around to it. But to refer back to your own affair...'

'Isn't it likely to come out anyway? I would have thought with the reporters around...'

'Ah, but you can give *zip* to the thing, you can ensure that members of the public will think henceforward of Trinity as a kind of Mozartian establishment, instead of as an adjunct of the heavy-jowled, black-beetled KGB.'

'Doubtless you have a strong point, Master. But some form of compensation to the young lady would be only a matter of common justice. Such I think would be the opinion of any reasonable person.'

'Compensation?'

'I was thinking of election to a Fellowship of the College.'

'I see,' said the Master, tapping his fingers slowly against each other. 'Election *summa cum laude*, as it were.'

Then after thinking for a while, the Master continued:

'It would need to be managed with a little care. When certain of the older Fellows are away, either on health cures or unfortunately in hospital. But with suitable staff work there is no reason why it should not come to pass. On condition, of course, that the scandal succeeds in lifting the roof off Fleet Street.'

Chapter 19

THE ORGAN NOTE MYSTERY – MURDER OR SUICIDE?

With headlines such as this appearing in the weekend press it was inevitable that the Coroner's Court would be crowded at the inquest, held, as Inspector Grant had foreseen, on the Wednesday, eight days after the death of Mike Howarth. Reporters had not found it difficult to ascertain the curious circumstances surrounding the discovery of

Howarth's body. And since Isaac Newton had taken no steps to prevent them from talking to Howarth's associates at the Laboratory, the general nature of his research work and the cancellation of his contract by CERC were also known. In the hands of even the least imaginative journalist such a story could not have failed to have caught the public attention, and of course the journalists employed on the matter were by no means the least imaginative members of their profession.

Because of the publicity which the case had already received, the Coroner's Court was held in the largest of the courtrooms at the Cambridge Guildhall, a room with a timber motif to it – panelled walls and wooden benches. Isaac Newton, arriving together with the Master of Trinity, overheard one official remarking to another with a touch of pride:

'We could have filled it ten times over.'

Filled it was, to overflowing. Isaac Newton and the Master squeezed along the second row, where seats had been reserved for them, directly facing the Bench.

'This is going to be the Coroner's moment of glory, the day he's been waiting for all his life,' observed the Master.

'What's his background?'

'Medical, with some jurisprudence, I suppose. I see you've got your plans well laid,' replied the Master, indicating the capacious briefcase which Isaac Newton had brought with him.

'It would be more accurate to say I'm prepared against the plans of others rather than having any particular plan of my own,' Isaac Newton answered, as he examined the faces around the courtroom, looking for any he could recognise. The Dean, the Chaplain of St John's, Mr Kent the night porter, the porter from St John's, two staff associates of Mike Howarth from the Laboratory – and Clamperdown. Clamperdown was deep in conversation with a legal-looking man. Since others joined their conversation from time to time, it seemed the Research Council was well represented.

The sergeant who had knocked Isaac Newton so summarily out of bed appeared, equipped with papers and a notebook. He seated himself quietly, showing that he was a professional well-used to the situation, and then remained immobile. Inspector Grant was not to be seen, however, from which Isaac Newton deduced that the police had decided to hold their hand for the time being – a policy which Clamperdown might have been wiser to have adopted, he thought. The press and the visual media evidently occupied a fair fraction of the seating capacity, partly because they knew how to barge their way into most situations, and partly because they had arrived at the Guildhall at a competitively early hour.

Isaac Newton allowed his mind to wander off as the Coroner arrived with a group of officials, and as the jurors were chosen and sworn in. Over the past week he'd had conversations with Frances Haroldsen, using telephones at hotels in the surrounding countryside lest the lines at the Laboratory were being tapped by the Post Office on the instructions of the Home Office, at the request of an intelligence group attached either to the Home Office itself or to the Foreign Office, or whatever. The possible ramifications were endless, as he delighted in emphasising to the Master. Isaac Newton didn't like it, and because he didn't like it he'd taken good care to make sure his calls to Geneva were not only from, but also to places that lay outside the imagination of officialdom, thinking it better to be over-cautious than foolish.

Frances Margaret had told him that the enhancement of the dot-dash signals was proceeding apace, and then she'd driven him half-insane by saying Kurt Waldheim had made a breakthrough towards interpreting the signals themselves. In response to his urgent request to be informed as to the nature of the breakthrough, he'd been told soothingly to bide his time, because the thing was too complicated to be explained over the 'phone. And without having the data themselves in front of him, any attempt at an explanation would be meaningless, Frances Margaret had added, which, Isaac Newton reluctantly conceded, was probably true.

So over the past four days he'd been racking his brains to think what it was that Waldheim had found, a frustrating process which had done his temper little good. Not to put too fine a point on it, he'd arrived for the inquest in a pretty foul frame of mind, with a few tricks not conceived of on the playing fields of Eton up his sleeve – or, more accurately, in his briefcase.

Mr Kent the porter was the first witness to be called. He described his macabre discovery of the body in the Chapel with more relish than he'd felt on the occasion itself. Isaac Newton, noting the avidity with which Mr Kent's opening shots were being recorded by one and all around him, began to have a guilty feeling that he was slacking on the job. Then his roving eye caught a familiar face – Featherstone.

Mr Kent had gone immediately from his discovery of the body to the porter's lodge at the main gate, from which he had telephoned the Dean, who being resident in College had arrived shortly thereafter at the lodge. At this point the Dean himself took up the story. Instantly he had 'phoned the police and a doctor of his acquaintance. Mr Kent and he had then returned to the Chapel, but to avoid leaving the lodge unoccupied they had asked the night porter at St John's – only a few yards away – to walk across and man the gate for them, so that the police could be admitted on their arrival.

A police constable had been the first to appear. Commendably, it took him little time to realise that the situation was so unusual as to demand a stronger police presence. He had therefore been through to his sergeant, Sergeant Atkinson, on his pocket radio. Thereafter, Sergeant Atkinson had arrived with another police constable.

A stage had come when the night porter from St John's had been unable to contain his curiosity. Going to the Chapel himself, he had recognised – or thought he had recognised – the deceased as a Fellow of his own College, Dr Howarth. So the Chaplain had been called from St John's. The Chaplain had then confirmed the night porter's identification, and in answer to a question from Sergeant Atkinson had said the dead man was a physicist employed at the Cavendish Laboratory, whereon the Dean had offered the information that the new head of the Cavendish Laboratory happened to be resident there in College, only a moment's walk away. Sergeant Atkinson had then proceeded to knock Isaac Newton out of bed, and Isaac Newton had also joined the party in the Chapel. Such was the story that unfolded.

Turning his mind back to the actual events, it had all seemed straightforward enough at the time to Isaac Newton, but in the courtroom, in the clear light of day, this toing-and-froing sounded overdone. Faced by a seemingly inexplicable state of affairs, the reaction had been to add one person after another to the party, apparently in the hope that the inexplicable would somehow become explicable with the arrival of each new individual. By the time Sergeant Atkinson came in with his testimony, describing Isaac Newton's own joining of the party, the Coroner had himself reached saturation point. Looking up from the pad on which he had been writing, the Coroner said:

'Sergeant Atkinson, can we get this straight? By now I have Mr Kent, the Dean of Trinity, the Chaplain of St John's, the night porter from St John's, Constable Green, Constable Reddaway, yourself *and* Professor Newton. Is that correct? Have I now got *everybody?*'

Sergeant Atkinson hesitated for a long moment, glancing up and down as if in embarrassment.

'Not quite, sir,' he eventually replied. 'There was also a young lady.'

Everybody except Isaac Newton and the Master of Trinity reacted in the same way to this item of news. They looked up if they had been writing, or became instantly attentive, if they hadn't. Although each made only a slight noise, because the noise was the same in each case, the effect was to generate a sharp pulse of sound within the courtroom.

'It hasn't taken long to come out. I didn't think it would,' the Master of Trinity whispered. It had taken one hour and five minutes to come out, Isaac Newton noted from the clock on the wall.

'Could I have the young lady's name? To complete my list,' the Coroner asked.

'I didn't take it, sir,' Sergeant Atkinson replied, revealing the source of his embarrassment. 'You see, she came suddenly out of the bedroom, just as we were on the point of returning from Professor Newton's rooms to the Chapel.'

'Bullseye, first shot,' the Master whispered again.

Isaac Newton caught Featherstone's eye. The man gave a slight shrug, to which Isaac Newton replied by raising his eyebrows. The thing to do was to be entirely unconcerned. Then you remained the boss, the lady in question had assured him.

With this tit-bit under its belt, the court turned its attention to the medical evidence. The doctor who had first examined the body explained that a time interval of about half-an-hour had elapsed between his being telephoned by the Dean and his arrival in the Chapel. He had found the subject dead, sprawled across the organ console. There was no visible sign of the cause of death, so far as he could tell under the prevailing circumstances and conditions of low-light intensity. A flash photographic record had then been made, and at the Dean's urgent request the body had been removed shortly before daybreak for eventual post-mortem examination.

Sergeant Atkinson had been left in charge of the non-medical aspects of the situation, especially the examination of the College organ, it being judged that finger-printing of the keyboard could better be accomplished in the light of day.

The doctor, who was thus the first medical witness, was then bowed out in favour of the official Police Surgeon. The proceedings settled down thereafter into a technical discussion between the Police Surgeon and the Coroner. Isaac Newton was concerned now with conclusions rather than with details. Howarth had not been found to suffer from any organic defect. No drugs had been found in the body, but an exceptionally high level of adrenalin was present in the blood. So far as an estimate of the time of death could be made, the Police Surgeon gave the opinion that it had not been before 11.30 p.m. and not after 1.00 a.m. – perhaps an hour before the discovery of the body by Mr Kent.

'Half-an-hour would be more like it,' Isaac Newton whispered to the Master of Trinity.

'How do you arrive at that?' the Master replied.

Whatever Isaac Newton's response might have been, it was drowned by an interruption from the legal-looking man beside Clamperdown.

'Might I ask the witness a question, sir?'

'Of course, Mr Sherbourne,' the Coroner agreed.

'They seem to know each other. All in the family,' the Master whispered.

'Could the witness state if he found anything that would definitely point to suicide as the cause of death?'

'No, nothing definite.'

'Thank you.'

Isaac Newton was surprised to hear his own voice ringing out through the courtroom.

'On the grounds, Mr Coroner, that Dr Howarth was a member of my staff, could I claim the Court's indulgence to ask a question?'

'Professor Newton?'

'Yes.'

'Since you have yet to be sworn in, Professor Newton, it would be a little irregular. But I will allow it.'

'Could the witness state if he found anything that would definitely point to any particular cause of death?'

'No, nothing definite.'

'But Dr Howarth did die, whether due to suicide or otherwise?'

'Yes, of course.'

'Thank you.'

'A declaration of war, if ever I heard one,' muttered the Master, with a satisfied growl.

The morning session came to an end. On the way out of the courtroom Featherstone was waiting, an almost self-deprecating smile on his upward-curving lips.

'That was quite interesting – I mean the medical part,' he said.

When Isaac Newton introduced the Master of Trinity, Featherstone nodded.

'You won't remember me, Master, but I was at your Feast, at the end of the Michaelmas Term last year.'

'I suggest we go along to the Lodge for a hunk of French bread and ham and a bottle of beer or two, if that suits you,' the Master replied. 'Featherstone, what was it that interested you about the medical evidence? To me, it was all my eye and Betty Martin; and I thought I understood a bit of Latin. But the way these doctors botch it up encourages me to keep out of their clutches,' the Master continued, once the three men were back at the Lodge with the promised bread and ham and a silver tankard of ale in front of each them.

'Well, for one thing there wasn't much said about the stiffness of the body. They talked round it pretty cleverly,' Featherstone began. 'My feeling is the afternoon session is going to be a bit more entertaining. Newton, I can see that Sherbourne lawyer gearing himself up for a few awkward questions once they've got you in the witness box. Better prepare yourself.'

'I have,' Isaac Newton said quietly.

The conversation lapsed for a while, but the Master, who preferred conversation to silence, eventually broke it by saying, 'It's no good you studying all this silver, Featherstone. Even if we have enough of it in this College to salt a mine, we keep it under lock and key. Otherwise, of course, we wouldn't have so much of it.'

'I wasn't thinking about silver, Master. I was thinking about adrenalin.'

'And what were you thinking about it?'

'In veterinary science we stand quite a bit in the shadow of the medical profession. For one thing they have a lot more financial support for research than we have. For another, we have many kinds of animals to study and they have only one. So, as a general rule, really we don't know as much about animals as they know about humans. But there are a few things we know that perhaps they don't, mostly because we can study animals under wild conditions, not always under domesticated conditions.'

'What's all that to do with adrenalin?'

'Well,' said Featherstone slowly as he put down his tankard, 'if an animal died with an exceptionally high concentration of adrenalin in its blood, but otherwise without anything wrong, d'you know what I'd say? I'd say that it died of sheer terror!'

Chapter 20

Although the very nature of the case had given him star billing, the morning's revelation by Sergeant Atkinson of the emergence of a young lady from his bedroom ensured that a pin could have been heard dropping in the courtroom as Isaac Newton took the witness stand and was duly sworn in. The Coroner, pointedly ignoring the biblical injunction to drink the best wine first, began with a number of humdrum questions. How long had Isaac Newton been in the country?

'About two weeks.'

'You returned to Cambridge from abroad?'

'Yes, from Switzerland.'

'So the deceased was not well-known to you?'

'He was hardly known to me at all. I met him only once, on the afternoon of my first day in the Laboratory. He declared himself very anxious to see me.'

'About what?'

'About his research interests, which he considered to have been seriously set back through the cancellation of a contract from one of the research councils. He was in a disturbed state of mind about it.'

'What was the purpose of his discussion with you?'

'He was hoping I would attempt to persuade the Research Council to reverse its decision.'

'Did you make such an offer?'

'No, I did not. I told him I thought the Research Council would be unlikely to reverse its position, which proved to be true. I did, in fact, discuss the matter on the following day with a representative from the Research Council. My efforts on Dr Howarth's behalf were, as I'd rather expected, unsuccessful.'

'So what was the conclusion of your discussion with Dr Howarth?'

'I encouraged him to investigate the scientific material which he already had, instead of being so concerned about acquiring additional material. The desire to accumulate more and more material is very strong in many young scientists. In a sense, the passion for acquiring data becomes a substitute for the harder job of interpreting it. I thought Howarth was suffering from this syndrome.'

'You are saying that he was in an emotive state of mind.'

'Yes, very definitely.'

'Did the thought that he might attempt to take his own life occur to you?'

'No, it did not, perhaps because I looked at the position from what I suppose one would describe as an everyday point of view. I regret I did not perceive the possibility.'

'Could you inform the Court, in simple terms if possible, what the scientific issues were?'

'Howarth believed he had detected pulsed signals with equipment mounted in a satellite, signals which had their origin in a passing comet. Comet Boswell.'

'Can you explain the term "pulsed signals".'

'Dots and dashes.'

'Thank you. Did this suggestion strike you as peculiar?'

'Most peculiar. When I raised a number of objections against it, Dr Howarth gave coherent answers to my points, although this would be quite usual. The authors of strange theories commonly have answers to the most obvious and immediate objections. Otherwise nobody would listen to them.'

'What objections did you make?'

'I pointed out that the signals might have had their origin in some other satellite.'

'To which the answer was?'

At this point there was an interruption from Sherbourne, the lawyer:

'I know you will understand, sir, if I make a request of the Court in regard to this line of questioning.'

'Yes, Mr Sherbourne?'

'The investigation is leading into what, from a security point of view, might be described as a sensitive area. If the questioning is to persist I would ask that the Court be cleared.'

Partly because of the unexpected nature of Sherbourne's intervention, and partly because of the loud buzz which erupted in the courtroom, causing an official to cry, 'Silence! Silence *please*!', the Coroner was momentarily nonplussed. Seizing his chance as the burst of sound died away, Isaac Newton held up a file.

'I have here transcripts of my conversations with Dr Howarth and with an official from the Research Council. Might I suggest that instead of your verbal questioning, Mr Coroner, these transcriptions be considered as read into the Court's record.'

'Are the transcripts verbatim?'

'Yes, and I also have here the recordings from which they were obtained, on which the actual voices can be heard.'

Isaac Newton held up for everyone to see two of the cassettes which Frances Haroldsen had obtained from her illicit bugging of his office. Sherbourne recovered quickly from the trap into which he had fallen, saying, 'Professor Newton's suggestion deals with the situation admirably, provided this material is treated as strictly confidential.'

'Of course, Mr Sherbourne. Professor Newton, you would have no objection?'

'I have no objection to this being given restricted access,' Isaac Newton replied as he handed the papers and the cassettes to a court official. 'But it would be difficult to guarantee that the several other copies which exist can all be gathered up and impounded. If that is even within the Court's jurisdiction?'

'It evidently is not,' answered the Coroner. 'The purpose of this Court is to determine the cause of Dr Howarth's death, not to address itself to problems of security, although the Court will naturally take whatever steps can be considered reasonable and prudent within the scope of its own jurisdiction. But there is no way I can order you, Professor Newton, to destroy or impound your own personal papers. That would clearly be a matter for others to deal with.'

'It will be,' Sherbourne responded tersely, almost causing Isaac Newton to cry out, 'Shut up, man! Don't you see you're hanging yourself!' There was no way now the press could fail to acquire copies of his conversation with Mike Howarth and with Clamperdown.

His line of questioning broken by Sherbourne's intervention, the Coroner turned to the discovery of Howarth's body and to Isaac Newton's visit to the Chapel in company with Sergeant Atkinson and his party.

'I am missing the name of the young lady who was accompanying you, Professor Newton,' the Coroner said, with the air of a man grasping the nettle.

'If you feel the name to be relevant to the objective before the Court, I will give it,' Isaac Newton replied. After thinking for a while, the Coroner smiled and nodded.

'It is possible I was only giving way to vulgar curiosity. So I will bypass the question, more particularly because your being late on the scene in the Chapel makes your evidence subsidiary to that of earlier witnesses. What I really have to ask is whether as a trained scientist you noticed anything which would not have been apparent to others.'

'I am unhappy to have to admit that my training as a scientist was insufficient proof against the peculiar circumstances of the occasion. I made the mistake of looking too much at Howarth's body and too little at the organ console.'

'For what?'

'To discover how the key that would have given rise to the wailing note heard by Mr Kent had been depressed.'

'Have you views on that?'

'Yes, but too late I'm afraid.'

'Nevertheless, the Court would be glad to hear from you, Professor Newton.'

'I consider it impossible that the key was depressed by the corpse itself, which I think was the idea of all of us at the time.'

'Yes?'

'So the key must have been depressed, in my opinion, by wedging it.'

'According to Sergeant Atkinson no wedge was found.'

'So the material of the wedge must either have melted, like ordinary ice, or evaporated away into the air, like dry ice. I should have examined the keyboard for traces of such a material.'

'The material being placed deliberately?'

'Yes.'

'Have you any idea by whom?'

'Either by Dr Howarth or by an unknown person.'

'Why would Dr Howarth do such a thing?'

'To add notoriety to his manner of death.'

The Coroner thought over this remark for a while, as apparently did most of those in the courtroom, which fell quite silent.

'As an indication of how much I missed at the time,' Isaac Newton continued, 'even though I've thought about it quite a lot over the past week, Mr Coroner, there was a possibly significant point which didn't occur to me until I heard the evidence this morning.'

'What was that?' the Coroner asked, his lips pursed.

'When I went into the Chapel I overheard somebody say that the organ gave you the "collywobbles" when it was switched on. I think that was the word. But none of the witnesses this morning has mentioned switching off the organ, which made me wonder if anybody ever did switch it off.'

There was rapt attention as the Coroner glanced at his notes and then said:

'You are right, Professor Newton, nobody did mention it. To save recalling all the previous witnesses, can I ask the person who switched off the organ to stand for a moment.' Nobody stood.

'It appears then as if we have another mystery on our hands,' the Coroner admitted in a puzzled voice. 'Yes, Sergeant Atkinson, do you wish to be recalled?' Sergeant Atkinson had his hand up. Then rising to his feet he said:

'It's just that when I examined the keyboard sometime later the organ was definitely off.'

'What have you to say to that, Professor Newton?'

'My guess would be that the wailing note heard by Mr Kent went off because some substance holding down the relevant key evaporated away like dry ice, but that the organ went off as a whole sometime later because it was on a time switch.'

'You see,' continued Isaac Newton, 'the organ is frequently played in the evening by musicians in the College. A time switch would be sensible, because otherwise somebody might leave it on through the night. Not that leaving it on would be particularly important; but then neither is a time switch particularly important, in the normal way of things.'

Isaac Newton's aim of thus throwing up a great big smokescreen was about to be shattered, he could see, for the irrepressible Sherbourne was on his feet again.

'While all this speculation on the organ key is doubtless very interesting, I would like the Court's permission to ask the witness one or two questions.'

'Very well, Mr Sherbourne.'

'I wish to return to the matter of the young lady who emerged from the bedroom in Professor Newton's rooms. Was this young lady a member of the staff of the Cavendish Laboratory?'

'Yes, she was.'

'A colleague, then, of Dr Howarth?'

'Yes.'

'Over the years?'

'I don't know for how long they had been acquainted.'

'But much longer than two days, the time which you and the young lady had been acquainted?'

'Yes, a good deal longer than that.'

'Mr Sherbourne, if you have something relevant to ask will you please ask it,' broke in the Coroner.

'I am about to suggest to the Court that, after his arrival in Cambridge, the learned Professor quickly replaced the deceased in the young lady's affections, and that the distress so caused to the deceased had a bearing on his unhappy death. Therefore the young lady's identity is germane to the case.'

'What have you to say, Professor Newton?'

'I have to say that the transcripts now in your possession, Mr Coroner, will show that no such issue was ever mentioned throughout my conversation with Dr Howarth.'

'May I ask another question?' continued Sherbourne, pressing the

slight advantage he felt he had gained. 'Professor Newton, the death of
Dr Howarth happened very shortly indeed after your return to
Cambridge. Has it occurred to you that there might be a connection
between the two events?'

'The simultaneity is apparent,' Isaac Newton answered, 'but I can
think of nothing that would make it anything but coincidental.'

'I still suggest the young lady's identity is germane to the case,'
persisted Sherbourne.

'I am reluctant to agree with you, Mr Sherbourne,' the Coroner said
clearly and with emphasis, 'because the issues you are seeking to raise
have all the aspects of a fishing trip. If this were a straightforward case I
would have little hesitation in dismissing them for that. But because
it's all too obvious the case is not straightforward, I feel it is right for
every aspect to be examined. This will I think best be achieved,
Professor Newton, not by pressing you further, but by calling the
young lady herself as a witness. Can you inform the Court of her
whereabouts?'

'She is at present at the CERN laboratory in Geneva, where I was
formerly employed myself,' Isaac Newton replied, conscious that he
was suddenly on delicate ground. 'I had intended returning there last
weekend in connection with several current projects, but in view of my
suddenly acquired and unexpected responsibilities here in Cambridge I
considered my going away to be impractical. Since the young lady had
expressed to me her interest in acquiring a post at CERN herself, and
since various calculations and designs of mine had to be transmitted to
a particular colleague there, I asked the young lady, Miss Frances
Haroldsen by the way, to make the journey in my place. It would
therefore be necessary to postpone the inquest if she were to be recalled
in order to answer questions which amount to nothing more than a
fishing trip by Mr Sherbourne.'

'Yes, Mr Sherbourne?' the Coroner asked, in response to an
exclamation from the lawyer.

'I wonder if the Court could be told exactly when Miss Frances
Haroldsen left the country?'

'A week ago.'

'That would make it last Wednesday?'

'Yes.'

'Which is to say the very day after Dr Howarth died. Another time
coincidence, Professor Newton! If the timing doesn't strike *you* as
remarkable, I'm sure the Court will take note of it.'

'There was no coincidence, Mr Sherbourne. I sent Miss Haroldsen
immediately, at the earliest possible moment, to free my mind for

dealing with the serious matters which I knew would arise from Dr Howarth's death, and which have been occupying the Court's attention today. And let me add this, please. If there were anything peculiar in my position, the very last thing I would have done would have been to remove the person who could give me a perfect alibi throughout the evening and the night when Howarth died. I hope the Court will take note of that.'

'Your point is well-taken, Professor Newton,' the Coroner acknowledged. 'Have you anything more. Mr Sherbourne?'

'Just this, sir. We have heard from the witness about radio signals obtained by the deceased and about altercations with the Research Council as a cause of stress and possibly even of suicide. Yet no such scientific material has yet been produced. Two officials from the Research Council visited Professor Newton on Wednesday last, the very day, I might emphasise, on which Miss Frances Haroldsen so conveniently disappeared to Switzerland. It was pointed out to Professor Newton that materials acquired through Research Council grants, although normally left for research purposes in the possession of the investigator or investigative body, belonged in law to the Research Council itself. After making Professor Newton aware of this fact, the two officials then asked that Dr Howarth's materials be handed over so that the Council could make a proper appraisal of their value, if any. Professor Newton refused to comply with this request, so placing himself some distance on the wrong side of the law. What I wish to ask now is that Professor Newton be asked to produce these materials. He has been very ready, as everybody in this courtroom will have seen, to produce verbal transcripts of conversations, but he has been very *unready* to produce the supposed causative agent of this tragedy. I ask, sir, that Professor Newton be ordered by the Court to be immediately forthcoming on this matter.'

'What have you to say, Professor Newton?' the Coroner asked yet again.

'That the radio signals in question consist of a sequence of dots and dashes, much of the record being blurred by what is known as a poor signal-to-noise ratio. Placing such a record at the Court's disposal would no more solve this case than the sequence of dots and dashes issued typically by a ship at sea. Secondly, I have not yet taken advice on the legal aspects of the position *vis-à-vis* the Research Council, nor has the Research Council taken any steps beyond a word of mouth message from two of its officials. Third, I was not satisfied that the material, if turned over, would have been safe from destruction.'

'But it *is* safe?' the Coroner asked.

'Yes, sir.'

The Coroner considered the matter for a while and then gave his ruling on Sherbourne's request:

'I accept your assurance, Professor Newton, that the possession of these materials by the Court would do little to assist it in arriving at a decision in this case. Nevertheless, the fact of the existence of the materials themselves is indeed relevant to the case. Mr Sherbourne has almost gone as far as to say the materials might not exist. This, I feel, is something on which the Court must have an explicit assurance. Normally I would have accepted your word, Professor Newton, as a sufficient guarantee, but we have here as puzzling a case as I can recall in a long career. Therefore, and with some reluctance as I hope you will understand, I have to ask that these materials be produced for the Court's examination.'

'Could I ask that the materials be then returned to me?' Isaac Newton asked.

'The materials would, I hope, be returned to their legal owner,' Sherbourne interposed.

'The transcript will show that Dr Howarth was most strongly opposed to the Research Council being given access to results that were the product of his own efforts, not of the Council's efforts,' Isaac Newton said firmly. 'I feel that in this respect it is incumbent on me to respect Dr Howarth's wishes, to the limit of what is possible.'

'I respect your point of view, Professor Newton, but I still must ask that the materials be produced. You have them?'

'No, I do not have them.'

'Did they ever exist? Or are they now in Switzerland?' exclaimed Sherbourne.

'I think I should make it clear to the Court what Mr Sherbourne's purpose has been in all this questioning, questioning that I have borne with more patience externally, Mr Coroner, than I have felt internally. Mr Sherbourne's purpose, and the purpose of those he represents, is to obtain Dr Howarth's materials – for reasons best known to themselves, reasons well-removed from the basic purpose of this Court.

'Mr Coroner, you asked me if I had the materials and I said no, which is true. Just because I realised possession of them was a matter of dispute I had them deposited with a third party of valid repute. They are with the manager of Barclays Bank, just around the corner, about a hundred yards from here.'

'Well, who won that Homeric battle?' the Master of Trinity asked, as he and Isaac Newton walked together across Great Square.

'Sherbourne won it. He wanted Howarth's data. Or at least his employers wanted the stuff, at all costs.'

It was at this point, through allowing himself to be deflected by his annoyance with Sherbourne, that Isaac Newton missed the chance to resolve the whole mystery by stepping across to the chapel to inspect the arrangements for turning off the organ. In a few hours it would be too late for quick proofs to be obtained.

Chapter 21

The guard at the gate had evidently been given Isaac Newton's name and informed of his appearance.

'When you see the house, bear to the left and you'll be right for the car park, if you see what I mean,' the guard explained.

'Expecting much traffic over the weekend?' Isaac Newton asked.

'There's a crowd coming in Saturday, tomorrow. But you and the Chancellor are the only ones this evening.'

The Prime Minister's country residence gleamed white through the trees as Isaac Newton drove his car a mile or so from the entrance gate along a shrub-bordered drive to the rear of the residence, where he carefully selected as unobtrusive a place as possible to park. The residence had the characteristic Tudor court construction, somewhat reminiscent of the familiar inner court of Queen's College in Cambridge – more ornamental, but with a plastered finish that tended to enhance the similarity.

Walking from the car with his suitcase and briefcase, Isaac Newton entered the courtyard through a gateway, and then chose from a selection of doors what seemed to be the main entrance to the house. A man in his late twenties dressed in formal clothes – a half tail-length jacket – answered his ring.

'Oh yes, Professor Newton? Will you come this way, sir.'

As one always does following a valet, Isaac Newton quickly lost his sense of direction as they ascended stairways and walked along corridors, avoiding larger rooms which opened off the corridors.

'Shall I unpack?' the valet asked when they reached their

destination, a room of moderately large size with nineteenth-century furnishings, except for twin beds that were clearly of modern origin.

'The bathroom is on the left, sir,' the valet added.

By the time Isaac Newton had explored the amenities of the bathroom, a young woman had arrived with a pot of tea.

'The fire is laid, sir, so you've only got to light it,' observed the man, who had stripped out the suitcase in a remarkably short time. 'If there's anything you want, you've only got to ring the bell.'

Then the two were gone, leaving Isaac Newton to drink a cup of tea in peace, as some say. Or to plot his strategy, as others say. He hoped the file he'd sent to Chequers Court two days earlier had reached the Prime Minister, whom he knew to be a voracious reader, and surely anything to do with the weird state of affairs in Cambridge would have seemed compulsive reading, even to someone who was not a voracious reader. In short, he hoped the Prime Minister was clued-up on the situation.

Finishing the tea, he gave way to an impulse to explore the house. Unlike the Cambridge Colleges, which have been at pains to preserve Tudor associations in their interiors, it was not so here. He was uncertain what to call the interior – a mixture of Georgian and Gothic, he supposed, with a dining hall that suggested a fantasy to his mind of Charles Dickens reading from *Wuthering Heights*, with a large portrait of the Lord Protector gazing sternly down upon the listeners.

A bronze bust of the composer Gustav Mahler caught his eye. For two reasons: it was by Auguste Rodin; and it was positioned immediately outside the toilets near the dining hall – an effective comment, Isaac Newton thought, on the decline of Viennese music from Beethoven to Mahler and beyond. It was strange how the declining political influence of Austria had been mirrored in the decline of its music. Was it the same with British science, he wondered?

There was a larger library with a smaller one leading off it.

'Ah, you're here,' the Prime Minister remarked as Isaac Newton was somewhat idly scanning the bookshelves. The Prime Minister led the way into the smaller library, which had two large armchairs, a big leather sofa, stereo equipment, and a bar set up in one corner.

'You haven't met Godfrey, I suppose, Professor Newton,' the Prime Minister continued.

The middle-aged man who rose from one of the armchairs was of spare build, of medium height and grey-haired: Godfrey Wendover, the Chancellor.

While Isaac Newton shook hands with the Chancellor, the Prime Minister took a handful of nuts from a dish on the bar. Handing the file which Isaac Newton had sent two days before to the Chancellor, the Prime Minister went on:

'Fascinating. Comets alive. Comets are alive because|– let me see if I've got it right – because they divide if they go near the Sun, which means they must be liquid inside. Then they can't be liquid inside unless they have a source of heat inside, which seems sensible. And the only source that appears feasible is something like the OKLO reactor, caused by bacteria two thousand million years ago. Do I have my catechism right, Professor Newton?'

'Excellent, Prime Minister, except for the signals.'

'Oh, yes, of course. They've found dot-dash signals coming from a comet. Only they don't know what the signals mean.'

'Would you mind if I had a look?' asked the Chancellor.

'Not at all,' Isaac Newton replied. 'By the way, how many portraits of Cromwell are there in this house?'

'I always say fifty-seven varieties,' the Chancellor answered, resuming his seat in the armchair.

'At least it's better than clocks,' defended the Prime Minister. 'When I was an unsuspecting child I was once taken out to a place with an impossible number of clocks – although I expect they've become very valuable these days.'

'Anything is valuable these days, provided it's daft enough and provided it's old enough,' added the Chancellor, as he opened the file and began to read. The Prime Minister took another handful of nuts, saying, 'I'm a compulsive nut-eater. You know, it would be a big thing for this country if those signals could be deciphered.'

'I'm aware of it,' nodded Isaac Newton dryly, 'which is why I wanted to ask for a little action on your part, Prime Minister.'

'Action! You need a drink? Godfrey?'

'Scotch and soda,' the Chancellor replied briefly, without looking up from his reading. 'Same for me,' agreed Isaac Newton.

'Better have a few nuts before I finish them. Once I start eating nuts it's impossible to stop me. Primeval instinct from ancient days in the forest, I suppose. What action have you in mind?'

'We need the heavies taken off our backs. Otherwise, they'll become a serious nuisance, or worse. Somebody has been pressuring both the Research Council and the police. I've had lawyers waving documents, trying to seize the tapes and disks carrying the signals, and my office has been gone through by the itchy fingers of some agency or other, an agency under your own ultimate control, Prime Minister.'

'Why would Intelligence be interested in comets?'

'Why wouldn't they? Anything unusual and you always have

Intelligence sniffing around,' observed the Chancellor, still without bothering to look up from his reading.

'If, as a member of an intelligence agency, you happen to think the signals come from a satellite instead of from the comet, consider the conclusions you reach, Prime Minister,' Isaac Newton began. 'If you're American, you think the Russians have made a breakthrough, and you want to know about it. If you're Russian, you think the Americans have made a breakthrough and you want to know about it. If you're British, you think somebody or other has made a breakthrough and you still want to know about it. It's like a pot of honey to bees, or to bears, or to whatever. As it happens, I'm serious about it, to the extent that over the past fortnight I haven't slept twice in the same place. My movements have had a sort of random pattern, because I happen to know that intelligence agents don't like that sort of thing. A bit like the thrush to the sparrowhawk.'

'I don't see the connection.'

'When a sparrowhawk hovers overhead, birds panic and those that fly away desperately looking for shelter often get picked off in mid-air. But the thrush stays on the ground out in the open, running a random pattern, daring the hawk to dive. Which it doesn't because it would bash itself into the ground if it did. The tactic is good, but after a while it gets a bit wearisome.'

'So you want me to do some leaning?'

'If we're to have a chance of deciphering the signals, yes.'

'For my money you can put all the heavies in a big black bag and drop the lot of them into the sea,' observed the Chancellor, still without looking up from his reading.

'You *do* have the money, Godfrey,' the Prime Minister returned immediately.

'I may have the money at the moment, but I won't have it for long, not after all the suppliant hands have reached into the till.'

'We're haggling over the budget,' the Prime Minister explained, taking another fistful of nuts. 'The big spenders are all coming in tomorrow morning. We're going to have a big-spenders evening and dinner tomorrow night. You'll be staying?'

'I'd like to leave Sunday morning and I'd like to ask for a car to Heathrow. If possible, I want to leave mine here, you see, because it would be harder to tamper with.'

'Seriously?'

'Yes, seriously.'

'Give me a week and I'll nail the lot of them, from the Research Council upwards,' the Prime Minister said firmly, adding, 'How's the reading coming on, Godfrey?'

'Fascinating. Could I have another drink please? It needs strong medicine to read your stuff, Professor Newton.'

The following morning, the Chancellor suggested a walk, the 'Aldbury Round' he called it. He and Isaac Newton drove through the small town of Wendover.

'Your family came from here?' Isaac Newton asked.

'Yes, back in the eleventh century, although it's pretty scattered by now, of course. And yours?'

'Oh, I'm a creature of geology,' was Isaac Newton's reply.

'Sounds very mysterious.'

'It's not really. You see about four hundred million years ago, when most of the British Isles was under the sea and Western Europe was somewhere near the equator, the sediments laid down in the sea happened to be coloured bright red. The grains of sediment then hardened into a richly-coloured sandstone rock which geologists call Devonian sandstone.'

'I see. So to cut the cackle, you come from Devonshire. I thought you'd a bit of an accent from that direction.'

'Then, about three hundred million years ago, a spike of granite rocks pushed its way up through the red sandstone, and that's the place we call Dartmoor today. Well, if you come down off Dartmoor on its south-western side, and if you notice the first few miles after you reach the red rocks, that's where I come from – the country near Tavistock. My family have been farmers there for a long time, centuries, I suppose.'

'What does your family think about it? Your being a scientist, I mean.'

'They think it's madness, and that no good at all will come of it.'

'Do you ever go back there?'

'Sometimes. I'm still enough of a Devon man to fight anybody who won't admit it to be the best county in England, and I'll fight anybody there who won't admit Tavistock to be the best town in Devon.'

They parked in Aldbury village, with the Chancellor saying, 'We can pick up a beer and a sandwich at the pub here when we get back from the walk. It's about four miles. By the way, you may have saved me a lot of money.'

'How's that?' asked Isaac Newton.

As they began to climb a little through woods the Chancellor continued:

'Your memorandum on those cometary signals set me thinking.

Let's begin by supposing that you're wrong. Suppose the signals didn't come from the comet. Suppose they came from a military satellite. Then we're at the beginning of a new space-wars kind of era, something in which Britain can't compete. Well, if we can't compete we might just as well save our money, it seems to me. Why go on spending it on weapons that are becoming more and more obsolete?'

'There's the usual deterrent argument.'

'Which becomes weaker the more we fall behind in the race. Of course, we can't change things overnight. It has to be gradual, from year to year. But it's an advantage, I always think, to know the direction one is travelling in. We might just as well sit back and let the superpowers beggar themselves. The Russians pretty well have already, and when I look at the size of the U.S. public debt I don't see too much hope there either.'

'Can you insulate yourself from a debt crisis in the U.S.?'

'You might think not, but the Swiss always seem to manage to insulate themselves from everybody, more or less. The remarkable thing about the international financial scene, you know, is that the margin between solvency and insolvency is closely equal to the amounts spent on armaments. Everywhere, in all countries, except a few like Switzerland and Japan.'

'So if all armaments were scrapped, the world would suddenly be prosperous. Is that it?'

'Something like it,' the Chancellor nodded as they reached a main road. 'We have to make a dog-leg here.'

'I'm not so sure I agree with you there,' Isaac Newton began when they had resumed their original direction along a broad track, still through woods. 'I think all communities consume their entire output. I mean the people spend it on themselves, either privately or on welfare – and by welfare I don't just mean handouts to poorer people. Let's not forget that university professors and even Chancellors of the Exchequer are paid out of the public purse. What happens is that having consumed its entire substance on itself, nothing remains to provide for a community's defence. So what is done is to borrow against tomorrow's productivity. But, of course, tomorrow never comes.'

'I'd rather suppose you've proved my case,' the Chancellor argued, as he strode out along the track. 'If everything balances without the armaments, cutting them would set things exactly right, I would have thought.'

'I doubt it. The compulsion to overspend would continue. Welfare would increase in a flash and you'd simply be back where you started.'

'So what's the remedy?'

'Inflation. You have to inflate at a rate which exactly compensates for the rate of increase of the public debt. Newton's first law, you might call it.'

'Not a popular remedy.'

'No, because inflation confiscates savings. The people who lend to Governments simply lose their money.'

'Yet the whole world is falling over itself to buy U.S. Treasury Bills, just at the moment.'

'Because the U.S. Government claims it can have zero inflation combined with an ever-increasing debt, which every Swiss peasant knows to be nonsense. The moral is, put your money into Swiss francs. We have a professor in Cambridge who understands these things, a chap called Boulton. He sees through a glass very darkly,' concluded Isaac Newton as they came into open ground in front of a large long house with turreted battlements.

'Henry VIII kept his daughters here, both Mary and Elizabeth. It was done up in the eighteenth century by the Duke of Bridgewater, who made *his* money from canals,' explained the Chancellor. 'The latest in technology at the time. Then came the railways and it was disaster for the canals. Railway stocks were seen as the equivalent of gilt-edged. Then came the motor car and the aeroplane, and it has been disaster ever since for the railways. What next, I often wonder? There will be a next, you know. There always is, and it always seems to be something people don't expect, something they laugh at to begin with. Which is why I was so interested in these signals of yours – they could be the beginning of something.'

As they resumed the walk back to the pub at Aldbury, the Chancellor began a soliloquy. 'I'm a historian by education. Oxford. I might possibly have stayed there, if I'd been determined about it. The trouble was my period – late Middle Ages. I grew more and more depressed with history the more I learned. You had a world in decline in every respect. By modern standards, even the fourteenth century was already pretty dreadful, as you can easily read for yourself in the letters of the Black Prince. But in the fourteenth century you still had accepted standards of behaviour, accepted codes. These were gone in the fifteenth century. The entire state of society had declined to disaster point – in England with the Wars of the Roses, of course. Francois Villon, the finest poet of the age, was a rogue and a vagabond. Perforce. Because there was nothing better for him. Yet about a century later, the greatest poet of the age, Shakespeare, was a noted visitor in the houses of the aristocracy. Conditions had changed drastically so that Shakespeare was able to put together a comfortable fortune for himself.

'The usual explanation for this huge change is that America was discovered,' the Chancellor went on. 'Not just the actual discovery itself, but the opening-up of the imagination which it brought to the European mind. But then you ask yourself by what coincidence was it that America happened to be discovered just as a disaster point was being reached.'

'I thought the Vikings had been there long before the fifteenth century,' Isaac Newton managed to interpose.

'One or two isolated voyages, perhaps — the Irish also claim one or two visits — but never a steadily maintained contact between Europe and America. It was the maintained contact which made the difference. And you know *why* this was so?'

'No, I'm afraid I don't.'

'Well, it wasn't because of Columbus, or Vasco da Gama, or Drake, or any of the famous seadogs. It was because of unsung and unremembered shipwrights. Ships had of course been improving steadily since Roman times,' the Chancellor continued, warming to his subject, 'and in the fifteenth century a three-masted carrack emerged along the Atlantic coast from Lisbon to Brest. But it was the shipwrights in the region of Bayonne who first reached the critical level of technology, just as critical as one of your nuclear reactors. Their ships reached the stage where they could ride out the biggest Atlantic storms.

'Of course, they were thinking at first only of vessels plying along the Atlantic coast, of the trading advantage of being able to ride out a storm instead of being obliged to run for port. But, you see, once a ship could do that it could cross the entire Atlantic or the Pacific. So within only a few more years you had Columbus and you had Magellan, and pretty soon you had the English in North America. It's one of the injustices of history that while it seems to have been the French who made the technological breakthrough, it was the Spaniards, the Portuguese, and eventually the English, who reaped most of the reward.

'Well, to cut a very long story very short,' the Chancellor concluded, 'I had an uncanny feeling as I read your little memorandum. I thought about those shipwrights of old Bayonne. They could never have foreseen the outcome of the improvements they were making. I wonder if you, Newton, have yet seen what the consequences of these signals might be. They could jerk our modern, rotting state of society, rotting just as society was rotting in the fifteenth century, into something very different.'

Chapter 22

There were more theories in the Sunday newspapers about the 'Cambridge affair' than there are days in the week, particularly as the open verdict reached by the Coroner's Court on the Friday had made any notion with an air of plausibility grist to the Fleet Street mill.

After leaving the Prime Minister's residence early on Sunday morning, Isaac Newton had been driven by special car to Heathrow Airport. There he bought an armful of newspapers, wondering with morbid anticipation what he would find therein. He'd restrained his curiosity until after boarding a British Airways flight to Geneva. Then, settling himself comfortably, he began scanning a series of articles on the 'affair' written by the 'Insight' team of the *Sunday Times*.

The desire of the Master of Trinity that the 'roof be lifted off' had been granted, but whether the Master would be entirely pleased by the manner of its granting seemed an open question. Instead of burying the spy-filled public image of Cambridge, the present uproar, he thought, was only too likely to enhance it. The investigative journalists had learned about the very long wavelength of the transmission intercepted by Mike Howarth, and they had also learned of its possible relevance from a military point of view – that such wavelengths could neither be jammed nor intercepted from the ground, which made very long wavelengths ideal for secret inter-satellite communications. A big point was made of this fact, and Insight did its readers the courtesy of explaining the technical situation in a specially-written article on the shielding effect of the Earth's ionosphere.

The possibility of the signals originating in a comet, Comet Boswell, was mentioned, but was dismissed out of hand as a device for throwing the credulous off the real scent. In view of the great disparity between standards of electronic technology in the U.S. and the U.S.S.R., it was far more likely that a breakthrough in inter-satellite communication had been made by the Americans than by the Russians – so it was credibly argued. So where did this leave Mike Howarth, the man who had intercepted and analysed the signals? It left him as a person with left-wing sympathies engaged in passing information to the Russians. So far so good, from the point of view of the Master of Trinity. The spy, this time, was from 'over the wall', from St John's.

The termination by the Research Council of Mike Howarth's contract fitted neatly into this scenario. The Council, having learned that espionage was proceeding under its own auspices, very naturally

put an instant stop to the business. Somebody a bit cleverer than
Clamperdown must have thought of that one, Isaac Newton mused. It
let the Council off the hook beautifully, so beautifully that it was all too
obvious where the investigative journalists had obtained much of their
information. The Council must have opened its mouth wide and sung
at least some parts of the song very loudly.

Enter, now, the new Cavendish Professor. To Isaac Newton's
amazement, the papers even had knowledge of his own involvement in
security matters on behalf of Government, at 'its highest level', the
papers informed their readers. Had this information been leaked from
the Foreign Office, Isaac Newton wondered?

What could have been more natural, in these circumstances, than
that the new Cavendish Professor should have been asked as an
immediate first priority to report on the security aspects of the work of
Dr Howarth? Did the new Cavendish Professor turn in an adverse
report, the journalists asked their several million readers? And having
received the new Cavendish Professor's adverse report, did British
Intelligence then send in a hit-squad? This was an important matter,
about which all citizens had a right to know. The Government must
come clean, or be made to come clean. If not, how was Britain a whit
better than the régimes of Eastern Europe which the Government
claimed so strenuously to oppose?

Isaac Newton had expected his liaison with Frances Haroldsen to
feature prominently, and it did – but in a way he'd not expected at all.
From his first meeting with the girl, Isaac Newton had dismissed
thoughts of her origin and family from his mind, except he'd surmised
in a general way that the family must have an army background. Here
he'd been on target, but not quite on the bullseye. He now learned
from the newspapers that her father, Rear-Admiral Sir James
Haroldsen, had retired only recently from Naval Intelligence. The
security aspect of the presence of the Admiral's daughter in the rooms
of the new Cavendish Professor on the very night of Howarth's death
could not be overlooked, the papers further instructed their readers.
Touché.

It was the stuff of good quality journalism. Facts that were
reasonably accurate had been woven together into a pattern at least as
plausible as the plot of a James Bond novel. The plausibility had been
achieved, of course, by carefully missing out the bits that didn't fit –
bits like Isaac Newton's courtroom duel with the lawyer Sherbourne.

Isaac Newton had no liking for being cast in the play as a signer of
death warrants. But it was not this distaste which caused him to send
back uneaten the breakfast which a stewardess brought him. He was

dismayed because he actually *had* signed a death warrant. When many newspapers converge on the same story, each individual journalist is under pressure to discover some new angle which the others have overlooked. It was no surprise, therefore, that journalists had discovered Mike Howarth's cottage near the Linton water tower, nor that they had managed to gain access to it. Somebody had connected up the outside power cable, which again was not surprising. The trouble was that somebody else, a journalist, had then electrocuted himself on the filing cabinet in the upstairs room of the cottage. The manner of this death was further confirmation to the newspapers of the role which Mike Howarth was supposed to have played, since it fitted very well the popular idea of the methods which an espionage agent might be expected to use. For his part, Isaac Newton cursed his own negligence. After cutting the power line outside the cottage and then opening up the filing cabinet, he should, he told himself bitterly, have ripped off the leads to the high-voltage transformer he'd found occupying the bottom drawer of the cabinet.

The world would evidently continue to believe in the thriller-type scenario thus concocted by the papers, unless really solid evidence could be presented to the contrary. And solid evidence would be hard to come by, although Isaac Newton had a suspicion it might exist. Only time would tell. Isaac Newton forced himself to turn his thoughts to what Kurt Waldheim might have discovered, the discovery Frances Haroldsen had refused to explain over the telephone. Taking papers from a briefcase, he looked over several sheets of mathematical equations. Then he began to calculate from the equations and to draw a number of line diagrams, among which was a sketch of a U-shaped curve.

Chapter 23

———————————

Nothing that had happened so far had quite prepared Isaac Newton for the scene which occurred as he emerged out of Customs at Geneva Airport. As Frances Haroldsen rushed up and embraced him vigorously there were several photo-flashes from nearby.

'These fellows have been dogging me for days now,' she muttered,

going immediately to where Rosie Waldheim was holding a bag of large
ripe peaches. Grabbing a peach Frances Margaret let fly at one of the
photographers with the vigour and urgency of a catcher throwing to
second base. Other peaches followed. Then a policeman arrived on the
scene, shouting loudly in Swiss German instead of in French, which in
itself was unusual for Geneva.

Kurt Waldheim was a firmly-set man, big with a broad forehead
surmounted by the quiff of fair hair he frequently brushed back into
place, in contrast to his wife who had a short bob of nearly black hair.
Eventually Kurt Waldheim managed to translate the policeman's
remarks, contriving as he always did to make everything sound like a
joke.

'He is not worried by your hitting the photographers but by the
mess caused by the peaches. Who is to clear it up, he wants to know?'

'Well, I will,' Frances Margaret answered immediately.

There was a further altercation in Swiss German, and Kurt
Waldheim again translated in his slow, deliberate way.

'He says he's not satisfied that you will do a proper job. So you must
pay for the cleaning. It is to cost five francs for each peach thrown. He
wants to know how many peaches you threw?'

'Seven, I think.'

Frances Margaret counted out thirty-five Swiss francs, and remarked
as she did so:

'No wonder their currency is very solid.'

Meanwhile the policeman gravely wrote out a receipt which he
handed over with a nod in exchange for the money.

They had walked across the foyer of the airport building when there
was a further shout from the policeman, who came running towards
them. After a short conversation with Kurt Waldheim, the man
disappeared, this time for good. After they were seated in the
Waldheim car with Rosie driving, Kurt Waldheim turned from the
passenger seat to Frances Margaret and Isaac Newton in the back,
and said in his wry voice:

'The policeman came back to ask if the young lady was a film star. I
said not to my knowledge, and he said as he walked away, "Then I
think she soon will be!"'

Four hours later, Isaac Newton and Kurt Waldheim were seated
on the balcony of the Waldheims' chalet above Wengen in the
Lauterbrunnen valley, which has been described as the one valley in
Switzerland where the landscape is Himalayan in scale. The Waldheims
had bought their chalet for another reason, however: this was the scene
of Rosie's greatest triumphs in her earlier ski-championship days.

The two women had walked down into the village to fetch supplies, leaving the two men sitting lazily on the verandah of the chalet, gazing towards the high mountain wall of the Jungfrau, much as they had done several months earlier. It struck Isaac Newton that of all the big mountains of the world the Alps were the only ones that were kind to man. The glaciers of the past million years had come and gone, cutting broad valleys instead of the intractable narrow ravines that otherwise would have been eroded by streams and rivers. Then the broad valleys had become covered by sediments, which permitted grass, crops and flowers to grow in profusion when aided by a warm summer sun. And even in the hottest summers there was never any shortage of water, because the hotter it became the more snow and ice melted off the high mountains. Everything worked here to perfection, to an extent that seemed too great merely to be ascribed to chance.

'Your young lady friend has more ability than the throwing of peaches. She is sometimes a little wild, I think.'

'Her father is an Admiral. I suppose she has reacted against her home background.'

'Ah, yes, the dreaded naval discipline,' Kurt Waldheim nodded. 'When I was in California I learned the American Navy was once on manoeuvres off Monterey Point. They had many ships-in-line on the same course. Unfortunately, the leading ship had the course wrong and piled itself onto rocks. Naval discipline was then so strong that the ships behind kept implacably to the course, piling themselves one after another onto the rocks. By the time the order was finally given to change course, eleven ships had been sunk or damaged. It was this incident, I believe, that led to the famous dictum "The U.S. Navy never makes any *trivial* mistakes".'

'So what has Frances Haroldsen done, besides throw peaches?'

'Well, when the data she brought to CERN had been cleaned up a bit, she noticed that there were really four kinds of pulse, not just two. She measured their lengths, finding them in strict geometrical proportions. Call the shortest a dot; the next shortest has twice the time duration of a dot; the next longest has four times the length of a dot; and the longest pulse has eight times the length of a dot. The more of the record she analysed the more accurate this progression became. So then she had the idea of inverting the situation. By assuming the pulses to have lengths progressively in the ratio one to two it was possible to clean up the record still more, until what had seemed fairly noisy in the beginning became very good in the end. It was then I began to get interested in these comet signals myself.'

'You're convinced they come from the comet?' Isaac Newton asked in some surprise.

'Yes, for reasons I will now explain. Although I didn't think so to begin with, of course.'

'Go on, I'm interested,' Isaac Newton urged as Kurt Waldheim stopped for a long, dramatic pause.

'I thought you might be. Well, Isaac, the reason why the longest and the next longest pulses weren't noticed until after the record had been cleaned up is that they're used very sparingly. About one pulse in thirty is of the longest kind and about one in ten is of the next longest kind. On the other hand, the shortest and the next shortest are about equally common, but with the next shortest having a slight excess of a few percent over the shortest. You see what this must mean?'

Isaac Newton thought for a while and then replied:

'Almost surely it would be numbers that were transmitted, and the most universal way to express a number would be in binary form, just as numbers are expressed in a computer. Well, if you wrote out a lot of numbers in binary form, the number of zeros and the number of ones would be about equal. Except the ones would have a slight edge over the zeros, because every number has to begin with one when it's expressed in binary form. So I would deduce that the shortest pulses are zeros, and that the next shortest are ones.'

'Yes, and you can also deduce that most of the numbers have to be rather long, with many digits, otherwise the excess of ones would be rather more than it is. Well, having got as far as that,' continued Kurt Waldheim, 'I next took a look at the longest pulses, and I found they were invariably followed by a one, never by a zero. Which told me that the longest pulses must mark the beginnings of numbers.'

'So what about the next longest pulses?' Isaac Newton asked.

Kurt Waldheim held up a hand, and speaking slowly and precisely, and always half-humorously, answered:

'It is here, Isaac, that the slight subtleties begin. What, I asked myself, would *you* do to express the decimal point in a number, or in this case the binary point? If you were transmitting the number to another human, you would simply stick in a point, just as we do in a letter or in a scientific paper – because you would rely on your correspondent to understand the meaning of it, without any explanation on your part being necessary. But if you were transmitting to some unknown intelligence you could not stick in a point, because you could not rely on your presumed correspondent understanding the conventions we adopt in the use of a decimal point, or of a binary point.'

Kurt Waldheim paused for breath, and to see if Isaac Newton was following his argument. On receiving a nod he continued:

'So, I asked myself, what exactly do we mean by a decimal point? For instance, by saying the exchange rate is 2.85 marks to the dollar? Well, we use the decimal point to separate-off the fractional part of the number. If I give you the first three digits of the number 3.14, what we mean is 3, plus 1 divided by 10, plus 4 divided by 100. From this you see that by using a decimal point we avoid specifying the operations of addition and division. Hence if we are to scrap the decimal point altogether we shall need to bring in symbols to denote addition and division, the symbols we usually denote by the plus sign and the divided-by sign.'

'I have no difficulty in following you, Kurt,' Isaac Newton interposed.

'Hence I decided that within the signals there had to be such symbols, and well, to cut the story short, I found a single near longest pulse stands for "plus" and a triplet of near longest pulses stands for "divided by". And I would infer that a doublet of such pulses stands for "subtract" and a quartet stands for "multiply". It was at this stage I also decided the signals must be coming from the comet, not from a man-made source.'

'Why?'

'Because from a man-made source the convention of the decimal point would surely have been used. Nobody human would dream of spelling out all the additions and divisions in the way they are spelled out in these signals. But there were other indications, too.'

'Such as?'

'It's obvious when you look at the actual numbers, after doing a computer conversion from binary to decimal to make them easier to read, that they form a very long sequence of pairs of the type (x,y). The numbers x and y in each pair are very different: but if you go from one pair to the next the number x varies smoothly; and the number y also varies smoothly from one pair to the next.'

'Whereas if we were dealing with some highly secret military transmission...' Isaac Newton tried to interpose.

'...the numbers would surely have been *scrambled*, so as to come out in a random sort of way,' Kurt Waldheim concluded triumphantly.

'That sounds very conclusive, Kurt, although I'm not sure if it would have an instantaneous appeal to the Research Council or to investigative journalists,' Isaac Newton remarked drily. 'So the big question now is to find the meaning of these (x,y) pairs. How far have you got there?'

'Nothing yet,' answered Kurt Waldheim with a broad smile, 'because that would have been rather unfair, wouldn't it? These signals

are your data, Isaac, if they are anybody's now. It would not have been
very moral of me to begin working seriously on them – not until I have
your permission. Although I have hardly been able to stop myself from
speculating just a little, naturally.'

'And where have your speculations taken you?'

Instead of answering immediately, Kurt Waldheim fetched a bottle of
wine and two glasses and said:

'The wine should be chilled now.'

Pouring generously into the two glasses, he went on:

'I ask myself what numbers could there be that would be the same
for any intelligence, anywhere in the universe.'

'Pi or e,' Isaac Newton said as he took a first sip of the wine.

'Yes, but not especially informative; or the square root of two, if you
like. These are all *mathematical* numbers. I have been thinking of
physical numbers, world invariants, coupling constants. You would
have no objection if I were to try that kind of thing? Because I expect
you will be trying something different yourself.'

'Possibly,' smiled Isaac Newton. 'No, I have no objection, provided
you supply me with a copy of these (x,y) pairs.'

'I have a copy prepared for you,' agreed Kurt Waldheim, fetching a
thick wad of computer print-out and handing it to Isaac Newton. 'I
think I hear the ladies returning,' he added.

In bed that night Frances Margaret remarked:

'I saw the Sunday newspapers before you arrived this morning – they
fly them from London overnight. It's awful, and it's untrue, nearly
every bit of it.'

'You could hardly expect anything else.'

'I hope you won't go back to Cambridge.'

'You'd prefer to stay here?'

'Much. There's a sort of undercurrent of malice back home. It
won't have been so obvious to you perhaps, until now, but I've had it
right through my career. On and on it goes,' she said.

'If this were an entirely personal matter, I'd agree. But suppose
these signals really are from the comet. Suppose we can prove it; prove
it up to the hilt, I mean, so that everybody believes us. There's nothing
we could then do if we stayed here, because CERN can't go into the
satellite business. That's just not on. So we would simply be handing a
great discovery to those who are in a position to capitalise on it –
NASA in America, the Research Council in Britain. You'd soon have
Clamperdown changing his tune, blowing out his chest – is that what
you want?'

'Not really. I was rather thinking of all this publicity.'

'If we can prove the signals came from the comet, this publicity will boomerang. But a different question: Kurt told me about these (x,y) pairs of numbers. What happens if you plot them as a graph? What kind of a curve do you get?'

Frances Margaret thought for a while and then answered:

'It would be a U-shaped curve, I suppose.'

Chapter 24

A week later, Isaac Newton and Frances Haroldsen had returned to England, the latter with some reluctance at first. Then, as the excitement of decoding the cometary signals took hold, Frances Margaret buckled down to it in earnest. She was at the Cavendish Laboratory helping Scrooge load a micro-computer into the back of Isaac Newton's Mercedes. When they had it safely in position, Scrooge remarked:

'Well, it wasn't too heavy. Now, there's just one more thing.'

'What's that, Scrooge?'

'A box of papers. I've been keeping them for the Professor. You know what, Frances Margaret?'

'What?'

'All sorts of people have been looking for those papers.'

'Like whom?'

Scrooge squared up his shoulders with a characteristic gesture and said with a suggestion of a wink:

'Like the police. Like people from London. Like all sorts. Like I said. And all the time they've been lying in my storeroom.'

Finding much humour in the situation, Scrooge gave a hoarse chuckle and went off to fetch the data files which Isaac Newton and Frances Margaret had taken from the filing cabinet in Mike Howarth's cottage.

Meanwhile, Isaac Newton was closeted with the Master in the latter's upstairs snug in the north-east corner of the Great Square of Trinity College. He had given the Master a quick rundown on Kurt Waldheim's discoveries, thinking it right that a third person in Cambridge besides Frances Margaret and himself should know about the situation. The Master had not been unduly impressed.

'Decimal points were always a dark and sinister mystery to me,' he admitted.

Then Isaac Newton showed how the pairs of numbers (x,y) could be plotted as a graph.

'Never did like graphs,' grunted the Master, still unresponsive.

Isaac Newton sketched a U-shaped curve on a piece of paper which also failed to excite the Master.

'Not very interesting,' he grunted again.

Isaac Newton grinned and quickly sketched a frog-like monster beside the U-shaped curve.

'I suppose you'd be more interested, Master, if the graph had turned out like that.'

'Frankly, I would.'

'Frankly, I wouldn't, because then we'd know for sure that somebody was playing a joke. But this kind of a U-shaped curve could be a different story – if it turns out to be the *right* U-shape.'

'What is the *right* U-shaped curve?'

'One connected with the comet, Master.'

'How can you find out?'

'A few days of calculation. That's why I telephoned to ask if you could get me the cottage.'

'I managed it from Howard Baker. He has a cottage somewhere out on the Norfolk coast. You remember Howard, the organist?'

'Of course.'

'The young devil should have been here by now, but he's always late,' the Master observed, glancing towards a silver carriage clock. 'What I can't understand is why you should need a remote cottage.'

'I need a place where I can be free from interruptions.'

'Can't you kick everybody out of your office? I do. I kick everybody ten miles when I have to get down to it.'

Isaac Newton thought for a while before replying.

'It's the spy business, Master.'

As if a switch had been pressed the Master roared:

'Not spies! I can't bear the thought of spies!'

'I even asked the Prime Minister to put a stop to all the poking and prying. Outwardly it actually has stopped, but only outwardly.'

'Explain.'

'I'm being followed around like an animal with a radio beacon around its neck. That's why I have to get away to some quiet place where I can't be found.'

'How are you being followed around?'

'My car is emitting blips.'

'Are you sure?'

'Of course I'm sure. A transmitter has been fitted to the car chassis. Quite a pro-job. Whoever did it even had the impudence to run the thing off the car's own battery. It only works when the engine is running so the battery doesn't run down.'

'Who's behind it?'

'Impossible to say. As long as people go on thinking military satellites are involved . . .'

'No! I can't bear it! The stuff from which tragedies are made. Have you ripped this transmitter thing out of your car?'

Isaac Newton shook his head.

'I'll do that in good time. As long as it doesn't matter where I go, it doesn't matter if somebody knows where I'm going. If you see what I mean?'

The clock on the Edward III Tower was striking noon as Howard Baker came out of the now-famous antechapel into Great Square. As he walked towards the Master's Lodge an observer would have described him as all hair and beard, almost to the point where only the eyes and the tip of the nose could be seen. On arriving at the Lodge he was shown by a College servant up to the Master's snug. The Master instantly rose from a large armchair in which he had been embedded.

'Ah, Howard, you've come! Fifteen minutes late as usual.'

'Sorry, Master, but I've been having trouble with my pedals.'

'Pedals?'

'Yes, the harmonies aren't right. They haven't been right ever since the police swarmed all over the place. I hope the big pipes won't have to be taken out.'

'Oh, my God, no! It'll cost a small fortune. A glass of iced white wine?'

The Master moved to a table on which there were three glasses and a bottle of wine in a big silver ice-bucket. Baker nodded cheerfully.

'I don't mind if I do. Thank you, Master.'

As he poured the wine the Master said:

'You've brought instructions about how Newton here is to find this cottage place of yours?'

In response, Howard Baker took a map and a sheet of paper from an inside pocket.

'It's actually quite hard to find so I've written out instructions.'

'It's very kind of you to lend it,' said Isaac Newton as he took the map and sheet of paper from Howard Baker.

'Glad to help,' Baker said with what appeared to be a smile, although this was hard to be sure of because of the beard. 'Glad to have someone look in on the place. It's out by itself on the coast, you see, not too far from Blakeney. I've been there for weeks on end and hardly seen a soul, except for the postman. You know, Master, I wrote quite a sizeable chunk of my book there.'

'On plainsong, wasn't it? More wine?' the Master asked.

'Thank you. Yes, on plainsong.'

As the Master recharged the glasses all round, Howard Baker produced a pair of lightweight binoculars which he handed to Isaac Newton.

'You might be glad of these. There are a lot of interesting birds coming in to the Norfolk coast at this time of the year – turnstones, purple sandpipers, goosanders and mergansers, amongst others. You'll find a book on birds in the cottage.'

Howard Baker finished the second glass of wine with a quaff and jumped to his feet, saying briskly, 'Well, Master, I'll be on my way. Hope you'll enjoy the place, Newton. Thanks for the wine.'

When Howard Baker had gone, the Master pointed to the map he had brought.

'That's young Baker! Always in-and-out. He never stays still for long. Hard to see why he should have a remote cottage like that.'

Isaac Newton was on his feet.

'I should be on my way.'

'I won't try to stop you. I'm expecting Witherspoon to drop in any minute now. He wants to dig up the College garden.'

'Whatever for?' Isaac Newton asked in amazement.

'He's looking for Roman remains.'

'But he can't dig up every place looking for Roman remains.'

The Master nodded emphatically.

'He can't, but he'd like to. That's Witherspoon all over.'

As the Master moved to accompany him, Isaac Newton shook his head.

'Don't bother coming down, Master. I'll let myself out.'

Isaac Newton made his way downstairs and was just on the point of letting himself out of the Lodge into Great Square when the bread-eating Professor of History came in.

'Morning, Newton,' said Witherspoon, his big white walrus-like moustache spreading into a broad grin, as if some memory of the recent past caused him great amusement.

'Morning, Witherspoon,' Isaac Newton replied, thinking that without a walrus-like moustache he couldn't really compete.

He walked out of Great Square by the exit in the north-west corner.

A moment later, after turning to the right, he reached Trinity Bridge where Frances Haroldsen was waiting with the car. He slipped into the front passenger seat.

'Won't you drive?' Frances Margaret asked.

'No. I've been drinking iced white wine.'

'Disgusting! At this time of day.'

Frances Margaret drove across Trinity Bridge, along the avenue and out into Queen's Road.

'Where are we going?'

'Ultimately, the north Norfolk coast.'

'Then we need the Ely road.'

'I'd sooner go via Norwich. I'll explain why later.'

It was one of Frances Margaret's good points, Isaac Newton thought, that she didn't demand an explanation there and then. Instead she simply said:

'Scrooge put the box in the boot, with Mike Howarth's data files.'

'Better check we have everything we need. Computer?'

'Check.'

'Printer?'

'Check.'

'The data tape from CERN?'

'It's in your briefcase.'

'And my briefcase?'

'It's in the back. I made sure.'

'We need the orbital elements of Comet Boswell.'

'I have the International Astronomical Union circular. It gives the latest update on the elements.'

'Food?'

'Stocks adequate, boss.'

'Drink?'

'After all that white wine? Disgusting.'

Frances Haroldsen drove along the fast A45 in an easterly direction to the fork of the A11, four miles beyond Newmarket, then along the A11 across the Breckland to Thetford and Wymondham. Eight miles more and she turned left onto the Norwich by-pass.

'Once you get past the University, pull up on the grass verge,' Isaac Newton told her.

Eventually, Frances Margaret pulled the car onto a fairly extended verge and cut the engine.

'Perhaps you'll explain what the mystery is all about, Professor.'

For answer, Isaac Newton got out of the car and after sorting through equipment in the back took out a portable radio receiver which he handed to Frances Margaret.

'It's on the ultra-short band,' he said. 'Walk twenty yards away and then switch on.'

As Frances Haroldsen moved away, Isaac Newton slipped into the driver's seat of the car. When he saw the girl switch on the radio he started the engine and then joined her, leaving the engine running. Blips could be heard on the receiver at about three-second intervals.

'They started when you started the engine,' the girl said. 'What goes on?'

'It's a beacon. Fitted to the car,' Isaac Newton answered, glancing up into the sky. 'Somebody is following us, probably from the air. I kept a close watch on the road but there didn't seem to be any car on our tail.'

Frances Margaret went back to the Mercedes and, squatting down, peered underneath.

'Where is it?'

Isaac Newton joined her, also squatting down, and pointed.

'On the chassis. It works on the battery.'

'Through the aerial?'

'Yes,' Isaac Newton replied as they both stood again.

'Why didn't you rip it off before we started?'

'Because the A11 is a straight road. We could easily have been intercepted and followed.'

'And now?'

Isaac Newton pointed along the by-pass.

'This has all sorts of roads branching off it, like spokes on a wheel, and between here and the coast it's a rabbit warren of smaller roads.'

J was the work of only a few moments to snip the wires leading to the car aerial, much quicker than actually finding the beacon would have been. Isaac Newton then took Howard Baker's map and sheet of instructions from a pocket, handing them to Frances Margaret and saying,

'I'll drive from here. We're heading for a spot near Blakeney. You'll need to navigate fairly carefully.'

Driving to instructions from Frances Margaret, Isaac Newton worked his way through a veritable labyrinth of smaller roads until eventually they reached a moderately broad road. Several miles along it he picked up a signpost to Blakeney, and several miles further still he received something of a shock.

'There's a police car behind,' he murmured.

At this, Frances Margaret looked up from the map and twisted around so as to get a good view through the rear window. After a brief moment she said:

'There is.'

'It can't be us. I haven't done anything,' continued Isaac Newton, assuring himself of his rights as a citizen.

'You're living in a fool's paradise, boss,' Frances Margaret informed him. 'It's a first principle – whenever there's a police car behind, it's always you they're after. I hope the Master's white wine is out of your system by now.'

'I hope so, too. But I still don't see . . .'

Whatever Isaac Newton intended to say was cut short by the police car, which came up alongside with its blue roof-light flashing. Resigned to his fate, Isaac Newton pulled up at the road side and opened the window beside him. A young police constable came and rested a hand on the window.

'Professor Newton?'

'Yes?'

'We've a message for you, sir, from your secretary. She said it was important, and it seems to be. We've had a hard job picking you up.'

The constable handed Isaac Newton a sheet of paper. He read it quickly and then grinned up at the policeman.

'Thanks very much, Constable. I'm sorry you had a hard job picking me up.'

The constable gave a wave as he returned to the police car. Frances Margaret bottled up her impatience until they were on their way again. Eventually she asked:

'What on Earth is it?'

'A message from the Prime Minister's office. We're expected at Chequers on Saturday.'

'Two days from now. Why?'

'I don't know. My guess is, curiosity.'

'At what?'

'At what's going on.'

'They can't know about the signals.'

'Not explicitly, no. But you don't become a top politician without developing an instinct for important happenings. They know about my trip to Switzerland, and perhaps even about our rushing out of Cambridge this afternoon. You wouldn't have to be a genius to put two and two together – if you were interested, and I think they *are* interested.'

'It could explain the beacon.'

'And why they had a devil of a job picking us up, once we disconnected it,' Isaac Newton agreed.

'Suppose we really try to give them the slip now,' Frances Margaret said, with an expression that made her look as if she were about to hit a winner on the tennis court.

'Agreed,' nodded Isaac Newton. 'I know now when that beacon was fitted on the car.'

'When?'

'The last time I was at Chequers. Didn't Shakespeare say something about...'

'...not putting your trust in princes,' Frances Margaret finished. 'From now on, I think we must watch everybody,' she concluded quietly.

Chapter 25

Howard Baker's cottage was at the end of a small lane. It nestled behind a dune among a multitude of gorse bushes not far from the sea. After they had unpacked the car of electronic gear, food and drink, sheets and towels and the like, Frances Margaret and Isaac Newton crossed the dune onto a shingle beach where the waves were crashing.

'Unfortunately the weather forecast isn't good,' Frances Margaret remarked. Then they returned to the cottage, where Isaac Newton lit a wood fire while the girl set about preparing a meal. When they had eaten and washed up they both squatted close to the fire.

'It seems pretty isolated here now it's dark outside,' Frances Margaret observed as she barred the door with a stout wooden spar.

'Yes, young Baker – he's the College organist – says you can stay here for weeks on end without seeing a soul, except for the postman,' Isaac Newton recounted.

'I can believe it. The place is a bit unlived-in. We'd better keep the fire high.'

So they concentrated for a while on getting a scorching blaze going. Sitting enjoying the warmth, Frances Margaret said:

'I've got the pairs of numbers on tape, ready to go into the computer. Here, by the way, is the graph. It's quite accurate.'

Isaac Newton smiled as he studied the U-shaped curve which the girl passed over to him.

'The Master wasn't too impressed when I told him about it. He would have preferred it if the numbers had graphed up into a bug-eyed monster.'

'Kurt Waldheim thinks it must be something very fundamental. He's working on SO (10) projections.'

Isaac Newton grinned again and piled more wood on the fire.

'Oh, is he? Frankly, I don't think it's anything like that.'

'What d'you think it is?'

'Something very clever but very simple.'

'Such as?' Frances Margaret asked.

'Kurt's idea of world invariants would be the kind of lofty message we might want to send to somebody at the far side of the Universe, just to show how intellectually-advanced we humans have become. But here we've got a comet passing close by the Earth, not at the far side of the Universe. Perhaps the comet has picked up some of our own radio signals, so it knows we exist. In that case, I think it would simply want to announce itself.'

'Announce itself?'

'Yes, announce itself. Like saying, "Hey, here's me. Boswell is the name."'

'I'd keep that idea strictly private, if I were you.'

'That's what Boulton, the Geostrophics man, is always saying – if I were you. Rest assured, Frances Margaret, I've no intention of broadcasting my views until I've got solid proof.'

'How can we get solid proof?'

'At first I thought solid proof would be impossible. Then I saw it might be possible. Then I saw it might be easy. But just tell me one thing before we go on. Had Comet Boswell been seen before? I mean, was it a known comet, like Halley's?'

'I got it mixed up at first with a Comet Bowell, but then I checked that the two aren't the same, although they've got nearly the same name. No, it seems Comet Boswell was a newcomer. There are one or two newcomers every year.'

'So there was no possibility of the orbit of Comet Boswell being known beforehand?'

'Absolutely not. But why would that be important?'

'Because it removes the outside possibility that the signals might have been put out deliberately by a man-made satellite. It would have been impossible if nobody could have known how to do it. At least, if

I'm right that's the way things will come out. I began by wondering what would be the most likely quantities for a comet to measure. Every living creature, even a mouse, must have some form of internal clock. So one possibility for measurement would be time. In your (x,y) pairs, suppose x represents the time measured by the comet. Next let's consider what y might be. It wouldn't need too much sophistication for a comet to measure the flux of sunlight on its surface. Because the flux of sunlight goes inversely as the square of the distance of the comet from the Sun, this would be equivalent to a measurement of distance from the Sun. Suppose such a measurement to be the number y. Then, as a comet comes inwards to perihelion passage and moves out again from the Sun, you would have y decreasing to a minimum and then increasing again. So that if you plotted the (x,y) pairs...'

'...you would have a U-shaped curve!' exclaimed Frances Margaret.

'So far so good,' nodded Isaac Newton. 'But do we have the *right* U-shaped curve? That's the big question. You see, each value for the ellipticity of the comet orbit gives different invariants along the curve, as Kurt Waldheim would express it. So, does the curve of your (x,y) pairs give invariants that correspond to the known ellipticity of Comet Boswell?'

'Which shouldn't be too difficult to find out,' Frances Haroldsen said, with a sudden rush of confidence.

'Not difficult, but a bit fiddly. We have to cope with three nuisances. We don't know the zero point of the comet's clock, and we don't know the units which the comet uses to measure either distance or time.'

'We can set our clocks together from the moment of perihelion passage of the comet,' Frances Margaret suggested immediately, 'by subtracting off from each x the particular x when y is least. But how about the units?'

'Well,' Isaac Newton went on, 'suppose we divide each value of y by the least value of y. We'll then have distances in terms of the perihelion distance as unit. When we've done both these things, call the resulting comet pairs (X,Y). Then we proceed to calculate pairs of our own like this: for each step of heliocentric distance from one (X,Y) pair to the next, we use the known orbit of the comet to determine the change of the heliocentric longitude. Then we use Kepler's law of equal areas to calculate corresponding steps in time, which we call T. So we arrive by calculation at a sequence of pairs (T,Y), with the Y values exactly the same as in the (X,Y) pairs of the comet.'

'And the question becomes whether our T values are the same as the comet's X values,' concluded Frances Margaret with a quick smile of comprehension.

'The same except for a scale factor due to different clock units. And if they really are the same, not all the sceptics in the Universe can deny that those signals came from Comet Boswell. OK?' asked Isaac Newton.

'OK!' Frances Margaret agreed. 'But why didn't we settle it in Geneva? The thing would have been easy.'

'Partly because I didn't want it getting spread around, and partly because when you've got a bottle of fine wine you don't drink it all at a gulp. Besides I still have an odd feeling...'

'What?'

'That there's something extremely peculiar we haven't seen yet.'

A high wind was hammering at the cottage door the following morning as Isaac Newton and Frances Haroldsen finished washing up the breakfast pots.

'Well!' exclaimed Frances Margaret when they had done, 'Today is likely to be a full day. Nose to the grindstone. The question is, do we go out before we start work? The radio is forecasting a real storm for this afternoon and evening.'

'We can work during the storm. It won't do any harm to walk on the beach for half an hour – to clear our heads,' Isaac Newton decided.

They muffled themselves against a mean wind. After crossing the dune between the cottage and the sea they made their way against the wind to within a few yards of the water's edge. Everywhere along the beach each successive wave broke with a sudden crash at just the same moment, each crash being followed by the strangely disquieting sound of rolling pebbles. They walked for the best part of a mile before turning back towards the cottage. Few birds were to be seen, and such as there were appeared to be in purposeful flight towards some kind of shelter. A thin drizzle changed to rain.

A dark figure had appeared between them and the cottage. Looking towards the figure, Frances Margaret pointed and said:

'It reminds me of the character in Ibsen's *Peer Gynt*. The one with the cloven hoof.'

'We'll take a closer look at it, then,' Isaac Newton grunted.

As they approached the figure it became apparent that he was a man wearing an astrakhan hat. Frances Margaret's remark about a cloven hoof caused Isaac Newton to look down at the fellow's feet. The chap, remarkably enough, was wearing natty shoes and a city suit half-covered by a thin plastic mackintosh. A rain-soaked, partially-smoked cigarette hung in the corner of his mouth.

'Have you seen the sunken trawler?' the man asked, gazing out to sea as they came up to him.

'Frankly, no,' Frances Margaret replied.

'We had a report that it's sunk with all hands.'

'*Who* had a report?' Isaac Newton managed to force himself to ask. For answer the man reached through his mackintosh into his suit, causing Isaac Newton to think the fellow might be reaching for a shoulder gun. But his hand emerged with a small white card about two inches by one inch, a business card.

'I'm Tommy Taylor. From the *Observer*. I had a tip-off about this trawler. Call me if you see it, or hear about it. Everybody knows Tom Taylor of the *Observer*.'

Then the fellow moved along the beach away from the cottage, gazing out to sea the whole while.

'Cloven hoof!' yelled Isaac Newton as he and Frances Margaret changed into rough woollens after their soaking. The girl was shaking with helpless laughter.

'I think he was wearing Gucci shoes!' she managed to yelp.

'Actually, it wouldn't be at all a bad day for drug smuggling, when you come to think about it. You'd need a trawler, wouldn't you?'

'Could he be an intelligence type?'

'If he is, the agency he works for deserves to succeed.'

At which remark from Isaac Newton they clutched each other for support against the downward pull of gravity. Even so, they were careful to bar the cottage door with the wooden spar, ostensibly against the storm.

An hour later they were dug into the problem of the U-shaped curve.

'I have all the equations now,' Isaac Newton eventually said.

'Then why don't you make the lunch while I start the programming,' Frances Margaret suggested, adding, 'I'm hungry after the blow on the beach – and the sunken trawler, of course.'

Isaac Newton finished washing up after lunch. He then stoked up the fire.

'I'm beginning to see why woman's work is never done. How's it coming?'

'Not so badly,' answered Frances Margaret from her position at the computer console. 'I'm about ready to go.'

It was some ten minutes later that she set the computer to

calculating in earnest. The printer was activated. It first typed out a table of numbers, and then a U-shaped curve emerged.

'Well, at least we've got a U-shaped curve,' Frances Margaret observed. 'But we had to get that, assuming your equations were right, and assuming my programme was right.'

'Suppose you take over the cuisine for a change, while I check one or two of these numbers by hand.'

'Are you doubting my programme, Professor?'

'I doubt everybody's programme. How about a pot of coffee?'

Isaac Newton sat by the fire examining the sheets from the printer and making calculations of his own with the aid of a small hand-held calculator. The storm appeared to be rising outside, and as Frances Margaret brought the pot of coffee to the fireside there was a heavy knocking on the cottage door. Isaac Newton jumped immediately up from his chair, saying with more calm than he actually felt, 'Now I wonder who that might be?'

'Didn't you say nobody calls for weeks on end?' Frances Margaret asked as Isaac Newton began to unbar the wooden spar.

'Except the postman.'

'Perhaps it's the postman.'

'And perhaps it isn't.'

When Isaac Newton opened the cottage door he found a grey-haired stocky man in late middle-age standing on the threshold. He was wearing a padded fawn jacket and a blue woollen bonnet with a big bobble on it. Around his neck were binoculars, tucked inside the jacket for protection. He stamped into the cottage with a certain air of proprietorship.

'Oh, I thought Howard Baker must be here. I saw the smoke from the fire. We often go bird-watching together.'

Isaac Newton hurriedly closed the door, replacing the wooden spar instinctively, and then felt an explanation was necessary:

'In this wind even the cottage might blow away.' Then he went on: 'Howard Baker let us have the place for a few days. I'm a colleague of his at Cambridge.'

'I didn't mean to barge in,' the man said half-apologetically as he freed the binoculars from the confines of his jacket.

'No trouble at all,' Frances Margaret came in, 'have a cup of coffee. We're just making it.'

'Well, thank you very much. The wind is a bit overpowering. I see you're in computers,' the fellow added, nodding towards the equipment which covered the cottage table.

'Yes, more than birds really,' Isaac Newton agreed.

'It must be very interesting. If you understand it. How long are you staying?'

'Until early next week – if I'm not called back to Cambridge. When we've got this job finished we'll have a bit of time for the birds. Baker told me to look for one or two quite rare species which come in here at this time of the year. Especially the purple mergansers.'

Adjusting his bonnet, the grey-haired man finished the coffee with a last quick gulp.

'You'd need to go a mile or two back from the coast on to freshwater for mergansers. I'll be glad to show you where. Later in the week, perhaps? Well, thanks for the coffee. I'd better be on my way. This storm is likely to get worse before it gets better.'

As soon as the grey-haired man was gone, Isaac Newton again barred the cottage door. Then he began moving around generally, closing the shutters with which the windows were equipped, and saying, 'The chap was quite right. This storm is likely to get worse before it gets better. Howard Baker said there was a book on birds. D'you think you could find it?'

By the time Isaac Newton finished closing the shutters, Frances Margaret had managed to discover Baker's book on birds.

'These books,' she said indicating a small bookcase, 'are horribly musty. Let me see, the index.' Then, running her finger down a page of the index, she went on: 'Mergansers, hooded; mergansers, red-breasted; but no purple mergansers. It was purple mergansers you said, wasn't it?'

'It was. I remembered Baker had told me to look out for purple sandpipers, so I changed it around a bit.'

'So the fellow was a phoney. Which leaves us where, boss? Trapped in a cottage with the door barred and the windows shuttered. But trapped.'

'At the end of a narrow lane, with nowhere to go in front of us except the sea,' acknowledged Isaac Newton. 'How about our friend who was . . .'

'Looking for the sunken trawler. You said they deserved to succeed, didn't you?'

'A mistake, I freely admit.'

'And this remote cottage has no telephone, naturally.'

'Which is just where you're wrong, young Frances Margaret.'

Isaac Newton rummaged among one of the boxes which Scrooge had packed into the car, and eventually came up with a piece of electronic equipment.

'A transmitter. We can call the police any time we want. And it works on a battery. So even if they cut the electricity . . .'

Frances Margaret didn't wait for the end of the sentence, but flung her arms compulsively around Isaac Newton's neck. After she'd kissed him, she moved back a pace and looked up into his face with her best 'Anyone-for-tennis' smile and said:

'Aren't you the cleverest man in the world?'

'Amazing, isn't it?' Isaac Newton grinned in reply. 'You see, when we unhooked the beacon on the car I realised we might be losing connection with our friends. So I thought some sort of compensation was needed.'

'If it was your friends who were following us, why did you unhook it?'

'Because I don't like being tracked around. Even by my friends.'

'So what do we do now?'

'Nobody is going to start anything in this storm. Therefore, we get back to what we were doing before.'

And indeed the storm had now broken with a vengeance. A gale force wind battered the cottage, causing a perpetual rattle from the shutters through which they could hear rain being driven noisily against the windows themselves.

'So what did you find before the interruption?' Frances Margaret asked.

'Well, our calculations look all right, so we'll move on to compare our U-shaped curve with the one from the comet.' Isaac Newton handed several sheets of paper to the girl, adding, 'I've written an outline programme for taking out the units and making the scale adjustments.'

Two hours later, from her position at the computer console, Frances Margaret looked quizzically towards Isaac Newton, who had just finished piling the fire with pieces of wood. She wrinkled her nose and said:

'Hopefully that's the last bug in your programme, boss. Let's give it a go.'

She punched the computer start button and watched for a while. Then, with satisfaction – since the computer continued to function – Frances Margaret stepped back from the table and hitched up the sleeves of her sweater.

'At least it functions this time. It shouldn't be long now.'

The printer started to operate. They watched as the numbers came out, with Frances Margaret standing in a better position to compare their calculated (T,Y) pairs with the comet's (X,Y) pairs.

'My God, they're the same. Our numbers and the comet's

numbers. Up to now I didn't really believe it, I suppose. But they're *exactly* the same,' Frances Margaret whispered. When the printer had finished disgorging numbers, she tore off several sheets which she handed Isaac Newton.

Isaac Newton reached for the sheets, but it was not Frances Margaret who stood there handing them to him. It was an object very tall, and glowing a bright orange colour, with a grotesque face like the Greek mask of Tragedy. Almost immediately the image cleared and he could see Frances Margaret again, but not before he felt a sharp flash of searing heat. Frances Margaret's face was screwed up with fear.

'I saw it *again*. You were it,' she shouted.

The sudden flash of heat was followed by an icy chill. Both of them were shivering violently as they reached the bedroom upstairs. Throwing off their shoes, they pulled blankets over themselves, clutching each other as the storm outside reached an unprecedented fury. Sheets of water were hitting the outer windows and were falling heavily on the roof of the cottage, as if the wave-tops of the sea itself were being lifted and dumped upon them.

An hour earlier, the grey-haired man in the padded fawn jacket, still wearing the blue woollen bonnet with the big bobble on it, had driven into the nearby village of Blakeney. He stopped his car beside a public telephone box on the outskirts of the village. An observer might have watched the man in the woollen hat with the big bobble on it move, a vaguely-defined figure under the dim street lighting, from his car to the telephone box. The observer would not have seen the well-satisfied expression on the man's face as he dialled a number. But an observer, if such there had been in the deserted village street, could not have missed a bright glow which suddenly enveloped the man, telephone box and all, so that it had the appearance of a huge orange-coloured apparition.

There were actually two observers, not in the village street but a quarter of a mile away, sitting in a police car. One of them was the same constable who had stopped Isaac Newton's car on the previous day.

'I wonder what that was?' he said to his fellow constable.

'We'd better go and look,' his companion replied in a practical voice.

The police car moved slowly through the village to its outskirts. After passing the telephone box, which was again but dimly-lit by a street lamp, the first constable muttered:

'There was something funny back there. About the telephone box.'

'Then we'd better go back and look,' his companion suggested in the same practical voice as before.

The two constables approached the telephone box together. A dark figure inside the booth could be seen poised at an abnormal angle. One of the constables opened the door to the booth, and the jerk which he applied caused the dark figure to swivel disconcertingly. The woollen cap with the big bobble on it was intact, resting on what had once been a head. The jacket was also intact, but what had once been the face of the grey-haired man with the binoculars was now without any feature. It was a dark-brown colour, charred like a newspaper held too close to a fire.

Chapter 26

It was disturbingly quiet when Isaac Newton and Frances Margaret tumbled out of bed close on 7.00 a.m. the following morning. They had maintained watches during the night with the short-wave battery-driven transmitter and receiver at the ready, tuned to the police waveband on which they heard instructions and responses passing backwards and forwards between various centres and a wide-flung network of police cars which could be detected most of the way to Norwich. They'd been comforted by the thought that it would be the work of only a moment to break into this network with an SOS sent out from the cottage.

After hastily packing together their essential items, Isaac Newton cautiously went to work opening one of the upstairs shutters after another. As soon as he was convinced that nobody was lurking in the immediate vicinity of the cottage itself, he unbarred the door and stepped outside. Knowing that Frances Margaret would immediately refix the bar on the door behind him, so as to give herself time to make a radio transmission unhindered if it were needed, Isaac Newton at last became acutely aware of the uncanny stillness of the morning. Everything, everywhere, was enveloped in a covering of water. When he put a few drops to his tongue it was salt. So the night wind had indeed lifted off the tops of the waves from the sea a couple of hundred yards or more away.

The Mercedes looked as if it had been standing under a waterfall. Although nobody was to be seen over the fifty yards or so of open ground which separated the cottage from dense gorse bushes, half an army could be concealed beyond his range of vision. But the Mercedes was the critical object, because hostile forces would have inactivated it, or worse. Isaac Newton first peered underneath. Then, after releasing the bonnet safety catch, he examined the interior, especially the electrical wiring. Satisfied eventually that no untoward attachment had been added, he slammed down the bonnet, slipped into the driving seat, fitted in the ignition key and turned it. The car started at a touch, which struck him as keenly anticlimactic. Quickly he swung it close to the cottage door and then held his hand on the horn for a few seconds. Frances Margaret emerged with a box into which the critical data files and papers and computer output had been packed and jumped into the passenger seat. As Isaac Newton immediately accelerated the car away, the girl said:

'That was a quick exit. We can leave the hardware to be collected later.'

The narrow lane from the cottage passed among the gorse bushes, giving Isaac Newton further anxious moments. Eventually the lane joined a small surfaced road that led before long into a larger road.

'Our friends of yesterday seem to have disappeared. I wonder why?' Isaac Newton mused in a puzzled voice.

Frances Margaret had no opportunity for reply because as they came into Blakeney village a police car lay ahead. A constable was standing beside the car; it was the one who had pulled them up two days earlier. Isaac Newton waved a greeting and the constable returned the wave by indicating that the Mercedes should stop. He then walked over and put an arm on the open window beside Isaac Newton, just as he had done before.

'I hope you don't mind me stopping you, Professor Newton?'

'D'you say that to everyone. New public relations?' Isaac Newton replied. The policeman did not notice the slight touch of humour, or affected not to notice, but went on:

'It's just with you being a scientist.'

The first constable was now joined by the same practically-minded colleague as on the previous evening, who immediately came into the conversation.

'We had a man hit by lightning, sir.'

'That's unlucky,' Isaac Newton replied.

'It was queer too,' the second constable added.

'How was it queer?'

'He was standing in a telephone booth when he was hit,' the first constable came in.

'And nothing else was hit,' added the second. 'The rest of the booth was untouched. Wouldn't you expect the stroke to have gone through the walls? Like it would do with people in a car.'

'Or in an aeroplane,' the first constable augmented.

Isaac Newton thought for a moment and then answered:

'If the stroke hit the booth it would surely go through the metal walls. Not through somebody standing in the booth. But how if it came along one of the telephone wires?'

'Wouldn't it fuse the wire?' the second constable suggested.

'A full stroke would fuse the wire, yes. But I suppose you might get enough inductive pick-up to electrocute a man.'

'I'm sorry for mentioning it in front of the lady,' the first constable then said, coming to the real source of his worry, 'but you see, Professor Newton, this wasn't like somebody being electrocuted in a house. The fellow was incinerated. Yet nothing else was damaged. Not even his clothes.'

'Even the bonnet on his head was OK,' the second constable remarked in a bewildered tone.

'What sort of a bonnet?' Frances Margaret immediately asked, leaning across Isaac Newton to look up at the two constables.

'A woollen bonnet.'

'Blue,' the first constable nodded, 'with a big bobble on it.'

'Well now we know, don't we?' Frances Margaret remarked, once they'd left the policemen a couple of miles back along the road.

'What do we know, Frances Margaret?'

'Why there was no showing.'

'A stroke of lightning?'

'It makes you really wonder, doesn't it?' the girl said in a small voice. 'The trouble is I can't put it into words. Not to make any sense.'

'I find myself pondering things a bit. Some I can put into words, some I can't.'

'What can you put into words?'

'Well, I wonder how Howard Baker managed to write a sizeable chunk of his book on plainsong in that cottage.'

Thinking over this enigmatic remark and not being able to make much out of it, Frances Margaret bit back the temptation to ask for an explanation and simply said:

'Where have we to get to?'

'Princes Risborough.'

After examining a road atlas for a while, Frances Margaret eventually said, in something more like her usual firm style:

'You know, if you designed a road system with the intention of making it difficult to get to Princes Risborough you couldn't make it worse. I suppose that's why Prime Ministers live there.'

'You appear to have made amazing and exciting progress since our last meeting,' said the Prime Minister, when Isaac Newton and Frances Haroldsen had concluded a brief account of their recent discoveries. 'I notice there was a piece about you in the *Observer*. Badly garbled as usual,' the Prime Minister added.

Except that Frances Margaret was now taking notes, the place and company were the same as they had been on an earlier occasion: the library with its corner bar at the Prime Minister's country residence.

'I'm baffled as to what can be done next,' the Chancellor came in. 'There has to be a next, I suppose. In science there always seems to be a next.'

'If there isn't, the thing soon atrophies,' nodded Isaac Newton.

'So what d'you propose?' the Prime Minister asked.

'We must return the transmission. Using the same wavelength, with the same pulse system, and with a similar message. Pairs of code numbers, giving the time and the updated distance of the comet from the Sun – as *we* measure them, of course.'

'Which would be evident proof that we had received and understood the comet's own signals,' nodded the Chancellor. 'What are the snags, if you don't mind my asking?'

'That Comet Boswell is moving further and further away all the time. By the time we can put a satellite in a position to make the transmission, the distance may have become too big. Then we'd have to beam the transmission at Comet Halley, which is now on its way towards us.'

'Comet Halley would be much better from a public relations point of view,' the Prime Minister said with enthusiasm. 'In fact Comet Halley would be terrific from a public relations point of view'– not that public relations should be a dominating concern, I suppose.'

'But it is,' said the Chancellor, 'it always is. And you'd hope for some kind of further reply?' he asked Isaac Newton.

'Yes, but we must take it like a game of chess, move by move. Assuming the first signals to be purposive, we can expect some kind of reply. When we see what it is . . .'

'. . . we make a further move ourselves,' nodded the Chancellor.

'You know, Godfrey, if we can produce some kind of reaction from Comet Halley. . .' the Prime Minister began.

'You can see yourself trailing clouds of glory?' the Chancellor smiled.

'Something like that,' the Prime Minister admitted.

'If we can get a satellite up in time – that's the logistic problem,' Isaac Newton interposed.

'Essentially the whole of the British satellite programme is under CERC. Is that also a problem?'

'If this were put under CERC, Prime Minister, it would be an insuperable problem.'

'Apart from the fact that you don't seem to hit it off with the Research Council, can you give me any other reason?'

'CERC has made it plain that the Council doesn't believe in signals from comets.'

'After your last results, it would surely have to believe.'

'Reluctantly, perhaps. But I don't think the Research Council would do much of a job in defeat, and because of the shortness of the time there would be an excuse for making a bungle of it. Besides, Prime Minister, not very long ago you asked me to return from Geneva, as a matter of principle you will recall – to help the universities. But if every time a university comes up with something important the Government takes it away, the principle becomes a bit hollow, doesn't it? This project started with Cambridge and it should stay with Cambridge.'

'How much will it cost? Ten million, or more?'

'I would think so. But we would need to shop around rather carefully before a decent estimate could be made.'

'Godfrey, how could ten million be made available to Cambridge?'

'A specific research grant can, in principle, be earmarked through the University Grants Committee,' replied the Chancellor. 'But a grant of this size would cause a lot of discussion and I doubt it could be done within the necessary time-frame.'

'It couldn't,' agreed Isaac Newton. 'Cambridge would spend months arguing about the fine print before even accepting a grant of that size. All my experience suggests that it would be wrong to work through a body like the University Grants Committee, which has to cast its net much wider than this particular project. What we need is an organisation related directly to the project itself, and to nothing else.'

'There's no way I can see,' the Chancellor said reluctantly, 'that the Treasury could make a grant directly to the Cavendish Laboratory. Monies must go from the Treasury to an accounting officer accredited by the Government. The University Grants Committee has the status of an accredited accounting officer, but individual universities do not, still less individual departments within a university.'

'Which, of course, is why we have the Research Council system, with the Councils acting as the accounting officers,' explained the Prime Minister.

Frances Haroldsen looked up suddenly from her notes. 'Can I ask a question please? Who was the accounting officer for the monies which operated the Prime Minister's think-tank? In the days when there was a think-tank, I mean...'

'The Treasury made a small grant available to the Prime Minister's office.'

'Why can't the Treasury make a larger grant available to the Prime Minister's office?'

'It would be more visible,' answered the Chancellor again.

'This project is going to be very visible indeed, however it's done. If it's done. So if it's done, a bit more visibility isn't going to make all that much difference. Better have a visible success through the Prime Minister's office than a failure through the Research Council,' concluded Frances Haroldsen firmly.

'Suppose I take orders for refreshments while we think that one over,' said the Prime Minister, walking from the table to the bar. 'Godfrey?'

'Gin and tonic, please.'

'Professor Newton?'

'Dry sherry, please.'

'Miss Secretary?'

'A large tomato juice with Worcester sauce, please. But let me see to it, Prime Minister.'

When they resumed, Isaac Newton took a sip of his sherry and began:

'I'd like to develop that idea a bit. Suppose the Prime Minister's office were to appoint a management committee, a kind of board of trustees for the project, perhaps with three members drawn from your side and three from the science side. The committee then appoints the Cavendish Laboratory to act as its project co-ordinator.'

'How about contracts? I mean, how are they to be let?' asked the Chancellor immediately.

'The Laboratory would make technical recommendations to the board, but the board would have the responsibility of actually letting the contracts.'

'And the Laboratory itself would be financed how?'

'On a "cost plus" basis.'

'Overseen by the board?'

'Yes, of course.'

'How is this board to be appointed?' the Prime Minister now asked with interest.

'Let's make a dry run at it,' answered Isaac Newton. 'Let's appoint a provisional board to be sanctified later. We obviously have the Prime Minister in the chair. The Prime Minister also appoints one other board member, and so does the Chancellor. Now since the Chancellor would never appoint himself, the Prime Minister appoints the Chancellor, and the Chancellor appoints an officer from the Treasury, an officer who keeps the board's accounts in impeccable order down to the very last detail.'

'Thank you for all these decisions, Professor Newton. By the time you've also chosen the science side, you'll have all six members sewn up in your pocket. Who, apart from yourself, is to represent the science side?' the Prime Minister asked.

'Someone I've worked with for many years at CERN. He's German, but I don't see why that should matter, especially as if we're to acquire a satellite in the required time we may have to work with the Europeans, or perhaps with the Germans themselves. For the sixth member, I'd choose someone to represent the University. The Master of my own College is, I believe, to become Vice-Chancellor next year. I'd ask him to join the board.'

There was a long silence, at the end of which the Prime Minister turned to the Chancellor:

'Well, Godfrey, you told me you could see this business turning out to be staggeringly important. What have you to say now?'

'I think this proposal of a controlling board would give such a project the best possible chance of success, although I'm not sure I could contribute very much to it myself.'

'You're much too modest,' Isaac Newton said decisively.

'The thing would be highly visible,' continued the Chancellor, 'partly because of the spectacular nature of the project itself, and partly because we would be departing drastically from normal procedures. So it could have quite significant political implications. With that said, if we consider it to be worth the candle, we should do it. That would be my opinion, Prime Minister.'

'Yes, well,' nodded the Prime Minister, 'it certainly would be different from the run of the mill, wouldn't it?'

There was again a long silence which was again broken by Isaac Newton, who said:

'I'm not sure whether we constitute a quorum, but there's a decision which should be taken immediately. Should the position up to
this point be published? Or should we reserve publication?'

'Why should we wait?'

'Some scientists like to have a result already in hand at the start of a
new project, so that they have something to offer in case the project
goes sour.'

'Is this project going to go sour?'

'We can't exclude that possibility.'

'I think it would be wrong to go in with the thought of failure in our
minds. So I would say publish. Godfrey?'

'I agree. Besides which, your results to date would make it easier for
people to understand what we're doing. The public relations side can't
exactly be ignored.'

'How far away in time is the denouement?' asked the Prime
Minister.

'About fifteen months.'

'In politics you *never* worry about things that are fifteen months
away,' concluded the Prime Minister.

When she and Isaac Newton were on their way back to Cambridge,
Frances Haroldsen said:

'I think we managed that quite well.'

While at the Prime Minister's residence, the Prime Minister said to
the Chancellor:

'I think, Godfrey, that we've just been sold a very clever bill of
goods. But if it comes off. . .who knows what the consequences might
be?'

Chapter 27

Dr Alan Bristow, the editor of the weekly science magazine *Nature*,
sat in the big black armchair in Isaac Newton's office in the Cavendish
Laboratory. He took a file from his briefcase, opened it and announced:

'You'll have guessed, Professor Newton, that I've come to discuss
the article "On the Reception of Signals from Comet Boswell" by
M. L. Howarth, F. M. Haroldsen, yourself and K. Waldheim. Because

the matters arising are somewhat delicate, I thought it better to discuss them here in person, instead of over the telephone.'

'Very considerate of you, Dr Bristow.'

'Yes, well, I hope you'll continue to think so. Let me come to the point straight away. *Nature* is willing to publish immediately without refereeing of the article, just as you asked us to do, provided the title is changed, and provided you remove any suggestion of signals coming from the comet.'

Isaac Newton felt his jaw falling open. Recovering himself, he managed to say calmly:

'Wouldn't that be a bit like *Hamlet* without the Prince of Denmark?'

'Possibly, but you can hardly expect us to publish a clearly unacceptable hypothesis.'

'Are you suggesting the calculation is wrong?'

Alan Bristow shook his head vigorously. 'Not at all. Although we haven't actually checked it ourselves, we're quite happy to accept the calculation.'

'Or that Waldheim decoded the record incorrectly?'

'No, no. We accept all that.'

'Then just what is the trouble? Incidentally, what *is* an unacceptable hypothesis?'

'An unacceptable hypothesis is one which is regarded as inferior to any other hypothesis that can explain the facts. It ranks last of all in order of preference.'

'Regarded as inferior by whom?'

'By the scientific community. *Nature* has to operate with respect for the goodwill of the scientific community. We stand or fall by our subscribers, more than a half of them in the United States, by the way. What I'm really saying is that if *Nature* were to fall on hard times, the Cavendish Laboratory would hardly dig into its pocket and come rushing to our rescue.'

'Even if we did, our pocket wouldn't go very far, I'm afraid,' Isaac Newton acknowledged. 'What baffles me,' he added, 'is the idea that any other hypothesis could explain the facts.'

'Oh, surely! Howarth might have faked the signals to come out the way you found them.'

'But the Research Council cancelled his contract because of the signals. Why would they do that if the signals didn't exist?'

'Oh, there were genuine signals all right. But they weren't the ones Howarth gave to you.'

'So what d'you want us to do?'

'To describe exactly what you did. No more, no less. You received the supposed cometary signals from Howarth. You analysed them into pairs of numbers which you then found to agree with pairs of numbers calculated from the orbit of the comet. But no inferences or conclusions – just the facts. You see, Professor Newton, if this is a fake it wouldn't be unique. Cases like it are coming to light at a rate of about one a month –'and this may be only the small tip of a very big iceberg. Mostly in the biological sciences, I'll admit, but the practice is spreading.'

'I must confess the possibility never crossed my mind.'

'Because you come from a part of physics where it's virtually unknown.'

Isaac Newton's thoughts came into a clearer focus. He tapped the desk top with a pencil and said:

'There has to be a way of checking what you say. The Research Council cancelled Howarth's contract because they had evidence of unauthorised signals being received. Howarth told me some other research group must have gone behind his back to the Research Council with the unauthorised signals. So the Research Council must have that original material, or some of it, at any rate. A comparison with our material would soon show if there had been any faking.'

Bristow nodded and said:

'You're coming now to the really sensitive point. The Research Council may have material which could shatter your whole position. Not just your article, but all the high-level political stops you've been pulling out.'

'They would have to wait until the article was published, I suppose, before they could move,' Isaac Newton remarked uncomfortably.

'They would,' Bristow nodded again. 'In view of your somewhat sticky relations with the Council, the position certainly bears thinking about.'

Isaac Newton smiled wryly and said:

'Well, I rather thought we were going to have quite a row. Instead I'd like to thank you, Dr Bristow. Would you care to dine with me at Trinity tonight?'

'Thank you, yes. But I'm driving back to town tonight. It wouldn't be an embarrassment if I was away by eight-thirty to nine?'

'Not at all. You could get away at the end of the dinner proper, before the Fellows go up for port.'

'Still the old Cambridge way of life.'

'That's right. I was away for thirteen years but you'd never know the difference.'

'Perhaps it's as well that a few places don't change. Would you mind if I changed the subject a bit?' said Bristow. 'Rumour has it that you're having difficulties in buying satellite space.'

'Lying rumour, or was it loud rumour, according to Shakespeare?'

'Loud rumour, I believe.'

'Negotiations are proceeding.'

'Delicate negotiations?'

'Rather obviously.'

'But you will be able to obtain space?'

'I've no doubt of it.'

'Then what's the problem?'

'You've put your finger on it yourself – when you said we're dealing with an unacceptable hypothesis.'

'By the way,' Bristow interposed, 'anything you say will be treated as confidential. But when these things break in the press, *Nature* is pretty well forced to comment, and when we do it's better for everybody to have informed comment, rather than speculation and kite-flying. With this Board being formed under the Prime Minister, you can hardly expect to avoid comment.'

'I haven't. In fact, I seem to have attracted little else but comment right from the first day I returned here from CERN. Obviously everybody with excess satellite space available next year knows we're in the market, and obviously the high-level political connections of the Halley Project Board imply that we might be willing to pay a premium to acquire space.'

'One doesn't need to be a genius to see that. So, in effect, you're over a barrel?' suggested Bristow.

'Yes and no. Although you mightn't think it, we're not being gouged. In fact, money isn't the problem at all. The amounts aren't big enough to be politically important. When Governments are dealing in money by the billions, the difference between ten and twenty millions isn't big potatoes. It's not even big by CERN standards.'

'Then I'm still missing the problem.'

'The problem lies with the unacceptability of the hypothesis. By the very nature of an unacceptable hypothesis, its consequences are shattering if it turns out to be true. So everybody in a position to sell satellite space to us would like to use their leverage to buy into the Project, provided, of course, that the hypothesis turns out to be true. On the other hand, they'd like to be a thousand miles away if it turns out to be wrong. Leave the poor old Brits with a lemon if it's wrong; join them if it's right. Hedge the bets, just as you're doing yourself with this publication of ours.'

'By writing an optional contract, I suppose?' nodded Bristow, ignoring Isaac Newton's gibe.

'Optional to join at a later date, yes.'

'So long as the decision date precedes the satellite launch, that would surely be OK?'

Isaac Newton laughed. 'Nobody would dream of being crude enough to ask explicitly for an option date *after* satellite launch,' he said. 'What you ask for is an option date related to your internal budgetary problems. You claim not to know yet whether you will be able to find the money to join, although you would desperately like to do so, of course. That's your story and you stick to it.'

'With the budgetary problems resolving themselves after satellite launch, I suppose?'

'That's the trick. Resolving themselves after the race is run.'

'I'm glad we only have to deal with sordid commercial issues,' said Bristow. 'I wish you luck.'

Glancing at his watch, Isaac Newton remarked:

'Oh, by the way, I've promised to call in on the Master of Trinity before dinner. There's no reason why you shouldn't come along – although if he wants to talk about a confidential matter, I'll have to ask you to excuse me for a while.'

'That's understood, of course,' nodded Bristow.

The Master of Trinity padded forward as Isaac Newton led Alan Bristow into the big upstairs drawing room at the Master's Lodge in the north-east corner of Trinity Great Square.

'Can I introduce my guest, Master: Dr Alan Bristow. Bristow is the editor of *Nature*. He came up this afternoon to discuss our publication.'

'*Nature*, the dreaded weekly!' exclaimed the Master. 'Actually it was about your publication that I wanted to see you, Newton. I've been trying to read it, as befits a conscientious Board member. So you can stay around, Dr Bristow, if you wish. Or you can pour yourself a drink from the sideboard at the far end of this room, if your eyesight carries to such a distance. Or you can study the silver. We have a lot of it in this College. Or, of course, you can do all three of these things,' welcomed the Master in his deep resonant voice. 'I've been worrying about your dot-dash signals, Newton. You make a big point of the wavelength of reception being very long – too long to be able to come down to ground level, down through this ionosphere, as you call it.'

'That's right, Master.'

'Well then, how were the signals ever received at ground level? Or was the satellite retrieved in some way?'

'No, the satellite wasn't retrieved. What happened was that the dot-dash pattern was received by the satellite on what is called a long-wave carrier. The pattern was recorded and then re-transmitted down to ground level on a shorter-wave carrier, which easily penetrated the ionosphere. This is the nature of satellite telemetry. It takes data acquired by various instruments in ways that are most convenient for the instruments themselves, and then re-transmits the data in the best way for reaching the ground. It's a two-stage process.'

'Ah, ha! I knew there had to be some explanation. There always is with you scientists. So this Dr Howarth was a telemetry whizzkid, an expert in playing around with dots and dashes. Although how he came to be sitting there at past midnight, dead at our organ, still beats the band. I'm thinking of making a play out of it. I'm still looking around for characters, which is why I've been very glad to meet you, Dr Bristow.'

It was close on 9.00 p.m. when Isaac Newton drew up his car in the driveway at Boulton's house in Adams Road. Frances Haroldsen was away, trying to charm the birds off the trees in Washington. Kurt Waldheim was similarly occupied in Germany. So he was left alone to agonise over the squall which Alan Bristow's visit had suddenly conjured out of a clear sky.

Isaac Newton was well used to scientists claiming more significance or more accuracy for their experimental results than was warranted. He was used to results being claimed that were illusory, mere instrumental effects. What he had not conceived of before was deliberate fraud prosecuted on a huge scale. For the past three hours one part of his brain had been searching for a refutation of the idea. The calculation which he and Frances Margaret had done at Howard Baker's cottage on the Norfolk coast fitted better to the claimed results when the updated elements of the orbit of Comet Boswell were used, rather than the earlier elements. So Howarth would not only have had to fake, but he would even have had to update his own fake. But then why not? Once you began to have such suspicions, there was no limit to the extent to which they could go.

For a long two hours, until after 11.00 p.m., Isaac Newton simply sat pondering the wreckage which might ensue. The high-level Board he'd caused to be set up would be brought into ridicule, with obvious political consequences. The sense of purpose now invading the Cavendish Laboratory would be gone, worse than gone. It would be a latter day Piltdown-skull situation, on a larger and more ludicrous scale.

The temptation was to dismiss such thoughts, to continue. But then if the situation really were wrong, it could only grow more wrong – rapidly more wrong. To date, no major sums of money had been spent, no major contracts signed. There was still time to pull back and avoid total wreckage, albeit with an enormous pile of egg on his face. Always he came around to the Research Council, with the proof of faking – or otherwise – residing in its files.

Boulton's house gave its customary creaking lurch, which it always seemed to do at this time of the day. It jerked Isaac Newton from his thoughts. There was nothing to be done, he saw, as he climbed slowly upstairs, but to eat humble pie. He must go and talk with the Chairman of the Council.

Chapter 28

It was an awkward cross-country drive from Cambridge to Swindon where the Research Councils were located, having moved there from central London a few years previously. The awkwardness of the cross-country route was eclipsed, however, by the difficulty which Isaac Newton experienced in finding North Star Avenue in Swindon itself. Somebody told him to make for a place which rejoiced under the name of the Oasis, but the instruction he received only contrived to get him on the wrong side of the railway, so that although he ended up only a couple of hundred yards away from his destination, he could find no way to get his car across the lines. In some irritation he managed to park the car, and then cross the lines by a footbridge, only to find himself among a number of large buildings with a style of architecture that reminded him of an artist's impression of ancient Mesopotamia. The Research Council building was among them, and as he stalked into its entrance he felt that none of his experiences since leaving Cambridge three hours earlier presaged a happy meeting with the Chairman of CERC, which Mrs Gunter had fixed for 3.00 p.m. sharp, so that he'd had to go without lunch – and this hadn't improved his temper either.

'I have an appointment with Sir Anthony Marshall,' he told a uniformed concierge, 'for three p.m. sharp.'

'Then you're exactly on time, sir,' the man said. After a moment on the telephone he added: 'They'll be sending someone down. If you'd like to take a seat...'

A secretary led the way to a lift; then along corridors to a heavily-carpeted outer office with several other secretaries and much glass panelling. Anthony Marshall was a man in middle age of middle height with a rather small round head and big horn-rimmed glasses. He had been the head of a chemistry department in a Midlands university, from which he had embarked on the by now well-trodden route to a Vice-Chancellorship via the chairmanship of a research council.

'I don't think we've met,' said Marshall as he came across to shake hands.

'No, I've been out of the country for quite a number of years.'

'Your secretary simply told my secretary that you wanted to see me, but she didn't explain why.'

'It's about the Howarth affair, as I think you'll have guessed.'

'Do you mind if I ask one or two of my people to sit in?'

'I'd sooner you didn't. To begin with, at any rate. Perhaps later, if a reason emerges.'

'Very well. But you can't rely on my knowing all the details. I wasn't concerned in handling the business.'

'That makes two of us, because I wasn't either. The thing was a *fait accompli* by the time I arrived in Cambridge. I tried to reverse the tide, but it didn't work.'

'I was told there was no possibility of that, under the rules. We had advice from both our Committees and our Legal Department as well.'

'Yes, I understood you had.'

'Frankly, I'm a bit mystified. I thought you'd everything running nicely your way at the moment. So what can we do for you? Howarth's dead, unfortunately, and that settles it. Surely?'

'You wouldn't accept any responsibility for his death?'

'Of course not.'

'No, I don't think I would if I were in your position,' agreed Isaac Newton, 'although, as I told your man Clamperdown even before the tragedy, I'd have handled things a little differently.'

'In Cambridge you would have more latitude than we had.'

'Perhaps. But there's a point I need to clear up about the cancelled contract between us, you for the Council and me for the Laboratory. Then the whole thing can be laid to rest, once and for all. What were your technical reasons for the cancellation?'

'The unauthorised use of facilities, of course.'

'How did you know the facilities had been used in an unauthorised way?'

'As I recall, we had a report from one of the other groups engaged in the project.'

'There must have been some pretty hard evidence, for the Council to take such a drastic step, I mean.'

'I'd imagine there was. But this is a sensitive area. The Council doesn't want to start a feud between groups in different universities. It's quite bad enough to have something of a feud between Cambridge and the Council itself.'

After this exploratory skirmish, Isaac Newton felt almost certain that Marshall wasn't behaving like a man with the ace of trumps up his sleeve. A secretary brought in cups of tea and a plate of biscuits. While accepting the tea and taking as many biscuits in lieu of lunch as he thought decent, Isaac Newton wondered if he should sign off the discussion in some plausible and reasonably gracious way. Then he decided that, in the interests of everybody engaged on Project Halley, especially the political authorities and the Master of his own College, he had to put a few cards on the table, even if Marshall interpreted them to the Council's advantage.

'As I read the affair,' he said, 'the Council would never have taken such drastic action unless it had cast iron evidence. The other university group must, therefore, have produced the hard evidence – in the form of the signals which Howarth obtained through his illicit use of the facilities. These must have been sent to the Council, I would suppose?'

'That is my understanding. Certainly.'

'And you would still have them on file?'

'I would think so.'

'Could you find out?'

'Obviously I could. But why?'

'I'd be glad to explain if you would first be kind enough to check that you really have those signals on file. Otherwise the cancelling of Howarth's contract would really have been quite wrong, wouldn't it? It would have been pretty high-handed, to say the least.'

'You're surely not doubting our *bona fides*?'

'No, I'm not, Sir Anthony. What I'm saying is that until we see the hard evidence on the table we're not in a position to bury the hatchet. After all, we do have a dead man on our hands.'

Anthony Marshall walked silently on the thick carpet from his desk to the door which gave onto the secretaries' office. Opening it, he called out:

'Mrs Brownlee, would you bring me the files on Dr Michael Howarth, and on our contracts with the Cavendish Laboratory.'

Marshall then turned to Isaac Newton and said with the air of a man taking the plunge:

'I'm a bit surprised you haven't asked us if we have any spare satellite space.'

'Because you have to buy your space just the same as we have to do, and I assumed you wouldn't have bought beyond your needs – not in these times of financial penury,' Isaac Newton answered. 'Only people who actually have launchers seemed to me to be in the market. Surely you have all your satellite space assigned years ahead?'

'On paper, yes. But when you have a pipeline going, it's always possible to stretch out some of the packages over a longer time-frame.'

'I'd hate to be seen shouldering other people aside; it wouldn't make me very popular.'

'That isn't a sentiment I've heard expressed very often in this office,' Marshall answered with a wry smile. 'The usual argument, and very plausible they always make it, aims to show why they should go ahead of the other fellow.'

Mrs Brownlee proved to be an older woman than the secretaries Isaac Newton had seen thus far. She came in with an armful of files which she set down carefully on Marshall's desk.

'I'm not interested in the personal or confidential stuff,' explained Isaac Newton reassuringly, 'only the signals, the hard evidence – if you've got it, and haven't imagined it.'

After a couple of minutes spent examining the files, Marshall exclaimed:

'There's a lot of technical stuff here. I knew we'd have it, of course.'

Isaac Newton got up from his chair, more calm outwardly than he felt inwardly. Marshall put the opened file on the desk and both men looked down at it. Isaac Newton saw that it was a signal record. He shifted the pages casually until he came to a good quality part of the record and then said:

'But you had something more important than this in mind. You seemed to be offering me some kind of a proposition.'

'Have you thought what you're going to do if your satellite blows up on launch?'

'Obviously we'll need another. But we'll need another anyway, irrespective of whether we run into trouble on the first shot. It's inevitable that we shall need another and another and another. So why don't we be crude about it? What d'you want in return?'

Anthony Marshall leaned back in the big swivel chair at his desk. He eyed Isaac Newton for a long moment and then said:

'Membership for the Research Council on the Halley Board.'

'I rather thought you would,' nodded Isaac Newton. 'Give me a few minutes to think about it; and while I'm thinking about it, could you photocopy that bit of the signal record for me.'

'Is that what you came about?'

'Yes, I hadn't expected to get into this much bigger issue you've raised. There was a gap in Howarth's record, you see, and we need this missing piece to connect the time-markers.'

Anthony Marshall picked up the file and took it into the secretaries' office, leaving Isaac Newton to deplore what a practised liar he was becoming. He then fell into a reverie, and did not notice Marshall's return. He wondered how a knowledge of the article by Mike Howarth, Frances Haroldsen, Kurt Waldheim and himself had jumped from the offices of *Nature* to the Research Council in Swindon. It must surely have done for Marshall to be so anxious to join the Project Board. He believed Alan Bristow's assurance that the article had not been sent to referees. But somebody who had seen it had spoken to somebody else. And so it had gone, flaming through the bush telegraph. There was only one way to keep a secret in science, and that was to keep it locked to oneself. Aloud Isaac Newton said:

'You must know I don't have membership of the Halley Board in my gift.'

'I understand that. But I think you can work it if you want to work it.'

'I can *try*.'

'And I can *try* to provide a back-up satellite.'

'Suppose you send me the specs. We shall be finalising design decisions fairly soon.'

Mrs Brownlee came in with a number of photocopied sheets in a file, which she handed to Isaac Newton. Giving no sign that the sheets were more precious to him than gold, he remarked:

'I'm surprised you're not concerned about involving the Research Council in a can of worms.' Marshall gave Isaac Newton a long, level look and then replied:

'I would be if I were carrying the can. But that's your privilege, isn't it?'

The same secretary showed Isaac Newton through the labyrinth of corridors and lifts to the entrance foyer of the building. As he walked across the footbridge over the railway line he thought quizzically that this was the first time in his life when he had won every battle, but had yet contrived to lose the war. The best he could achieve was to set to rest the horrible doubt which Alan Bristow had raised, whereas the best the Research Council could achieve was to insinuate itself into the Project. But there was no way he could have acted otherwise, without breaking faith with his backers, he decided.

Half an hour after reaching his car, he was out on the M4, headed for London. He still had ample time to catch a late evening flight to Geneva. It would be the work of a morning to have the photocopied sheets digitised, and then the work only of minutes to discover if the genuine bit of the signal record was homologous with a part of Mike Howarth's record. If it was, the ghost would be laid and he could be back in Cambridge by tomorrow evening. If it wasn't, then he'd better stay in Geneva . . . permanently.

Chapter 29

A helicopter flew low along the line of the Sussex Downs to the south-west of Midhurst. Two men were walking on a path which led them through open, bush-dotted ground. One of the men turned to look upwards.

'It's the third time they've flown directly over us,' said Isaac Newton.

'I must confess I don't take much notice of that sort of thing. We do have some kind of security protection, but I find it best for my peace of mind to ignore it,' replied the Chancellor. 'So we've a bit of difficult decision-making ahead of us,' he mused, 'although quite when in life one doesn't have difficult decisions to make, I've still to discover.'

'We have to take it fairly quickly now.'

'What better than this afternoon?'

'Without the rest of the Board?'

'I have discovered,' the Chancellor said, 'that when two members of a small committee agonise over a decision and reach a sensible opinion on it they usually manage to carry the rest of the members. So let us agonise. Where exactly do we stand?'

'There are two sensible alternatives: the Germans and the Americans. Both would like about a quarter share of the project. In a discreetly concealed sort of way – with us taking the limelight - because of the unacceptable nature of the project.'

'Unacceptable! Why unacceptable?'

'It's a word used by Alan Bristow, the editor of *Nature*. It means something which everybody pretends to disbelieve, no matter how suggestive the evidence for it may be.'

'Oddly enough,' remarked the Chancellor, 'I wouldn't be the least bit interested in this project if it weren't unacceptable in that sense, and neither, I suspect, would you.'

'You may possibly be right. In fact, it's pretty well the same with everybody. They all want to have a finger in the pie...'

'...while pretending there isn't any pie, I suppose.'

'I had an approach the other day from Anthony Marshall, Chairman of the Research Council. He wants to trade satellites in exchange for a seat on the Board.'

'How did you react?'

'Equivocally, but I promised to put it to the Board.'

'It would make things easier politically, take some of the sting out of our critics. Will we actually need more satellites?'

'Quite probably, yes. But if we're successful the political problems will disappear. The problem with admitting a Board member from the Research Council may not disappear, because it will mean infiltration. Very slowly at first, but more and more as time goes by.'

'You know,' said the Chancellor, digging at the sides of the path with his stick, 'if this were a steady, stable, ongoing project you'd be right. Civil servants have nothing better to do with their time than to infiltrate. It's their way of life. But this isn't a stable project. It's either going to die, which God forbid, or it's going to explode. If it dies you might be glad to have the Research Council sharing a bit of the odium. If it explodes, then likely enough it will soon become bigger than all of us.'

'What would you suggest?'

'That you put the matter without prejudice to the Board, just as you promised. Now let's come back to the Germans and the Americans. More precisely, where do we stand?'

'We stand a bit like the ass in the children's story, the ass which starved to death because it couldn't decide which pile of hay to eat first. Because the Americans have more experience of satellite launches, we'd run less risk of a malfunction that way. The European Launcher Programme has had a rather chequered history, although it's getting better now. This is a plus on the American side. The Americans, on the other hand, might object to the active side of our package.'

'I'm not following you.'

'Well, in order to transmit efficiently on this very long wavelength I'm always talking about, it's essential to run out a long aerial. So our package can't be passive. It has to interact fairly decisively with the satellite controls. There's nothing particularly difficult about it, of course, but when time is so short the area becomes sensitive.'

'You think the negotiations would go easier...'

'...with the Germans. Yes. I've been in the middle of European projects at CERN, so obviously I'm more than a bit prejudiced on this point. Where I don't think I am prejudiced is in my conception of what will happen if the project is successful. The American follow-up would inevitably be far stronger than ours could ever hope to be. After a first success, we'd soon be in a minor role. The story would be pretty much the same as it was in physics, until CERN got into its stride.'

'On the political side,' added the Chancellor, 'we have the Common Agricultural Policy forever with us. The Germans are our natural allies in pressing for reforms. This Halley Project is still much too small to be relevant in a CAP context, but if it *were* successful, it could conceivably become a significant piece in that game. I wouldn't urge it as a decisive consideration. But if you tell me the scientific pros and cons are fairly equally balanced, then I might feel it relevant.'

'If we opt for a European policy,' Isaac Newton acknowledged, 'there would be an immediate spur to NASA to become involved on its own. So we could expect competition in short order.'

'Worried?'

'Not for the moment. But if our first shot blows up on the launching pad, and if our second has some equipment failure, we might never get a crack of the whip at all.'

'This pessimism doesn't sound quite like you.'

'Because I'm a bit edgy, I suppose. The projects I'm used to were bigger and harder technically than this one, but if anything ever went wrong with them, as it usually did, you had all the equipment there on the ground, under your nose. You could always poke around and set things right. It's this business of committing oneself irretrievably in advance that I find a bit unsettling.'

'Being able to play around adjusting things is a luxury we don't always enjoy in politics either. Sometimes you have to move and, having moved, to abide by your decisions. I don't feel that kind of strain,' said the Chancellor, 'otherwise I'd be in a different job.'

'What kind of strain do you feel?'

'Reality in politics is what people believe, not what is true. I find it a strain being forced to take things seriously which I know not to be true,' the Chancellor replied. 'But short of bad luck, you think we're likely to keep ahead?'

'I think the unacceptability of our position is a powerful defence, in a way. After this *Nature* publication, it's inevitable that NASA will begin probing – but with a primary motive at first to disprove our position. If things then go our way, the next motive will be to relegate our present position to the level of conjecture.'

'How can it be reduced to conjecture?'

'The *Nature* publication has a tentative element to it.'

'But that wasn't of your choosing.'

'It would be hard to establish exactly what happened. As Bristow pointed out very cogently, *Nature* has its circulation to think about.'

'I'd no idea science was such a dog-eat-dog business.'

'Then you're likely to have a few surprises as this project develops. But seriously, though, I see the position as rather favourable. Nobody will be trying for two-way communications, yet, because they're all still firmly locked into the unacceptability syndrome.'

The two men reached a lane which descended from the crest of the Downs to the north, where the Chancellor's farm lay. Isaac Newton was a weekend guest there. At the sides of the lane were thick bramble bushes which channelled the way down. About half-way towards a surfaced road which led to the village of Bepton, they encountered a small party on the ascent. One of the party was wearing Gucci shoes and an astrakhan hat. The members of the party had binoculars slung around their necks.

'Bird watchers,' said the Chancellor briefly.

'Did you see the chap in the Gucci shoes and the astrakhan?'

'I saw the astrakhan, naturally, but the shoes rather escaped me. Why?'

'He's a reporter from the *Observer*. Or at least he says he is.'

'Why so suspicious?' asked the Chancellor. 'Don't Gucci shoes, intellect, the *Observer* and trendy views in politics all go very well together?'

Chapter 30

The eleven members of the Politburo and the eight candidate members were all heavy men, a description which, in the Russian idiom, did not imply an excess of weight – although excess weight was not in itself forbidden – but tough men, men you couldn't deceive with any old party trick. The ease with which ordinary people were deceived by the waxwork of Lenin in the Mausoleum in Red Square was a standing joke among members of the Politburo, and it gave them an abiding contempt for the people.

Every one of the nineteen was clean-shaven, as also was everybody in the Soviet Union who aspired to be anybody at all. The reason was Karl Marx. Marx, ironically, was an unpleasant thorn in the side of the Russian bear. Commentators in the West, who should have known better, spoke of Marxism as if it had become the political and economic philosophy of the Soviet Union, whereas the thing the Soviet Union wanted most was to get Karl Marx, and his jungle of a beard, from out of its system.

The trouble lay in the Marxist prediction that the West would collapse through the supposed contradictions of capitalism, whereas all the time the economies of Western nations went on and on accelerating like a fleet of formula one racing cars. The Soviet Union could hardly have been more misled if Karl Marx had been a CIA agent spreading his damaging disinformation everywhere east of the Iron Curtain.

The big difficulty for the Soviets in this situation was that, having mistakenly got Karl Marx into their system, it was impossible to get him out. This was because nobody in the Soviet Union from the highest to the lowest could admit to making a mistake, so that any beetle like Karl Marx which managed to burrow into the Soviet woodwork could never be gotten out of it. The Marxist beetle just kept on gnawing and gnawing, spreading its rot everlastingly. All any self-respecting Russian could do by way of silent protest was to go clean-shaven.

All members of the Politburo used the same kind of razor, a white disposable razor manufactured in France by the Bic company. Bic razors were available at far lower levels in the *nomenklatura* than the Politburo, available, indeed, to anybody who boasted a supply of certificated roubles. On the day in question, all members of the Politburo shaved themselves successfully with Bic razors except Number Ten, who, after giving himself a nasty cut just below the right-hand corner of the lip, had fallen into a sour mood.

The numerical system of designating members of the Politburo had begun, quite simply, as a ranking according to length of membership. Because ordering according to straightforward seniority is always in some degree a pecking order, the system had eventually developed into an overt pecking order, with factors other than seniority taken into consideration – making it easy to see who was up-and-coming and who was down-and-going.

The way things tended to work out was that the adoption by the Politburo of a half a dozen of your suggestions would usually be good enough to move you up a position; the telling of a dozen jokes which amused everybody, more or less, would hold your position stable; while being the butt of somebody else's joke only twice or thrice would move you down a rung of the ladder. Avoiding voting on the losing side over contentious issues was also important, of course, although this could be avoided simply by listening to the views expressed by Numbers One through Five.

The very large, black, highly-polished cars with their special MOC number plates in which Politburo members moved around Moscow and its environs had stormed that morning through the streets and avenues of the city. There had been nothing at all secretive in their passages. A visitor from outer space who had chanced to land in Moscow, for instance in Granovsky Street, would surely have picked them out at a glance. They travelled faster than the rest of the traffic down the very centre of the roadway, and on this day of melting snow they sent great bow-waves of slush high into the air, hitting unwary pedestrians full in the chops. Such was the position which the 'century of the common man' had reached in the nation which claimed most stentorously to promote it.

The highly-polished black cars had accelerated from the various streets and avenues into Red Square at nearly the same time, so that even the visitor from outer space would have deduced that something was afoot, such as the deployment in Czechoslovakia of the SS-21 missiles which the disarmament conference in Geneva was supposed to be abolishing. A meeting of the Politburo would have been suspected, and a meeting of the Politburo, scheduled for 9.30 a.m., it was. The cars turned into the Kremlin grounds at close on 9.00, which would give members time to deposit their fine furry overcoats, to confer briefly with the secretariat, to make certain their papers were in order, and to grimace broadly at each other from the teeth outwards.

The early items of the agenda were concerned with fomenting disruption in Central America, with financing the European antinuclear movement in a suitably well-laundered style, and with spreading disinformation and chaos over the Earth generally. Frankly speaking, they were old hat. Everybody was waiting for Item Seven on the agenda, but cups of coffee were drunk in abundance before it was reached. There was the usual sparring to see who could get his joke in first, and up-and-coming Number Twelve noticed with satisfaction that every time members laughed, Number Eleven was always a little slow on the uptake. True, Number Eleven managed to conceal his lack of sharpness by a whacking great guffaw which echoed around the room, but up-and-coming Number Twelve wasn't deceived; otherwise he wouldn't have been up-and-coming, of course. The truth he perceived was that Number Eleven was going deaf.

Item Seven was the most improbable of this or any other year – a report from England of an intelligent message from a comet...a comet! In this modern era of launching pads and space locks, who but the English, with their thoughts on bows and arrows no doubt, would have had such an idea? With his thoughts on scoring a point over the pressing Number Twelve, when Item Seven was introduced, Number Eleven let loose a bellow of laughter which ricocheted around the walls of the room.

Number Three came in as thinly and meanly as ever; he lacked a sense of humour, like all associated with the KGB. He explained at some length that detailed information had come from agents in England who operated under the cover of a furniture removal business. Mistaking his cue, and determined to be first in the field for once, Number Eleven let out another wild snort at this statement, much in the style of a neighing horse.

Number Three continued, even more meanly than before, by pointing out that a large diversion of effort towards cometary research had been made both in the United States and in Germany. The Japanese, who had previously had a strong programme in the field, were reported to be increasing their efforts still more. All this had occurred immediately following events in Britain, which in the opinion of AOK (Extra-Terrestrial Disinformation) went to show that those events were being taken seriously. With these remarks delivered, Number Three sniffed. It was only a small sound, but to members it sounded just as loud as the erstwhile laughter of Number Eleven.

Number Two now wanted to know how Number Three could be certain they were not dealing with a case of disinformation, a trick to divert Soviet effort in high technology into a useless activity.

'Remember,' he told the meeting, 'the Greeks only tell the truth once a year.'

This old Russian proverb triggered a brainstorm in Number Twelve. Here it must be explained that whereas most societies invent four or five classes into which their people are divided, the Russians had invented a hundred. There was even a class division within the Politburo itself, with those up to Number Eleven being styled 'full members' and those from Number Twelve to Number Nineteen being accorded the inferior status of 'candidates'. Thus Number Twelve was on the verge of a major quantum jump. Hence the brainstorm which provoked his immediate response to Number Two, which did not allow Number Three time for a reply – but in some degree relieved him of the need to do so.

'It occurs to me,' said Number Twelve, 'that if we tickle ourselves we can laugh when we like.'

At this, Number Eleven let loose with his loudest bellow of the morning. But since no one else joined him, Number Eleven knew that he had made yet another mistake and the roar died in a gulp, as if he had suddenly run out of breath.

'What I had in mind,' continued Number Twelve smoothly, 'was that at little cost to ourselves we can turn this business to our advantage.'

At this he stopped, whereon Number One nodded and asked:

'What have you in mind?'

Number Twelve now spoke slowly, carefully emphasising each word:

'I have in mind that if intelligent signals are reaching the Earth from outside, it might be a good plan to arrange for some signals of our own. It would be easy to arrange for a vehicle of ours to transmit a message with an intelligible form, a message that *we* can decode but others cannot.'

'What would be the advantage of that?' Number Three wanted to know.

'The message could have an important sociological involvement.'

'Which would be apparent to our people, who would be in a position to profit from it, even if others did not,' agreed Number One from the chair.

So it came about that the meeting agreed to launch a space station dedicated to transmitting back to Earth a Marxist-Leninist interpretation of society, of life generally, and of the Universe at large. Number Ten, who had been unfortunate enough to nick himself with the French-manufactured razor that morning, inadvertently jolted the small blood clot, causing it to bleed again. It wouldn't be long, he thought as he dabbed himself, before Number Twelve was treading on his own heels, since it was patently obvious that poor old Number Eleven was down-and-going. Number Ten tried hard to think of a proverb that would come close to matching Number Two, but all he could think of was: 'In the pond of lies only dead fish swim.'

Chapter 31

'It is unacceptable for civilians to be involved in any form of extra-terrestrial activity in respect of intelligible signals,' said the five-star General to the NASA Chief Administrator.

'We hardly know yet that we're dealing with intelligible signals,' the NASA Chief Administrator replied calmly, hoping the old adage about soft words soothing the savage breast would prove to be true on this occasion.

'Comets or whatever,' the five-star General continued, drawing steadily on his cigar.

'It would mean discontinuing a promising programme,' the Chief Administrator countered, 'which in any case the British and Germans are engaged in already.'

'The British capability is nil, and the Germans not much better. So I'm not losing any sleep in those areas,' the General boomed, smoking his cigar in passable imitation of the Chairman of the Federal Reserve, whose money-bags the General had every intention of having allocated to the Pentagon, in imitation of his counterparts in the Soviet Union.

'I think it would be as well if we had rules which defined exactly where we stand,' the Chief Administrator continued, more mildly than he felt.

The problem for the Chief Administrator was not so much where NASA stood with the Pentagon as where NASA stood with the White House. His suspicion, and hence his mildness, as well as the fact that he had come cap-in-hand to the Pentagon at the General's request instead of telling the General to come to NASA headquarters if he had anything to discuss, was that the White House must already have reached an unfavourable decision. In the present state of international tension, this was only too likely.

From the late sixties onwards, NASA's only real *raison d'être* had
been investigations in pure science, although of course the most
strenuous efforts had been made to invent all manner of pretences. But
neither pure science nor pretences had proved much of a bulwark
against the encroachment of the military into space. Spy satellites,
with all the refinements that the term implied, had turned out to be so
exceedingly important to the superpower struggle that the balance in
space had inevitably swung away from NASA to the Pentagon. As had
happened so often before, an activity which started for predominantly
civilian reasons had come to be controlled more and more by the
military, a situation that would surely continue for as long as the
superpower struggle continued. This made the Chief Administrator
wonder if it was not in the interests of the military, both in the U.S.A.
and the U.S.S.R., that the superpower struggle should indeed continue.

'Let us say this about that,' the General replied, sweeping his arm
over the extensive smooth surface of his very large desk so as to brush
particles of cigar ash onto the carpet, 'we keep the area of *science*,
which I define to mean sterile investigations, clear of the area of
intelligible communications. You keep to the sterile investigations and
we keep to the communications. Then nothing is likely to get fouled up
between us because we both know just where we stand. OK?'

'What's going to happen to the present programme then?'

'I want it frozen, frozen solid, until we've had the opportunity to sift
the details,' the General replied, emphasising his words by tapping the
desk top with the end of the first finger of the right hand, 'and I want a
cordon drawn around both the personnel and the *matériel*.'

The words slipped out of the Chief Administrator before he realised
it:

'But we have foreign nationals working on the project.'

'Precisely,' nodded the General, staring straight ahead as an ac-
cumulation of ash dropped from his cigar, 'which is why I want that
cordon drawn tightly and immediately, drawn from A to Z. I'll look
through a list of personnel just as soon as you can get it from your
office to mine.'

The tidal wave of the Chief Administrator's anger broke when he
reached his office at headquarters, so that his immediate assistants and
secretaries were instantly sent into a buzz of activity, collecting files
and materials and making telephone calls which inevitably became
amplified in number as they penetrated the network of NASA
institutions throughout the United States. Communication was
established almost immediately between the NASA headquarters in
downtown Washington D.C. and the Goddard Space Flight Center only

fifteen miles away at Greenbelt, near the north-eastern portion of the main Washington bypass road.

Dave Eckstein was a bearded man of about thirty with the gift, which some people have quite mysteriously, of hearing everything in the wind. So it came about that Eckstein was the first to hear the news. He stormed along a fifth-floor corridor in the Goddard building and burst in anger into an office, almost shouting:

'The military's taking over.'

Frances Haroldsen looked up from her desk and asked:

'Rumour or fact?'

'Fact. It's all over HQ. Even the secretaries know about it. There seems to have been a White House directive. Which doesn't surprise me the way things are going. The military are getting every disposable dollar in this year's budget.'

'How are they going to take over?'

'They're going to put a *cordon sanitaire* around the whole thing, people and all. You'll be OK, of course, but the rest of us seem likely to be gagged.'

'If I have the opportunity to publish the interferometer idea, should I put your name on it, then?' Frances Haroldsen asked as she began to unlock the drawers of a small desk.

'There's no way I can see you could be stopped, and there's no way I could be blamed for what you care to do. So I'd say go ahead, however you see fit. They're making it seem as if we're all spies and that kind of garbage.'

Frances Margaret Haroldsen forbore to explain that a spy was exactly what she was. She had come to the United States six months earlier, to present the *Nature* publication by Mike Howarth, Kurt Waldheim, Isaac Newton and herself at a space science conference held in Houston, Texas. From there she had wheedled her way into a short-term appointment at the Goddard Flight Center, where she had been able to monitor the NASA cometary programme in respect of Comet Halley. Although personally lost from the Halley Project in Britain, the critical information she'd accumulated, especially over the past few weeks, had well justified the policy. Besides which, she'd been able to sow disinformation concerning the British Project, representing it as an attempt only at verification of the earlier results, rather than as an overt endeavour to return information from Earth to Comet Halley, a project which in military eyes would have seemed far more significant and far more ominous than the passive policy of merely receiving signals. A comet was, after all, an enormous missile, vaster by far than all the weapons in the arsenals of the U.S.A. and U.S.S.R. If a comet were to lock itself onto a radio transmission from Earth, the damage it could wreak on impact with the Earth would be almost beyond comprehension. It would be supermilitary in its scale.

Frances Margaret glanced at her watch.

'Look, Dave,' she said, 'I've got a dentist appointment at four o'clock. D'you think you could whip around and get me change for this five-dollar note. I want to make one or two 'phone calls. In view of what you say, I'd prefer to make them from outside the perimeter. And to be frank, I'd advise you to avoid expressing your opinions over the 'phone. I guess you know what I mean.'

'I didn't like the smell of it, and I like it less when you tell it like that.'

'Can you get me the change, please?'

As soon as she had Dave Eckstein out of the office, Frances Haroldsen emptied the contents of her handbag into a drawer, except for her purse, credit cards, a small notebook, her passport and a pen. Into the space thus made available she slipped three tapes which measured about eight inches across. She would like to have taken more comprehensive material, *matériel* the five-star General would have called it, but bulkiness and the need for quick movement precluded anything more ambitious than the three tapes. She had learned from her home background the need to be prepared for action at any time, whatever the circumstances, and now the policy of being in a constant state of readiness had paid off, she thought, as she locked the door to her office and stepped into the corridor outside.

Dave Eckstein was there with a handful of small change which she slipped into her purse.

'Suppose you come along with me to my car, Dave,' she then suggested. When they reached the car, Frances Margaret held out her hand:

'You're not going to see me again for a while, Dave. So you'll understand that I take the position a bit seriously. So should you, and so should your wife. Keep absolutely quiet about your opinions. If they ask about me, how I disappeared so quickly, just say the news was all over the Center, that I'd have been a fool if I hadn't heard it for myself. Don't worry too much if there's blackmail over your job here, because you can get a job anywhere – in Germany, or in Britain, or France, or whatever – because the interferometer idea is a darned good one. People aren't going to forget it when they hear about it, which they will.'

Then Frances Margaret accelerated out of the parking lot in a

General Motors Cutlass, which was of a more modern vintage than appointees to junior research positions were usually able to afford. She did so leaving behind a thoughtful heavily-bearded young man, a young man who incidentally would not be/able to reach his office 'phone before she was clear of the police control at the main gate of the Center. Not that Dave Eckstein, with his liberal anti-military views, was likely to advertise her precipitate departure. But with her family background to the fore, it was instinctive with Frances Haroldsen to take no chances at all in such matters.

On the outskirts of the Maryland town of Greenbelt, she drew into a large shopping complex where she parked and then monopolised a public telephone box for upwards of twenty minutes. Only after she had given certain very explicit instructions to a contact at the Embassy, and had checked and double-checked the instructions, did she return to the car. Then, as an afterthought, she went across to a supermarket and bought a bag of readily eatable foodstuffs.

Within a few minutes of leaving the shopping complex, Frances Margaret was driving westward along the Washington bypass. She continued to its most western section, quitting it at the U.S.29. Heading eastwards into Falls Church, she pulled off the road into a Best Western motel, where she booked a room in the name of Joanne B. L. Johnson, paying cash for it. Parking in the space in front of her room, she noticed an old, somewhat beat-up car half-a-dozen spaces away. Since it would be a long time before she could expect a cooked meal again, she took the opportunity to eat an early dinner in the restaurant attached to the motel.

It was about 7.00 p.m., about two hours after dark, when there came a knock on the door of her room. A young man of Frances Haroldsen's age was standing there when she opened the door. Since he had evidently arrived in the large limousine standing outside, which bore diplomatic number plates, this appeared to be the contact she had arranged with the Embassy in the telephone call from the shopping complex near Greenbelt. Nevertheless, Frances Margaret took the precaution of checking the young man's credentials.

'I'm Tim Bassett,' he explained, somewhat superfluously. 'We've got the tickets,' he added. 'You're to take the nine-fifty p.m. flight from National Airport to Miami, where you join in with a package tour back to London.'

Frances Haroldsen took one of the three tapes from her handbag and told him :

'It's important for this to go in the diplomatic pouch. I want it taking straight to the Embassy, as soon as you leave here.'

'We're to leave together, so that I can take you to the airport. Somebody will collect your car tomorrow morning.'

At this, Frances Margaret went to the telephone and dialled quickly, so that Tim Bassett realised she must be dialling another motel room. A moment later there was a tap on the door. Tim Bassett jumped to open it, and standing there was a fair-haired girl not unlike Frances Margaret herself.

'Meet Maisie Cooke,' Frances Margaret introduced, 'as you can see, she's my *doppelgänger*.'

'What's the idea?' Bassett asked uncertainly, when the door was closed.

'As my luck would have it, Maisie is working here in Washington for a few months. She's taking my place. I mean she's going to Miami and she's joining your package tour there instead of me. Don't think I'm being over – cynical but . . .'

'You don't think we're penetrated?' asked Bassett incredulously.

'You'll be able to find out, won't you? I expect it will be all right, but I'm taking no risks. You and Maisie are going to the Embassy with the tape. Then you can go straight to National Airport. OK?'

'It's a pity we can't wait here. Then we could have a couple of torrid hours of it, couldn't we, boy?' Maisie leered at Tim Bassett. 'Assuming it works out, and I keep out of jail, I'm asking for first class on the way back.'

'But they'll trace you. Through your car, the number plates!' Bassett almost yelped at Frances Haroldsen.

'They won't, because I've changed 'em over. Come on now, boy,' Maisie said, putting an arm around the young man, 'if we hurry we may be able to squeeze together for a few minutes in the car at the airport.'

Frances Haroldsen drove off in the Cutlass, after checking that Maisie had fixed the plates taken from the beat-up specimen firmly enough. She drove at no great speed, there being no hurry. On the bypass again, she went as far as the north-west corner and then took Route 270 west, which dissolved in about an hour into Route 70. After another hundred miles, she turned directly north onto Route 219. It was coming up to midnight when she reached the town of Du Bois, where she turned into a motel once more. Instead of booking a room, however, she parked the car in the darkest spot she could find and settled down in the rear seats, with the doors locked, to sleep as best she could.

She was on her way before dawn, still driving north on Route 219, dawdling along and eating from the food she had bought the previous afternoon. It was 9.30 a.m. when Frances Margaret parked in a multi-storey building in the centre of the city of Buffalo. After drawing cash, of which she was running short, on an American Express card she hailed a taxi and told the driver she wished to make a trip to see the Canadian side of Niagara Falls. Half an hour later she was in Canada, without the slightest fuss, this being a trip made by hundreds of people every day, even without passports. The likelihood was that she had been ahead of officialdom, but there had been every reason to take no chances with the tapes. The one she had given to Tim Bassett was a blank.

Chapter 32

As John Jocelyn Scuby took a seat in the big black armchair in Isaac Newton's office, he said:

'I am a worried man, Professor Newton.'

'I'd have thought with all our new-found prosperity you would have been a very happy man,' Isaac Newton replied.

'No, no. In bad times one has reason to be worried. In good times one has reason to be very worried.'

'Why should that be?'

'Because it is in good times when expectations are built up. My experience has always been that the greater the expectations, the greater the disappointments which come later.'

'So it's our "cost plus" acquisitions from the Government that lie at the root of your agony, is it, Mr Scuby?'

'Not the costs. Costs are straightforward and the General Board will see no problems there, I hope. Although you can never quite tell what issues some Board member or other will raise, as I have learned to my dismay over the years. No, it's the "plus" part of the situation where the problem lies.'

'I haven't seen any problem yet, myself.'

'It is a question of how you propose to dispose of the receipts.'

'Re-equipment, and the establishment of a contingency fund, I would think. Frankly, I haven't given too much thought to the matter.'

'I'd hope that thoughts of staff increases would not be in your mind.'

'Staff increases *are* in my mind, Mr Scuby. But not to be funded by what one might describe as a windfall. In my own poor man's accountancy, windfalls shouldn't be used to take on commitments for the future,' Isaac Newton remarked.

The beginnings of a smile appeared on Jocelyn Scuby's face. 'Ah! Then on my first point we are in agreement. You would be surprised at how many problems in the University have arisen because appointments have been made on grants of limited duration.'

'Like lending long and borrowing short?'

'Exactly,' nodded Scuby, 'but you would be surprised at how many people fall into that trap.'

'You have a second point?'

'It is a matter of some delicacy.'

'I hope it's fit for my ears.'

'Well, I have been wondering still more about the "plus" receipts from the Government.'

'Yes?' Isaac Newton asked briefly, with a quizzical look.

Scuby shifted in embarrassment from the left to the right side of the big armchair, and then went on:

'It would seem to be arguable that some fraction of your profit should be passed to the University. You see, we have many calls from other departments not as large or as strong as your own. You don't mind my raising the issue, I hope?'

Isaac Newton thought for a while and then said:

'No, raising it is quite reasonable, Mr Scuby. The Laboratory couldn't exist by itself. It exists in relation to the University as a whole. Didn't you once tell me that overheads in the University average out at something like a hundred percent?'

'Yes, I believe I did.'

'Well then, suppose we agree on a fifty/fifty split?'

A look of astonishment spread across Jocelyn Scuby's face. Holding up a hand, he exclaimed:

'But I had been thinking of seventy-five/twenty-five.'

'Seventy-five percent to the University?'

'No, no, twenty-five percent.'

'I don't quite see that,' said Isaac Newton, tapping his desk with a pencil as he often did when about to press a point home. 'If it's one-to-one on the overheads it should be one-to-one on the profits. The principle, I would think, is more important than the money.'

The smile on Scuby's face broadened in spite of the stern internal effort he seemed to be making to suppress it. In a seemingly dazed state he struggled from out of the armchair.

'Have you any idea of how long it may go on?'

'There's no certainty beyond the short-term. But the latest news from the United States looks rather favourable, I'm glad to say.'

'Well, I'll be on my way,' nodded Scuby, 'and thank you for your point of view.'

An hour later, Isaac Newton looked up from the transmitter design details he was checking, hopefully for the last time.

'Good God, you're back!' he exclaimed as Boulton the Professor of Geostrophics erupted into the room, as always avoiding the normal entry route through Mrs Gunter's office.

'Ah, I'm glad to have caught you,' Boulton began. 'I was wondering about the house.'

'It's still standing.'

'I was wondering how long you'll be needing it. There's a lot going on just at the moment – with all the scandal you've been having, and the drilling in the Celtic Sea. I was in on the ground floor on that one. Are you buying shares now? I'm selling mine.'

'How was California?' Isaac Newton asked.

'There's a lot of talk there about comets. NASA doesn't seem to have been finding them very communicative.'

'When did you hear that?'

'Just before I left. There was a big seminar on it, heavily attended. People swinging from the chandeliers. How's the cat, by the way?'

'It comes and goes.'

'Don't you think you ought to pay a surcharge on the house?'

'Whatever for?'

'Notoriety. I gather the people in Adams Road were stirred up quite a bit – with things in the newspapers all the time. It'll be a bit awkward for me. When are you thinking of leaving, by the way?'

'When the rental period expires.'

'I was rather afraid you might want to hang on. Don't you find the foundations a bit of a bother?'

'I did at first, but now I rather look forward to the nightly visitations.'

'You will consider the surcharge idea, won't you? I mean, it's going to take some time, getting back on track, back to normal.'

'Yes, I'll be happy to consider the surcharge idea.'

'I'd take notice of these NASA people if I were you. They've been in business a long time. You could be digging yourself quite a hole. Not the sort of position I'd like to be in myself, dependent on fair-weather friends. What d'you think would be a reasonable surcharge? I don't want to be overbearing about it.'

'Twenty pounds would be a fair charge. The amount you borrowed from our petty cash and didn't repay,' said Isaac Newton. 'And by the way,' he added, 'I took the trouble to look into your foundation problem. I'd tackle it straight away, if I were you. Otherwise it can only get worse.'

Mrs Gunter came in as Boulton departed.

'Whatever is going on this morning, Professor? Mr Scuby went out in a sort of trance, and now there goes Professor Boulton looking as if you'd just lifted the wallet right out of his pocket.'

'I hope I haven't done Scuby permanent damage by offering him more money than he'd expected; by raising his expectations for the future. And Professor Boulton, he needs to grout. Urgently.'

'To do what, Professor?'

'To pump concrete into the foundations of his house.'

'He needs to pump concrete into his own foundations, if you ask me,' concluded Mrs Gunter.

'Ahoow!' shouted the Master of Trinity. 'This darned coffee-pot! I'm always burning myself on it,' he told the Chancellor as he padded back from the sideboard where the hot-plate rested, in the large upstairs drawing room of the Master's Lodge in the north-east corner of Great Square, carrying two late-morning cups of coffee.

'Which reminds me, I have a conspiratorial proposition to put to you,' the Master added. 'I have decided that you and I are exactly the men to corner the world's supply of silver.'

There was a tap on the door and the Master jumped again to his feet. 'Ah!' he boomed in his resonant voice. 'Here comes Bad-News Newton. What's gone wrong today, dare I ask?'

'Nothing I'm aware of, Master. Ah, good morning, Chancellor,' Isaac Newton greeted him.

'I thought we'd keep the lunch just to the three of us,' the Master explained, 'because the Chancellor has some worries he wants to talk about. Shall we switch from coffee to sherry?'

'Dry for me, Master,' requested Isaac Newton. 'What are these worries, might I ask?'

'It's just that I find this crescendo of denials from the U.S. disturbing,' said the Chancellor.

'What's this?' the Master asked immediately.

'There's something of an orchestrated campaign claiming that NASA has found nothing – no cometary signals. There's a bit in this week's *Nature* – the "News & Views" column – unsigned, of course.

And apparently there are people giving seminars around the U.S.,' explained Isaac Newton.

'But I thought you told me . . . ' the Master began.

' . . . that NASA found signals from Comet Halley about a month ago? So they did. We have their Comet Halley wavelength and the pulsing system. They're both a bit different from our own results for Comet Boswell. We were glad to get the new information.'

'You weren't misled?' the Chancellor asked cautiously.

'No, not a chance. I understand from Kurt Waldheim that there's clear-cut proof the signals really came from Comet Halley; besides which, our information was obtained straight from the centre of the NASA organisation,' answered Isaac Newton decisively.

'But why would they pretend now that it was different?' the Master wondered.

'Because the military recently took the programme over from NASA proper. Their first thought must have been to stop things dead, and I must say they certainly don't seem to have lost much time about it.'

'Can you explain how they've been able to pull so many strings?' asked the Chancellor.

'Suppose we interrupt the discussion for a moment,' interrupted the Master. 'I have a signal that lunch is ready. Why don't we go through to the dining room and find out what the kitchens have managed to devil-up.'

The long table in the dining room was set with three places at one end, set with much cutlery and with three patterns of wine glass, in keeping with the Master's reputation as a *bon viveur*. A waiter served the first of the wines as they began the first course, a plate of whitebait.

'I asked my secretary to put together a file on the business,' Isaac Newton continued in reply to the Chancellor. 'The first thing I noticed was that there's been no official statement from NASA itself. Everything is innuendo, most of it either unsigned or tip-offs to newsmen. Broadly speaking, any organisation with a huge income can pull a lot of strings.'

'Why would scientists lend themselves to that sort of thing?' asked the Master, setting down his glass and nodding at a waiter for a refill.

'Because they become over-extended. Universities encourage their people to secure research grants and contracts. Research groups get built up with staff, secretaries and technicians, many with wives and families. When the pressure piles up, the leader of such a group isn't in much of a position to resist.'

'What's the answer?' the Master wanted to know.

'Stay poor but honest. The trouble in experimental science is that the poor are only too likely to stay undistinguished.'

'I knew you had strong views on the financing of science,' the Chancellor nodded, 'and now I'm beginning to see why. Where the shoe pinches . . . If you were asked to refute all these reports, could you do it?'

'Yes, easily. You see, we don't just have information from NASA. We have their actual signal records, or at least a part of them.'

'How . . .' the Master began.

'Don't ask me how, Master,' Isaac Newton answered, shaking his head.

'We have a Summit coming up three weeks from now. I'm certain it would be useful to the Prime Minister to have your refutation. Not necessarily to use it, but to have it,' the Chancellor continued.

'Yes, and we have our launch coming up six weeks from now.'

'Even so, it would be well worth it,' the Chancellor nodded.

'I'm a bit annoyed with *Nature* for publishing such rubbish, but as Alan Bristow said, half their subscribers are in the United States. The irony is that he was talking about the pernicious effect of rumours. "Loud rumour", he called it,' Isaac Newton remarked.

' "Open your ears," ' boomed the Master, ' "for which of you will stop the vent of hearing when loud rumour speaks? I, from the orient to the drooping west, making the wind my post-horse, still unfold the acts commenced on this ball of earth: upon my tongue continual slanders ride, the which in every language I pronounce, stuffing the ears of men with false reports." But why should loud rumour speak this way? Granted there may be some tension between NASA and the U.S. military, but of what consequence is this affair to the military?'

Isaac Newton thought for a while and then answered, speaking more slowly than usual:

'Well, I suppose every profession has its instinctive reactions. Your instinct, Master, is to quote Shakespeare. Mine is to ask for experimental facts. The Chancellor's is to wonder what the effect will be on people. The instinct of the military is to think in terms of destructive power. And the destructive power of even a fragment of a comet, if it hit the Earth, would exceed that of a million megaton H-bombs. In such an event it would seem highly important that the impact occurred in the U.S.S.R. to the American military, and that it occurred in the U.S. to the Soviet military.'

Chapter 33

The security men placed at strategic points along the road from St Moritz over the Moloya Pass, down through the Bergel to Chiavenna, and thence to the narrow road between the mountains and Lake Como, might have been noticed by a skilled observer, but scarcely by the general public. Nor was there any reason for the general public to trouble itself with such matters, since the nature of what was going on could easily be learned from the media. The Summit Meeting was being held at a splendidly situated villa on the east bank of Lake Como in the region of Varenna. The Summit was a little unusual in its composition. It was not an official NATO meeting, since a NATO meeting would have excluded France; nor was it an official EEC Summit, since that would have excluded the United States of America.

Every chancellery in Europe, as well as the massed ranks of Government employees in Washington, had counselled strenuously against holding the Summit in such a place. A library shelf might have been filled with the reasons offered. There was, however, just one overwhelming reason why every bureaucrat in his senses objected to it in a voice loud enough to serve as an air-raid siren. There is so little physical space between the mountains and Lake Como itself that the villages along the lakeside are necessarily small, and lack the extensive hotel space needed to accommodate the several thousands of functionaries who normally settle on such meetings. Worse, from the point of view of the functionaries, was the suspicion, nay the certainty, that the venue had been deliberately chosen by the politicians precisely in order to reduce the number of bureaucrats who could attend the Summit, thus permitting a little useful business to be transacted.

Switzerland being an orderly country, the political leaders all flew to Zürich Airport, whence they were driven via St Moritz to the Italian border nearer Chiavenna and thence to Lake Como. This had been judged a safer route by security experts than entering Italy at Milan, because security can be made much tighter in a narrow restricted setting than it can in an open network of roads.

Isaac Newton and Frances Haroldsen travelled via Geneva, however, the aim of their presence at the meeting being to reassure the British Prime Minister on the reality of the cometary signals. This was as a preparation for deprecatory remarks being made publicly or privately to the Prime Minister – not to put too a fine point on it, remarks emanating from American sources following changes of policy in the United States – the switch in control over the Comet Halley Programme from NASA to the Pentagon.

They were picked up at Geneva Airport by Kurt and Rosie Waldheim, and driven to the Waldheims' chalet at Wengen in the Lauterbrunnen Valley. There still being snow on the mountains, they took off on the lifts for a day's skiing before getting down to the details of Kurt Waldheim's most recent discoveries, discoveries which had emerged from the tapes smuggled out of the United States by Frances Haroldsen.

After dinner that night, in front of a roaring log fire, Kurt Waldheim said:

'Well, it is interesting that Comet Halley disdains to use decimal points – because it has a much smaller time unit and a much smaller distance unit than the other comet. So everything is rounded off into integers.'

Isaac Newton knew by long experience not to hurry Kurt Waldheim towards the main issue. So he contented himself by asking, 'Has the time unit any relation to the period of revolution of Comet Halley around the Sun, about seventy-six years, isn't it?'

'By combining powers of two, with pi thrown in, you could always invent that kind of story, I suppose.'

'Or the time unit could be related to the spin of Comet Halley,' Frances Margaret interposed.

'But the good thing is the interference calculation invented by Frances Margaret here and her American colleague Eckstein, who by now has probably been sent to Alaska or some such place,' continued Kurt Waldheim, in his slow, half-humorous way.

'I wasn't sure how clean the reflected signal from the ionosphere would be,' Isaac Newton remarked.

'It is a problem of marvellous complexity,' Kurt Waldheim nodded.

'Which would make any reasonable person's head ache,' Frances Margaret added.

'For we have three distinct processes which cause the interference pattern between the direct signal from the comet and the reflected signal from the ionosphere to vary,' Kurt Waldheim continued.

'I'll bet you have,' nodded Isaac Newton, with a wry smile.

'The fastest variation comes from the motion of the satellite itself. Then there is a change of the reflected signal with respect to the time of day. On top of all that there is a slow variation resulting from the motion of the comet. The problem is. . .'

'. . .to disentangle it all.'

'Ah, you always spoil my conclusions, Isaac,' exclaimed Kurt

Waldheim, shaking his head disapprovingly. 'The calculation would be elementary and not very interesting,' he went on, 'if it were made directly. The good thing about it is that everything can be done backwards. Instead of starting with Comet Halley and working towards the expected signals, it is excellent to start with the observed signals and then to find the position and the motion of their source. A fine, big and delicate calculation.'

'I can imagine it. So you found that the source must be Comet Halley?'

'Didn't I say you spoil it always! Why can't you be more patient, Isaac?'

'Because I've got our political benefactors breathing down my neck. You see, the Americans have gone into reverse about the whole business.'

'Why?'

'To delude the tax-paying public, I suppose – for the public's own good, they would say.'

'I still don't see why,' repeated Kurt Waldheim. 'The world is the way it is, and nothing Governments may do can change it.'

'Thereby hangs the real issue,' Isaac Newton replied seriously. 'In politics, the world is the way people believe it to be. In science, the world is also the way people believe it to be, at any rate in the short term, so far as grants for research and publications acceptable in the literature are concerned. There's actually very little perception of the existence of a real truth in the world, a truth irrespective of human opinions and emotions.'

'That isn't the way I care to think about it,' Kurt Waldheim replied, again in his disapproving voice.

'The way it's being seen, I think,' broke in Frances Haroldsen, 'is that a few odd bods of scientists shouldn't be given the leading role in what may turn out to be quite a spectacular show. That was the problem for Mike Howarth. He didn't have enough weight to carry it through even in Britain. When we took it over, the stakes were raised high enough to get things started in a smallish way, as an Anglo-German project, but not at all as a superpower project. With the military dominant now in both superpowers, the aim must inevitably be to discredit us – to rub us out so that things can go ahead, if they go ahead, in what are believed from their point of view to be more reliable hands.'

'Those are sombre words, Frances Margaret,' grunted Kurt Waldheim. 'Where, then, do we stand?'

'We stand as strongly or as weakly, whichever way you care to see it, as two leading politicians stand in Britain – politicians who are under pressure for associating themselves with what is claimed to be a crackpot project,' answered Isaac Newton.

'But we have proofs! Clear-cut proofs!' Kurt Waldheim almost shouted. 'From a detailed analysis of the interference patterns we have the orbit of the source of the NASA signals, the ones brought from the United States by Frances Margaret. The position of the source and its orbit are just the position and orbit of Comet Halley. There cannot be the smallest doubt about it.'

Isaac Newton got up from his chair. Standing with his back to the log fire, he nodded and said:

'Which gives us breathing space. We'll get our shot at Comet Halley all right; perhaps even two or three shots. But somewhere along the line we've got to produce some form of practical demonstration. We can carry people a little way by arguments and calculations, but only a little way, I'm afraid. What we need is something which hits everybody straight in the eye; something which brands the opposition for exactly what they are.'

'I don't see how that's to be done,' Kurt Waldheim remarked, shaking his head dubiously.

'Nor, I'm afraid, do I,' admitted Isaac Newton. 'Let's hope I'm being too pessimistic.'

From Wengen, they travelled by car to Andermatt and thence over the St Gottard Pass to Bellinzone and Lugano. From Lugano they took the road south, crossing the border into Italy just north of the town of Como. Another hour's drive brought them to the site of the Summit Meeting on the east bank of Lake Como, near Varenna.

Security was an issue of primary importance to the Summit Meeting, both personally for the participants and on an international scale: for this was a meeting which it would have been in the interests of the Soviet Union to prevent, since a principal topic for discussion was to be a Soviet proposal for the 'Finlandization' of Germany – an epithet not flattering either to Finland or to Germany. It was an issue that had bobbed up and down for more than a decade, the idea being for the Soviets to offer a union of East and West Germany in exchange for the demilitarisation of the resulting reunited Germany. There were plenty of people in the West who saw the creation of a demilitarised buffer between the two superpowers and their allies as a good thing. There were also plenty of others who saw the proposal as a trick to lift the Red Army in one move to the western border of the combined Germany, and to do so without a shot being fired.

It was towards the end of a torrid morning session, a session which had heard a sobering presentation of the strategic situation from the NATO Commander-in-Chief, that the American President made a statement. The French President being in the chair, the American President said:

'If you'll pardon me, sir, I'd like to make a little announcement. It's just an inconsequential matter which I thought might ease our minds after the difficulties we've been discussing this morning. You'll all know, sir, that a very famous comet, Comet Halley, is now approaching the Earth. What I have to say is that radio signals of an organised kind have been detected from Comet Halley by workers at the Goddard Space Flight Center, under the direction of Professor Helen Salome Johnson.'

'Clearly a *femme fatale*,' the British Prime Minister instantly interposed in a loud clear voice. When the splutter of laughter had died down, the British Prime Minister went on:

'Radio signals of an organised kind were detected several months ago in Britain, not from Comet Halley, but from Comet Boswell. As everybody knows, of course, Boswell comes before Johnson.'

After lunch that day, the German Chancellor was walking the grounds of the Italian villa with the French President.

'Why is the British Prime Minister so anxious always to be in confrontation?' wondered the French President.

'Something to do with the weather, perhaps? I once met an Englishman who said he thought they had the best weather in the world,' replied the German Chancellor in a gloomy voice.

'That was the worst *volte face* I've ever heard. A little announcement indeed!' snorted the British Prime Minister.

'It means we're only one shot ahead now, not two or three. Which is a pity,' replied Isaac Newton.

'Why would they have switched like that?'

'Once the struggle between NASA and the Pentagon resolved itself, they must have seen it made no sense to try freezing the situation – particularly as they know that we're going ahead regardless. So the best policy was to switch, and then try to pip us at the post.'

'What post have you in mind?'

'I wish I had a clear idea of an answer to that question, Prime Minister. The obvious goal is to make the first transmission to Comet Halley. What happens then is another matter. Unless we get some sort of a reply it's going to be a rather hollow business.'

'What sort of a reply could there be?'

'I can't imagine. But I keep telling myself that the signals would never have come in the first place unless some two-way exchange was intended.'

'You're assuming there's a rationality in it all,' observed the Prime Minister.

'The faith of the scientist, I suppose.'

'So how long do we have to wait?'

'Twenty-three days to countdown, assuming everything goes well.'

After all the careful preparation they'd made for countering an assault from the opposite direction, Frances Haroldsen was even more annoyed by the *volte face* than the British Prime Minister. Disregarding the cluster of people hovering around the American President and disdaining to wait for a lull in their conversation, she let loose in her most audible voice:

'That was a most *courageous* announcement, Mr President. About Helen *Salome* Johnson, what with her being so *mouse-like* and this being an *election* year.'

The thought of it being an election year riveted the President's attention. 'Why should an election year signify?' he asked with a frown. The numerous other bystanders were stricken by the ease with which this bold young woman had cut, like a scalpel through butter, across their stumbling attempts at conversation with the President.

'Well, you can hardly *want* the media to hear about it, can you?' Frances Margaret continued. 'I mean, you don't want the *White House* to become a *haunt* for *UFOs* and *comets*. Not with all the *cartoons* in the *media*. The ones with *balloons* coming out of your *mouth*, saying all sorts of *ludicrous* things about *astrology* being *rampant* at the White House.'

'I guess you have a point there, young lady. I must get my staff to work on it.'

'They don't need to *work* on it, Mr President. All they need to do is to tell these *NASA* people to *piss off* with their astrology. Tell them that *astrology* will not fool *all* the people *all* the time. Which is what *really* matters in an *election* year.'

'Yes, ah...' struggled the President, looking around for help. Seeing aides coming rapidly forwards, Frances Margaret added:

'I think you ought to *rest* a little, Mr President, after that simply *courageous* statement. Give my regards to Helen *Salome* Johnson...'

Chapter 34

The countryside around the European Space Organisation's launching site near the coastal town of Kourou in French Guinea was lush with tropical rain forests, monkeys and flocks of brightly-coloured parrots. The countdown for the Ariane launcher had been interrupted twice due to equipment problems, and Isaac Newton's nerves had pretty well reached snapping point.

There was no technical reason for him to have attended the launching at all, since immediate communication from Cambridge by a short-wave radio link was available to the Comet Halley Project. News of its triumphant success or abject failure could therefore be flashed five thousand miles or more in a tiny fraction of a second. In fact, arrangements had been made to control the details of the experiment itself remotely from Cambridge. Before then, however, it was necessary that the launch should put the satellite into its assigned orbit, that the satellite shouldn't end miserably in the ocean, or that one or other of the various stages of the launching rocket shouldn't explode in the upper atmosphere – disaster in its most spectacular form.

The first two days had been relatively relaxing. The great scale of the engineering equipment, the rocket itself, the enormous cranes, the fuel tanks, pipes, gantries and scaffolding, were in tune with Isaac Newton's experience in the assembly of high-energy accelerators of vast dimensions. Very different from the minute detail of the satellite package itself, minutiae in which he had been immersed over the past year.

It had been a haunting conviction which had mainly been responsible for bringing him to the launch, a conviction that far more depended on it than anything he would care to put into words. On the face of it, failure would simply mean postponement, postponement perhaps only for a few weeks. So why did it seem to matter so much that this first attempt should succeed? If the new NASA-Pentagon axis were to take over from this first effort, would anything be different – setting aside the affront to his own ego? On the face of it, no. Yet Isaac Newton had a conviction, amounting almost to a neurosis, that it did matter. It was a conviction he could not explain. It was easier to explain his presence at the launch on the psychological grounds that, if disaster should occur, he could at least be seen to have done everything within his powers to avert it – on the principle of the doctor receiving an 'A for effort' at the deathbed of his patient.

The first of the delays was said to be caused by a defect in the electrical circuits. The second was mysterious. Isaac Newton found himself being brusquely interrogated as to his credentials and the purpose of his presence at the launch. His papers were examined and then taken away, apparently for some kind of verification procedure. When the papers were returned with a curt nod by the inspector of the security guards, he was also issued with a special yellow-coloured pass. In this regard he evidently fared better than all but two or three of the other visitors, since the rest of the initially quite large posse of outsiders was missing as the time for the third attempt at a countdown arrived. For some reason, which Isaac Newton could only guess at, the rest of the visitors had been summarily booted out. His guess was that his own insistence on security lay at the root of the affair.

The yellow pass carried Isaac Newton into the actual flight control room. The control room was not nearly as large as television viewers of NASA spectaculars, spectaculars like the Moon landings, would have supposed. There was seating accommodation for about twenty-five persons, with the launching director and his immediate lieutenants occupying the first row, facing a battery of television monitors.

Time passed in what seemed to Isaac Newton to be impossibly drawn out units of about a quarter of an hour. The operational crew were perpetually engaged either in terse conversations among themselves or in passing instructions to engineers outside, who made adjustments or took readings which then appeared on the television monitors. Gradually the units of time shortened, until Isaac Newton was measuring it on his watch in five-minute steps. Outside it would be well past dawn now; the launch was scheduled for two hours after dawn.

The units of time contracted more and more, to minutes and at last to seconds...ten...nine...eight...seven...six...five...four... three...two...one...zero. Even though he knew exactly what to expect, Isaac Newton's eyes were glued compulsively to the particular screen which showed the rocket. Flames appeared at its base and, for what seemed an eternity, nothing else happened. Then the sleek cylinder began to rise, at first with an agonising slowness. The upward motion increased and now, all in a moment it seemed, the thing was on its journey at a speed with which the cameras were scarcely able to cope. All that could be seen on the monitor was a bright flame from the exhaust of the rocket.

Isaac Newton sat back in his chair suddenly aware that his mouth had gone quite dry. The first of many hurdles was over, for at least the rocket carrier hadn't blown up on the pad. More and more he was wishing himself back in a straightforward, decent, honest-to-God business like high-energy physics. High-energy physics was like mountaineering, he decided. A mountaineer can plan his route and choose his weather, controlling his risks almost to the point where failure may be said to be a consequence either of misjudgement or of a lack of technique. But this rocket business was like riding the rapids of a steep river flowing swiftly between canyon walls. Once you pushed off in your boat, you were at the mercy of the current and of the rocks in the river-bed, with the difference between success and disaster only slightly dependent on judgement and technique.

Isaac Newton counted first the seconds and then the minutes following the launch, looking anxiously for signs of crisis in the talk and mannerisms of the crew. Nothing happened, and he had just begun to relax when the director of the crew turned towards him, saying, 'Monsieur Newton, it will soon be your turn. We would like to eject your antenna wire at the next passage of the satellite – about three quarters of an hour from now.'

So Isaac Newton moved from the rear of the room to the front row, where he checked his telemetry tape yet again on the monitors. Step by step, with the aid of the controls on a small console in front of him, he went for the last time through the instructions for actually operating the satellite. Eventually he turned to the director and nodded: he was satisfied that the last critical part of the launch could begin.

Once again there was an agonising wait until the satellite was judged to be in the optimum position for this most delicate phase of the launch – the ejection of the long wire, reeled off in the fashion of a fisherman's line, that was needed to make radio transmission at a very long wavelength feasible. The reeling out had to be done very gently to prevent the wire from recoiling into an imitation of a ball of wool. The trick had been to enclose the wire inside a thin tube of plastic through which gas was blown, so that the tube and the wire within it straightened in the manner of a well-known toy – the kind which uncurls and makes a rasping noise followed by a hoot when you blow it out in the face of your neighbour at a Christmas party.

It had also been necessary to use a metal alloy without any spring in it, so that after once being straightened the wire would stay straight, the way that solder wire does – except that the alloy had to have a high electrical conductivity to avoid unnecessary wastage of power from the satellite's solar cells. With these problems all solved in the laboratory well in advance of the actual launch, difficulties had been minimised to a point where success could be expected. Even so, Isaac Newton had a bad half an hour of it until the thing was done. If anything fell apart now, he himself would be fairly and squarely to blame, whereas up to this point the blame would have fallen on those who produced, maintained and launched the rocket which had acted as the carrier for his satellite package.

Suddenly the control erupted into shouts and back-slapping and hand-shaking, as it always does at the end of a successful launch. There were bottles of wine with the late-breakfast party in a nearby refectory. Everybody behaved as if it had been a run-of-the-mill launch, which, of course, no launch ever really was. Eventually Isaac Newton excused himself to catch a charter flight – one which would connect with a commercial flight from Caracas in Venezuela, scheduled to reach Heathrow by the afternoon of the following day. He shook hands once again all round – with the director and his crew, and with the engineers responsible for the detailed work on the various stages of the rocket. As soon as he was airborne in the small charter plane, Isaac Newton reflected with satisfaction that, short of shooting down the satellite, there was nothing which anybody outside the Cavendish Laboratory could now do about it. This was because it would respond only to the code which it had been instructed to obey, a code known to nobody outside himself and three other persons in the laboratory. Nothing now could prevent a first transmission being made to Comet Halley.

He was met at Heathrow Airport by Frances Haroldsen.

'You'd forgotten about the College Feast, I suppose,' she said as soon as they were started in Isaac Newton's Mercedes on the infuriating drive along well-nigh impassable roads around London.

'What about it?'

'The Master has invited all Board Members. Even such a small worm as I am has been invited. The Chancellor is coming and is going to speak.'

'Sounds interesting.'

'It will be. Ever since the Master heard of the successful launch he's been hell-bent on turning it into a Roman triumph. You can expect all the flags to be flying and every trumpet to be blowing.'

'Oh, my God, no! We're still a thousand miles from any real success.'

'Oh, my God, yes! If the Master calls it a triumph, then a triumph it will surely be. I wouldn't put it past him to have radio and TV in on the job,' Frances Margaret said with evident relish.

Since Boulton had repossessed his house in Adams Road, Isaac Newton was back again in the Old Guest Room, and Frances Margaret was back – ostensibly at least – next door in King's. In evening dress they both made their way from the Old Guest Room through the cloisters and down the steps past the Hall to the Master's Lodge. The reception there was for 7.30 to 8.00 p.m., and they were just in time to enjoy the last moments of it.

As soon as they appeared the Master, dressed in tails with white tie, padded towards them booming,

'Ah! Here comes Bad-News himself! Except that it isn't bad news for once.'

The Chancellor was there with a hearty handshake. 'Well, we seem to be over the first hurdle. A pretty big hurdle, I'd imagine,' he said.

Because Isaac Newton had just travelled upwards of five thousand miles, some of them hard won, the occasion had an unreal quality to it, almost a fairy-tale atmosphere, which persisted into the main dinner itself. All the Project Halley Board members, with the exception of the Prime Minister, were there, seated at the first table immediately below the Holbein portrait of Henry VIII. That the past and present should thus be brought together was a fairy tale in itself. Comets and satellites and telescopes and telemetry were a far cry indeed from Holbein and Henry, a vast separation of the mind.

After the Loyal Toast had been given and drunk, the Master rose for what the Fellows appeared to have been given to understand would be a humdinger of a speech. At least, this seemed to be the implication of the hoots and bangings from the younger Fellows and their friends, male and female, seated at the lower tables. But it was to introduce the Chancellor that the Master now rose.

'Fellows and Guests, it gives me great pleasure to ask you to drink a toast to Her Majesty's Government, represented here tonight in the person of Sir Godfrey Wendover, a man of many parts, disposition, and *departments*. Both departments and deportments, should I say? A *minister* to us all in times of anything else but trouble? Yet, as we all know full well, trouble – cauldron boil and bubble - builds character. Which is why we in this College have so much character, as well as silver, much of which you see splendidly displayed here on the tables in front of you (*loud laughter*).

'So, Fellows and Guests, I give you the toast: Her Majesty's Government, long may it survive.'

The thought of toasting the survival of the Government, any Government for that matter, did not sit too well with the younger, heavily-bearded and anarchically-inclined section of the body of Fellows, who let loose with a ferocious banging of the tables as the Chancellor rose to respond.

'Master, Milords, Fellows, Ladies and Gentlemen,' he began

soothingly, 'it is with humility, surprise and a sense of anticipation that I speak to you tonight. Humility, because as a *sometime* historian myself I am acutely conscious of the many famous persons who have spoken in this Hall before me, during the long and distinguished history of this most noble foundation (*polite tapping of tables*). Surprise, because as a graduate myself, of another place I must admit (*polite tapping*), I never cease to marvel at the sheer scale of your Cambridge Colleges, a scale shown nowhere better than in the magnificence of your own Great Square. Anticipation, because, as you may possibly know, over the past year I have been associated with a project based here in Cambridge, of which I in particular and the Government in general, entertain great hopes (*banging of tables*). Quite why I, as the most non-scientific of non-scientists, should have become involved in such a project remains something of a mystery even to this day.

'But at all events, I have enjoyed the experience, an experience not without its moments of anxiety, I might add. Shortly, as I intend to be brief myself, you will be hearing details from the Master of the very recent successful satellite launching, masterminded, I should emphasise, by a Fellow of this College, Professor Isaac Newton (*more tapping*). There is something of an analogy between satellite launching and drilling for oil, which as you will know is reckoned in business to be a chancy affair. *Unsuccessful* satellite launching is a little like drilling a dry hole, except that in unsuccessful satellite launching you lose your money a million times faster than in drilling for oil. In fact, there is no way that I have been able to discover in my time as Chancellor of the Exchequer of losing money more speedily than in the unsuccessful launching of satellites, for which merely trying to *burn* money is only a poor man's substitute (*laughter*). But enough of this unproductive talk. We were successful, *not* unsuccessful. No money has been burned, the well is *not* dry (*general applause*).

'In this vein,' continued the Chancellor, 'I would like to remind you of a certain Scrope Davies, a Cambridge student in the days of Lord Byron. Davies was a great gambler who had the peculiar habit of attempting to cut his throat after every Newmarket meeting at which his bets met with failure. On one such occasion, the doctor who was sent for insisted on finishing his dinner when he heard it was Scrope Davies' throat that was cut. For, as he said, "There is no danger of him dying, for I have sewn him up six times already!" '

It was now the Master's turn.

'It is my pleasure this evening to propose a toast to a name which has for long been associated in the minds of people all over the world with this College,' he began. 'I refer, of course, to the name of Isaac Newton. Not to Isaac Newton senior, the successful planet calculator, but to Isaac Newton junior, the successful satellite launcher (*applause and more banging of tables*).

'Let me be the first to admit that I am no scientist (*more loud applause*). I came to science a year ago thinking it to be a case of heads I win, tails you lose. Or to put it more poetically, I began by thinking of the scientist that:

> Where he falls short, 'tis Nature's fault alone,
> Where he succeeds, the merit's all his own.

'Then, as I began to carry a little responsibility myself, I came to feel much more like the story told about Marshall Joffre, who was credited by some, but not by others, with winning the First Battle of the Marne in September 1914. Asked if he had really won the battle, Joffre replied: "I can't say, but I can say that if it had been lost the blame would have been on me." So indeed it would have been on Isaac Newton if this launching business had turned out to be the speediest loss in the history of the British Treasury (*table rapping*).

'I confess I would be dumbfounded, an unusual condition for me (*laughter*), if you were to ask exactly where we go from here. Something, *I think*, to do with Halley's Comet (*more laughter*). Edmond Halley was born in the year 1656. He became, I regret to say, a student in that other place to which our guest has already referred, a student of Queen's College, Oxford (*groans*). He is best known, not for the comet which bears his name, but for his wise role in encouraging the publication of *Philosophiae Naturalis Principia Mathematica* – by Isaac Newton senior, of course. It is, however, peculiarly fitting that Edmond Halley should have had connections both personally with Isaac Newton senior, and through the comet which bears his name, with Isaac Newton junior, and with that other place to which our guest belongs (*applause*).

'It would be remiss of me if I were to recount to you a story about statues (*pause followed by loud laughter*). I will relate it nevertheless (*more laughter*). The Roman writer Cato, observing that statues were being created in honour of many others, remarked: "I would rather people should ask why there is *not* a statue to Cato, than why there is." Perhaps this story suggests that the College would itself be remiss if it did not add a second marble monument in the name of Isaac Newton (*applause and laughter with table banging*).

'Success breeds success, they say. Piling Pelion on Ossa – which, I might add, were mountains, not a male-and-female situation as some of you might have hoped (*table banging*) – the story in mythology has it, was a device by which the sons of the god Poseidon sought to climb to the sky, an endeavour on which we are still engaged to this day (*applause and then laughter*). None amongst us more than Isaac Newton junior, to whom I ask you to rise. I propose the toast of, Isaac Newton junior; for the Universe and St George!'

There was pandemonium in the Hall as Isaac Newton rose to his feet, suffused with a horrible inner vacancy, except that the story of an entomologist floated mysteriously into his consciousness. The time had been immediately after the Second World War, and the entomologist had been persuaded by the Foreign Office to tour occupied Germany, giving educational lectures on bugs and beetles to the troops. Arriving one day at an American base, he was introduced by the camp commander there with the remark, 'He's the British Bob Hope. Boys, he'll slay ya.'

Which expressed exactly Isaac Newton's own feelings now as he looked along the first table and then down the Hall. All that now occurred to him was that the bread-eating Professor of History's moustache was indeed remarkably walrus-like. To Isaac Newton's amazement, the bread-eater put the first finger and thumb of the left hand into his mouth, and then let forth a shrill whistle, after which he beamed up and down the table and repeated the performance. Whereon one of the oldest of the Fellows blew into cupped hands and, a moment later, began to hoot like an owl.

'Masters, Milords, Fellows, Ladies and Gentlemen,' Isaac Newton began, 'I cannot do better, it seems to me, in replying to the toast you have kindly drunk, than to tell you how what has become known as "Project Halley" now stands (*table tapping*). The Project had its origin in an intelligible message received from an earlier comet, Comet Boswell. Of the intelligible nature of that first message there was never much doubt, and what little there may have been was removed when NASA intercepted a somewhat similar message from Comet Halley.

'The plan of our Project has been to direct a return message towards Comet Halley, using the same form of radio transmission and coding, with the return message constructed so as to convey the same form of information as that which has been received twice from the two comets. In this way, there should be no problem of interpretation should our transmission be made successfully, and should it be received.

'The situation so far is that the satellite from which this transmission is to be made has now been successfully launched, as indeed you have already been apprised by the previous speakers. Its power supplies are working and its aerial system is in the correct position. What remains is to test the electronic circuitry, which I hope will be done tomorrow from the Cavendish Laboratory (*applause*). After that, perhaps as early as tomorrow evening, the first transmission will be made. With what result, you will naturally ask?

'If we already knew the answer to that question, the Project would have been pointless, and I can do no better to satisfy your curiosity than recall a conversation I had in the early days with the Chancellor. He said that the situation today reminded him of the Europe of the fifteenth century, a Europe shut in on itself, without any depth of perspective. It was the discovery of the Americas which then transformed the medieval age into the Renaissance. The thought was that in a similar way our present activities may prove to be the small beginning of a new, more hopeful age. The time is not too far away when we will put this thought to the test.'

Chapter 35

The world is full of jubilees, so much so that the public has long since become jaded with them⎮– especially as the media cannot wait until a jubilee really arrives, but must always be milking it long in advance.

So it had been with Comet Halley, which in any case was something of a flop from a public relations point of view. This was because the Earth's position in its orbit was less suited to.a spectacular display from the Comet than it had been at the previous return in 1910. There was also the great increase in the brilliance of street lighting which had taken place since 1910: the sky this time was artificially bright in the very places where most people lived, making the light coming from the Comet's head and tail seem far less impressive than it had ever been on any of the returns of Comet Halley from time immemorial. In these circumstances, the existence of intelligible signals⎮– or otherwise, for there was still a considerable body of so-called respectable scientific opinion which denied such a possibility ⎮– had proved a boon to the media, especially as the spectacular death of Mike Howarth had set things off to a dream start for the newsmen. All aspects of the Project

Halley Board had been carefully watched both at home and abroad, particularly in view of the exalted status of its political members.

The successful satellite launch was, therefore, headline material for the morning papers and, as one might have expected, the speeches which had been made at the Trinity Feast were known and were freely reported, with the result that a sense of spectacular events in the offing took root overnight.

When Isaac Newton turned up at the Cavendish Laboratory at 9.15 on the following morning, it was to find several of his assistants standing waiting in his office in a state of revolt.

'Reporters are swarming all over the place. We've simply had to lock everything away that's sensitive, and it's impossible to do any testing at all,' said a fresh-faced young fellow of about twenty-five called McClelland.

'In that case I want you all to think of yourselves as actors in a play,' Isaac Newton told them. 'Between now and twelve o'clock convince these media types that they've seen everything. Put on a good show without laying it on too thick, because these fellows aren't stupid. They may not know too much about circuitry, but they can tell a phoney when they see one.'

'And what happens then?' someone asked.

'After twelve o'clock you'll get a couple of hours, three hours maybe, to do all the checking.'

'How will that be?'

'Never you mind. Just smile, and keep on smiling. I'll join you in about half an hour.'

When the posse of younger staff members had filed out of the office, Isaac Newton called Mrs Gunter and said:

'Will you get me the Master of Trinity, please?'

'Bad-News! My God you *are* bad news,' groaned the Master when he came on the 'phone. 'I've got a head like a football.'

'I wanted to ask you to organise a sumptuous lunch, with three or four wines.'

'Do I really need to tell you that I've got a mouth like the bottom of a parrot's cage,' came the hollow reply.

'It's all that port-drinking, Master, the higher alcohols. The kidneys can't filter them.'

'Stop! Stop! The thought of lunch is like the hangman's noose to a condemned criminal.'

'A pity, Master. Because it's the press.'

'The press, did you say?'

'I did, and if we can't entertain them for two or three hours it's goodbye to any shot at the Comet tonight. Besides, there's a reporter from the *Observer*. He's wearing Gucci shoes and an astrakhan hat. He's wearing the hat here in the Lab, and I want to find out if it's stitched to his skull.'

'God, Bad-News, I've got gimlets stitched to *my* skull.'

'I was thinking of shipping 'em out of here close on noon.'

'You're not shipping anybody. You're bringing them. I'm not doing this thing alone and that's flat.'

'But I need to check the circuits.'

'And I need to check this headache. Three or four wines, you said, didn't you?'

'And cigars.'

'Oh, no, not cigars. I couldn't bear it. I couldn't face everybody lighting up with bland smiles on their wine-drunk faces. Oh, no, I can't face anything at all,' groaned the Master again.

There came a click, which concluded the conversation conclusively. Thereupon Isaac Newton walked through into Mrs Gunter's office saying, 'Mrs Gunter, will you circulate among the press reporters and any other media personnel, telling each one in turn that they've been invited to a special lunch by the Master of Trinity, for twelve o'clock. Make it sound confidential. When you have a list of them all, phone the Master's secretary with the number. Add two or three in case of late arrivals, and then have taxis ready for them at twelve sharp, please. We'll pay the taxis out of petty cash, if Professor Boulton has left us with any.'

'Very good, Professor. Do I make a separate list of any who don't wish to go?'

'An excellent idea. We ought to know the names of them all. I hate the idea of having to install guards at the Lab entrance and that sort of thing, but if this goes on I don't know what else we can do.'

Firmly forcing himself to smile broadly, he then joined the throng. Pretty soon the mere looking over of equipment in the various laboratories palled. Time was then eked out by the serving of coffee and snacks in the canteen, following which the information was spread around that a press conference would be held in the large lecture room.

Isaac Newton began the press conference by more or less repeating what he had said in his speech at the Feast on the previous night, ending with, 'The plan of the Project has been to return a very long wavelength transmission to Comet Halley, using the same kind of coding and incorporating the same kind of message as we ourselves received.'

'Could I ask a question about that, Professor?' a woman reporter in the second row came in.

'Yes?'

'As I understand it, your message consists of pairs of numbers, one being the time and the other being the distance of the Comet from the Sun.'

'That is correct,' agreed Isaac Newton, glad of the accuracy of understanding implied by the question, and noting that the reporter from the *Observer* was still wearing the astrakhan hat, which suggested that perhaps the man, Tom Taylor he had called himself, had a radio transmitter concealed underneath it.

'Is your transmission in real time?' was the next question.

'Yes, it is.'

'Measuring time in what way?'

'Atomic units scaled by a decimal multiplier, and the same for the distance unit.'

'How d'you get the Comet's distance from the Sun? By measurement or by calculation?' someone else asked.

'Really by both,' answered Isaac Newton. 'The Comet's orbit has already been obtained by measurement. Then, knowing the orbit we determine the distance of the Comet nucleus from the Sun by calculation – the distance at the present moment, I mean. If you look at things from the point of view of an intelligent recipient of our transmission,' he went on, 'it would be possible to arrive at quite a number of interesting conclusions. First, that we had understood the Comet's own message. Second, that we understand atomic physics. Third, that we count our numbers in the scale of ten.'

'How would you do that?'

'From the decimal multipliers used to scale the units. Mathematically speaking, counting in the scale of ten is an absurdity. So you could conclude that the reason for such a practice must be primitively physical and not intellectual. The fingers . . .'

'Starrattson of the *Daily Record*,' broke in a voice, in a tone which told you instantly that all these finicky details were not of concern to anybody with his feet firmly on the ground.

'Yes, Mr Starrattson, you will find a few pin-ups in the workshops that might possibly be of interest to your paper,' returned Isaac Newton smoothly, but instantly regretting that he'd allowed his irritation at being summarily interrupted to come out so clearly. When the laughter had died down, Starrattson continued:

'What I'm interested in, Professor Newton, is what all this has to do with the ordinary man?'

'I would suppose that, if correctly reported, all this would be of considerable interest to the ordinary man.'

'I doubt that readers of the *Record* would see it that way.'

'Possibly not. But then the question, Mr Starrattson, is whether your readers should be described as ordinary. Or are they not more properly described as extraordinary?'

'There you go, giving yourself upper-class airs. What many people object to about this University is that it gives itself airs from one end to the other. Sneering at the tax-payers who foot the bill.'

'This University receives just the same treatment as other universities, Mr Starrattson. What this University stands for uncompromisingly is an intellectual attitude of mind, whereas what you appear to stand for is an anti-intellectual attitude of mind, which you then proceed to confuse with the attitude of ordinary people. Ordinary people are not anti-intellectual when things are explained to them in a proper way, which is surely the job of the media? My job is to explain things to you, which is exactly what I was trying to do before you replaced science by sociology.'

'Nevertheless, Mr Starrattson has a point,' broke in another voice. 'This project has, in fact, been supported by tax-payers' money...'

'*Not* through the University, so let's leave the University out of it,' interrupted Isaac Newton.

'Very well, not through the University, so let's leave the University out of it. But what is the tax-payer going to get for his money? That's surely a valid question?'

'It is, and I'll give you a valid answer to it. If we're successful, and I say "*if*", the tax-payer will get a doorway out of it.'

Since this reply produced a moment of silence, Isaac Newton continued:

'In Roman mythology, Janus was the god of doorways, openings, avenues to new prospects, new paths, but without any signposts to tell you where the paths will lead eventually. Without doorways, society would soon stagnate, which was why the Romans made a god out of their opener of doorways.'

'That isn't something which any *ordinary* man would give tuppence for. I can tell you *that*, Professor,' Starrattson remarked sarcastically.

'It's something which ordinary people would give more than tuppence for,' Isaac Newton answered as calmly as he could, 'because ordinary people have supported unusual things from time immemorial, whether at Stonehenge, or in building the temples of ancient Greece, or in modern scientific laboratories. Your trouble, Mr Starrattson, as I have already explained, is that you persistently confuse ordinary people with anti-intellectual people – of which there are nowadays a fair number, I'll grant you, but not a majority, I'm happy to say.'

'I think what may be worrying some people here is that Project Halley wasn't funded in the usual way,' broke in Alan Bristow, the editor of *Nature*, whom Isaac Newton now recognised sitting towards the back of the lecture room.

'What would be the source of the worry, Dr Bristow?' Isaac Newton asked.

'Well, that quite a lot of privilege was involved. Rather obviously from the composition of your Board.'

'Where d'you see privilege in a project sponsored by the highest democratically-elected representatives of ordinary people? Is there any other way you can suggest of coming nearer to democracy, Dr Bristow?'

'I suppose not, acknowledged Bristow, 'but there's no avoiding the fact that everybody sees the situation as unusual. Perhaps people might even see it as a little arbitrary. You see, if everything were done this way, everything would come down to privilege for those, like yourself, who happen to have the ear of influential politicians.'

'But everything isn't done this way. Aside from Project Halley, *nothing* is done this way.'

'It might be if you're successful. Then we should have democracy turned into a kind of aristocracy.'

'How much of the world's great art and music, and great science, was done in any other way?'

'You have the logic, Professor Newton. What you don't have is the principle which many of us believe important nowadays.'

'The principle of maximum decadence, I suppose. Yes, I don't have that,' agreed Isaac Newton.

'Well, let's drop this part of the argument,' continued Bristow with surprising calm. 'What I'm really interested in is what you're going to do if nothing happens when your transmission to Comet Halley is made.'

'We'll try again, repeatedly.'

'And if nothing happens?'

'Then the attempt will have failed.'

'Doesn't it worry you that it might fail?'

'Of course it does, as a scientist. But not personally very much.'

'Don't you think it should?'

'No, I don't.'

'Where is your sense of responsibility, man?' Starrattson shouted.

'My sense of responsibility lay in pondering this project as carefully as I could before it began. Once it was started, my being worried personally would only have decreased the chance of its success, just as mountaineers committed to a climb do best if they can avoid becoming scared by its difficulties. Worrying personally would really mean being concerned for my own skin, which in my view, Mr Starrattson, would be neither helpful nor admirable.'

It was at this point that Mrs Gunter appeared at the back of the lecture room, and Isaac Newton immediately held up an arm, saying in conclusion, 'Ah! I am receiving signals from my secretary that our transport to lunch has arrived. For those with deep concern about taxpayers' money, let me explain that lunch at Trinity College will be privately financed. So please enjoy it without allowing remorse to spoil your digestion.'

As the press corps filed out of the lecture room, Isaac Newton congratulated himself on having held his tongue, comparatively speaking. Otherwise he might have pointed out that through the descent of media personnel on the Laboratory the spending of taxpayers' money had been impeded for a whole morning. The reporter in the astrakhan hat caught his eye once more. It wasn't a radio transmitter that was concealed in the hat, of course, but one of those miniature Japanese tape-recorders. Perhaps the whole hat was really a tape-recorder in disguise?

Chapter 36

The circuitry had been checked out during the luncheon in Trinity, and over five hours had elapsed since Isaac Newton's return to the Cavendish Laboratory. He'd delayed making the first transmission to Comet Halley in the hope, a vain hope as it turned out, that the number of people milling around the Laboratory would die down. Indeed, members of the general public began to arrive as darkness fell, their numbers swelling as each hour passed, as if people generally had acquired some mysterious foreknowledge of events to come. Eventually, such a crowd had gathered that the police were called in, partly to direct the traffic and the parking of cars, and partly to provide a guard, not for the Laboratory in general, but for the special small room from which the transmission to Comet Halley was to be directed.

In conformity with the best traditions of experimental physics, Isaac Newton left the actual details of the transmission itself to the younger members of the Project staff. Thus do the younger members acquire experience and responsibility, just as Isaac Newton himself had done a decade before. At the rear of the operations room, all the Board Members were assembled, with the exception of the Prime Minister, who was speaking in London that evening at the Lord Mayor's Banquet.

Isaac Newton sat by himself between the younger people in front and the Board Members behind. Paradoxically, he was worried that he wasn't worried. He could see the worry on the faces of the others: the Chancellor who had stayed in Cambridge through the day; Frances Haroldsen among the young people, pressing switches and reading from television screens; Kurt Waldheim showed it, although his reputation was hardly at risk; even the Master of Trinity had fallen silent as the implications of failure suddenly became clear to him. If ever a body had teed itself up to become the butt of public opinion, it was the Project Halley Board. The Chairman of CERC, who had recently joined the Board, so consummating his unofficial arrangement with Isaac Newton, now felt he'd made a ghastly mistake. It wasn't the money spent that was really at stake, because the money spent on Project Halley had been less than CERC expended in other directions with little discernible effect; it was the unacceptable nature of the Project itself.

'We'll go at nine o'clock exactly,' Isaac Newton told the group in front of him. 'The Comet will be at about its best position then.'

Although no launching was involved, and although the exact timing of the transmission was not particularly relevant, it seemed natural to everybody that a countdown procedure should be adopted. The countdown was broadcast on loudspeakers throughout the Laboratory, and in the large lecture room there was also a television display showing the situation in the operations room. The actual transmission itself was converted, moreover, into a sound-show – an impressive rapid-fire sequence of dots and dashes broadcast in the large lecture room where the press corps was assembled together with members of the public. To increase the dramatic effect of the transmission, a picture of Comet Halley itself was projected onto a screen, the picture being obtained in real time by electronic devices fitted to one of the telescopes at the Observatory on the north side of Madingley Road.

In the operations room it was a matter now of checking to make certain that the long-wave transmitter in the satellite was functioning correctly, and it was some moments before everybody seemed satisfied that this was so. A telephone rang. The fresh-faced youth called McClelland who had been in Isaac Newton's office that morning answered it. Then turning to Isaac Newton he said:

'It's the Observatory. They're asking for you, Prof.'

All eyes were turned towards the telephone as Isaac Newton picked up the receiver. He listened for a moment and then said simply:

'My God!'

All eyes were still on Isaac Newton as he replaced the telephone.

'They've detected a sudden brightening from the centre of Comet Halley. The amazing thing is, it happened just as soon as our transmission reached the Comet.'

'I can see something now on the monitor!' shouted Frances Haroldsen.

'Dim the lights!' called another voice.

Sure enough, a bright point of light could be seen within the hazy head of the Comet. As they watched, the point of light became noticeably brighter.

'They said at the Observatory that it's growing brighter all the time,' added Isaac Newton.

'Better go now and face your public,' the Master advised.

So Isaac Newton, the Master and Kurt Waldheim left the others in the operations room, making their way to the crowded lecture room. The hubbub they could hear as they approached showed that the bright point of light had been noticed already.

The Master addressed the audience.

'Let me tell you what has just happened in plain language. A transmission was sent to Comet Halley at nine p.m. precisely. Allowing for the travel time of our signal to the Comet, Comet Halley immediately made the reply you can see on this screen. Each one of us in this room is now witnessing a scene that is likely to be a big turning point in human history. For what it means, I'm going to hand you over to the two wise men who stand here beside me.'

While the Master was speaking, Kurt Waldheim went to the big blackboard and, picking up a piece of chalk, began to calculate thereon, while Isaac Newton took up a Rutherford-like stance behind a bench which lay between him and the audience.

'Any questions?' he asked as calmly as he could when the Master had finished.

There was an instant concatenation of many voices, which led the Master to hold up a hand and to boom out in his resonant voice:

'Order! Order! Let us have nothing to do with John Milton when he wrote:

> Chaos umpire sits
> And by decision more embroils the fray
> By which he reigns: and next him high arbiter
> Chance governs all.

One question at a time please!'

'Has the Comet exploded?'

'I would doubt it,' Isaac Newton replied in the terse tone of a scientist on duty.

'It is more like a sudden emission of many small particles which are picking up the light of the Sun,' added Kurt Waldheim, turning from the blackboard to face the audience.

'How bright is it going to get?'

'That will depend on the quantity of particles. I have been trying to make a calculation on the blackboard,' Kurt Waldheim went on. 'From what we have seen so far, I think the amount must be at least a thousand tons,' he added.

'Of small particles?'

'*Ja*, and that is a lot of small particles.'

'Are these particles glinting like bits of dust shining in a beam of sunlight?' someone else asked.

'That's right. And the cloud of particles is growing brighter because it's expanding outwards from the Comet itself,' Isaac Newton answered.

'*Ja*, and as the cloud expands it grows brighter because the outside of it doesn't shield the inside of it quite so much.'

'When will it stop growing brighter?' asked the Master.

'It will stop growing brighter when the particles become so dispersed that the cloud becomes what is known as optically thin – which simply means the particles don't shield each other any more from the sunlight,' answered Isaac Newton.

At this point, there was what seemed an inexplicable dash of people from the lecture room.

'Don't worry,' boomed the Master when he saw the puzzled look on Isaac Newton's face. 'It's the press deadline. Even if the heavens fall, as they appear to be doing, the press deadline reigns supreme.'

An excited fair-haired man arrived from the Observatory with the information that the point of light was now as bright as a first magnitude star, that it was growing brighter all the time, and that it could now be easily seen outside with the naked eye. At this, the remainder of the audience surged out of the lecture room and hurried towards the Observatory, where viewing by telescope was available.

When he himself stepped outside the Laboratory, Isaac Newton noticed that Featherstone, the Professor of Veterinary Science, was there, equipped with binoculars. Then Frances Haroldsen, together with the Master and the Chancellor, came up saying, 'We were thinking of driving somewhere south of Gogs, so as to be well away from the town lights.'

'I'm not sure I should leave the Lab,' Isaac Newton replied doubtfully.

'With most of the people gone and with the police around, I don't see why not,' the Master argued persuasively. 'And with that dragon of a secretary of yours on the loose...' he added.

They piled into Isaac Newton's big car, the Chancellor, Featherstone and Frances Margaret in the back, and the Master adjusting himself in the front passenger seat.

'Where's Kurt Waldheim?' someone asked.

'I am here,' Waldheim replied, poking his head inside the driver's window. 'I shall follow in my own car.'

'I'll come with you,' Frances Margaret said immediately, getting out of Isaac Newton's car and adding through the window, 'Let's meet on the old Roman road where the road from Hildersham to Balsham crosses it.'

Isaac Newton drove out of Cambridge, yet again via Hills Road and the Gogs, as he and Frances Margaret had done on the night they'd raided the cottage of the dead Mike Howarth. Before reaching Linton, they turned off the main road into the village of Hildersham and climbed the hill beyond.

During the drive, the Comet had grown even more brilliant than the planet Venus. The particles expelled from it now formed a disk easily visible to the naked eye, and large and bright like the full Moon when viewed through Featherstone's binoculars.

'Yeeow! A fearsome thing indeed,' announced the Master. 'No chump of a critic will be able to deny this any more.'

The Chancellor gazed for a long time up into the sky and Isaac Newton said to him out of the darkness:

'A signpost leading us out of the twentieth century?'

'It begins to look so, but leading us where?'

'A long way, as you yourself guessed it might.'

'Have you any idea at all of what it might really mean?'

'I can only speculate,' answered Isaac Newton.

'Then speculate, God dammit!' demanded the Master, also from out of the darkness.

'Imagine yourself,' Isaac Newton began, 'spinning helplessly in space, disoriented, with nothing but blurred impressions of the world outside yourself. Imagine there to be as many of you in a like predicament as there are of us humans – a large population of individuals, each of enormous potential for achievement, but every one of you unable to achieve it.

'You are aware of nothing outside yourself except a bright smear of light, the Sun, which will mean a fiery death if you approach it too close, a fiery death just as surely and as painfully as any human burnt at the stake would experience a terrible and painful death. Yet perpetually a few of your population must sacrifice themselves by going in close to the Sun, as moths to a candle. They must do so on the chance, the tiniest chance, that little creatures such as ourselves have evolved on one of the inner bodies of the solar system. Little creatures, but with the intelligence to provide you with the eyes and ears you lack, so that you can orient yourself, and for the first time discover the meaning of your life and of your place in the universe.

'The fiery deaths have gone on and on, a few each year, not just for centuries or millennia, but for billions of years. The eras have rolled by and the contact has never been made. Until tonight. A little after nine o'clock. It was the end of a long road, a road more than four thousand million years old for you and your fellow creatures,' Isaac Newton said, speaking upward to the sky, 'which is why you are now celebrating, because what had come to seem impossible has actually happened. Comet Halley is celebrating the end of the long road.'

'But the beginning of a long road for us,' added the Chancellor.

'To which I will say, amen,' concluded the Master.

PART TWO

The Day Came Swiftly

Chapter 37

Isaac Newton did not think to connect the great flare-up of Halley's Comet with the disarmament talks in Geneva, which he had attended more than a year ago, and which had now become a distant memory. He parked his car and prepared to make the quickest possible dash through bone-chilling rain to the main door of the Cavendish Laboratory.

'No comet today!' remarked the familiar voice of Scrooge, the Laboratory storekeeper.

'I hope everything is in order, Scrooge,' Isaac Newton replied as he shook off the rain, 'no raids on your storeroom?'

'Trust me to keep everything tightly battened down, Professor,' Scrooge grinned in reply.

Boulton from Geostrophics was waiting in Isaac Newton's office.

'You're missing a great chance, you know,' Boulton began.

'What would that be?'

'With all these people milling around the Lab! Reporters from all over the world! They'd pay a tenner apiece without turning a hair.'

'Frankly, that never occurred to me. But then I'm doomed to die poor, I'm afraid.'

'Oh, I wasn't thinking of it personally. I was thinking of all the odds and ends around the Lab – coffee for the assistants and that sort of thing. It's a perpetual drain if you don't watch it.'

'How are your German marks doing?'

'I was out of those a long time ago. Japanese yen are where you should be at the moment. If I were you, I'd shift my Swiss francs into yen. Besides, the Swiss banks don't pay much interest. Or you could think about the peso. They say it's likely to go up.'

'Or down, as the case may be. You sure you don't prefer the drachma?'

'That's a tricky one. It depends on the olive crop, and quite a bit on the nut crop, too.'

'I imagine it might.'

'The thing is that comet toys for children look like a good bet at the moment. I've been on to one or two companies about it. We need a few ideas. It seems to be right in your line. I've also thought about comet fireworks. But of course you don't need to come in if you don't want to – except that it's always important to get in on the ground floor. Once everybody gets interested it's too late.'

'How much would I stand to lose?'

'Oh, you wouldn't lose anything, because you wouldn't be risking anything except your ideas.'

'That's a relief.'

'It's quite a chance, really. By the way, I'm thinking of buying The Ragamuffin. It's freehold you see, so either the University or one of the Colleges might be interested in the land eventually. But of course it pays for itself as a going concern.'

'Then why would anybody want to sell it?'

'All sorts of reasons. Death duties, arthritis, aching bones as the proprietor gets older, that kind of thing.'

'Have you ever thought of switching over to a chair in economics?'

'Not likely. Economists always lose money – the thing is a by-word. You see the stock market is really a zero-sum game, so if you win somebody else loses. Mostly it's the economists who lose. To everybody's benefit. Even widows and orphans do very well out of them.'

Mrs Gunter, Isaac Newton's secretary, appeared in the doorway to announce:

'We have a visit from Mr Scuby on our hands, Professor.' Instantly Boulton was at Isaac Newton's personal exit door, saying, 'Then I'll be on my way. Think about the comet toys. I'll be on to Pocombe – he's in Chemistry – about the fireworks, I mean.'

Boulton the Professor of Geostrophics just managed to make his exit before John Jocelyn Scuby, the Secretary of the Faculties, came in from Mrs Gunter's office.

'Might I ask if the figure who disappeared just now through the door . . .' Scuby began.

'Was Professor Boulton? In fact it was,' Isaac Newton replied to the incompleted question.

'I am almost impelled to chase after him. With remarkable skill he has evaded me now – let me see, it must be fully a year since I was last able to track him down,' Scuby continued.

'I think he must have had heavy losses on the markets, in German marks.'

'Quite possibly. But it is not his personal affairs with which I am concerned. The turmoil in his department is a grievous headache to us all.'

'Who is Pocombe of Chemistry?'

'The name is familiar but the connection escapes me, I'm afraid.'

'Could it be fireworks?'

'Ah! Fireworks. Yes, fireworks of course. Pocombe is something of an expert in that particular field. He makes them for charity displays, I believe.'

'Well, Mr Scuby, I hope you have managed to sort out the turmoil in this department.'

'Hardly turmoil, Professor Newton. A few irregularities perhaps, before your arrival, of course. No, I called to enquire if you would look with favour on a proposal, popular in many quarters I might say, that you be appointed to the University Financial Board.'

As always, Scuby managed to make the word 'board' rhyme with 'bard'. Isaac Newton delayed his reply for what he judged to be a polite interval and then said:

'Unfortunately there are only so many hours in the day.'

'I am aware of that, Professor Newton, and have often remarked on it to my wife. The problem for the University is that its most able officers tend very naturally to be the busiest. If they all refuse to serve, well, you can see what happens,' Scuby concluded, with a note of appeal in his voice.

'You wouldn't consider appointing Professor Boulton instead?'

'Heaven forbid!' Scuby exclaimed, his mouth remaining open as he pondered the full horror of the idea.

'I think you'd hardly deny that I've got a pressing state of affairs on my hands just at the moment, Mr Scuby.'

'Of course, Professor Newton. But pressing affairs come and go. I've seen very many of them over the years. In the University, however, change comes more slowly but just as decisively. Shakespeare, you will recall, said: ''Small showers last long, but sudden storms are short''.'

'The present situation may fade away, or it may not. We still don't know.'

'I think you will find public interest to be fickle. Unless it is constantly titillated, memories soon fade.'

'But the University goes on?'

'Exactly so,' nodded Scuby, 'which is how we must all think about it. I hope you *will* think about it, Professor Newton.'

'I promise to do so,' Isaac Newton nodded.

Scuby stood to take his leave.

'I wasn't looking for an immediate answer, of course.'

After the door had closed, Isaac Newton continued to stare into the distance, thinking that Wordsworth had got it all wrong. The shades of the prison house closed, not about the growing boy, but about the aging academic.

Chapter 38

'We believe you have some things wrong, Isaac,' said Kurt Waldheim as he and Frances Margaret Haroldsen came into Isaac Newton's office. Waldheim was carrying a large mug of steaming hot coffee with which he constantly warmed his hands.

'This wet cold you have in Cambridge is, I think, worse than the top of Mount Everest,' he said.

'So what is it I have wrong?' Isaac Newton asked.

'This spinning blindly in space,' Kurt Waldheim said. 'In your learned exposition to us all the other night, you referred to comets as spinning blindly. Disoriented, you said. But why should there not be sensors at the surface of a comet? Sensors all over the surface of every comet, like eyes – like a thousand eyes, or a million eyes. Eh, Isaac? What have you to say to so powerful an idea?' Waldheim ended with his usual half-humorous smile.

'Comets move in orbits which take them very far away from the Sun. In fact, they spend the overwhelming fraction of their time very far away from the Sun, so far away that the temperature at their surface can't be much above absolute zero. It's just that I don't see eyes working very well near absolute zero,' Isaac Newton answered.

'Not biological eyes, of course,' agreed Waldheim, 'but electronic eyes. Why not, Isaac?'

'Electronic eyes need a manufacturing industry. To separate their materials – elements like selenium, semi-conductors and so on.'

'Still, why not? Biological cells are especially efficient at separating the different elements. Your own argument about biological nuclear reactors inside comets depended on exactly this point. Or did I get you wrong, Isaac?' Waldheim persisted, still with his quiet, humorous smile.

'There would have to be some kind of wires or conducting channels connecting the frozen surface to the warmer insides,' Isaac Newton continued, 'otherwise the information from the sensors couldn't be processed.'

'Again, why not? You know, Isaac, you are beginning to have the look of a man who is hard-pressed in an argument. A desperate look is starting to glaze your countenance.'

Frances Margaret was perched on one of the arms of the large leather chair.

'The sensible thing,' she said, 'is to suppose the best, to suppose that whatever *might* be possible *is* so, if you see what I mean.'

Isaac Newton tapped the desk top with a pencil, and then nodded somewhat reluctantly.

'Very well then, let's suppose the best. Suppose Comet Halley has sensors of some kind all over its surface. You'd want the sensors to be phase-correlated, I suppose?'

'Why not?' agreed Kurt Waldheim.

'So the comet could correlate its sensors....' Isaac Newton continued.

'To act like a large telescope,' Frances Margaret concluded.

'At all wavelengths?'

'Not all at once, perhaps,' Waldheim acknowledged, 'unless the comet's surface is divided up into a number of telescopes, some for short wavelengths and others for longer wavelengths.'

'And with broadcasting as well as receiving facilities?'

'Again, why not? What's the matter, Isaac?' Waldheim asked.

'Just the flash of an idea.'

'Would it be proper to ask what it might be?'

'No, it would not. The idea was one that some people might not particularly like.'

'Better we know nothing about it?'

'Like little children,' Frances Haroldsen interposed.

'Much better,' nodded Isaac Newton. 'What the eye doesn't see, the heart doesn't grieve over.'

'Thank you,' she grimaced, shifting her position on the arm of the chair.

'In short,' Isaac Newton went on, 'the comet can either receive signals in a beam or transmit them in a beam. So it can form a picture of the world outside itself.'

'The sky at night,' agreed Frances Margaret. 'A clear sky, too, without clouds.'

'Even though the comet is spinning around.'

'Yes, even though the comet is spinning around. Even though it spins around in three or four hours. The situation wouldn't be much different from ours here on Earth.'

'Except,' emphasised Kurt Waldheim, holding up a hand, 'if there are several arrangements equivalent to telescopes, there could always be one of them on the dark side, pointing away from the Sun.'

'A veritable hydra-headed monster you're trying to sell me, Kurt. Eyes in all directions.'

'A fine situation, is it not?'

Isaac Newton seemed lost in thought and a silence descended on the

three. Kurt Waldheim went to a blackboard on one of the office walls
and began to calculate in a small neat hand, while Frances Haroldsen
adjusted her position once again on the arm of the black leather chair.
At length, Isaac Newton got up from his desk, walked to a window,
then turned and said in a distant voice:

'I can see the Comet could decide how to beam these telescopes if it
were looking out into space. It would look towards interesting things,
just as we do ourselves. But how would it decide to beam its
transmissions?'

'Well, if it can see the Earth, why should there be any difficulty?'
Frances Margaret replied.

'What Isaac is getting at, and I can see it coming at us from no great
distance,' Kurt Waldheim began with his slow smile as he turned from
the blackboard, 'is how would one comet know to beam a transmission
to another comet?'

'That's right!' Isaac Newton exclaimed. 'Comets mostly inhabit the
far recesses of the solar system, where they're essentially invisible.'

'Optically, perhaps, but how about radio?' asked Frances Margaret.

'If one comet knew just where another one was, they could
communicate by radio, of course. But they don't and they can't,' Isaac
Newton answered. 'If there were only a hundred comets, I could see
ways for them to learn each other's positions: by transmitting towards
the Sun they could find Comet Halley, for instance. Then Comet
Halley would know where each one was and could inform the others.'

'It would be necessary to determine distances as well as directions,'
Kurt Waldheim pointed out.

'Agreed. But it could probably be done, so long as only a few
comets were involved. Comet Halley is a doomed comet, evaporating
steadily away into space. It could cope with finding the positions of a
handful of the others, but that would be only a drop in the ocean
compared to all the billions of comets.'

'What in all this obscurity are you getting at, Isaac?'

'I was thinking of each comet as the cell of a giant brain, a truly
giant brain. Even a single comet is likely to be a giant brain by our own
standards, but think of a brain with hundreds of billions of distinct
parts, each component a whole comet. But at present it is a brain with
all its cells disordered, out of communication with each other. A giant
brain in what we might call a vegetable condition.'

'Go on,' Frances Haroldsen encouraged when Isaac Newton
hesitated for a moment.

'Ever since we began this business, I've felt a sense of urgency – as if
there was something crucially important to be done. In a way, I think

everybody has the same feeling. Not about comets, but about there being a purpose of some sort.'

'In human life?'

'In human life, yes. People have felt it down the ages, which is why they built churches, why they had an instinctive belief in a relationship between themselves and a mysterious purpose somehow connected with the sky. – a purpose connected with the world outside the Earth.'

'This is very mystic, Isaac. It isn't something we can calculate.'

'That's just where you're wrong, Kurt. Suppose I argue that we humans have a pre-programmed sense of purpose. When identified properly, it isn't mystic at all. The purpose is to build a sort of cosmic telephone exchange, a nerve centre that would wake a truly giant brain out of its present vegetable condition into a dominating factor in our Galaxy. Perhaps even a dominating factor in the whole Universe.'

'Fine words, Isaac, but how do we calculate?'

'We calculate if the thing is possible.'

'Very well, let us calculate if the thing is possible.'

Kurt Waldheim rubbed out carefully and slowly the symbols he had written earlier on the blackboard, and he then turned to Isaac Newton with a serious expression.

'So?'

'The first thing to be decided is how many telescopes we would need for our cosmic telephone exchange. Suppose there are a hundred billion comets in all, and suppose each telescope could provide channels sufficient for . . . say a thousand comets. Then we should need a hundred million telescopes.'

'That is a lot of telescopes, Isaac!'

'I'm aware of it. But that's only a value judgement, not a calculation. Let's begin by estimating how much space we'd need. Say a square kilometre for each telescope, which would surely be more than ample. So the requirement is for a standing space of a hundred million square kilometres. How does that compare with the Earth's surface?'

'The whole of the Earth?'

'Yes, the whole of the Earth. If we need more space than the whole of the Earth then the idea is impossible. Otherwise it's possible.'

Kurt Waldheim calculated for a moment and then said:

'The whole Earth is about five hundred million square kilometres, of which two-thirds is ocean. Therefore the available land surface is somewhat less than two hundred million square kilometres. Your idea survives, Isaac, but not by much.'

'It survives. That's all we need to know for the moment. Besides which, I was very conservative in the area I took for each telescope.'

'How about cost? It would surely be preposterous,' Frances Margaret came in.

'Right. Let's look at the cost. How much for each telescope?'

'Well, you wouldn't want them cheap and nasty. Present cost would be a hundred million dollars a crack,' Frances Margaret continued.

'That would be for telescopes ordered in ones and twos. Ordered in bulk, with improvements in technology as the project went along, they'd come down quite a bit. Say ten million dollars a crack,' Isaac Newton decided.

Kurt Waldheim immediately jotted down a figure of $1,000,000,000,000,000 on the blackboard, and said with his humorous grin:

'You are not given to small thinking, Isaac.'

To which Isaac Newton replied:

'A thousand billion is about a hundred times the annual income of the whole world. But we're not concerned with a single year. What matters is that humans should construct the complete telephone exchange, not in one of *our* years, but in the orbital periods of the comets themselves, which run to about a hundred thousand Earth years. So we'd be on track if we said this is a project for many millennia, not for a century or a decade. Then it would cost no more than a few percent of the human economic turnover. Which would be dead right, because it would provide a directive influence for the whole of human economic activity.'

'That's very odd,' said Frances Margaret thoughtfully.

'What's odd?'

'Well, when you look at economics, it's like a ship without a rudder – out of control, with all sorts of people rushing to snatch at the tiller. I mean politicians, economists and soothsayers generally. Yet the thing is like a greasy pole. Nobody seems able to come to grips with it.'

Isaac Newton nodded as new thoughts struck him in rapid succession.

'Yes,' he said at length. 'It all fits. It fits almost uncannily, doesn't it? If the project had been smaller it wouldn't have done much. But this would supply a steady direction...'

'...with a great pressure forward in electronics,' Kurt Waldheim agreed.

'And steady, purposeful employment for a large number of people.'

'But it can't be done, I'm afraid,' Frances Margaret said regretfully.

'Why not?'

'Because of the politics. You couldn't have people mounting such a huge project and have a superpower confrontation at the same time.

Economically it wouldn't work.'

There was a long silence, broken eventually by Isaac Newton.

'It all comes into focus,' he began. 'Humans have a choice. They can oppose each other in superpower confrontations, leading probably to disaster and extinction, leaving the solar system as a perpetual vegetable; or they can lift the importance of our system to a level of which it is hard even to imagine.'

Kurt Waldheim wasn't to be drawn by these high-flown sentiments.

'I find it à little bit strange,' he said, 'that the economic scale comes out rather the way it was for the Pharaohs when they built the pyramids, which also lasted for a millennium or two. Proportionately to our technology, it is the same.'

'And the same as the military budgets of the Earth,' Frances Margaret added. 'The same controlling effect on people in general; the same as the building of Stonehenge in really ancient times, I suppose. But how could it ever happen? People just wouldn't buy this kind of thing. It's been quite difficult enough so far for us to get just one small satellite.'

'There's a big difference,' Isaac Newton countered. 'Previously we were working in the dark, without knowing what we were looking for.'

'And now that we know . . .' Frances Margaret asked.

'. . . or think we know,' Kurt Waldheim added.

'We've got to do it,' Isaac Newton replied, giving the simplest possible answer.

'Just like that! We've got to do it. Change everything!'

'Well, what else is there to do, except attend to one or two little tactics without losing any more time in trying to convince a pair of unbelievers like you?' Isaac Newton concluded.

'What might these little tactics be?' Kurt Waldheim wanted to know, but any reply that Isaac Newton might have made was interrupted by the telephone.

After listening for a short while, Isaac Newton replaced the receiver and said:

'Back to reality. It was the Prime Minister's office. They've decided to call a general election.'

Chapter 39

A log fire crackled pleasantly in a large open grate as Isaac Newton sank into an armchair, scotch and soda in hand. He had driven from Cambridge to Godfrey Wendover's farm near Midhurst in Sussex.

'I'm sorry if I've deflected you from the campaign trail,' he said.

'Frankly, I'm not too unhappy about being deflected from that particular trail. We've still got another week of it, and the last few days before an election are always a bit of a nightmare. There's always a chance of making some horrible gaffe which you haven't time to live down before polling day,' the Chancellor of the Exchequer replied.

'I rather thought all the voters have their minds made up already, so it doesn't matter too much from here on what anybody says.'

'Mostly that's true. But there's always a last few percent who remain undecided. And even the very last percent can make all the difference in the marginals. In the old days we used to think about an election as a whole, which was tolerably restful. Now all the talk is about the marginals, where it may come down to the last few hundred votes.'

'Well, Chancellor, I don't want you to lose those last few hundred votes because of me. Which is why I came down here,' Isaac Newton explained.

'How could that be? Frankly, we've gained quite a bit from Comet Halley. Sorry about it, really. But with the comet showing up so brilliantly now, and with all the ballyhoo in the media about it – it was just too tempting.'

'Flesh and blood could hardly resist, I suppose.'

'Not the Prime Minister's flesh and blood, anyway. Not with only another year for us to run.'

'The point is, I've got into hottish water, and I thought you should know about it,' Isaac Newton said, the expression on his face more bellicose than contrite.

'I thought you were tolerably used to being in hot water,' remarked the Chancellor, settling himself into an armchair on the opposite side of the fireplace.

'I want to cut out of this satellite business,' Isaac Newton began. 'I'm uncomfortable with satellites.'

'Why?'

'Because we're in other people's hands all the time: other people's hands for the launcher, and even for package space.'

'It wouldn't be your old feud with CERC rearing its ugly head?'

'To some extent, yes. CERC is the Government's main channel for space satellites. So inevitably the balance is likely to tilt that way – away from the University and into the clutches of civil servants.'

'Pity me, for I'm in their clutches all the time,' mused the Chancellor in a wistful voice. 'But how is it possible to avoid satellites, if I may ask?'

'You'll recall we needed a satellite . . .'

'. . . because Comet Halley used a very long wavelength. Yes, I remember. It's written on my heart. That way all manner of radio interference at ground-level was avoided. You see, I learned my lessons very well.'

'Fine,' nodded Isaac Newton. 'The point is that ground-level interference can be avoided in another way.'

'Then why did we go to all that trouble?'

'The comets forced it themselves in the beginning. But now the position is different because we have a two-way transmission going. You see, Chancellor, I sent out a shorter wavelength in parallel with the longer wavelength. The short wavelength signal had the advantage of going directly to Comet Halley, instead of being relayed through the satellite.'

'Which you could do from the ground?'

'Yes, easily. We did it directly from the Cavendish.'

'What happened to interference from other ground transmissions?'

'I used a forbidden band – one of the bands reserved for radio-astronomers which nobody is supposed to use for transmission. It's prohibited by international treaty.'

'Between Governments?'

'Yes, it's forbidden not just to commercial traffic but even to the military. Warsaw Pact nations as well as NATO, and, of course, forbidden to Governments themselves.'

'Then you'd better not do it again!'

'Too late, Chancellor. The fat's in the fire already.'

Godfrey Wendover shifted himself and took a sip from his gin and tonic.

'How can the fat be in the fire already?'

'Because Comet Halley seized on the shorter wave transmission immediately. It must have interpreted the change of wavelength as an invitation, a sort of guarantee that it could use the channel without there being an interference problem.'

'Which you say there isn't?'

'That's right.'

'So what's the problem?'

'The problem is that Comet Halley is now transmitting on the shorter wavelength. It's coming straight through the ionosphere to ground-level, and it's swamping the radioastronomers. They've lost their channel.'

'And they're not too pleased about it, I suppose?'

'To put it mildly, Chancellor. I'd expected some sort of a protest, of course, but not quite the uproar they've actually stirred up. It's being done through ICSU.'

'ICSU?'

'The International Council of Scientific Unions.'

'Who represents ICSU in this country?'

'The Royal Society.'

'I see,' said the Chancellor thoughtfully. 'What exactly is happening?'

'I expected things to build up over a period of two or three months, but it's happened at almost lightning speed. The Royal Society's Scientific Information Committee is meeting tomorrow. By itself it isn't a particularly formidable committee, but ICSU representatives from abroad will be there, as well as the Society's own senior officers. So the Committee has been puffed up into something a lot bigger than its normal complement. And of course the radioastronomers will be there, thumping the table as hard as they can.'

'You've been invited?'

' "Summoned" might be a more correct description.'

'I don't quite see what I can do.'

'I wasn't expecting any action by the Government. It's rather that I'm suspicious about the haste. From the point of view of the radioastronomers the damage is done. It can't be retrieved except by allotting them a new band, which doubtless will be done – although the allocation procedure may take a little time.'

'Couldn't you have asked for the allocation of a band yourself? It might have been better to go through the usual international channels. With strong Governmental support I'd expect an international application for a band to succeed,' the Chancellor remarked.

'It took the radioastronomers years to succeed, with pressure from scientists in every country, Soviet scientists as well as Western scientists. I doubt, Chancellor, that the Russians or even the Americans could have been persuaded to push their own commercial and military interests to one side. Not quickly, anyhow – not before Comet Halley moves away from us. By the time we had a band free from interference, the opportunity would have been lost.'

'I'd hardly have thought there would be any particular political motivation from the Royal Society.'

'Not the Royal as a whole, certainly not,' agreed Isaac Newton. 'A canvas of the Fellows would show supporters for all the main political parties. But at the time of a general election, the fraction who support your opponents. . .'

'Might have pushed this business along. . .'

'That would be my suspicion. After all, the Government is getting some advantage out of its support of the Comet Halley Project. So why shouldn't your opponents snatch at a chance of unravelling your position?'

'There's no possibility tomorrow's meeting will be kept confidential?'

'Doubtless confidentiality will be the Society's official position, but with so many attending the meeting, so many visitors, the opportunities for leaking the business will be legion,' Isaac Newton told the Chancellor.

'I see.'

'What would you advise, Chancellor? To start with, do I attend the meeting at all?'

'Are you a Fellow of the Society?'

'Yes.'

'Then you must go. But say as little as possible. You'll have a taste of what it feels like to be under attack in the House.'

'Without any support from my own side.'

'Ministers don't always get support from their own benches. Then the position is doubly grim, I can tell you.'

'It won't be easy for me to say as little as possible; it would really mean saying nothing at all.'

'Obviously you must defend your position, but make your defence as short and as clear as possible. Then stick to it. Don't wander off into sidelines. Repeat and stonewall. Long experience shows the best tactic is to be as slippery and smooth as black ice. Don't lose your nerve, which is the worst thing. After all, you've got this waveband and they've lost it. Try to feel sorry for them.'

'I'd hate you to lose those marginals.'

'We'll brace ourselves for it. Try to give the media as little to latch on to as possible. Think of the media ferreting around to make whatever you say look bad; we have to cope with that sort of thing all the time. The safe lines are to be high-minded, and to wave the flag, of course. If you can bring yourself to be unctuous, praise everybody for their concern in the matter, but keep stabbing away at higher purposes

and that sort of thing. Which, I suppose, is not too far from the truth,'
the Chancellor remarked as he put more wood on the fire, stoking it to
a greater heat.

Chapter 40

Isaac Newton swung his car into a vacant metered parking space in
front of the Royal Society building in Carlton House Terrace. Frances
Haroldsen fed the meter, saying, 'It goes for two hours. Will that be
enough?'

'Possibly, but there's no telling how long this affair is going to last.'

'Then it might be better to leave the car stranded out in the traffic.'

'Out in the traffic?'

'Yes, to cause a bit of a blockage. You leave it with the bonnet open
so that everybody thinks it's U/S. You have to pretend to tinker with it
when you return, and it's better to be wearing overalls and have oily
hands.'

It was just like Frances Margaret to talk about overalls and oily
hands on one of the rare occasions when she was dressed in her
smartest city clothes instead of the usual slacks and shirt. The porter
on duty immediately inside the door of the Royal Society building
looked up as they entered, and without prompting announced:

'Science Information Committee. In the Council Room, sir.'

Isaac Newton handed the porter a banknote.

'Could you feed the meter? Likely enough the meeting will run
over.'

'Likely enough, sir. It promises to be a real meeting, by what I can
tell. If you see what I mean, sir.'

Frances Margaret's shoes made a loud clicking noise on the tiled
floor as they walked towards the staircase which led up to the first
floor. At the foot of the staircase the girl put her arms around Isaac
Newton's shoulders, kissed him, and said:

'You're going to need that. I'll see you at lunch. And remember,
the best policy is to attack. The trouble is you're more tactful than I
am – which is why you've got further in life.'

A buzz of voices guided Isaac Newton along an upstairs corridor and into an almost full Council Room. Since the actual Committee itself, together with its ICSU Sub-Committee, hardly counted more than fifteen, an appreciable number of visitors had evidently been invited. Many of the places at the large Council table had been 'bagged' through the device of depositing briefcases on the table, after which the attendees had gone to a corner where coffee was being served. They were now standing chatting to each other as they drank the coffee. From the sudden freeze which his entry brought in the apparently free and easy atmosphere of the room, Isaac Newton knew he was in for a difficult meeting. After choosing one of the remaining seats he went himself to fetch a cup of coffee. A moment later the President of the Society, Sir Alistair Airey, came in. He nodded towards some, shook hands with others, and eventually came around to where Isaac Newton was sitting.

'It has been suggested I should take the Chair – in view of the visitors from abroad.'

'It would be very appropriate,' agreed Isaac Newton.

'We have Artimovich from the Academy of Sciences of the U.S.S.R., O'Donovan from Washington, and Langevin from Paris,' Airey went on.

'ICSU members?'

'That's right. The Germans didn't send their ICSU man. Perhaps because they're involved with your satellite. Would you like to meet them?'

'If you think it could change what they've come to say. Otherwise there might be some embarrassment,' Isaac Newton replied.

'Then perhaps we'd better not.'

Shortly thereafter the meeting was convened and the minutes of the previous meeting were instantly nodded through. Without further ado the Co.nmittee then came to the agenda item entitled 'Transmissions in the reserved 408 MHz band'. The President explained that the 408 MHz band, reserved by international treaty for radioastronomers, was now jammed out by Comet Halley, and that the meeting had been called at the request of ICSU to discuss the situation. It had been called in London, partly because of British interests in radioastronomy, and partly because the first transmissions to and from Comet Halley had been British-inspired, especially through the Comet Halley Board and the University of Cambridge. Professor Newton had been invited to the meeting because of his associations both with the University and the Board. When the President had finished his opening remarks from the Chair, a dark-haired, slightly-built man sitting immediately to the President's right compulsively flung up an arm.

'Yes, Professor Trugood?'

'I would hope, sir, that we shall not take too much time over preliminary niceties. Some here have travelled a long way because of the enormous gravity of this situation, for which reason I think we should come straight to the basic issue before us.'

From the Society's yearbook on the table, Isaac Newton could see that Trugood was from the radioastronomy department of the University of Winchester. No help there, he decided.

'If I may come to the nitty-gritty of this matter, Mr President,' a grey-haired man continued quickly – evidently from his accent it was O'Donovan from the U.S. Academy, and evidently he was joining an attack premeditated with Trugood – 'I would like to ask Professor Newton if transmissions in the 408 MHz band have been made from Cambridge?'

'That's rather a personally-directed opening question, Dr O'Donovan, but one central to the agenda item, I must agree. Professor Newton, would you care to answer?' Sir Alistair Airey asked.

'On request from the Chair I will answer, sir, even though I take exception to Dr O'Donovan asking a question to which he must already know the answer,' Isaac Newton replied. 'Because of the great sensitivity of radiotelescopes, it must be perfectly well known that transmissions have indeed been made from Cambridge, or from a place very near to Cambridge. So the question really isn't a question.'

'Was the first transmission made from Cambridge?' Trugood broke out again. 'Did you start it or did the comet? Is *that* really a question?'

'Sir Alistair, I would like to remind both members of the Information Committee and members of ICSU that I am here at this meeting on invitation. I came to the meeting as a matter of courtesy...'

Isaac Newton waited for murmurs around the table to subside, and then went on:

'...as a matter of courtesy. I did not come to be subjected to a barrage of intemperate questions and remarks. If the meeting would like me to do so, I am prepared to describe what happened at Cambridge. Beyond that I am not prepared to go.'

'Yet you *are* a Fellow of this Society, Professor Newton, and through your Fellowship you are responsible for the undertakings of the Society, of which our membership of ICSU is a particularly important undertaking,' the President said firmly.

'I am aware of that, Sir Alistair, which is exactly why I have come here this morning, and why I am prepared to make a statement to the meeting,' Isaac Newton answered as calmly as he could manage.

'Very well, Professor Newton. The Committee will hear your statement.'

'Doubtless, Sir Alistair, everybody here will be aware of the circumstances in which communication with Comet Halley was established,' Isaac Newton began. 'Unfortunately the technology used was temporary, partly because of the limited lifetime of the satellite employed, but more particularly because our linking transmission from the satellite to the Comet was too weak to reach very far out into the solar system. Connection with the Comet would necessarily have been lost, and could not have been re-established for another seventy years unless a new system of communication was established.

'A new system, namely transmission from ground-level using a wavelength short enough to penetrate the ionosphere, was to hand, provided the problem of local interference at the new wavelength could be solved. One way to solve this problem was to use an existing interference-free band, which is to say one of the bands made available to radioastronomers. Another possibility was an application by the Project Halley Board through this Society and Committee for a new interference-free band, a band reserved for communication between Earth and Comet Halley, a band that would need to be agreed internationally. This second possibility would evidently have been preferable if it could have been negotiated with sufficient speed. Unfortunately there is no example in the past of such an international agreement being reached within the available time scale, a matter of months only.

'I was therefore faced by an unpleasant choice. Either to lose contact with the Comet or to use one of the reserved radioastronomy bands. I judged that use of the 408 MHz band would be the least disruptive, because research work in radioastronomy is done nowadays very largely in the bands reserved at still shorter wavelengths. My choice in this situation is known to the meeting.'

'Your choice was deliberate?' the President asked in a serious tone.

'Inevitably it was,' Isaac Newton admitted.

'Would you act the same way if you had to make the choice again?'

Isaac Newton thought for a moment and then nodded.

'I cannot answer that I would not.'

Trugood made no attempt to speak through the Chair. His voice rang out:

'If ever there was a statement replete with conceit, replete with self-righteousness, then this was it! I think the meeting should pass the strongest possible condemnation of Professor Newton and all his ways, which by now are becoming notorious!'

The President was wondering how best to cover this emotive outburst when he caught the eye of an incisive-looking, grey-haired woman.

'Yes, Professor Worthing?' he asked.

This must be Wendy Worthing, a mathematician from Manchester of whom Isaac Newton had heard.

'I came to this meeting with a quite open mind,' the woman began, 'fully prepared to make it up in accordance with what I heard. Unfortunately, I have heard nothing from Professor Newton that shows the smallest measure of contrition for what is very clearly a grave breach of the Society's international undertakings. You, sir, have already drawn Professor Newton's attention to his responsibilities as a Fellow of the Society. In a similar spirit, I would like to ask Professor Newton if he is aware of statute twenty-seven on page one-eight-seven of the Society's Yearbook?'

'I would rather not proceed quite so directly, Professor Worthing,' the President cautioned warily.

'But this is the whole essence of the matter, is it not?' Wendy Worthing persisted sharply, refusing to be put down, even by the President. 'In case Professor Newton is not aware of statute twenty-seven, I will read it:

> If any Fellow of the Society shall contemptuously or contumaciously disobey the Statutes or Orders of the Society or Council; or shall, by speaking, writing, or printing, publicly defame the Society; or advisedly, maliciously, or dishonestly do anything to the damage, detriment, or dishonour thereof, he shall be ejected out of the Society.'

'It appears to me that Professor Worthing has put her finger precisely on the point,' nodded O'Donovan vigorously. 'I trust it will not be regarded as improper if the Academy I represent should express itself in a very similar manner.'

There was now a long speech from Artimovich, the Soviet member of ICSU. Although Isaac Newton did not understand the details of the Russian words, it was easy to tell from Artimovich's face and gestures that nothing favourable to himself was being said. And so it proved when a translation was eventually provided. Like Wendy Worthing, Artimovich was rule-minded, with much being said about the treaty undertakings of members of ICSU. It was while Artimovich's speech was being translated that the meeting became conscious that Isaac Newton was tapping lightly on the table with a pencil.

'Would you like to respond, Professor Newton?' the President asked when the translation was finished. The tension heightened as a silence followed, a silence broken only by the steady tapping of Isaac Newton's pencil.

'Yes, I would like to respond, sir,' Isaac Newton eventually said. 'First, I would like to respond to Professor Worthing. I would like to respond by doubting the truth of her statement that she came to this meeting with quite an open mind. As a mathematician, she will appreciate that it would be more accurate to say that she came here with not quite a closed mind.

'Next, let me say, Sir Alistair, how much I appreciated your attempt to prevent Professor Worthing from reading statute twenty-seven to the meeting. By doing so, Professor Worthing gave the impression that all our actions and responsibilities fall within the purview of this Society, or, in Dr O'Donovan's case, the purview of the Academy he represents, and similarly in Dr Artimovich's case. Unfortunately, life isn't as simple as that, as the treasurers of all societies and academies are well aware. I would think it unnecessary to remind this meeting that front-ranking scientific societies the world over depend very considerably on the patronage of their respective Governments. Consequently, no such society is an island in itself. Not even the whole of science is an island in itself. Attention in some degree must be paid to what is of interest and importance to the respective Governments and to people generally. Since I myself have lived in this atmosphere for most of my academic career, it is perhaps clearer to me than it may be to some others.

'Before I withdraw I should finally like to leave the meeting with what I believe to be a helpful statement. Nothing that has so far occurred is more than a temporary inconvenience. But if the situation should become public knowledge, due to leaks from this meeting, people up and down the world are going to seize on other reserved wavebands, and the impulse to transmit and to receive a reply from Comet Halley in those bands will be irresistible. So it might happen that radioastronomers will lose *all* their reserved bands.'

'And whose fault would that be?' Trugood almost shouted.

'Not mine,' answered Isaac Newton as he stood up to leave. 'So far as I was concerned, nobody would ever have known. The situation was completely safe until it was stirred up by this Committee. The fault will lie in your own sense of self-righteousness, and in your attempt to exercise a little power.'

Frances Haroldsen was waiting downstairs. She came forward, her heels clicking as before.

'I finished my shopping early. How did it go?'

'Badly. I lost my temper and said terrible things,' Isaac Newton grinned wryly.

'Good!' grinned Frances Margaret in return, linking her arm into his.

'An interesting meeting, sir?' the hall porter asked with his eyebrows raised quizzically. Remembering his promise to say nothing, Isaac Newton answered by raising his own eyebrows. Then he and Frances Margaret walked arm in arm out into Carlton House Terrace.

Chapter 41

Over breakfast the following morning, Frances Margaret handed Isaac Newton a newspaper.

'Take a look at this.'

The paper was open at a page which carried the headline: ICSU IN CALL-GIRL DEBACLE. The piece read:

> Members of the prestigious International Council of Scientific Unions foregathered yesterday in London. During daylight hours they occupied themselves with what one scientist has called 'The Row of the Century'. But once darkness had fallen other ideas appear to have entered the heads of the learned men...

Printed there were pictures of Trugood and of the Russian Artimovich, each in close proximity to a girl who was, to the evident delight of the paper, *déshabillée* in the extreme.

'What the devil's been going on?' exclaimed Isaac Newton in astonishment.

'Maisie has been going on. That's the sort of thing she's particularly good at. Getting into hotel rooms and fixing the photography. It's going to cost you five hundred pounds.' Frances Margaret smiled.

'I beg your pardon. Did you say five hundred pounds?'

'I did indeed.'

'The situation is appalling.'

'On the contrary. It's just the way they do it in Russia, which must have made this Artimovich man feel quite at home. Actually it's very decent of Maisie to turn over the pictures at cost, because I'm sure she could have got much more for them otherwise. Very decent.'

'Decent or not, I'm not paying for them,' Isaac Newton stated brusquely.

'Not even for the Trugood man? Wouldn't you pay, just to please me?'

'No, I would not. Can't you imagine what it would look like if it came out?'

'Poof! One day you're full of talk about re-directing the whole Universe. Then the next day you run scared of what people might say about one or two quite tastefully-taken photographs. Fixing the Russian would make you a national hero overnight.'

'Even that splendid prospect doesn't change my mind.'

'Well, if you won't pay I'll have to look for someone who will. I'm sure John Jocelyn Scuby will pay. He knows which side his bread's buttered. Once he understands these ICSU people were threatening your contract, Scuby will open up the University Chest before you can say Jack Robinson.'

'The situation is impossible. Besides it's the University Treasurer who controls the Chest, not Scuby.'

'The more the better. Or I could try Professor Boulton. I hear he's bought The Ragamuffin, so he must be in funds.'

Isaac Newton put on his coat in a determined fashion and prepared to leave. As he reached the door he called back:

'I'm not paying for anything so completely disgraceful. And that's flat.'

'Can I use the rest of those Swiss francs you made out to me. The ones I didn't spend?' Frances Margaret called in return.

'Make sure they go through the numbered account then,' was Isaac Newton's last word.

There was a pile of posters on Mrs Gunter's desk bearing the inscription in large letters: EAT PORKYS AT THE RAGAMUFFIN. Below the inscription was a fresh-faced youngster biting into an indefinite concoction from which a red material dribbled.

'I can't make out whether it's supposed to be jam or tomato ketchup,' Mrs Gunter remarked.

'Where did they come from?' Isaac Newton asked.

'Professor Boulton brought them. He said he'd like the posters displayed all over the Laboratory.'

'I've a better idea, Mrs Gunter. Have them sent over to Professor

Featherstone at the Vet. School. He probably has a goat or two that would think the paper a delicacy.'

'There's a visitor, Professor. Dr Bristow from *Nature*.'

'Oh, is there? I wonder what he can be wanting? Have you seen the morning papers, Mrs Gunter?'

'Not yet, Professor.'

'Then you have a treat in store.'

'What's that, Professor?'

'Save it for the coffee break, Mrs Gunter. If we ever manage to stagger as far as the coffee break.'

'Ah, Dr Bristow! To what good fortune do I owe the pleasure of your visit?' Isaac Newton enthused with more affability than the exact state of his mind warranted.

Alan Bristow rose from the big leather armchair in Isaac Newton's office.

'Well, I'm glad you see the position as fortunate.'

'Don't say my geostrophical colleague, Professor Boulton, who I understand has just bought The Ragamuffin, has suffered a sudden set-back on the markets. You wouldn't like to run this in *Nature*, I suppose? It would make a handsome cover picture,' Isaac Newton remarked, handing Bristow a copy of the poster.

'Extraordinary!' Bristow remarked, after examining the poster. 'Is this Boulton really the 'strophics man?'

'The same. Would you consider mounting it in your office? Perhaps in one of those dark mahogany frames, alongside a nineteenth-century painting of stags in the glen?'

'I rather gather you had a difficult meeting yesterday at the Royal,' Bristow replied, evidently determined not to be deflected from the object of his visit.

'Oh, did I?' Isaac Newton answered, smiling amiably as he seated himself at his desk.

'I don't want to keep my cards under the table, so let me say that I had dinner last night with Trugood. He seemed to think you'd taken quite a drubbing.'

'Did he now? Well, suppose we find out how he feels about it this morning,' Isaac Newton responded, lifting the 'phone. 'Mrs Gunter, would you please get me the radioastronomy department at the University of Winchester.'

Isaac Newton kept his ear to the phone for a couple of minutes and then held the receiver out to Alan Bristow.

'The situation sounds chaotic. You'd better handle it yourself.'

Instead of troubling himself to listen to Bristow's staccato monosyllables and questions, Isaac Newton studied Boulton's poster more carefully than its artistic quality merited. Eventually Alan Bristow put down the receiver.

'I agree it sounds a little curious. Trugood doesn't seem to be available.'

'Even to the editor of *Nature*! That's rather unusual, isn't it? Considering how we university professors try to curry favour with you, Bristow.'

'I often wish it wasn't quite like that.'

'Ah, but the system of welfare support from the research councils forces it on us, you know.'

'Your quarrel with CERC has become well known, and I sometimes wonder where it's likely to get you.'

'I sometimes wonder, too.'

'And now you're taking on the world establishment of senior scientific societies. The position can hardly be comfortable, especially with every radioastronomer on your track.'

'I haven't noticed any particular discomfort, but perhaps I'm missing something important. Hopefully you can enlighten me. Tell me, Bristow, d'you think the man in the street cares very much about radioastronomy? Cares as much as he does about Comet Halley being alive?'

'Doubtless the man in the street cares more about Comet Halley. But that hardly matters, does it? What matters is what the Royal Society thinks, what ICSU thinks.'

'And what *Nature* thinks?'

'To some extent, yes. And what the research councils think. You may be happy to forget about the research councils, but you shouldn't.'

'Bristow, you're a remarkably contradictory fellow. Only a couple of weeks ago you were criticising me for being too autocratic, for lacking the spirit of democracy. Yet now you're doing just what you criticised before, saying that although the man in the street pays the piper, he does not, and should not, call the tune.'

'If I said that science is a democracy then of course I was wrong. Science is an oligarchy. Your fault, if I may say so, is that you are monarchical in spirit.'

'I see. Let the man in the street go out in the cold of a winter morning to earn the money we scientists spend; then let's all sit around sharing out the spoils by mutual consent and be damned to democracy. Shares all round for everybody with the scientists' trade union card. You know, Bristow, my family have been farmers for as far back as I

know their history, and they really have gone out in the cold of a
winter morning, the cold of every winter morning. So I don't see
things at all your way. Whatever is put in my hands, whether it was a
scholarship when I was young, or a piece of scientific equipment, and
now this whole Laboratory, I see as a trust by the people, a trust that I
do what I think right, irrespective of what your card-carrying friends
may say. You've made it clear you don't like my way of doing things,
which is your privilege. What is not your privilege is playing the game
both ways. Supporting the card-carriers and at the same time coming to
my office looking for tit-bits of information. Do I make myself clear?'

'Very clear. Unwisely clear, I might add,' Bristow replied, with a
sharp edge to his voice, as he took his leave by the door which gave
immediately on the corridor outside.

Isaac Newton picked up a pencil, tapped the desk for a while, and
then said to himself:

'That's could hardly have happened in Rutherford's day.' After
which he added:

'Which only goes to show how democratic we've all become.'

Chapter 42

'Yeeow!' howled the Master of Trinity as he withdrew his hand hastily
from the hot silver coffee-pot which occupied its usual place on the
sideboard of the large upstairs drawing room of the Master's Lodge in
the north-east corner of Great Square.

'It's the daftest idea I've ever heard,' the Master said, padding back
to where Isaac Newton was sitting. 'You'd better pour the coffee, Bad-
News. I've burned my fingers off. I'm finished with that damned
coffee-pot. My nerve ends have become supersensitive.'

Isaac Newton walked in turn to the sideboard and, using a muffler,
poured the coffee, with which he returned, announcing, 'There's one
thing wrong.'

'There's more than one thing wrong. But what in particular have
you in mind, Bad-News?'

'You should get yourself a set of silver coffee cups, Master.'

'Oh no, I can't bear the thought of silver coffee cups,' groaned the Master, blowing vigorously on his fingertips. 'Where are you living now?' he then asked.

'In what you might call a *bijou* cottage, out at Grantchester. Rosie Waldheim spotted it. She's amazingly good at ferreting around for houses. Then I took the place over when the Waldheims left.'

'He's gone has he, Kurt Waldheim?'

'Yes, you couldn't keep him away from CERN for long, not once the action here was over. But he'll be back as soon as we get moving again.'

'Well, you're not likely to move very far with this daft proposal of yours. Building millions of telescopes, God rest us. Haven't you enough enemies as it is?' grunted the Master, again blowing ostentatiously on his fingertips.

'I seem to accumulate enemies like insects on a car windscreen in summer. I just had a set-to with that fellow from *Nature*, the chap I brought here one night.'

'What was the trouble?'

'Nothing of my causing. At least I don't think so. He came along and started asking questions. It's a sort of pattern. They all come along asking questions about what I'm going to do next, and saying they didn't like what I did last. Then I boot them out and they don't like that either.'

'I'll bet they don't! You can't expect to push their favourite political party around without being pounced on. Come off it now,' the Master roared.

'Tomorrow will tell. Are you going to sit up for it, Master?'

'I always say I won't, but I always do. Although the outcome tomorrow is already a foregone conclusion – we know it from the polls. Then they'll do a computer analysis of the first ten thousand voters, with interviews of course. Then the computer will tell you the result and you can go safely to bed knowing the answer. But you don't. You sit around hour after hour waiting for the constituencies to dribble in, getting more and more bleary-eyed and drinking more and more beer. Or coffee, and that's worse, because then you really can't sleep. I'd write a play about it, only no theatre would put it on – it would be too dull. Yet everybody does it on election night, because everybody else does it. The thing is as daft as your telescopes. Get me another cup of coffee, will you. If you can face up to that coffee-pot again.'

'I've got the Treasury interested,' Isaac Newton remarked as he brought two more cups of coffee back from the sideboard.

'In telescopes?' asked the Master incredulously.

'In the economics of it. I've been thinking about economics recently, and that's a really daft subject for you.'

'The thing that's difficult about economics,' observed the Master as he sipped his coffee, 'is to distinguish the daftest aspect of it. Among so much that is silly it's trying to pick the darkest spot in a dark pool. Well, what's your choice, Bad-News?'

'Value, I think.'

'Expound thereon, with cheerful eye and ready wit.'

'The value of a company's products is said to be determined by what the products can be sold for in the market.'

'Good Adam Smith kind of sentiment. I can understand that – partially anyway. Some of the best books sell for little, while some of the worst sell for a great deal. But proceed, good auncient Pistol.'

'Then what is the value of the money for which the goods are sold?'

'The problem is yours, Bad-News, and the answer shall be yours.'

'The value of money is what it will buy in the market. So what might have seemed like a sensible beginning turns out to be nothing but a circular statement.'

'A tautology by God! I always knew it.'

'So I puzzled about value. Survival value to start with: food, clothes and shelter. I gave high marks to food, clothes and shelter, but lower marks to everything else. The next step down the ladder took me to things like dishwashers and cars, things that have a clear convenience, but which are not absolutely necessary. But the big step down the ladder took me to articles which depend for their supposed value entirely on our state of mind, which may change quite arbitrarily as time goes along.'

'Examples please.'

'Your television set. It has value if a programme is being shown that you really want to see, but it has no immediate value if all the channels are showing rubbish; paintings that fetch millions nowadays at auctions weren't thought worth more than a quid or two at the time they were painted; or so-called defence items like guns, tanks, ships and 'planes. They have value if you think you need them, but none at all if you think you don't.'

'Who thinks they don't need guns and tanks?'

'For more than thirty years the Japanese have done very well from thinking they don't, and the Russians have done very badly from thinking they do.'

'How profound is all this, Bad-News?'

'My remarks so far are introductory.'

'Then let's have the rest of it,' grunted the Master, swallowing the last of his coffee with an audible gulp.

'Things became interesting when I began to do a bit of arithmetic on my three categories of value – survival value like food, convenience value like dishwashers, and conceptual value like guns. First, I found that a surprisingly large fraction of what we're pleased to call our national product is only of conceptual value. Second, I found most of what we call progress over the years has simply been an increase in the proportion of the economy taken up by items of conceptual value. Which means that if people were to change their ideas of what they think important, quite a large fraction of our national product would go up in smoke. It would become an illusion.'

The Master considered this speech for a while and then nodded.

'It gels. Which is why we've a feeling we're being swindled by all this supposed progress, why we feel the economists haven't got their sums right. It's a Goddam mess all right, from which we in this College are largely sheltered, I'm glad to say. But what led you into all this analytical profundity?'

'Because I wanted to orient myself before approaching the Treasury.'

'With what? A hand grenade?'

'I wanted the Treasury to do an in-depth study of the effect of changing our conceptual values from guns and tanks to telescopes.'

'Does it make any difference?'

'Yes, it does. For one thing, there's a big difference between a steady situation and sporadic projects like building a ship or working a mine. In the old days when a battleship was ordered there was work for a lot of people, but only for a while. People flooded into the port where the ship was being built. Wages were spent immediately, without any development being put into the area, and at the end of the job there was unemployment and devastation. The same for a mine. Temporary prosperity, lots of building of mean little houses, and then a blot on the landscape as soon as the mine was worked out. Sporadic prosperity always leads to a bad end-result, however great the prosperity may seem for a while. But prosperity at a lower level that's maintained indefinitely has a different atmosphere to it, producing the kind of solid development you can see in a hundred market towns throughout the country.'

'And you're arguing, I suppose, that your daft proposal would give steady employment?' grunted the Master again.

'Yes, not just over years and decades, but over centuries, with constantly improving technical spin-offs. So it seemed to me.'

'And with this preposterous notion you went to the Treasury?'

'I did. At first they really did think I was mad. But with a nod from the Chancellor I got them to look into it, and the more they looked into it the more interested they became. Hopefully, we'll have their report in time for the next Board meeting.'

'You're not seriously going to try selling it to the Board? Oodles of telescopes?'

Whatever might have been Isaac Newton's reply was interrupted by the telephone. The Master answered it. A moment later he turned to Isaac Newton with an expression very different from his usual bouncy mien.

'It's your Laboratory,' he said. 'I'm afraid there really is bad news. There's been an explosion, a bomb they think, and some people are badly hurt.'

Chapter 43

The facade of the Cavendish Laboratory had been blown away, and the windows over most of the western elevation were broken or blown in – worst affected were the many windows of the ground-floor canteen. But it wasn't the physical damage that attracted the attention of Isaac Newton and the Master of Trinity as they walked from the more distant part of the car park to the building. In front of the main doors were two ambulances, and a third arrived in the brief moment which it took them to reach the building.

A stretcher was being brought out. It had a red-stained sheet over a body which lay beneath. Somebody touched Isaac Newton on the arm. Looking up, he saw it was Featherstone, the Professor of Veterinary Science.

'I got my people over straight away – we have some experience . . .' Featherstone said.

'Of course. Thank you.'

'We attended to the injured first, and they're nearly all on their way now to the Hills Road Hospital.'

Isaac Newton stepped forward and lifted the sheet. The body lying there inert, the eyes glazed, was Scrooge the storekeeper. Scrooge, who had worked faithfully and conscientiously day after day ever since the year that Rutherford died. Scrooge, who had found him a second galvanometer twenty years ago, in his scholarship examination on his tremulous first visit to Cambridge.

'Mostly it's cuts from flying glass,' Featherstone went on, 'which looks awful, but hopefully doesn't usually turn out to be as bad as it looks. One or two were in the corridor leading from the door, unfortunately, and they seem to have got the full blast. There was nothing we could do for them, I'm afraid.'

Another stretcher was carried out. Groans indicated that the man on it wasn't dead. He was swathed in a blanket with only the head showing.

'Good God, that's Boulton,' Featherstone exclaimed.

Isaac Newton watched as the stretcher was manhandled into one of the several ambulances, with Boulton still groaning.

'He appears to be badly hurt,' said the Master of Trinity.

'I don't remember Boulton being in there,' Featherstone added. 'It must have been one of my people who attended to him.'

Isaac Newton handed his car keys to the Master.

'Would you drive out to the hospital, Master. I can't just at the moment.'

'I suppose I can still drive. I don't do much of it nowadays,' the Master replied. 'I'll telephone,' he added as he made his way rather stiffly back to the car park.

'Would you thank your staff, Featherstone? I'll come over later to thank them individually.'

'You'll be wanting to look around for yourself. I haven't had time to notice the physical damage.'

'The physical damage isn't important, although I suppose I must take a look at it,' Isaac Newton replied in a hollow voice, as the two men went into the Laboratory.

It was obvious the pressure wave from the blast had ripped through the main corridor. The blast and the following suction effect had even torn doors from their hinges. Isaac Newton walked slowly with his head down, forcing himself through his nausea to remember details. He arrived eventually at the control area for the transmissions to Comet Halley. Because it was situated towards the eastern side of the building, with a considerable number of doors separating it from the main entrance on the western side where the explosion had taken place, there had been little damage to the control area itself. Isaac Newton examined the electronic equipment for several moments, then closed and locked the several doors which barred the area from the main part of the Laboratory.

Mrs Gunter wasn't at her accustomed desk, and a wind was blowing through a shattered window pane, reaching with its cold into his own office. Isaac Newton moved like an automaton to his desk, where he picked up the telephone with the intention of calling the hospital; but the line was dead. Something was peculiar but he couldn't think what it was. He couldn't think at all. Eventually he lifted both his fists, crashed them on the desk, and shouted:

'It's my fault. It's all my fault.'

'What's your fault, sir?' asked a voice from the open doorway to the office. Standing there was a figure in police uniform. The police of course. There had been police cars along the access road to the Laboratory. He hadn't bothered with them because they were too late.

Isaac Newton recognised the man standing there, a solidly-built man of about fifty. He recognised the Inspector first by sight, and then recalled the name.

'Inspector Grant, isn't it?' he managed to say.

'Yes, we had some business before, if you remember, sir.'

'I do remember. Naturally I remember.'

'You were saying it was your fault, sir. What might you have meant by that?'

'I meant we should have had a guard on the door long ago.'

'There wasn't anybody? Not even a receptionist?'

'It is a tradition of the Laboratory, going back to the very beginning a hundred years ago. Anybody can simply walk in through the doors. In Rutherford's day when the discoveries were being made that have produced the nuclear age – with all the nuclear age implies – there was still no guard. I suppose we must be unique nowadays in keeping to the old tradition. But I should have seen that times have changed for the worse. Especially with Comet Halley and all the publicity we've been getting. It was bound to attract every crackpot in creation.'

'So you think it was a crackpot?' asked the Inspector, seating himself in the big leather armchair.

'Obviously. We've harmed nobody. Who else could it be except a disoriented lunatic?'

'I just wondered, sir.'

'I'd have thought this was more a time to worry about the people who've been hurt.'

'Everything that can be done for them is being done, sir. You can rest assured. The point is you might be able to give me an idea that would help us in our enquiries. It's better if we can move now rather than later.'

'Then put a block on the M11 into London. And examine all the cars going into town.'

'Unfortunately that's hardly practicable.'

'Well, it's your best bet. With the M11 only a few hundred yards away it must have been easy to make a quick getaway. I should have seen the danger of the M11. It was damn stupid of me,' acknowledged Isaac Newton.

'I'm not so sure, sir. I mean about this being a job done by some lunatic.'

'Who else could it be?' Isaac Newton asked.

'That's what I'm wanting to find out, sir. This bomb wasn't a simple home-made job. You can see that from a glance at what happened. This building isn't a ramshackle construction, and you don't do this amount of damage with a firework. It looks like a pro job, not one of your crackpots. Which is why I'm wondering if you have any knowledge of who might have wanted to do it?'

'Frankly, Inspector, I can't pretend I'm widely loved.'

'I'm well aware of that, sir,' Grant remarked dryly.

'But I don't have real enemies, I mean enemies who would conceive of violence on this sort of scale.'

'Can you be certain, sir?'

'I can imagine someone wanting to hit me in the eye, yes. But nothing like this.'

'I see.'

'What d'you see?' Isaac Newton asked.

'It wouldn't have anything to do with this Comet Halley?'

'That was my feeling, Inspector. Certainly we've had a lot of publicity over the Comet. So somebody might have thought it a way to draw attention to themselves . . .'

'Too simple, sir.'

'So you say, but I'm not convinced. I don't see why a crackpot couldn't have used a lot of explosive. Deliberately or by mistake — through ignorance.'

'You can take it from me it wasn't a crackpot, sir.'

Isaac Newton looked up to see John Jocelyn Scuby standing in the office doorway.

'This is the most dreadful thing I've ever seen,' said Scuby.

'I'm horribly distressed by it, Mr Scuby. Can I introduce Inspector Grant.'

'I'm sorry we meet in these terrible circumstances, Inspector. What I was wondering, Professor Newton, is d'you have a list of everybody employed here. Doubtless we have the details down at the Old Schools, but it would be quicker if you have a list. Then I can make enquiries as to what has happened to each one of them.'

'The Master of Trinity has gone out to the hospital.'

'Good, but the Master will hardly have *all* the names.'

Isaac Newton took Scuby into Mrs Gunter's office. Then he realised he'd no idea at all how to search the files.

'I must have a list in my desk,' he half shouted in frustration. Then a frenzied search through the drawers of his desk produced the required list.

'Thank you,' nodded Scuby. 'Where can I contact you?'

'I'll either be here or at the Master's Lodge.'

'When I have details from the hospital I'll come again in person,' Scuby said. A moment later he was gone, leaving Isaac Newton alone once more with the Inspector.

'You were saying, sir?' Grant continued.

'I wasn't saying anything of importance, Inspector. It is the lives of the injured that are important.'

'I accept that, sir. If there was anything I could do about it, I'd be doing it.'

'I take it, Inspector, that your men will keep an eye on the Laboratory overnight?'

'Of course.'

'And overnight I'll consider your questions. The only thought which occurs to me at the moment is that the attack might have had political overtones – what with excitement at its height over tomorrow's election. But something of the sort has probably occurred to you already.'

'Certainly it has, but I'm working in the dark on that one,' answered Inspector Grant.

Isaac Newton stood up to leave.

'Since I'm in just the same position, Inspector, I think I'd like to make enquiries at the hospital. You see I was expecting a 'phone call but the line is dead. The Master of Trinity has my car, so I wonder if I could ask you to detail one of your men...'

'If you have nothing further...'

'I don't. I'm just too distraught to think clearly, I'm afraid.'

'I can understand that, Professor. Yes, one of our cars will take you to the hospital. I doubt you will find you have lost any time because the reports on the injured persons will only be coming through about now.'

Isaac Newton led the way downstairs to the shattered entrance hall of the Laboratory. As he and Inspector Grant emerged into the open air, Featherstone could be seen hurrying towards them.

'There was a call from the Master of Trinity,' he shouted while still twenty yards away.

Isaac Newton felt his shirt sticky on his back.

'Yes?' he managed to say.

'It was about your young lady friend,' Featherstone gasped, having evidently been running. 'She was one of the lucky ones. They've discharged her from the hospital, and the Master is taking her back to Trinity. But I'm afraid there have been three deaths, two of your assistants and a young man named McClelland.'

'Was there anything about my secretary?'

'He didn't say, but I understood quite a number have been discharged. It was more or less as I said. Bad for those in the direct blast, but more secondary for the others – cuts and shock.'

'Was there any news about Boulton?'

'If there was the Master didn't say,' Featherstone replied.

Chapter 44

Frances Haroldsen rushed forward as soon as Isaac Newton reached the upstairs drawing room of the Master's Lodge. He kissed her gently and then lifted her face. Her left arm was bandaged from wrist to elbow.

'They put in a few stitches. Lucky the glass missed my face,' she said, her eyes filling with tears.

'You should be in bed, young lady,' the Master growled from the background. He had a thick blanket over one arm. Coming forward with it he added: 'But at least you can put this around your shoulders.'

'I've had aspirins and that seems to take the throbbing off. What happened to the others?'

Isaac Newton caught the Master's eye and replied:

'According to Featherstone it wasn't nearly as bad as it looked. I haven't heard anything about Mrs Gunter yet. I wonder if I could use the 'phone to enquire?'

When Isaac Newton returned from the telephone at the far end of the drawing room, he saw that Frances Margaret had acceded to the

Master's request and was now tucked up on a settee with the big
blanket around her shoulders.

'They haven't discharged her,' Isaac Newton announced, 'but they
say she's comfortable, although heaven knows just what that means.'

'Being older, she's quite likely to suffer more from shock,' the
Master added in a controlled voice.

'Boulton didn't suffer from shock. They discharged him.'

'Oh, I rather thought he'd been badly hurt,' the Master replied.

'Apparently not.'

'I think I'd really like to lie down,' Frances Margaret suddenly
announced. The Master immediately sprang to his feet.

'That's very sensible.'

When Isaac Newton moved to accompany Frances Margaret and the
Master, the girl said:

'I'll be all right. They gave me a sedative to take. But don't go far
away. What I wanted to say is that you should try to get a military
guard on the equipment. And make sure they're regular troops, not a
special detachment.'

'I think you'd better go through into the snug,' the Master
remarked to Isaac Newton as he and Francis Margaret left the drawing
room.

Isaac Newton made his way to the snug, just as he had been told to
do. He was so deeply sunk in thought that he hardly noticed two
College servants bringing in trays with beer, coffee and sandwiches. In
fact, he only noticed when one of the servants stayed to light a fire. It
was a while before the Master returned, saying as he came into the
snug and sank into a big plum-coloured armchair, 'I thought you
wouldn't be wanting dinner. So I got them to send over a few
sandwiches.'

'I doubt I'll be wanting anything, Master.'

'I feel much the same way, but we should have something. I've
promised to meet the guard at ten o'clock at the back of the College. I
rang one of our honorary Fellows who's in the Army High Command.
You'll have to validate things from the Prime Minister's office, of
course, but he's willing to stand in for a day or two, until it can be
fixed up officially.'

Isaac Newton stared blankly into the fire, which did not suit the
Master's talkative disposition, the Master being eventually provoked
into asking directly,

'What's the matter? I know it's bad, but there seems to be something else.'

'There's a lot else, Master,' Isaac Newton eventually replied. 'I told the Prime Minister not long ago about how when I was a boy I used to watch the way a thrush deals with a hawk. Other birds try to fly away and are then picked off in mid-air. But the thrush runs a random sort of pattern on the ground, so that the hawk does not dive for fear of crashing and ruining itself. I've always thought the thrush's system was a good one, and I've used it myself throughout this business. But now with five people dead...'

The Master was silent for almost as long as Isaac Newton had been.

'*Five* dead you said,' he eventually said in a deep slow voice. 'Today I count three. A year ago there was the man Howarth, whose death was never cleared up properly. But who's the unfortunate fifth?'

'A grey-haired man in a padded fawn jacket. He wore a woollen bonnet with a big bobble on it.'

'For God's sake what has that to do with it?'

'He was killed by lightning, or so the police maintain.'

'I'd be glad to hear how a grey-haired man in a woollen bonnet, killed by lightning, has anything to do with this affair in the Laboratory,' boomed the Master, before biting into a sandwich.

'It hasn't, not directly.'

'Then why raise it?'

'Because it had to do with Howarth's death.'

'I'm listening.'

'I don't quite know how to begin.'

'Don't bother. Just begin.'

'Then I'll begin by asking whether you've heard from Howard Baker lately?'

'Not lately. He landed himself a very nice job, you know – organist at Chichester Cathedral. But what...'

'It would be interesting to put a call through to the Bishop.'

'Whatever for?'

'Just to ask how Baker is getting on.'

'Good God, you're not suggesting Baker had anything to do with it?'

'It would be interesting to know if there really is a Howard Baker at Chichester Cathedral. If there is, I'll lay heavy odds you'll find him clean-shaven.'

For once the Master was totally at a loss for speech. Isaac Newton took the opportunity of the intermission by taking a sandwich himself. He then went on:

'I've just made another mistake, Master. I said five people have died. The number should be six. There was a reporter, you remember, who was electrocuted at Howarth's cottage. But he didn't have anything to do with it.'

At last the Master's voice broke loose like a damburst.

'I think you take a devilish delight in all this obscurity!'

Biting into his sandwich, Isaac Newton affected not to notice the Master twisting and turning in the plum-coloured chair.

'Actually, Master, I'm so deep in it now that I suppose I'd better go on.'

'You had!' the Master exploded.

'Just before I came to the Cavendish from CERN I'd been involved in what you could call a sensitive matter.'

'I heard about it.'

'So it would hardly be surprising if one or two curious folk decided to keep an eye on me. In fact, I soon located one such person.'

'Baker.'

'No, not Baker. I'll come to him in a moment. But for the unlucky chance of my becoming involved with Mike Howarth the curiosity would soon have fallen a bit flat. The thing which sparked the trouble...'

'...was the possible military aspects of Howarth's discovery. You told me that a long time ago.'

'I soon realised the position was going to be quite sticky, and it was. Until we got a visible response from Comet Halley, most people believed the thing to be military. Suppose *you* were an intelligence type in that climate of opinion, Master. What would you do to get a finger in the pie?'

'Stir things up a bit, I suppose.'

'As a hawk stirs up the small birds, hoping to pick off something in mid-air.'

The Master moved to the fire and began stoking it.

'What I suppose you're hinting at is that removing Howarth in some comparatively unobtrusive way, like in a car accident, wouldn't have stirred things up, not sufficiently.'

'Killing Howarth in a car accident would have been almost pointless, which was why nothing happened to him until I arrived. The essential thing was to connect me with the business, visibly and publicly in the media.'

'So it was done in the Chapel, right under the nose of the statue. Is that what you're saying?'

'It was what Frances Margaret said right from the beginning.'

'A clever girl that,' grunted the Master, pouring beer from a big jug into two glasses.

'You know, Master, I never got those disks back – the ones at

Barclays Bank. The Coroner collected them on my authority.'

'Are you now suggesting the Coroner was involved?'

'I doubt it. What I am suggesting is that once the disks were away from Barclays they were up for grabs. Somebody got them.'

'That lawyer. What was his name?'

'Sherbourne? I don't think so.'

'The people he represented?'

'The Research Council? I doubt that too.'

'Why?'

'They would have told me. If only to score a bit of a victory. Somebody bamboozled both the Coroner and the Research Council. Even at the time I could see something of the sort coming. One reason why I'm pretty sure they weren't in it, you see, is that Sherbourne provided the key to everything. It was his questioning which almost brought the whole business into the open.'

'That's the last thing that would have occurred to me.'

'But it was. D'you remember when we both walked back here from the Guildhall that afternoon?'

'After your set-to with Sherbourne?'

'Yes, after my set-to with Sherbourne. I was so annoyed that I couldn't think straight. But you could have seen it, Master, so could Featherstone, so could Sergeant Atkinson.'

'Seen what?'

'Seen that we only needed to walk into the Chapel.'

'I'm not remotely with you,' growled the Master.

'We only had to see if there was a time switch on the organ.'

'I remember you pointing out in the courtroom that there had to be a time switch because nobody had mentioned switching the organ off. Yet it was off.'

'It was certainly off, because with everybody milling around Howarth's body one of us must have messed the keys – inadvertently, if not deliberately. Yet nothing was heard from the organ – after Mr Kent's wailing note had gone off, it stayed silent.'

The Master took a long pull on his glass of beer and then said in a puzzled way:

'I follow the argument, but I don't see the conclusion.'

Isaac Newton looked the Master straight in the eye.

'Suppose, as I feel certain was the case, that we'd found no time switch. What conclusion would you have reached, Master?'

Although the Master's *amour propre* as a story-teller and playwright was now aroused, the best he could think of was:

'I would conclude that somebody not in the Dean's party must have switched the thing off. The murderer you're doubtless going to tell me. I can see it in your eye. But why?'

'Because if the organ had boomed out we would have turned our attention from Howarth's body to the organ itself. Then we'd have found the wedge in the key which produced the wailing note. You see, Master, the murderer had to give the material of the wedge time to evaporate. It was a cool late autumn night and Mr Kent and the Dean had the police there quickly, sooner than the murderer probably expected.'

'I'm still vague about why discovering, or not discovering, a wedge was important,' the Master said as he drained his glass.

'Because it would have removed a sense of mystery. The Coroner could hardly have avoided a verdict of murder. The police would have had a clear target to aim at, and the connection with me would have been gone – I had a perfect alibi, you remember. And it wouldn't have been long before everybody began to ask what person knew his way around the organ in the darkness better than the organist. The man must have been waiting there. Not a pleasant situation, with the moonlight flickering sporadically through the antechapel windows. We all had a curiously spooky feeling, even the police.'

'When did you come round to it?' the Master now asked gravely from the depth of his capacious plum-coloured chair.

'The moment I saw the grey-haired fellow in the woollen bonnet. It had a big bobble on it.'

'Never mind the bobble. Just explain why.'

'He was waiting for us, bobble and all.'

'At Baker's cottage?'

'Yes, we walked straight into it. I managed to persuade Frances Margaret that we'd been discovered by accident, but...'

'But you don't believe in accidents...'

'Except in a play, Master.'

'What happened then?'

'Luckily for us, the man in the woollen hat was hit by lightning, as I told you before. The strange thing was that the bobble on his cap wasn't disturbed.'

The Master sat deep in the plum-coloured chair, transfixed. At length he brought his jaws together with an audible snap and said in a voice rising quickly to a crescendo:

'Lightning! Don't take me to be *daft*!'

'Daft or not, that's what the police will tell you.'

'And what d'you tell me?'

'Nothing that makes any sense, I'm afraid; except that when I returned to Cambridge I had a look at the organ.'

'Finding what?'

'As you might expect, it now has a time switch. The switch had been fitted recently, very recently, I would have said. Then I remembered Baker had been extremely ready to emphasise that people had swarmed all over the organ.'

'But he came out with his suspicions about the key being wedged.'

'Only when it must have been clear what my own suspicions were. Actually, he did it so well that I never suspected at the time...'

'Nor did I,' grunted the Master, 'not at all. Then he said he was having trouble with his pedals. He said the big pipes might have to be taken out, didn't he? How d'you think Howarth was killed?'

'At a guess, something taken through the mouth, possibly in a drink.'

'Something which produced a lot of adrenalin,' nodded the Master, adding, 'it wouldn't be too difficult to deceive a local Coroner's court, not if expert forensic people were behind it. I did once write a play on that.'

'You wouldn't like to telephone the Bishop?'

'Not just now,' the Master replied with a shake of his head. 'More beer?'

'Thank you.'

'I don't see how Baker could have had anything to do with this afternoon's affair,' the Master then went on as he padded from his chair to the table where the rest of the beer was standing in the big jug.

'Very likely not,' agreed Isaac Newton, coming over to the table to collect his beer. 'There isn't just one hawk in the world. My devastating mistake in this case was that a bird I took to be only a sparrow turned out to be a sparrowhawk. But before I come to that I'd like to tell you exactly where we stand with the Halley Project.'

'Don't say you've been keeping more cards close to your chest?'

'Very close to my chest, I'm afraid. You see, Master, I've been running my patterns like the thrush on the ground. Perhaps that's where I've gone wrong,' Isaac Newton acknowledged. 'The essential point about transmissions to Comet Halley,' he continued, 'is that nobody except ourselves has been able to establish communication.'

'Why not?' the Master asked after he had returned to his chair.

'Because the Comet won't reply, except to *our* callsign.'

'Why don't the others use your callsign? I know the sort of thing: this is Spotlight calling, Spotlight calling,' chanted the Master, back to his usual exuberant self.

'We seem to have satellites overhead all the time, these days, so a lot of people are trying to decipher our callsign. But that's essentially impossible, because it's being changed all the time.'

'By what magic formula d'you do that?'

'Well – and this is the remarkable bit of the story – really at the Comet's own suggestion. We've been trying hard, of course, to decipher the messages we receive. Mostly we haven't been too successful. But we did succeed with this callsign business, probably because we had rather the same sort of idea ourselves.'

'So you really have a two-way interchange going?'

'To a limited extent, yes.'

The Master whistled loudly, and then boomed out:

'No wonder the dovecotes have been stirred up a little more than somewhat.'

'I doubt anybody could ever anticipate in advance just how our callsign is going to change from day to day,' Isaac Newton continued. 'It's a bit like using a one-time pad, except that we work wholly in numbers without any translation into words.'

'A one-time pad by God! I should think the dovecotes are stirred as by our dreaded hawk hovering in a darkening sky. Why, the Comet might be passing on the most devastating information. You know it's always the disposition of Government to believe the worst. You might almost say that thinking the worst is the primary business of Government. God knows what might be going on between Comet Halley and its Board. Yowee!' exclaimed the Master, sucking in his breath with an inverted whistling sound.

'The only way to deal with a one-time pad,' Isaac Newton remarked, 'is to steal it.'

The Master thought about this for a while. Then he scowled and glowered up at the ceiling, snapped his jaws tightly again, got up from his plum-coloured chair and paced for a while before saying, 'Am I to understand that if someone got into that control room of yours it might be possible to steal this one-time pad?'

'You are to understand exactly that, Master. You are also to understand that the bomb explosion this afternoon caused a massive diversion which provided someone with just that opportunity. Immediately after you left to go to the hospital I went to the control room. Two critical disks were gone. But fortunately the wipe-out circuits must have made them useless.'

'Wipe-out circuits?' the Master asked.

'A device rather like the clear-store instruction in a computer. If anybody tries to shut down the operation or to remove vital information in anything but exactly the correct way, a clear-store instruction comes automatically into operation, and a record of it is made. I saw the record immediately I went into the control room,' Isaac Newton explained.

'So you definitely know somebody had been tampering?'

'More than tampering. As I've just said, Master, two disks are gone.'

'Although they'll be useless to whoever took 'em,' the Master persisted.

'That's right,' Isaac Newton nodded.

'Who could have done it?'

'Somebody who knew the Laboratory, obviously. An outsider wouldn't have known where to go or where to begin. But it couldn't have been anybody in the Halley Project itself.'

'Because they wouldn't have activated your wipe-out circuits,' the Master nodded thoughtfully, adding, 'but they would need powerful outside support. To organise that bomb, I mean.'

'That's right,' agreed Isaac Newton in a disturbed voice.

'Very awkward.'

'What makes it still more awkward was that I had that policeman on my doorstep before you could say Jack Robinson.'

'What policeman?'

'Grant, the Inspector we had dealings with before.'

'Did he suspect anything?'

'He always seems to be trying to find out what we're doing. He behaves more like an intelligence officer than a police officer.'

'Which may be true,' grunted the Master.

'Which is why Frances Margaret's idea of a military guard on the equipment is a good idea,' Isaac Newton remarked.

'Unless my memory has gone to pot, as recently as this morning you were telling me the military had only conceptual value.'

'Yet another of my mistakes, Master.'

'As a penance, suppose you come clean about the insider.'

Isaac Newton thought for a long time before he replied and then said:

'If you must know, it was Boulton.'

The Master also thought for a long time before he responded to this revelation. Then he enquired in a deliberately matter of fact tone:

'Why Boulton? Why not Featherstone? He seemed to be dug in pretty deeply when we arrived.'

'Featherstone has never been inside the Lab, except with me. In fact, I've been in his place more often than he's been in mine.'

'But he was there very quickly.'

'You couldn't miss an explosion of that size from the Vet. School. It must have been heard immediately, and it only takes five minutes or less to hurry across.'

'Boulton looked to be hurt.'

'If he was, the hospital doesn't know much about it. They have him down in their notes as having bruises and shock. Not much for a man groaning the way he was.'

'What was all that groaning in aid of then?'

'In aid of the blanket which covered him. It was quite thick. Remember?'

'So you think he got your missing disks out under the blanket,' the Master mused as he quaffed his beer.

'Yes, but he overdid the moans and groans. From the time I first arrived in Cambridge, Boulton has been in and out of the Lab, and always unannounced. He had a sort of minor genius for sliding in and out.'

'But you rented a house from him, if I remember rightly?'

'Partly because I needed some place – he must have known that – and partly out of curiosity.'

'Curiosity killed the cat.'

'Don't say that, Master!' Isaac Newton almost shouted. 'I'm only too aware of it. You see, I found a bug planted in the house and still I didn't take the man seriously. Even in the last few days he's been roaming around the Lab trying to stick up posters.'

'What posters?'

'Ridiculous adverts for a café he claims to have bought, a place called The Ragamuffin.'

'I know it.'

'And Boulton was always rushing off, out of Cambridge. Scuby will tell you he's never where he's supposed to be.'

'The trouble is that all this stuff is circumstantial.'

'One of the deaths wasn't circumstantial, Master.'

'What about it?'

'It was a young member of the staff called McClelland. He was on duty at the time of the explosion.'

'On duty where?'

'In the control room.'

'But the control room is at the back of the building, about as far as it could be from the explosion. Why would McClelland have left the control room?'

'I doubt that he did,' Isaac Newton replied.

The Master paused in the middle of another quaff from his glass.

Then he wiped his mouth with a napkin and said in a deep tone:

'Are you trying to say this McClelland was also murdered? Deliberately, in order to get at the disks?'

'It would be my expectation that a careful autopsy on McClelland would show that he didn't die from the explosion.'

'Which is saying the same thing.'

'The problem is whether I ask for a careful autopsy. If I do, I'll also have to do a lot of explaining, more than I feel I want to explain because I can't see what good can come of it. It can't bring McClelland back.'

'It's for the police to decide. You don't need to start telling them their job.'

'That's rather the way I feel about it.'

'How long do you see a necessity for this guard?'

'Until the Halley Board has had time to re-orientate itself.'

The Master scowled, took a deep breath, and said with a shake of his head:

'Hopefully that won't be too long. You see a more or less permanent military presence in the University would raise a lot of questions: among the students, in Regent House. People would start saying such activities have no proper place in the University. Not that I agree with such a sentiment but, knowing how things are, it would be said.'

'I suppose so,' Isaac Newton replied wearily.

A silence fell, leaving both men listening to the crackle of the fire. Isaac Newton suddenly felt desperately thirsty. He was just in the act of picking up his glass when the Master shouted in sudden alarm:

'But if everything is wiped, if your disks have gone, where do we go from here? The thing is over!'

'No, Master, my mistakes have been psychological, not technical. I learned long ago how to keep copies of things where people won't go looking for them. Once we have your guard in place we can be back on the air in a couple of hours.'

Chapter 45

The Prime Minister and the Chancellor of the Exchequer threaded their way through the bushes which grew along the crest of the Downs above Midhurst, a few miles to the south of the Chancellor's farm, where a meeting of the Halley Board had been scheduled for the following day. A helicopter flew above their heads on a course which seemed to be parallel to their own.

'I don't like that damn thing,' frowned the Prime Minister.

'Oh, the helicopters? I hardly notice them,' replied the Chancellor, striding out and idly swishing at one of the bushes with his stick.

'How many seats d'you think we owe to Comet Halley? Thirty or forty?' the Prime Minister asked.

'It's impossible to say. My guess is that instead of our actual majority of sixty in the House we'd have been down to twenty or thereabouts – without the Comet, I mean. The big point was that our communication to Comet Halley was a British first, and we haven't had too many firsts to brag about in recent years.'

'So we owe the Comet something?'

'In a manner of speaking,' nodded the Chancellor.

'Well then, I'm inclined to go along with this proposal of Professor Newton's.'

'The telescope proposal, I suppose you mean?'

'Of course. What else should I mean?'

'It's a bit odd, isn't it? Newton seemed to have the idea the Treasury report on his proposal would come out the way it did – the more telescopes the better. The strange thing is, it doesn't help the economy to do things on a small scale. The gain only comes if the project is big enough, otherwise it's marginal. Like the usual grants for scientific research.'

'There's no possibility that Professor Newton and your economists were in step, deliberately shall we say?'

'None, I would be sure.'

'Then we should do it. For one thing, a defined project is much better than an open stimulus. You never know what will happen when people are motivated, but to no particular end.'

'Until you see the project raising its ugly head in the inflation rate,' agreed the Chancellor with another swipe of his stick.

'What d'you think of the latest reports from Cambridge?'

'The bomb was a very nasty business. I know Newton feels badly about it. We shall be hearing from him at the meeting.'

'We should have put a proper guard there before. It was as much our fault as his – if it was anybody's fault.'

'What does Intelligence say?'

'Opaque. Desperately opaque, Godfrey. I can't form a real opinion, except that somebody seems to be sheltering somebody else.'

'At home or abroad?'

'Abroad, I would say. Our own agencies, even down to the local police, are only inclined to be nosey...I think.'

'A bit like water-divining?'

'Just a bit. You know, Godfrey, the more I go along, the more I appreciate the wisdom of the legal oath.'

'What wisdom in particular?'

'About telling the truth, the whole truth, and nothing but the truth. I doubt that what I'm told is ever really untrue, but I also doubt that I'll live to see the day when I'm told the whole truth – about anything.'

'Nobody knows the whole truth. There's the rub, I'm afraid.'

'Except after the event. After the event everybody seems to know the whole truth, especially the papers.'

'Well, we didn't do too badly.'

'In the election? No, we didn't. Actually I feel quite bouncy about it.'

They reached a lane which descended to the north where the Chancellor's farm lay. At the sides of the lane were thick bramble bushes which channelled the way down. About half-way towards a surfaced road which led to the village of Bepton, they passed a lone figure ascending the lane. It was not until they had gone another hundred yards that the Chancellor stopped short and exclaimed:

'Good God! Did you notice the fellow we just passed? He was wearing an astrakhan hat. That's Tom Taylor of the *Observer*.'

'It hardly seems the right time of the year for such a hat, I must admit,' the Prime Minister acknowledged, with a wrinkle of the nose.

'The strange thing is I met him at just this spot when I was out walking here with Newton several months ago.'

'Perhaps he camps around here,' the Prime Minister suggested.

'That's quite possible,' agreed the Chancellor. 'He must believe he's on to something. Newton told me a story about a sunken trawler.'

'Well, there are no sunken trawlers around here,' the Prime Minister said decisively.

'Perhaps in the eyes of the *Observer* there are,' murmured the Chancellor, giving another swipe with his stick.

Chapter 46

The Board met in the large kitchen of the Chancellor's farmhouse, a kitchen with polished brasses gleaming on the walls. The Board members were seated around a long rectangular table, the Prime Minister at one end and the Master of Trinity at the other. Isaac Newton was on the Prime Minister's immediate right, and on his own right was Kurt Waldheim, who had travelled from Geneva for the meeting. To the Prime Minister's left was Sir Harry Julian, the Treasury mandarin appointed to the Board by the Chancellor, who sat himself down on Julian's left.

Frances Haroldsen had a separate small table, to the left and slightly behind the Master of Trinity, on which she kept the records of previous meetings and made notes on the present meeting, her writing arm luckily being uninjured.

'I have an apology for absence from Sir Anthony Marshall,' the Prime Minister began. 'In strict confidence I might add that Sir Anthony is leaving CERC – for a Vice-Chancellorship, of course. Not Cambridge, where the Board is already fully represented. Why the Chairmen of our research councils should be perpetually gravitating to vice-chancellorships might merit comment from the Master of Trinity.'

'The path is evidently seen to be paved with gold, Prime Minister. Although if it is, I haven't noticed it,' the Master immediately replied, producing smiles all round the table.

'Matters arising,' the Prime Minister continued. 'Professor Newton, I believe you have quite a few things, some very serious, to report.'

'Yes, thank you Prime Minister. I would like to mention at this early stage the serious explosion which occurred at about four-fifteen p.m. on the twenty-fifth of last month,' Isaac Newton began. 'A forensic report on the explosion is on the table, so I will only say about the explosion itself that it is believed to have been caused by a bomb of considerable power.

'Of immediate concern to the meeting,' Isaac Newton went on, 'are the injuries suffered by the Cavendish Laboratory staff. In all, thirty-seven persons were injured, mostly due to flying glass, as in the case of our Board secretary. By the worst of luck three persons exposed to the direct blast were killed. All injured persons were covered by normal University insurance, but in so far as the Board judges its own activities to have played a role in causing the explosion, I wish to raise later in the meeting the question of payments being made through the Board to the injured, and especially to the families of the deceased.'

'How could the Board be involved?' Sir Harry Julian asked immediately.

'The Board might be involved because Comet Halley communicates its transmissions to us and to no one else.'

At this the Prime Minister sat up involuntarily and said:

'That's the first I've heard of it, Professor Newton. How does the Comet distinguish us from them?'

'Because of a continuously adjustable code which exists between us and the Comet.'

'Call it a one-time pad, Prime Minister,' boomed the Master of Trinity from the far end of the table. 'We possess a one-time pad, and what Professor Newton is saying is that somebody may have tried to steal it from us, using the explosion as a cover. If that is so, then the Board has a responsibility to those who have been injured, and particularly to the families of the dead.'

'Is the University wishing to divest itself of responsibility?' asked Sir Harry Julian.

'The University has no wish to do other than meet its obligations,' the Master declared.

'Is there any proof of a baleful intervention of the kind hinted at by the Master?' asked the Chancellor.

'I arrived at the Laboratory approximately half an hour after the explosion to find the control room unmanned. It was unmanned because the person on duty there was among the deceased. To cut a long story short, I found some unauthorised person had been there ahead of me, presumably during the preceding half-hour,' Isaac Newton answered.

'How can you be sure of that?'

'There had been interference with the electronics of a kind which could only have come from an intruder,' Isaac Newton answered.

'The electronics are of such a design,' Kurt Waldheim broke in, 'as to give a clear warning of interference by an outsider. There can be no question about it.'

'Have the police been informed?' the Chancellor wanted to know.

'No. Because of the sensitive nature of the situation, I thought it right the Board should be informed first,' Isaac Newton replied.

'If we are receiving signals from the Comet on a more or less secret basis, the situation appears to me to be highly sensitive,' nodded the Prime Minister.

'Distinctly so,' the Master agreed. 'We have a club of two, with all the others excluded. No wonder they were after it.'

'The reason we're being difficult, Prime Minister, is that it makes a big difference to the Treasury whether the operation in Cambridge is to be treated on an overt or a covert basis,' explained Julian, a man not unlike G. K. Chesterton in appearance.

'There's no way we could make payments on a covert basis,' the Chancellor explained further.

'Ah, I see now what your trouble is,' interposed the Prime Minister. 'Surely this is one of those little problems whose solution delights the subtlest minds at the Treasury?'

'I'm afraid it isn't really subtle at all, Prime Minister,' insisted the rotund Julian. 'If we come out with this business in the open, through the police, then we can make payments, such as we decide to be reasonable and proper, directly through the Board's accounts. But if we decide to maintain a covert status, as I rather think we may, no moneys can pass through the Board's account. Whatever is done must find its way through the Prime Minister's own unaudited account, the unaudited account in respect of covert activities, I mean. In effect, Prime Minister, the moneys must pass under the table between yourself and Professor Newton.'

'With the possibility that I might then decide to emigrate?' Isaac Newton asked in some amazement.

'Exactly so,' nodded Julian. 'It may seem odd, but that's exactly the way it must be done.'

'I think I'm very glad to be doing only physics and not governmental finance in public view,' said a puzzled Kurt Waldheim with his slow, humorous smile.

Two women from the nearby village came in at this point, one bearing a tray of thermos flasks containing tea and coffee, the other with two trays of sweetmeats of various kinds and descriptions.

'Ah, this is where we must watch our figures,' said the Prime Minister brightly, and then bit off the remark, realising belatedly that with Julian's figure so plainly in view a gaffe had been made. The gaffe was instantly covered, or not covered according to one's point of view, by the Master of Trinity who boomed out:

'Getting rid of one's figure can be reckoned a primary achievement in life, Prime Minister. It releases one from unbearable stress.' With which the Master bit into an enormous cream puff that momentarily whitened his lips in the fashion of a stage comedian.

The Prime Minister soon called the meeting to order, insisting, 'We must press on. The next item is future developments. Professor

Newton, we must call on you again.'

'The developments intended for this item have already been overtaken by events,' Isaac Newton began. 'Principally, we're concerned with decoding messages from Comet Halley. The thought isn't visionary, because we are succeeding more and more. At the present rate of progress, we should have developed fairly extensive interchanges a year from now.'

'What exactly has happened?' the Prime Minister asked.

'Comet Halley has directed us to other comets out in the region of the planet Neptune, and we've actually made contact with them. Until this morning I thought in seven cases, but Kurt Waldheim tells me that the number is now up to nine. This has been done by using radiotelescopes at Jodrell Bank and the Bonn telescope in Germany, as well as our own facilities.'

'We had instructions, of course, from Comet Halley on where to look,' Kurt Waldheim added.

'Where to look?' the Chancellor asked with a puzzled expression.

'It was a little bit subtle,' Kurt Waldheim acknowledged. 'We eventually realised that Comet Halley was giving us a catalogue of directions in which to look, and the question was whether the directions started from Comet Halley itself, or from the Sun, or from the Earth.'

'Only directions from the Earth would be much use, I suppose?' the Chancellor suggested.

'Yes, but we didn't get them that way. The catalogue turned out to be of directions from Comet Halley,' Kurt Waldheim told him.

'To begin with we had to shoot in the dark,' Isaac Newton came in. 'We made the conversion of the catalogue to Earth directions, and this was really quite hard. Not the mathematics of the conversion, but the distance of Comet Halley which had to go into the calculation. But one of the things we're operating now is a transponder system.'

'*Ja*,' said Kurt Waldheim, beginning to enjoy himself. 'We send out a signal to Comet Halley which immediately triggers a reply. Then by timing the transmission accurately we know the distance of Comet Halley. Then we know the directions of these other comets on the outside of the solar system. In effect, Comet Halley is acting like a sentinel, like a shepherd.'

'So what happened?' asked the Prime Minister, trying to short-circuit the scientific subtleties.

'We alerted the Anglo-Australian telescope in Australia and they kept watch visually when we made our transmissions.'

'They watched in the same direction as you made a radio

transmission, is that it?' the Prime Minister asked.

'Exactly right, Prime Minister,' nodded Isaac Newton. 'And in each case we got the same sudden flare-up from the comet – the distant comet in this case – that we got before from Comet Halley.'

'You mean that sudden burst of particles? Like a whale blowing off?'

'That's right. It seems to be a kind of agreed recognition signal.'

'And you say this has happened nine times?'

'Nine times,' Isaac Newton confirmed, 'and now our telescopes are beginning to get saturated – in Germany as well as in this country.'

'Why is that?'

'Because the comets are beginning to chatter a great deal to each other.'

'And they weren't before?'

'No, because until we established the contacts the comets couldn't find each other.'

At this the Chancellor held up a hand and said slowly:

'Am I to understand that, while the comets can't find each other directly, they can communicate by locking on to your radio beams?'

'Yes, one comet sends a transmission of its own back down our beam, which the comet is receiving, of course. Then we re-transmit the message along another beam directed to another comet,' Kurt Waldheim said, drawing a triangular diagram on a piece of paper, with the Earth at its apex, the two communicating comets at its base, and arrows to show the directions of the radio transmissions.

'I see,' said the Chancellor again slowly, 'in fact, I begin to see a great deal.'

'What d'you see, Godfrey?'

'Perhaps still a little darkly, I see what is going on, and it is rather terrifying. We've just taken the first step into an extra-terrestrial communications system.'

'You've got the point exactly, Chancellor,' agreed Isaac Newton.

'A tele-interchange system by God,' the Master broke in. 'But can we decipher these messages which are flowing through our telescopes and transmitters? That seems to me to be the big question. Otherwise what good does it do us?'

'It is my view,' answered Kurt Waldheim, 'that eventually we will be able to decipher as much of these messages as we may want. But that will not be all of it, because to decipher all of it would be impossible for us.'

'Frankly, I can't understand that, Professor Waldheim. Could you explain either more clearly or in more detail? Because this really is a most important point the Master has raised,' the Prime Minister declared with some gravity.

'I give you two different atoms as examples: the simple atom hydrogen, and the extremely complex atom uranium,' Kurt Waldheim began, reverting to his familiar smile, and brushing back a quiff of hair from his broad forehead with a sweep of the hand. 'We humans are capable of understanding the hydrogen atom completely. When we do so we understand the essential principles on which all atoms are constructed, and information of *this* kind, I think we shall be able to decipher. But the details, not the principles, of the uranium atom, the full details, are too complicated for us. Too many numbers to be sifted through by any method known to us – clouds of numbers, like the clouds of numbers that would be necessary to describe the movements of all the molecules in the air of this room, or like the atoms in our bodies. Principles, yes; clouds of numbers, no. That is what I mean.'

'What I think Kurt is saying,' Isaac Newton interposed, 'is that we shall be able to decipher all those things which seem important to us, the basic principles of situations. But what we tend to consider to be huge and irrelevant detail will escape us. Not because we couldn't decipher it, but because we couldn't cope with the huge volume of numbers if we did.'

'Why are these wretched clouds of numbers relevant at all then?' the Master asked.

'It's the difference between understanding something and making it. Every time we make something – a car or a 'plane or a computer – we have to calculate a cloud of numbers to begin with. But small clouds compared to what is involved here. The gory details, you might say.'

'The difference between an idea for a book and the mechanics of writing down all the words?' the Master then suggested.

'That's essentially the thing, Master. If you think of it in terms of a book, there's a limit to the size of book that an individual writer can cope with, because otherwise the cloud of words gets too big. And if you take all writers together and put their books into a library, there's also a limit to the size of the largest cloud of words that a library can cope with.'

'And you're saying this thing may go far beyond human capacity?' the Prime Minister asked again.

'*Ja*, that is the position exactly,' nodded Kurt Waldheim.

'But what would the end result, the product, be?'

'Something big. Something very big,' Isaac Newton insisted.

'Which is rather what I thought,' remarked the Chancellor. 'What I sensed from the beginning. Prime Minister, may I suggest that we break for lunch at this point. It's still a little early, but I feel we've all had something so important to chew on as it were, that we ought to digest it a little before coming to the later items on the agenda.'

'I must be back in town by six o'clock at the latest,' the Prime Minister warned.

'I'm aware of that,' returned the Chancellor, 'but we'll push the lunch along. I've arranged for us to eat at the local. It's quite good and they're very obliging.'

Isaac Newton climbed into the driver's seat of his car, expecting to drive Kurt Waldheim and Frances Haroldsen to the hotel in the village, but the Master of Trinity hopped with surprising agility into the front passenger seat.

'Come on. The others can follow. I want to talk to you alone.'

When they had moved off a hundred yards, Isaac Newton asked: 'About what?'

'About the money for all those telescopes, that daft project of yours. You've got it. I could see it in Godfrey Wendover's eye. So don't go mucking things up this afternoon.'

Chapter 47

After lunch, the Chancellor and the Prime Minister drove back together from the hotel to the farm.

'Do you really find it terrifying?' the Prime Minister asked.

'When you consider that we've barely peeped through the curtain yet, don't you find it terrifying?' the Chancellor returned the question.

'What else can there be?'

'I don't know. Even Newton and Waldheim don't know. They're feeling their way just as we are. But I think it's extremely unlikely we've seen everything there is to be seen, all in the very first moment.'

'This telecommunications system...'

'What about it?'

'Well, I was wondering if it could eventually go outside,' the Prime Minister pondered.

'Outside the Earth?'

'No, outside the whole solar system.'

The Chancellor thought about this idea for a while and then shrugged.

'Why not?'

After driving for a further half a mile or so, the Chancellor continued by asking mundanely:

'How are you going to take the meeting this afternoon?'

'Well, we've decided already, haven't we? There's no point in having a long argy-bargy on whether we do or we don't. So I'll concentrate rather on ways and means: the organisation of it, especially.'

'Even though we may be decided,' said the Chancellor, 'I'd appreciate it if you didn't cut Julian off too short. He's put a lot of effort into his report, so give him his head for a while.'

In spite of the Chancellor's claim that the lunch would be early, it was coming up to 2.00 p.m. when the meeting reconvened.

'We really must start firing on all cylinders,' announced the Prime Minister from the chair. 'So we will come now to the central issue of the meeting, the agenda item on telescopes. This morning we heard that instruments presently available are already approaching saturation point, both in this country and in Germany – just when developments are becoming most interesting. I propose to the meeting that we consider the need for further instrumental resources to be an established case. Our concern now must be ways and means, economic ways and means, logistic ways and means. First then, the economic ways and means, on which Sir Harry Julian has prepared an extended report, for which I wish to thank him and his staff on behalf of the Board. Sir Harry, would you care to take us through your report?' the Prime Minister concluded, thinking that if Julian could be kept to between half an hour and forty minutes, the next critical matter could be rolled through by four o'clock. An hour and a half against the traffic back to London should be sufficient, leaving a margin of thirty minutes before the impending arrival at 10 Downing Street of the Indonesian President.

Julian's account of his report was remarkably similar to Isaac Newton's conversation some days before with the Master of Trinity. Steady purpose was the theme of Julian's exposition. Steady purpose in the economic field, as well as in other walks of life, brought its reward, a moral which Julian emphasised with a steady waving of his pince nez. The Master of Trinity could not forbear making a number of interventions, which the Prime Minister laboured to prevent from mushrooming into full-blooded discussions. These interruptions apart, the Prime Minister's attention wandered, wandered into a picture of the room, the Chancellor's farm, the whole of Britain, being slowly overwhelmed by the steady purposeful advance of an enormous glacier, a glacier of bureaucratic dough. As Julian droned on, they all fell into a hypnotic state of the kind to which all committees and boards fall prey from time to time. Realising it was already 3.00 p.m., the Prime Minister decided to cut the Gordian Knot.

'Rarely, if ever, have I listened to so cogent a case as the one put forward by Sir Harry. It had been my intention to call on Professor Newton to present technical arguments in its support, but so thorough has Sir Harry's exposition been that anything further would surely be superfluous.'

'I agree, Prime Minister. It would be carrying coals to Newcastle,' the Master of Trinity intervened in his deepest, most decisive tones.

'Thank you, Master. Pressing forward then, we arrive at the question of how we can best go ahead with the imaginative programme proposed by Professor Newton and analysed so deeply by Sir Harry, assuming, as I think we can, that financial support from H.M. Government will be forthcoming. Let me not try standing angels on a penny piece,' continued the Prime Minister with an eye to the clock. 'At the risk of disturbing the existing state of affairs, let me say that basing activities in Cambridge as at present would not be the best arrangement for a continuous and extended programme of telescope construction. Our universities are best occupied with research activities, not with contractual work, unless it happens to involve a unique scientific instrument. What are your comments on that didactic proposition, Professor Newton?'

Isaac Newton thought for a moment, trying to recall exactly what didactic meant, and then said:

'So far as construction is concerned – by which I mean the overseeing of design details, the letting of contracts, and the continuing negotiations with manufacturers – I think I'd acknowledge that a university wouldn't be an ideal centre of activities. Construction activities, I must emphasise, not operational activities. Universities might well be the places, however, where the telescopes should eventually be located.'

'Not just Cambridge?'

'No, not just Cambridge. We're already making heavy demands on Jodrell. Obviously all universities who wish to do so should be encouraged to join.'

'Master, wearing your hat as Vice-Chancellor of Cambridge, what have you to say?'

'I agree entirely with the discussion to this point.'

'Possibly a consortium of universities might be the correct form of organisation, Prime Minister,' Isaac Newton suggested.

'The problem, frankly, for the Government is that we already have an organisation,' the Prime Minister returned. 'Not one that you approve of particularly, I'm afraid. I mean CERC.'

'I rather thought the resurrection of CERC would be somewhere in the offing,' grunted Isaac Newton.

At this point the Chancellor came in. Looking across the table squarely at Isaac Newton he said:

'I think you'll agree this project greatly transcends any purely personal issue.'

'If it were only a personal issue, not one of performance . . .' Isaac Newton countered.

'There is an easy way to guarantee performance,' the Prime Minister said.

'From CERC? How would that be?'

'I said at the beginning, in confidence of course, that Sir Anthony Marshall is leaving CERC. Which provides the Government with the opportunity to appoint you, Professor Newton, in his place. Such a course would provide you with the opportunity to ensure the performance you are looking for in the implementation of your own proposal. Can I possibly say fairer than that?'

Instantly there came a groan from the Master of Trinity:

'Oh no, I can't bear the thought. Are we to be left in Cambridge without visible means of support? To quote the good book, Prime Minister:

> O give me the comfort of thy help again:
> and stablish me with thy free Spirit.
> Then shall I teach thy ways unto the wicked:
> and sinners shall be converted unto thee.'

'A fine sentiment, Master,' replied the Prime Minister evenly. 'You hardly need to lift your eyes unto the hills to receive the help for which you crave. If you look a little to your left you will find a very present help in trouble. I refer, of course, to Professor Waldheim. Appoint him to the Cavendish and you have the right wavelength immediately, with everything then going forward at maximum speed.'

'Ah, but it is not so simple . . .' Kurt Waldheim began.

'It *is* simple, Professor Waldheim. After all, this is *your* project, you two gentlemen. My role is only to show you how best to implement what you so much want to do.'

'My wife,' gasped Kurt Waldheim, 'you see she has many votes, which in a democratic household can make for a little difficulty.'

'Let me follow the precept of the Master,' the Prime Minister continued, in full stride, 'by quoting the old saw: ''Where there's a will there's a way''. Which brings us to the end of business, remembering that on Sir Harry's advice the serious issue of compensations to be paid to injured persons at the Cavendish Laboratory is to be settled directly between Professor Newton and myself. Unlike a well-remembered remark of William Cobbett, I think we can say we have today transacted a great deal of profitable business,' the Prime Minister concluded, snapping files closed with a relish that suggested that all was now signed, sealed and delivered.

Ten minutes later the Prime Minister, the Chancellor and Sir Harry Julian were all on their way back to London in a large black chauffeur-driven limousine. Before leaving the Chancellor said:

'Stay on as long as you please.' Then with a cheery wave he was gone.

'Ho,' roared the Master, 'a deep-wrought fix, if ever I experienced one. The temptation, as with birds who spy a hawk overhead, is to scatter our forces. Waldheim back to Geneva, the other three of us helter-skelter back to Cambridge. But we are booked into the hotel for the night, since we had expected this meeting to run into tomorrow, having no thought of course that the Government was preparing to spend hundreds of millions, if not billions, of pounds on itself. My proposal, citizens of Rome, is that instead of disintegrating helter-skelter we in fact stay for the night. My proposal is that we repair to the hotel for extended council. Let us trust in God and keep dry the baccy for our pipes of war.'

Chapter 48

When Frances Margaret, Kurt Waldheim, the Master of Trinity and Isaac Newton assembled in the hotel dining room it was to find a table reserved on which four opened bottles of wine had been placed, two of them – the whites – in buckets of ice.

'I don't know about anybody else,' announced the Master taking a chair, 'but I'm going to drink myself into a damnable hangover.'

'Childhood's passing,' said Frances Margaret, taking a seat beside the Master. 'It really ended with the explosion, didn't it?'

'*Fin de siècle*,' nodded the Master, pouring from one of the bottles of white wine. 'I've ordered salmon all round for starters. No point in us fussing about courses, because we've too much to talk about. We've been outmanoeuvred. But nagging common sense tells me there's not much we can do about it.'

'I can refuse,' Isaac Newton said shortly.

'You can't, and you know you can't. People would say you'd funked confronting the civil service, for one thing. And you'd lose control over everything: control over building these damn telescopes, and then control over where they're to be sited; a series of battles all lost. No, you're in a cleft stick and you know it,' the Master asserted as he began to drink the wine.

'It is better to think what we can achieve, and how soon,' Kurt Waldheim remarked.

'If it were just a matter of heading a Government agency with the job of building telescopes the prospect wouldn't be so bad. But CERC has its sticky fingers into every aspect of British science,' Isaac Newton replied gloomily.

'Then you'll have an opportunity of getting their sticky fingers out!' Frances Margaret grinned unhelpfully.

'Not so, neither. The most notable aspect of the civil service is its amazing ability to frustrate anyone who seeks to change things.'

'So say all of us,' agreed the Master, pouring more wine and continuing, 'I'm going to get drunk. So I can start throwing things.' He quaffed from his glass and then groaned, to the consternation of a waitress who was bringing the salmon.

'Oh no, I can't bear it. The agony of it. Just when we were within sighting distance of the towers of El Dorado. I can't bear it at all.'

'Rosie will not bear it either. You see, there are no snow mountains near Cambridge,' Kurt Waldheim said, also in a gloomy voice.

'It's odd, isn't it?' mused Isaac Newton. 'I didn't really want to return to Cambridge, and now I don't want to leave.'

'It grows on you,' agreed the Master.

'Kurt, you asked what we can achieve. I'll tell you. Knowing the inertia of human institutions, we can gear up eventually to the building of about ten telescopes a year, when really we should be building hundreds. We can do it by holding tight to the reins and gritting our teeth, though all around us howl perpetually with derision.'

'Contumely is the correct word,' the Master managed to insert into

Isaac Newton's disconsolate speech.

'We can make sure the telescopes are sited in the right places and we can set up a group of universities to oversee their operation. We can push ahead with the decoding problem so that by the time we reach retirement age the thing may have enough momentum to continue. All this is assuming we can fight off changes of Government. And provided the superpowers don't annihilate each other, taking everybody else with them.'

'It isn't as much fun as science,' Kurt Waldheim nodded in agreement. 'You will need to persuade Rosie, Isaac. I know I cannot.'

'You will do it, the Cavendish?' Frances Margaret asked.

'I haven't yet been asked,' said Kurt Waldheim, avoiding the question.

'No, but the Prime Minister has a long arm.'

'I would have to do it, because of the way things are. If Rosie will let it happen, which I doubt. Tomorrow you must come back with me to Geneva, Isaac.'

The Master re-charged glasses all round.

'Let us eat, drink, and be merry. Why is the world never the way we would like it to be? We've been out-generalled if not out-fought, I fear. Oh no, I can't bear it, the thought of it, the disgrace of it.'

'I'm not so sure about all that,' observed Frances Margaret.

'Expound thereon, rare wench.'

'Well for one thing, they've agreed to fund the programme, which wasn't by any means a foregone conclusion. And for another, it's a step up the ladder of command, grisly as it looks. To make this thing go properly it has to be done from the top. Besides, there's something you're all leaving out.'

'What are we leaving out, Frances Margaret?' Kurt Waldheim asked.

'The comets themselves. You all seem to take it for granted that they'll be content to stay passive.'

'Brave comment, but what can the damn things do?' the Master asked.

'I don't know, of course. But if there are whacking big intelligences out there, I'd expect some kind of a demonstration from them sooner or later. I wouldn't expect them just to sit back and leave it to small fry like us to carry the whole load.'

Chapter 49

The five-star General always had difficulty in his meetings with the President, especially when the meetings were held in the Oval Office. It was a matter of principle with the General to scatter ash from his cigar indiscriminately wherever he went. Indeed, subordinate officers sometimes remarked *in camera* that the General had really based his whole career on this little idiosyncrasy. In the Oval Office, however, the General usually showed his deference to the President by making ostentatious use of an ash-tray. But not on this occasion, by God, especially as on this occasion he hadn't got himself a single trump card in his hand; and equally because he had to listen on this occasion to a lemon squirt like the Secretary of State talking, ineffectually as usual.

'The problem, Mr President,' the Secretary of State said, adjusting his steel-rimmed spectacles, 'is to see how much more we can do to put a run on the pound than we're doing at the moment. The budget deficit and our high interest rates have run the pound down already, and besides, the British have a credit trade balance, so the fundamentals are on their side. Experience shows it is never wise to fight the fundamentals. A little gentle pressure, perhaps, but this can't be our main thrust, I'm afraid,' the Secretary of State ended lamely, just as a discharge from the General's cigar landed on the table, spraying ash in his direction.

'Goddam it, man, can't you screw them for every dollar they've got? The Brits need dollars the same as everybody else needs dollars,' the General exploded.

'They don't,' the Secretary of State replied as abruptly as he could manage, blowing vigorously to clear the cigar ash from his papers.

'That's just it,' continued the Secretary of Commerce in a snuffly voice. 'You see, General, the Brits happen to have oil. So unlike most other people they don't need dollars to buy oil. In fact, they receive a tidy income in dollars by selling oil, so it helps them to have the dollar riding high. Nor do they need dollars for food, because Europe happens to be overwhelmed by mountains of beef and butter, as well as inundated by seas of wheat, and lakes of whisky, beer and wine. The Brits might need dollars for certain kinds of weapons, but up to now the Pentagon seems to have been only too glad to get its latest and most deadly weapons into Britain free of charge. To whit, mark you, we even pay the Brits dollars to keep our armed services in Britain, where they maintain, again free of charge, all the weapons which the

Pentagon is perpetually, urgently, avidly, shipping there – in British ships, doubtless, for which the Brits again receive dollars. So does the Pentagon make its bed, General. It only remains for you, and those excellent cigars of yours, to lie in it.'

'Yes, well, let's take this thing at a steady pace,' the President suggested in a soothing voice.

'It can't be taken at a steady pace, Mr President!' exclaimed the General, aghast. 'The security of the United States is involved.'

'I don't see there's any evidence at all to show that the Brits talking and chattering to this comet thing is doing us the slightest harm,' the Secretary of Commerce stated nasally.

'Then why would they be doing it all in an unbreakable code?' the General asked in a rumbling volcanic voice as he blew out a remarkably large cloud of smoke, seemingly in the hope of choking the Secretary of Commerce into a paroxysm of coughing.

'Unbreakable, did you say, General?' the Secretary of State asked rhetorically, his attention being restored now that he had cleared the ash from his papers. 'I thought the Pentagon could break anything.'

'Everybody knows there are codes that are unbreakable, and this is one of them. Which shows exactly what's going on!' the General replied, convinced that he had scored with a heavy punch.

'It does look strange, very strange,' agreed the President. 'It's hard to see why an unbreakable code should be used, unless something important was involved, isn't it?'

'Exactly, Mr President,' the General continued, 'and they can hardly be kissing each other can they, the Brits and this comet thing.'

'The thought excites my imagination,' the Secretary of Commerce said, blowing her nose loudly on a paper tissue.

The General again produced a copious eruption of smoke, causing the Secretary of State to sit back firmly and wonder if the General's infernal cigar and apparently overpowering smoke clouds could possibly combat the greater subtlety of the Secretary of Commerce, who must surely be shedding many millions of viral particles into the air. So thinking, he took a sip of water, noting gloomily that fine particles of ash were floating in his glass. The great thing, he perceived, was to wash the viral particles down from the throat into the stomach, where, being only cold virus, they could hardly do him much harm. He took his small private notebook from an inner pocket and made a note to seek an appointment with his doctor. A check-up would not come amiss, he felt; the Secretary of Commerce again blew her nose on a tissue, but more delicately than before.

'Suppose, then, we turn for a little while from exposing our cards upwards on the table to other ways of achieving our objectives,' the President directed. 'Suppose you fill us in on the score and on your game plan,' the President continued, looking up towards the Director of the CIA.

The Director of the CIA had a big shock of white hair and vivid blue eyes. He was held in great esteem throughout Washington, from the President downwards, for the skill with which, several years before, he had cornered the world pepper market, violently squeezing a rival syndicate organised out of Zürich, Switzerland, by a man who went under the curious alias of Kaufman St John.

'The British position is both strong and weak,' the Director of the CIA began in an impressive voice.

'How can it be both strong and weak? Would you describe yourself as both tall and short?' the Secretary of Commerce asked caustically, with those curiously-altered resonances in the voice that come from a cold in the head.

With a mental note to make certain that the tax returns of the Secretary of Commerce were audited exhaustively, the Director of the CIA continued:

'The position is strong because a knowledge of the coding system used to communicate with Comet Halley is confined to only one place and to only a few individuals.'

'Where?' asked the President.

'At the Cavendish Laboratory in Cambridge, England.'

'And the individuals?'

'The Professor there and several of his staff, and a German who works in Geneva, Switzerland. I have photographs of them all,' the Director of the CIA replied, handing a package to the President, who looked casually through its contents until he came to a picture of Frances Haroldsen, whereon he exclaimed:

'Great jumping cats! I've met this woman before. She didn't sound like a coding expert at all. More like a column writer for the movies.'

'No doubt, Mr President,' nodded the Director of the CIA, 'but there are a few interesting little details you might like to know about this young lady. She happens to be the daughter of a former Chief of British Naval Intelligence. First strike. She was recently hired in a temporary position at the Goddard Space Flight Center. Second strike. At the very moment, the same day, that the General here took control over the comet mission – at your own directive you recall, Mr President – the young lady left Goddard without any word to the administration there. We became curious about her as soon as that was reported to us, and we took immediate steps to find out exactly how she exited from the United States. It was very professional. Third strike, Mr President.'

'Who is supposed to be pitching?' asked the Secretary of Commerce in her curiously muffled voice. Ignoring the Secretary of Commerce, the five-star General brought his fist down with a thump on the table, asking in a loud voice as ash sprayed in all directions, 'What did she get away with?'

'We don't really know, General. We intercepted a Goddard Center tape in the British diplomatic pouch.'

'Then you do know,' persisted the General, angrily stubbing out his cigar on papers belonging to the Secretary of State.

'No, we don't, General,' persisted the Director of the CIA, 'because the tape turned out to be a blank.'

'Ha ha!' the Secretary of Commerce croaked, shedding more viral particles in the vicinity of the Secretary of State.

'This is very serious, very serious,' the President said gravely.

'Why is it serious, Mr President?' the Secretary of Commerce sniffed. 'I should have thought that if the tape was blank it wasn't serious at all.'

All this was gall and wormwood to the Secretary of State. With the United States economy striding along in fine shape, the Secretary of Commerce could afford to be sassy, even to the President, who couldn't risk firing her in an election year. The situation at State was very much otherwise, however, with disasters happening somewhere in the world every month, if not every week. The Secretary of State took another sip of water, again taking care to swill the liquid around the back of the throat so as to wash viral particles down into his stomach.

'Because it was a come-on,' the Director of the CIA explained to the Secretary of Commerce as if she were a child.

'Well, at least it means there's no holds barred and we can proceed with a clear conscience. What do you suggest?' asked the President.

'I said the position was weak as well as strong.'

'Why is it weak?'

'Because the Laboratory in Cambridge is exposed.'

'No electrified fence around it?' the General asked.

'None.'

'Then what's the problem?'

'The problem is that about three weeks ago there was a bomb attack on the Laboratory. Someone tried for the code but failed to get it. We're pretty sure of that.'

'Our beastly bear-like friends?' suggested the President.

'There are several possibilities. The KGB obviously, but there are others I can think of. Following the explosion, guards have been brought in.'

'So what?' asked the General.

'The guards are field troops, General, and you know what that means better than I can tell you.'

'What does it mean?' the Secretary of Commerce asked, just before sneezing violently.

'It means they're trained to kill,' the Secretary of State told her lugubriously.

'Worse than that,' continued the Director of the CIA, 'it means they're hard to infiltrate. If the Brits had used one of their security agencies, the situation wouldn't have been so tough.'

'Then what's so secure about security agencies?' the Secretary of Commerce asked, whereon the Director of the CIA glanced towards the President, hoping he would kick this thick-headed woman out of the meeting. But the President simply said:

'Well, well, it means we must move by degrees. With a little financial pressure here, a little diplomatic pressure there, and infiltration in Cambridge, of course, as best as we can manage.'

'Mr President, this is serious. We have a crisis on our hands!' the five-star General suddenly roared, throwing his cigar in an arc through the air with such skill that it landed fair and square in a wastepaper basket, which soon began to smoulder, only to be quenched by the President's aides.

'There is no telling where this will end,' the General continued, with more percipience than he realised.

'Yes, well,' continued the President in the soothing voice which did so much to appeal to voters, 'let's hope that all ends well.'

'All's well that ends well,' nodded the Secretary of Commerce in a voice which had developed more and more into a harsh croak.

'You should go to bed with that cold,' said the Secretary of State.

'To bed – yeah,' leered the Secretary of Commerce, leaving the Secretary of State to adjust his steel-rimmed spectacles.

Chapter 50

For every full-blown comet that becomes a public news item, there are many small comets which go unreported. Comet X would have been one of these had it not been for a rather close approach to the Earth, and for an accidental sighting of it by a Japanese astronomer. This first sighting was then confirmed by the Tonanzintla Observatory in Mexico and by a Soviet observatory in the Pamir mountains. There was nothing, however, from the world's largest astronomical institutions, which were all deeply engaged on what they believed to be more important business. Europe, moreover, was covered almost entirely by heavy cloud during the critical few days when Comet X might have been seen by the many European amateur comet-watchers.

It was some five weeks after the passage of Comet X when a meeting of the Politburo again featured an unusual item. Two outsiders joined the meeting for this particular item, Igor Lobochevskii, Professor of Microbiology in the University of Moscow, and Alexander Krilov of the Extra-Terrestrial Division of the KGB. Both ranked high enough in the *nomenklatura* for their wives to be admitted by the policemen who guard the special shopping centre in Granovsky Street. Yet neither had remotely expected ever to be called, if only for a single item, to a meeting of the Politburo itself, and both were understandably nervous about it, especially as one of the committee members seemed to be in the habit of suddenly gulping great volumes of air. This was the erstwhile Number Eleven, who in the few weeks that had elapsed since a previously reported meeting had been demoted to Number Twelve. The up-and-coming erstwhile Number Twelve had now vaulted into eleventh place, thereby bringing him into a position to breathe hard down the neck of Number Ten, the member with a penchant for cutting himself on the imported Bic razors to which the higher categories of the *nomenklatura* were entitled.

Igor Lobochevskii and Alex Krilov both rated explicit names rather than numbers, since each in his own special way had achieved a measure of distinction based on survival in the Soviet system. Lobochevskii had, for almost forty years, survived the outrageous system by which without using the lift it is impossible to communicate between one floor and another in the building which houses the University of Moscow, a building erected in a form known among architects as late-Grotesque. Igor Lobochevskii had never summoned the courage to calculate how much of his life had been wasted in waiting for never-appearing lifts, for they operated with such astonishing inefficiency as to have become a by-word even in the Soviet Union. Instead, he contented himself with thinking about his small *dacha* in the countryside, a hundred kilometres to the west of Moscow. It was a single-storey *dacha* without any lifts. It was the way people used to live before they thought of erecting buildings with more than a hundred floors in them, topped by a red star that lit up at night. There was no red star on Igor Lobochevskii's *dacha*, and not likely to be either, unless one were ordered there by the Central Committee, which was unlikely.

Alex Krilov considered himself fortunate in working more on the civilian side of the Extra-Terrestrial Division (VOK) than on its diverse seamier sides, which is to say he was mostly concerned with sieving and sorting the kind of information about the world which appears openly in the non-Communist newspapers of Europe and America, apparently simple information which if properly sorted and collated could often be useful to the KGB. He was ranked 173rd in the exceedingly strong list of Soviet chess players, which made him of the master class. Being resident in Moscow, and with his Party connections, he had ready access to the larger chess events and had, on one occasion, in the game of a lifetime, handsomely defeated a Soviet grandmaster well known to the public at large. He had a shock of dark hair that went straight up from the forehead like a cap or hat, quite unlike Igor Lobochevskii, whose hair, atop a remarkably round face, was flat and grey. Both men wore suits specially pressed for the occasion, dark suits so alike in cloth and cut that in the non-Communist world the two would have been taken as representatives of the same multi-national corporation. And both had a truly remarkable story to tell.

Igor Lobochevskii had considered it best and safest to prepare a written draft of his testimony, which he proceeded to read in a completely flat voice. In this way he could never be accused, he and his wife had decided after careful discussion, of implying, if not saying, anything wrong.

'On the 3rd of May,' he began, 'a curious disease broke out in the city of Onega, which lies at the head of the gulf of Onezhskoye in the White Sea, about a hundred and fifty kilometres to the south-west of the major city of Arkhangel'sk. The curious aspect of the disease can best be described by the following quotation from the Ancient Greek writer Thucydides:

. . . the internal fever was intense – the sufferers could not bear to have on them even the lightest linen garment; they insisted on being naked, and there was nothing which they longed for more eagerly than to throw themselves into cold water... They were tormented by unceasing thirst, which was not in the least quenched whether they drank much or little. They could find no way of resting, and sleeplessness attacked them throughout...'

Lobochevskii looked up for a moment as he finished the quotation, and then continued in the same monotone as before:

'I, Igor Lobochevskii, was called on by the Central Steering Committee of the Academy of Sciences of the Soviet Union to investigate this acute outbreak of disease in the city of Onega, for the reason that I have made a study of ergot, a disease with symptoms similar to the foregoing. Ergot, sometimes known as St Anthony's Fire, is caused by the fungus *Claviceps purpurea* which is occasionally present in baker's flour, the disease resulting from the eating of bakeries, usually of bread.

'On May seventh, I travelled from Moscow to the city of Onega, where together with the local doctors I examined a number of those who were suffering from the disease. While at first sight there were similarities to ergot, there were also discrepancies which caused me to entertain suspicions that some other disease might be involved. To this end, virological tests were performed on swabs and other specimens, these being immediately sent back to Moscow. There, a new form of herpes virus was successfully isolated by comrades at the Institute of Virology. The new form has been termed ''pseudoergot'', in analogy to the form of herpes virus known as ''pseudorabies'', which causes the disease of ''mad itch'' in cattle.

'It remains for me to end my testimony on a more cheerful note,' Lobochevskii continued in the same grey voice as before. 'Unlike ergot, which leaves serious circulatory problems that can cause eventual gangrene in the legs, nose and ears, the new disease took a benign course, leaving its victims none the worse in the long run. Technical details are given in the appendix to my descriptive report.'

As soon as Lobochevskii indicated with a slight wave of his hand that he had finished, Number One asked:

'In summary, Comrade Lobochevskii, in what respects was this disease unusual?'

'It was unusual in the intensity of its attack, in the peculiarities of its symptoms, and in the new form of the virus which was its causative agent.'

'The disease was easy to recognise?'

'Once it had been described it was unmistakable, sir.'

'Before I ask Comrade Lobochevskii to leave the meeting, are there more questions?' Number One went on.

There was a brief silence, broken after a few seconds by the new Number Eleven, the erstwhile Number Twelve, who asked a question so pertinent and so confidently assured as to be a cause for worry to members ranging upwards as far as Number Seven.

'Was the disease infectious?'

'Not so far as observers could tell,' Lobochevskii answered, and then, at a short nod from Number One, left the room, feeling that he had negotiated an obstacle with no harm done.

'Now I call on Comrade Krilov from VOK, who will speak in the light of what you have just heard,' Number One announced, with the same brief nod towards Alex Krilov.

'On May twenty-first,' Alex Krilov began, 'the computer at VOK, which is dedicated to searching for correlations and connections between world-wide events. . . '

'Of whatever nature?' broke in the self-confident Number Eleven.

'Too confident by half. He's headed for a bust and, with a bit of luck, perhaps even for a shit,' Number Five thought to himself.

'Of whatever nature,' agreed Alex Krilov. 'In this case the correlated events were two acute outbreaks of disease, the outbreak in Onega, of which you have just heard, and an apparently similar outbreak on Marion Island in the South Indian Ocean. Marion Island is a South African dependency, on which we have an agent – in safe placing, for obvious reasons.'

'To monitor a possible South African nuclear test,' broke in the demoted Number Twelve in a loud voice addressed to nobody in particular, ending his peremptory interruption with a gulp of air which suddenly reminded Alex Krilov of the proverb he had been searching his mind for ever since he had noticed Number Twelve at an earlier stage of the meeting: 'What has fallen off the cart is gone.'

'There was no doubt about the similarity of the disease?' Number Two asked.

'The descriptions were sufficiently alike for the computer to notice them,' Krilov continued. 'But when I became interested in the computer's findings I enquired more closely. The result was that, as far as it is possible to tell, the disease was the same in both places. At that point it was natural to put out a world-wide search for more reports of the same thing. Fortunately, the situation was given an alpha-alert status, in view of its singular peculiarity.'

'Why did you consider it so peculiar?' Number One asked.

'Because both outbreaks were in more or less isolated places separated by a huge distance: latitude sixty-four degrees north for Onega and forty-seven degrees south for Marion Island. Yet both have almost exactly the same geographical longitude. It seemed odd, the same queer disease.'

'Go on,' grunted Number Two.

'The disease which Comrade Lobochevskii described as being like "mad itch" is very noticeable, with people moaning and groaning and throwing off their clothes, very noticeable,' Krilov continued. 'So I thought that if it had occurred elsewhere it should have been commented on in public. Thereupon my small department put out an alpha-request to our agents world-wide for information on occurrences of the disease. To cut a long story short, we turned up two outbreaks and only two, and they also were most peculiarly situated, both of them in remote locations, as the first two outbreaks had been. The third report came from the extreme eastern tip of the Solomon Islands in the Pacific Ocean, and the fourth from the Galapagos Islands off the coast of South America, also in the Pacific Ocean.'

'Why, if the disease did no harm, go to all this trouble?' asked Number Twelve with a gulp not unlike a belch.

'Because it sounds like the ideal form of biological warfare, comrade, causing whole armies to down weapons and throw off their uniforms,' answered Krilov, to the annoyance of Number Ten, who would much have liked to defend his position against the advancing Number Eleven with this obviously sensible reply.

'Go on,' grunted Number Two again.

'The really striking thing about the third and fourth outbreaks was that they occurred very nearly on the same parallel of latitude. The first two were on the same line of longitude and the second two on the same line of latitude.'

Krilov was then asked to explain this curious circumstance, whereon he asked an attendant to bring a large package which he had brought with him to the table. When unpacked in front of Number One, it turned out to be a blue plastic globe on the surface of which the continents and oceans of the Earth had been marked in outline. The sphere contained an electric battery and other equipment, and when Krilov pressed the switch of a small radio transmitter, which he was carrying in his pocket, four lights appeared around the surface of the globe.

'Those are the places where the disease struck, one in our own remote northern city of Onega, the others in remote oceanic islands. When I marked all four places on a geographical globe, as you can see here, I was struck by the regularity of their arrangement. At first I was a little puzzled by what my eyes were trying to tell me, but then in a sudden flash I saw that if the four places were connected by lines running through the Earth the resulting figure would be a tetrahedron.'

At this, Krilov pressed a second switch and six lines lit up inside the globe joining the points on its surface. Now that the arrangement was demonstrated in this practical way, the regularity of the tetrahedron so formed was instantly obvious to the eye.

There was a loud murmur around the table and Number Two summed up the general feeling in a few words, as he usually did:

'This must have been deliberate, Mr Chairman.'

Greatly daring, Alex Krilov broke the resulting heavy silence by saying, 'That was also our thinking, Mr Chairman. We therefore referred the exact positions where the disease had appeared to our mathematical advisers, asking them to determine how exactly the four places corresponded to the four vertices of an ideal regular tetrahedron. They reported that to within small margins the situation was ideal. They also reported that because of irregularities in the forms of the land masses of the Earth, and because oceanic islands cannot be placed to order, it would be hard to find four remote localities which formed a stricter tetrahedron than these.'

'Which was why I thought it important to bring the matter to the Committee's attention,' broke in the hatchet-faced Number Three, moving in now to skim off for himself the credit for Krilov's discovery. With his subordinate Krilov having thus excited the general attention, Number Three continued:

'We also know the outbreaks were deliberate from their timing, for within at most an hour they occurred contemporaneously with each other.'

'But how could the Americans do such a thing?' asked Number Five.

'By submarine. You notice, comrade,' replied Number Three, 'that every one of the four locations, even our own city of Onega, is easily accessible from the sea. We have a carefully validated report of some kind of fireball being seen over the city of Onega in the very early morning, and of a similar fireball being seen at Marion Island, at the same time on the same day. A natural thought would be that the Americans exploded a biologically-loaded device contemporaneously over each of the four places.'

'But why would they want to do that?' Number One asked in a puzzled voice, so human in tone as almost to justify him being awarded a name. 'I can see,' he went on, 'that it would be a motivation for the Americans to test their device against our city; perhaps also as a warning to the South Africans in connection with Marion Island; perhaps even some issue with the French over the testing of nuclear weapons in the South Pacific Ocean. But why the Galapagos Islands, and why this strange arrangement?' Number One pointed to the lighted tetrahedron on the table immediately in front of him.

'We would need to suppose the Americans were playing some kind of a joke,' responded Number Three with a shrug.

'The Americans do not play jokes. They have no sense of humour,' Number Two asserted in a lugubrious voice.

'In that case, Comrade Krilov has an alternative theory which may please you better,' Number Three replied.

'Yes, Comrade Krilov?' Number One invited.

'Well, it was just this, Comrade Chairman. The time when these outbreaks of disease occurred was just at the moment Comet X, sighted by our astronomical observatory in the Pamir mountains, passed close by the Earth. The coincidence is suggestive.'

'But such a view would imply intelligent and deliberate action by the comet,' Number Two objected.

'Yes, Comrade, it would. But is that not exactly what the English keep on saying?'

There was a deep silence around the table, from which Alex Krilov dared to hope that perhaps he had just played the second great game of a lifetime. Then Number One brought the item to a close on an appropriate note:

'To be able to hit humans with a mad itch,' he said, 'at any precisely specified place on Earth, would be a formidable and decisive power that we should all think carefully about in the interest of the preservation of Marxist-Leninist thought, and of the inalienable rights of the workers of the world.'

Chapter 51

A man with a face which an unkind person might have described as a ripe tomato came into the room.

'Ah, Jamesboro', you're here at last,' said Sir Arthur. A broad-bladed fan turned relentlessly on the ceiling above his head.

'I thought Smithfield was supposed to be coming,' John Jamesborough remarked.

'I have been spared that calamity as yet,' Sir Arthur grimaced. 'So what have you to report, Jamesboro'?'

'Heavy transatlantic pressure, Sir Arthur.'

'About this Cambridge thing?'

'Yes, Sir Arthur.'

'Does Washington offer any *quid pro quo*? You know when I was at Harrow, Jamesboro', I once wrote *quo pro quid*. In an essay. Got an awful wigging for it. Ah ha! Thought it rather witty.'

'Too subtle for them,' nodded Jamesborough, his startlingly red face half-hidden in the shadow cast by a large fern-like tropical plant which constantly threatened to break loose from the huge pot in which it was entrapped.

'The stakes could be high, according to our spies in Washington. There are hints of possible reductions in armament shipments to South America.'

'Which would go down darned well with the PM, Jamesboro'.'

'Exactly, Sir Arthur. It would be quite a feather in our cap.'

There was a perfunctory knock on the door and then, without waiting for a call from Sir Arthur, in came a thin man, slightly shorter than middle height, wearing a suit that was a touch on the baggy side, an effect enhanced by the cigarette which hung loose in the left-hand corner of his half-open mouth. It was Smithfield, looking even more carcase-like than usual, Jamesborough thought. How such a man had ever secured a post at the Foreign Office was an abiding mystery, although there were cynics in Whitehall who said that Smithfield was actually well down the list of peculiar Foreign Office cases – it was just that others were better camouflaged. Because Smithfield sported no camouflage or bright feathers of any kind, he had inevitably been assigned to the Desk of Uncommon Activities overseen by Sir Arthur, out of Oxford by Harrow and sometime President of the Jockey Club of Ranjipur. God help England, Smithfield was fond of saying, knowing there was no possibility of Sir Arthur ever getting rid of him, for the simple reason that nobody else would have him. Besides which, Smithfield knew himself to be of the stringy long-lived type, so that he would easily live to see Sir Arthur boxed up, as well as James- borough, who would, as likely as not, pop off at any moment you cared to name.

'Bloody mess of a situation,' Smithfield announced gloomily, as he sank into a chair chosen to be as far away as possible from the fern-like monstrosity.

'What especially is a mess, Smithfield?' Sir Arthur asked.

'Try to get yourself into that Laboratory in Cambridge and you'll find out soon enough.'

'What would I find out?'

'That you could get your head blown off easy as winking.'

'Have there been more bombs?' Jamesborough blurted out, breaking his rule not to ask Smithfield any questions.

'Not on your fat nelly. They've moved the SAS in.'

'Good lord,' Jamesborough exclaimed in surprise, 'they must be taking it seriously.'

'Some people do take things seriously, although around this place you mightn't think so,' Smithfield replied.

'That's enough lemon in the drink,' Sir Arthur reprimanded. 'By whose order was the SAS moved in?' he then asked.

'The Prime Minister's. Which isn't any great deduction, is it? Easy question for the nursery-school class.'

'I said that's enough lemon in the drink, Smithfield,' Sir Arthur repeated.

'It was all the pressure that did it. Made the PM mad. See?' Smithfield returned.

'And it lifts the bisque, doesn't it?' John Jamesborough said thoughtfully.

'Why would that be, Jamesboro'?'

'Makes the thing seem more important. Increases the *quo pro quid*, Sir Arthur.'

'Oh, I see what you mean. Yes, ha ha! So it does, by Jove. Any more progress, Smithfield?'

'One step forward, two steps backward. If you call that progress. The police are co-operative and we know now who caused the Cambridge explosion.'

Smithfield paused to light a new cigarette, which he did at some length.

'I'm waiting,' Sir Arthur said eventually. 'The Russians I suppose?' he queried.

'The Russians aren't taking this thing seriously. Not yet, anyway. They have agents floating around, of course, but they have agents floating around everywhere. The bloody Russians seem to have more bloody agents than the whole human race put together. But it wasn't them. Try again.'

'From what we hear the Americans are very interested.'

'The Yanks might try rough stuff in out of the way places like Panama or Timbuktu. But they wouldn't in Cambridge, 'cos the media might get hold of it and then it would be curtains for re-election hopefuls. The Yanks will obviously try a run on the pound, the way they always do. So if you feel like speculating the family fortune you know what to do,' Smithfield suggested, blowing out two individual fine streams of smoke lazily through his nostrils.

'So where does that leave us?'

'It leaves us with a middleman job. Sell to the highest bidder. Does that strain your imagination?'

'Didn't I say...'

'Less lemon in the drink. The trouble is I've got bile on the stomach.'

'You amaze me,' Jamesborough interposed.

'Don't trouble yourself on my behalf,' Smithfield grinned sarcastically, 'I was born with it.'

'Do we know who this middleman is?'

'No, we don't, but I do,' Smithfield replied. 'A nasty bugger. Operates out of Switzerland. As they all do...'

Smithfield stopped as Sir Arthur suddenly stared upwards, his mouth open. For a fleeting second Smithfield thought it was a heart attack. Then he saw the broad-bladed fan had stopped turning.

'Damn it!' Sir Arthur exclaimed, 'there's been a power cut.'

At this point there came a firm knock on the door. On a call from Sir Arthur, the door opened and a girl came in, a girl whom a casual observer might have mistaken for Frances Haroldsen. She set papers down in front of Sir Arthur.

'These have just come in.'

'Thank you, Miss...er. You know, I don't think I've seen you around before.'

'No you haven't, Sir Arthur. I'm new. My name's Maisie. Maisie Cooke.'

'Well, thank you, Maisie. Ah ha!'

As soon as the girl had withdrawn, Sir Arthur continued:

'You know, I have an idea.'

'You know, that girl reminds me of somebody,' Smithfield said, more to himself than to the others, staring up at the now stationary fan.

'I was thinking, Smithfield, that it would be a good idea to infiltrate these people in Cambridge,' Sir Arthur concluded, with what he felt to be a well-earned smile.

Chapter 52

The party was well muffled up against the cold, because the curling rink close by the Derby Hotel in Davos, Switzerland, lay by early afternoon in the shadow of a February day. Everything looked innocent enough, and for the most part it was. Whenever someone with a surge and a slide set off a curling stone across the cleared patch of smooth ice, someone else rushed alongside the moving stone, polishing the ice ahead of it with a small soft broom, attempting to fine-tune the shot.

The party was made up of many nationalities, and the game was thus accompanied by ejaculated monosyllables in many languages. Because of the cold it lasted for little more than an hour, whereon the party broke up, its members moving away in sundry directions, proving that its composition had no directly sinister purpose. Two chunkily-built men wearing woolly caps stamped their way to the nearby Derby Hotel, where one of them said tersely to the receptionist:

'The usual, *Fraulein*.'

The two went into a small lift which took them to the second floor, where they were soon casting off their outer garments in a suite of rooms that was one of the larger sets possessed by the hotel. There was a tap on the outer door of the suite. It was a maid with a tray on which there were two glasses of hot *gluwein*.

Outside the hotel the lights of Davos were going on. Skiers were returning from the upper slopes. They could be seen in the main street with skis slung over their shoulders, walking with extreme clumsiness in their unyielding boots. Below the municipal conference hall, horses with dressed tails pulling sleighs with bells were arriving back from afternoon trips through woods and side valleys where mountain taverns were kept prosperous by the never-failing stream of visitors that arrives each year in Davos over the winter.

Here and there were armed policemen dressed in fur hats and big fur overcoats, who had little idea of what might be going on at the Derby Hotel, just as the amiable proprietor of that hotel had little idea of what might be going on, or the maid who had just delivered the two glasses of red *gluwein* at one of the largest of the hotel suites. While outside on the curling rink the two men who now sipped the *gluwein* had looked similarly bulky, with their outer garments removed it could be seen that while one was genuinely bulky with a great chest on him, for the other the bulkiness had been mere padding. The second man was actually quite thin, of middle height with close-cropped grey hair, and with a curious bird-like posture that made him look as if he was about to become airborne whenever he moved. It was Boulton, the Professor of Geostrophics from Cambridge.

As soon as the man with the big chest had removed his woolly cap it was apparent that one was in the presence of a big personality. The effect was greatly enhanced by the combination of piercing blue eyes, a bronzed face and a bald skull. Normally the big-chested man was to be found on the upper snowfields, where he invariably ran the slopes straight as a bullet, after choosing their gradients with circumspection – a measure of caution he took good care to hide from his acquaintances, just as he took care to hide many things from his acquaintances, and more still from the authorities.

But it was the shape of his skull that really caught the eye, a shape which students of anthropology would immediately characterise as Neanderthal, by which experts mean large and box-like, not primitive. This is a matter on which a whole treatise might be written, but which is most easily comprehended by watching a sculptor at work with clay. About two hundred and fifty pounds of clay go into a full-sized statue of a person, of which the first two hundred does little more than establish a trunk, a head, and four appendages, which might as well belong to a bear standing on two legs as a man. The next forty-five pounds of the clay go into establishing the statue as upright man, but it could still as well be *homo erectus* from a million years ago as modern man. It is only then, with the last pound or two of the clay, that modern man emerges as the front of the face is more carefully modelled. Now at last comes the question of which particular man the statue is to represent, and the answering of this intimate and subtle question can be seen to turn on the application of only the last ounce or two of the clay, on the last few smears even. Verily, if scientists in the past had only troubled themselves to watch a sculptor at work they would have seen the process of mammalian evolution unfold before their eyes. But in that case, evolution would have become an obvious trivium, instead of something that could be passed off on an easily-deceived public as a great and profound discovery. Had the public seen through the deception, sculptors rather than scientists might have been permitted to plunge their hands deep into the public purse, and the world then have been full of statues and gargoyles instead of the nuclear warheads over which the superpowers were currently negotiating in Geneva, only two hundred miles away from the Derby Hotel. Or not negotiating, as the case might be.

It will therefore be understood that the Neanderthal skull of Kaufman St John implied nothing primitive. Whereas it is normal for the skull to be egg-shaped above the ears, the skull of Kaufman St John tended to flare out above the ears, destining him for the important role he was to play in human affairs, a role greatly transcending, as it turned out, the roles of the negotiators in nearby Geneva.

For those having no patience with such a metrical analysis of the skull of Kaufman St John, let it be said that his teeth were large, white and strong, and the fact that they were quite evenly spaced showed immediately that something was unusual, for there would simply not have been room for teeth that were so large to be evenly spaced inside a normal skull.

'But, Kaufman, I *did* get the tapes,' Boulton said, sipping the *gluwein*. 'Are you sure your people didn't wipe them out by mistake?'

'Of course I am sure, my friend. They had what are known as protective circuits.'

'But I *did* get them,' Boulton insisted. 'I kept to my bargain, Kaufman.'

'You got them, but useless. For which reason you will not expect to receive the contracts.'

'I don't quite see why. But if you say so, I suppose. . .'

'That is wise. You will wait until my alternative arrangement is satisfactorily completed. You understand what is required? It would need some genius to bungle your part again.'

An Englishman would have described the accent of Kaufman St John as German, a German would have described it as Hungarian, and a Hungarian would have said either Bulgarian or from the Prippet Marshes. There was another tap on the door and the same maid appeared with a second tray on which there were two more glasses of warm *gluwein*, the glasses this time tall and slender. When the maid had gone, Kaufman St John took one of the glasses and said with a bland, broad-toothed smile:

'So. Down the hatch!'

At which he drained the glass in a single draught, leaving Boulton little alternative but to do likewise. Kaufman St John simply stood smiling, smiling with large, perfectly-spaced teeth. Then, nodding with seeming placidity for a while, he suddenly exclaimed, 'Enough!' and dismissed Boulton precipitately from his room.

From the window of the suite one could look down on the snow-and-ice-covered lane which led from the main village street to the Derby Hotel. Kaufman St John stood at the window of his suite watching Boulton stumble along the lane as the heavy charge of *gluwein* hit him in the cold afternoon air. It was a longish slippery walk to the Poste Hotel at the far end of the town where Boulton was staying, with ample opportunity for falls along the way. Perhaps a serious fall with a broken leg? In which case Boulton would no longer be of use. In which case Boulton would not leave Davos alive. A simple injection would suffice, the perfect painkiller, Kaufman St John thought, smiling to himself.

There was a louder tap on the door. It was a strong-looking girl wearing outdoor garments.

'Ah, you came, my dear,' murmured Kaufman St John, busying himself with the girl's coat. The golden tan on her face spoke of the upper snowfields and of ski runs through the lower forests. Kaufman St John continued to busy himself with clucking sounds and little solicitations. Then, in an instant, as if a switch had been pressed, he jerked a thumb towards the inner bedroom. When the girl hesitated for a brief moment, he instantly hit her a stinging blow across the face. As Smithfield of the Foreign Office had said, a nasty bugger, whom Boulton the Professor of Geostrophics from Cambridge would have done better to avoid. Just as Kaufman St John had a plan for the girl, who now rushed to the bedroom to strip herself as fast as possible to avoid a serious beating, he had a plan for Boulton — the one plan obvious, the other not quite so obvious.

Chapter 53

After three days in his new post as Chairman of CERC, Isaac Newton had discovered how to find his way around Swindon, to the extent at least of navigating successfully into North Star Avenue. He'd even learnt to recognise the Oasis when he saw it, and to pilot his car to the park outside the curious building with its architectural suggestion of ancient Mesopotamia that was the HQ of CERC. He was not yet used, however, to the plush carpet in the Chairman's office into which one sank inches deep. Nor could he yet comprehend the mystic significance of carpeting to the Civil Service mind, nor the purpose of the apparently never-ending bevy of secretaries and messengers that swarmed perpetually over the building, making it like an anthill, a Mesopotamian anthill.

He'd toyed with the idea of bringing his own secretary, Mrs Gunter, from the Cavendish Laboratory, but had desisted because on reflection he'd decided the grim Scotswoman would be only too likely to set off unrest in the clerical workers union. Likewise he'd insisted to Frances Margaret that it was better for him to come alone, because as a lone beetle it would be easier for him to burrow into the CERC woodwork. Besides which, the Master of Trinity had proved to be as good as his word – he had secured a Fellowship of the College for Frances Margaret, so that she could now march in a big cowl at 1.00 a.m. from the antechapel to the cloisters whenever the Master and Fellows took it into their collective mind to parade with bell, book and candle.

Seriously though, this was the first time in Isaac Newton's working life when he'd spent even a single day within an organisation that was not dedicated to some form of real scientific activity. The main pattern had always been for the staff to be engaged either in the research laboratories, or to be rushing off to give lectures and demonstrations to students, not for the staff to be an entire secretariat engaged in the pushing of pens across paper. This was the uncanny quality of the Mesopotamian-style building which had hit Isaac Newton immediately on his arrival there. Everybody in it was either a messenger or typist, a telephonist or telephonee, or a reader or writer of administrative documents. The notion that the scientific fate of the country could be successfully planned and controlled from such a place was, in Isaac Newton's opinion, madness. Wheat does not grow from tares, or apples from thorn bushes.

He'd begun by examining the financial accounts of CERC, in the form in which they had been presented to the public over the preceding ten years. Bearing in mind the inordinate attention to detail which CERC itself demanded from the universities to which it made research grants, the paucity of information that CERC offered in its own accounts seemed to Isaac Newton the worst of bureaucratic impertinence. It clearly implied that the so-called Public Accounts Committee was little better than a facade, a watchdog without teeth, and that the real details of public expenditures on science were outside the knowledge and control of the responsible Ministers of Government. John Jocelyn Scuby might be considered an old washerwoman in Cambridge, but what was needed in Whitehall, Isaac Newton decided with a wry smile, was a whole trainload of John Jocelyn Scubys. No wonder the University survived, whereas Governments came and went with little in the pages of history to mark their passage.

Details were not necessary, however, for one to see that the £300 million which flowed from the public purse to CERC each year flowed out through three main channels. First, by way of subscriptions to international organisations like CERN in Geneva, where Isaac Newton had himself been employed; second, in research grants to universities; and third, to CERC's own research establishments, which were sited throughout the country in locations as diverse as Sussex, Berkshire, Lancashire and Lothian. With the first of these channels, the Government was simply using CERC as its accounting agent, without CERC being permitted significant control over the activities in question, for these were decided by international agreement. Because of the Council's failure to achieve control over the first channel, the upper echelons of CERC would have been generally happy to see the international expenditures reduced, provided the monies could then be transferred to the second and third channels, over which CERC had indeed succeeded in establishing almost complete control.

The disposition of resources between grants made to universities and the recurrent budgets of the Council's own establishments had been an open scandal for more than a decade, and it was plain evidence of the pusillanimity to which British science had been reduced that nothing had been done about it. When the research council system was adopted in the mid 1960s, CERC had been given a charter that plainly directed the Council to promote research in the universities. In addition to this first duty, the Council had also been required to take over a handful of hitherto disconnected Government-operated research establishments, an addendum which had been tacked on almost as an afterthought, without any suggestion that the arrangement might impede the support which CERC was supposed to give to the universities; nothing was further from the minds of the planners than that the flow of funds to the universities would gradually become diverted into the coffers of these adjunct establishments. The long-standing causes of this perversion of original intent were strong union activity within the establishments, which successive Chairmen of CERC were unwilling or unable to face down, and the rather obvious fact that civil servants at the HQ of CERC were birds of just the same plumage as those employed in the establishments themselves, with like very naturally flocking to like.

To make an already bad situation worse, the morale of scientists within universities had been put under increasing strain by devices that came as natural as breathing to the CERC administration, such as elevating inferior and incompetent scientists into positions of judgement on the work of their superiors, as well as encouraging the worst of the universities to think themselves the equal of the best, always with one or two chosen favourites being permitted to scoop the pool – or what remained of the pool after CERC's own establishments had drunk their fill.

The once-proud ship of British physical science had already been three-quarters sunk by the time Isaac Newton had arrived from CERN at the Cavendish Laboratory. By the device of short-circuiting CERC through the Project Halley Board, and by the Board's success in contacting Comet Halley, a little in the way of baling out and righting the ship had been achieved. But even this little seemed now to be lost, Isaac Newton reflected, as he picked up his briefcase from the passenger seat of his car and began walking the fifty yards or so to the CERC building. Both the Prime Minister and the Chancellor had erred in thinking that the Council could be reformed in its ways through his appointment as Chairman. It was an error deeply entrenched in the whole British system, an error which the system actually encouraged as a means of perpetuating itself, that attempts at reform almost always ended by increasing the abuses they were supposed to remove. One might just as well seek to reform a patch of bishop's weed rooted deeply in the ground, Isaac Newton thought sourly to himself as he approached the Mesopotamian edifice. The only effective thing to do with bishop's weed was to root it out. Completely. Leave only one or two strands of the stuff and it will spread itself again, to become just as bad as before. The last time when this simple point was understood was back in the reign of Henry VIII. To deal appropriately with CERC one would need executioners in black masks with axes and thumbscrews.

However, deal with the situation he must; if not completely, partially at least. Whenever a person of high reputation is cajoled into accepting an unwelcome appointment it is always possible to make conditions of acceptance – one or two conditions, not a whole fistful of them. And this must be done beforehand, not after the appointment is accepted. So Isaac Newton had burned much midnight oil thinking about conditions. He'd started by writing down everything, but since everything he would have liked would have amounted to CERC being hung, drawn and quartered (which mindful of the media and commentators like Alan Bristow of *Nature* the politicians would never sanction), Isaac Newton had set about whittling down his list. Eventually he got it down to just two conditions, to which the Prime Minister and Chancellor had then agreed. These were the shots in his locker with which he now consoled himself, as he entered the CERC building for his first major confrontation with the higher echelons of the Council.

Chapter 54

Remembering the ICSU affair, Isaac Newton reflected that he seemed to be making a habit of attending meetings without his being able to see a single friendly face around the room. There were the heads of the five main Council divisions, augmented for the occasion by the station heads of all seven of the Council's own research establishments, making a total of thirteen including Isaac Newton himself. An unlucky number for someone, he reflected, giving a pat to one of the pads of white foolscap paper which the secretariat had distributed around the table in advance of the meeting. In spite of the Government charter to promote research in the universities, not a single person from any university had been invited to the meeting, which had been called by the permanent officials of the Council, not by Isaac Newton himself.

The foolscap pad suggested an idea. Making signs that he was drawing the meeting to order, Isaac Newton ostentatiously sketched the table on the pad, marking the positions of the various individuals present. Then he went systematically round the table asking for names and for the spelling of names. Nobody could make an issue of this esteem-puncturing procedure, for being the new Chairman he had every right to insist on knowing the composition of the meeting – even to the point of pedantry, and even though he'd already been briefly introduced to everybody except for two girls and a young fellow with a ginger beard who were sitting at the lower end of the table preparing to take notes of what was said.

The agenda for the meeting had been drawn up without reference to Isaac Newton himself, and it had a number of items placed early on the agenda about which he knew nothing. The crucial item on telescope building appeared at number eight, when his acuity could be expected to be a little impaired, and where continuity of discussion would quite likely be interrupted by the lunchtime break.

'I notice we have a considerable number of agenda items,' Isaac Newton began from the Chair, 'of which item eight on telescope-building is much the most important. Possibly previous Council Chairmen preferred to defer important matters for as long as possible, but for myself I prefer to deal with matters in their order of significance. We will therefore start the meeting with item eight.'

'It is rather that unfortunately I have to excuse myself later from the meeting, Chairman, and there are one or two matters I would like to raise before then,' said Dr Falconer, Head of CERC's Biology Division.

Isaac Newton immediately countered:

'Perhaps, Dr Falconer, you will raise these matters immediately following item eight. Mr Hoddinott, would you like to begin? For Dr Falconer's sake, we must press on with dispatch.'

Charles Hoddinott was the Head of the Administrative Division.

'Yes, well,' he began, 'we obviously need to understand much more of the shape of this telescope project which has been proposed by the Halley Board, of which you are a member yourself, Chairman. Particularly, of course, we need to consider how what appears to be a very large undertaking can be related to the other ongoing commitments of the Council. I believe Harry Henderson has some thoughts on that subject.'

Hoddinott used words rather in the fashion of a player dealing cards from a pack. On the face of it his remarks seemed sensible, and the grave manner of their delivery made the words seem important. But on reflection you could see that it was all so much wind, without a single relevant point in it. Isaac Newton reflected gloomily that he appeared to be destined over the next year or two to listen to a great deal of this kind of stuff. Harry Henderson was the Head of the Physics Division, and because of connections with CERN was much the best-known to Isaac Newton of all the Council officials.

'It appears to make good sense, Chairman, for us to breathe for a while without losing momentum,' Henderson said in a modulated voice, with a dying cadence on the word 'momentum' which Isaac Newton resolved to practise in some quiet corner. Restraining himself from laughing openly, he asked:

'How d'you propose to do that?'

'We are in a position to mount a considerable design effort, a *very* considerable design effort, I might say.'

'For what?'

'To ensure, Chairman, that by the time we emerge into the actual construction programme we're fully guaranteed the best design of telescope.'

'I was thinking of simply copying the NASA deep-tracking radiotelescopes,' Isaac Newton said quietly. At this there were pursed lips and a shaking of heads around the table that might have quenched the spirit of any but an obstinate fellow like himself.

'NASA had a lot of windage problems, and big problems with the final surfacing of their dishes,' the Station Head of the Council's Astronomy Division remarked in the manner of a doctor making an unfortunate prognosis. The trouble with this kind of statement, Isaac Newton reflected again, was that it departed so far from the truth that either you had to accept it or call the man a liar to his face. Focusing his attention back on Harry Henderson, he asked:

'How long would this initial breathing spell of yours be expected to last, Mr Henderson?'

'We were thinking about a year.'

'To which you can add another year for teething troubles, assuming your design manages to solve the problems which caused NASA such serious trouble. So we could be facing a delay of two years or more.'

'Hardly a delay, Chairman.'

'Then I must be missing something somewhere, because if we decide on the NASA design we can order straight off the peg.'

There were murmurs of dissent around the table.

'You're failing to understand, Chairman, if I may say so,' Henderson persisted, 'that we can't simply jump into this project overnight. You must subtract from your delay of one to two years a reasonable transition period.'

By now Isaac Newton felt he'd just about got the measure of CERC, and likely enough of much of the method of bureaucracy. It consisted in a number of people, all of them of rather exceptional intelligence, directing their efforts systematically towards a clever misrepresentation of the truth, and doing so in a pack which it was difficult to pick apart. As if to confirm this opinion, Hoddinott came in:

'Besides which,' he said, 'I think we have to see how the operating costs of the instruments are to be financed by Government. Until we've formulated an operating plan, actual construction might be said to be a little premature.'

As well as having the measure of the procedures of CERC, Isaac Newton felt to his satisfaction that away in the distance he could now descry the towers of El Dorado, which was to say he saw a device whereby he might conceivably rid himself of CERC in short order. He began his ploy by summing up what had just been said:

'So you think design work on the telescopes should go in parallel with the formulation of an operating plan, and meanwhile this Council should make suitable adjustments to its present activities? Is that the sense of the meeting?'

There were nods around the table. Now came the critical move. Making an effort to keep his voice flat, Isaac Newton continued:

'Would you formulate this proposal of yours in writing, Mr Henderson? Perhaps in consultation with Mr Hoddinott?'

Isaac Newton knew that not even the political convenience of associating the telescope project with CERC would persuade the Prime Minister and the Chancellor to stomach the nonsense he'd just been listening to himself. If he could only get the thing set down in writing, he reckoned there was a good chance of being back in Cambridge before the month was out.

But whether Isaac Newton had given himself away by an odd catch of the voice, or whether Hoddinott's instant covering of the position came from the experience of a lifetime, it was impossible to say.

'With your approval, Chairman,' Hoddinott nodded, 'of course we will put a paper together.'

This left Isaac Newton to hide his disappointment with a swift change of direction.

'I'm missing an important document,' he remarked, with a seemingly distracted frown. 'I mean the official Department of Education and Science letter informing Council of this project.'

For the first time there was a slight air of unease around the conference room. After shifting for a second in his chair, Hoddinott attempted to field this further shot by saying, 'Well, actually we don't have a letter yet, Chairman. In that sense our deliberations today might be said to be a little premature, which would of course be a reason to defer our writing a paper – unless it was for internal circulation only.

You see, Chairman, a dialogue between ourselves and DES has often proved an advantage... I mean before the situation becomes defined on paper.'

'But you are expecting a document from DES?'

'Eventually, of course.'

'Why are you expecting a document?'

'I don't understand, Chairman,' Hoddinott replied with a discernible edge now in his voice.

'I should have thought my question was clear enough,' Isaac Newton insisted, tapping the table with a pencil. 'This meeting wasn't arranged by me, as you all well know. I've been in this office for three days only and in that time I haven't had occasion to arrange any meetings. Yet the agenda involves telescope-building, which happens to be the business of the Project Halley Board. I'm simply asking, Mr Hoddinott, how a knowledge of the business of the Board reached this Council? Since it didn't come through the Board itself, I'm asking if it came through DES.'

There were murmurs that seemed to suggest that Isaac Newton's remarks were somewhat improper and therefore unwelcome.

'Well, yes,' Hoddinott eventually acknowledged.

'By what official channel, Mr Hoddinott?'

'Again, I don't understand.'

'I think you understand perfectly well, and I think everybody here understands perfectly well. On the basis of rumour, which leaked as usual through the Whitehall sieve, you arranged this meeting. You did so with considerable care, since some here have travelled from as far away as Scotland to attend it, apparently for the purpose of pre-empting the situation.'

Hoddinott reddened visibly at this and, conscious now of Isaac Newton's steady gaze and of his pencil tapping sharply on the table, answered in a markedly raised voice:

'I can assure you that my sources are extremely reliable. Besides which, why else would you have been appointed Chairman in place of Sir Anthony Marshall?'

Having fallen into the temptation to raise the temperature of the meeting, Isaac Newton knew he'd no alternative but to follow up by playing the first of his big cards. He regretted having to play it so soon, but if he was to maintain the initiative there could be no avoiding setting the card firmly down with as big a thump as possible.

'There never will be an official letter from DES, Mr Hoddinott. The letter will come from the Project Halley Board, and it will be signed by the Prime Minister.'

'I would have thought that an impossible scenario,' said Dr Falconer, his voice clipped and final.

'I'm sorry we're being so long in arriving at the matters of special interest to you, Dr Falconer,' Isaac Newton countered, trying hard not to laugh openly. 'Perhaps I should explain the situation this way: if an industrial corporation wished to consult CERC on some customer/contractor basis, it would write to the Council Chairman, which is to say to myself, not to DES. Communication with DES would then go from myself to the Minister of State. Correct me if I am wrong, Mr Hoddinott.'

Had the carpeting of the conference room been less luxurious, you could have heard a pin drop. People living normal lives, which is to say people making things and growing things, would have been hard put to it to understand the bombshell which Isaac Newton had just exploded. It is difficult for normal people to appreciate that power in Government comes not from wielding sticks or offering carrots, but by controlling the channels of communication within and between departments.

'You mean the Treasury is channelling funds directly to the Project Halley Board?' Hoddinott asked in a strained voice.

'And the Halley Board will then operate on a customer/contractor basis,' nodded Isaac Newton. 'I will of course report the suggestions of this meeting to the Board, and the Board will decide, quite quickly I would think, whether to accept your proposal of a two-year delay, or to turn elsewhere.'

'So the design of the telescopes wouldn't be Council's responsibility,' Harry Henderson said, giving a clear signal to his crew for a smartly executed tack.

'The Halley Board intends to take responsibility for the design. Of course it would be entirely in order for you, Mr Henderson, to send to the Board any doubts you may have on the design. Indeed, the points which have already been raised, the points about wind stability and surfacing, will be referred to NASA for comment.'

'If the Council is not to be concerned with design matters, then I think we should keep our opinions to ourselves,' the Head of the Engineering Division remarked.

'I concur with that. What exactly would be required of Council?' Hoddinott asked, covering again.

'Project management generally: to call for tenders, and to let and supervise contracts; but especially to keep a close watch on quality control.'

'What rather mystifies me, Chairman,' continued the quick-thinking Hoddinott, 'is that in all these matters you yourself are something of an expert. We all acknowledge that. Why then, with your expertise available to the Project Halley Board, isn't everything being done through the Board?'

'Frankly,' Isaac Newton began in reply, 'I would have preferred it so myself. But I had to give way to other Board members who argued that our job on the Board is to establish what we call a Cometary Network. The argument is that a major concentration on the building of hardware would deflect us too much from our main purpose.'

'The picture is coming into focus, Chairman. I wish we could have been brought into it at an earlier stage. So that rumours might not... if you see what I mean,' Hoddinott remarked, changing his stance a little more.

'Forestalling rumour is surely a counsel of perfection, Mr Hoddinott, especially where Whitehall is concerned. I would rather have thought we were pushing ahead at quite a rate of knots,' Isaac Newton smiled benignly, feeling he was getting the patter off reasonably well.

'What order of management fee has the Halley Board in mind to offer?' Hoddinott continued.

'Well, as you know, Mr Hoddinott, management fees on special one-off jobs come in at about twenty-five percent. But this is a permanent job, so Council will have to come in below fifteen percent to be reasonably competitive. Personally, I'd say about ten percent would be right, in view of the repetitive nature and magnitude of what is involved. But I expect we shall fight about the exact number.'

Hoddinott looked around the table for signals from his colleagues, but since there were none he went on:

'It would be helpful if you could fill us in on the actual amounts. I mean on an annualised basis.'

'You mean how much might flow to this Council?'

'Yes. Just as a sighting shot, Chairman.'

'Let's say one hundred million pounds.'

'Annually?'

'Yes, annually.'

There was now a long silence around the table, broken eventually by the Station Head of the Council's Astronomy Division who burst out:

'But that means an awful lot of telescopes.'

'Yes, it means a lot of telescopes,' agreed Isaac Newton.

'But what can you *do* with them?'

'If you could give me a thousand today, they would all be operating full-time in the Cometary Network before the end of the year,' Isaac Newton answered calmly.

'Economically, it's going to be an enormous item,' Hoddinott said in a voice which implied that for the first time he was beginning to grasp the true magnitude of the business.

'We've had a Treasury report done on the economic aspects, by Sir Harry Julian. I don't see any reason why the report shouldn't circulate among senior staff of the Council, on a confidential basis. So I won't discuss it now, beyond saying that the conclusion reached is that the economic effects will be strongly positive. The report is rather long.'

'Sir Harry is a member of the Halley Board I believe?' Henderson observed.

'Yes, indeed,' answered Isaac Newton, his lips twitching as he recalled Julian's attempt at a brief description of his report, accompanied by much twirling of Chestertonian pince-nez.

'But how will the operating cost of all these telescopes be funded, and where are they to go and who is to get them?' the Station Head of the Council's Astronomy Establishment asked in a voice that was made shrill either by anger or puzzlement – it was impossible to say which.

'The short answer to that question,' Isaac Newton said evenly, forbearing to remark that the question was not one for CERC at all, 'is that universities and perhaps polytechnics competent and willing to operate within the Cometary Network will get the telescopes, and will receive grants earmarked for the purpose. But I see no reason why the establishments of this Council shouldn't also be involved to the extent that it suits Council's policies for them to be so.'

'When is it proposed to start?' asked Henderson.

'As soon as Council decides if it wishes to act as project manager.'

'I see one major snag,' said Hoddinott, shifting his stance still more. 'It hardly needs the wisdom of Solomon to see that the Treasury may wish to reduce our vote in compensation for the fee we receive as Project Manager. I'm only too afraid we may not be allowed to keep very much of it.'

Isaac Newton nodded.

'I take your point, Mr Hoddinott, and if this were a one-off job there might well be some such danger. But I can hardly see the Treasury skimming off Council's management fee year after year.'

'Why not?'

'Because spin-offs from the programme are inevitable. They will become important both economically and scientifically.'

'You mean, Chairman, that Council's fee should be used in developing the spin-offs?' the Head of the Engineering Division asked.

'That would be my intention, subject to Council approval,' agreed

Isaac Newton.

'And the Project Halley Board itself?'

'Spin-offs aren't the business of the Halley Board, unless they affect the Cometary Network itself. Spin-offs are the business of industry and of this Council. You'll find it all set out in Sir Harry Julian's report. And now shall we pass on to the matters of particular consequence to Dr Falconer?'

Twenty-four hours later, the young man with the ginger beard brought a draft of the proposed minutes of the meeting to Isaac Newton's office. After reading the papers through quickly, Isaac Newton said:

'I have a few points of correction. Why don't you leave these minutes with me for an hour or two. John Brownrigg, wasn't it?'

'That's right, Professor Newton,' the young man smiled.

'I notice you've left out the whole first part of the meeting. I mean the part where we were all a bit at sixes and sevens.'

'Well, nobody wants that to go on record. I mean, it didn't come to anything.'

'I suppose not. How long have you been with CERC?'

'Since I left university, nearly three years.'

'And the girls who were taking down the shorthand. I suppose they must be fairly recent?'

'I'm not sure, Professor. A year or two, I suppose, but not quite as recent as you are yourself,' replied Brownrigg, with another smile as he moved towards the door of the office.

When Brownrigg had gone, Isaac Newton sat there visualising a great pyramid with many tiers or storeys to it, leading upwards from a broad base to a narrow top: the Civil Service pyramid. Those at the top of it disdained to take notes of meetings, which they delegated to those in the tier below them, which persons then proceeded to delegate to the tier still further down – and so on, until the very bottom of the pyramid was reached. So it came about that the many persons on the bottom tier knew exactly what was going on at the top. So it also came about that the pyramid spurted leaks in all directions. Not that Isaac Newton had any reason to suspect leaks in this case; and yet here were John Brownrigg and two girl assistants with a close knowledge of matters which officially speaking hadn't yet been communicated to CERC at all.

Newspapers were constantly hinting darkly at Government moles in high places. The mystery to ordinary folk, whenever the perpetrators of important leaks happened to be discovered, was that such supposedly sinister moles turned out to be rather innocuous persons in quite junior positions. The Civil Service pyramid was the explanation, an explanation so obvious and inevitable that Isaac Newton found himself angry with politicians, even the Prime Minister and Chancellor, who complained constantly about the situation but never did anything effective to stop it.

As regards stopping it, little *was* possible, Isaac Newton had to admit, except the bishop's weed treatment: strip the nuisance out, root and leaf. It was just about twenty years since Isaac Newton had cleared the weeds from a field in order to earn the money to buy the clothes with which he had first gone up to Cambridge. The field had carried a fair quantity of bishop's weed, ground-elder some people called it. By the time he'd finished the job there wasn't much about ground-elder that he didn't know. Even to this day he recalled the words of a sixteenth-century writer that summed up the situation admirably, words entirely suited also to the Civil Service pyramid he thought:

> It groweth without setting or sowing, and is so fruitful that where it hath once taken root it will hardly be gotten out again, spoiling and getting every yeere more ground, to the annoyance of better herbes.

Chapter 55

Igor Lobochevskii was the most frightened man in Moscow and, after he'd told his wife in whispers about the situation, she was the most frightened woman. The stark truth was that the highest in the land were smitten with the mad itch. The Motherland was without government. If this stark and dreadful fact were to leak out there would certainly be the devil to pay. As the sole acknowledged expert on the new virus, acknowledged from his observation of it in the city of Onega, Igor Lobochevskii had been called in repeatedly for diagnostic purposes. So, perforce, he was better placed than anybody else to blow the whistle on the situation. Which made him an obvious target for deportation or for detention in a psychiatric hospital, which was why he was the most frightened man in Moscow. What made it worse and infinitely serious was that, unlike the outbreak in Onega, the new attacks weren't passing off after a few days only. The virus had mutated so as to induce a chronic condition. It had found a way around the immunity systems of its victims, with the result that, as Igor Lobochevskii put it crudely to his wife:

'They're all scratching like pigs.'

At an extremely restless and uncomfortable meeting of the Politburo, only one decision was reached before the gathering broke up in disarray: full mobilisation of the army was to be set in train forthwith. Actually it had become overwhelmingly clear to the secretariat that a total news black-out on everything related to events in the Kremlin would simply have to be imposed. Mobilisation of the army was instantly seen as an excellent and welcome cover for its enforcement.

Only the air-gulping Number Fourteen, recently demoted from Number Eleven via Number Twelve, was not suffering from the mad itch. And he thought it prudent for the time being to disguise his good health beneath a flurry of agonised scratching.

The black-out of news from Russia, the extreme restrictions placed in Moscow on foreign correspondents, and the evidence from surveillance satellites of the mobilisation of the Red Army, created tension in Western capitals that amounted to crisis proportions.

The British Prime Minister returned to 10 Downing Street from the Houses of Parliament in a grave state of mind, to find Pingo Warwick, the PPS, walking up and down with an anxious look on his face.

'There's a man from the Foreign Office waiting to see you,' Warwick began.

'About what?'

'About the Russian black-out.'

'Oh good, I'm glad to learn that the Foreign Office has views. Who is it?'

Pingo Warwick shifted his stance uncomfortably.

'I'm not happy with him. He says his name is Smithfield. I've checked, of course, and there *is* a Smithfield – works for Sir Arthur Fotheringham on the Desk of Uncommon Activities.'

'Well, this is uncommon enough, isn't it? What's wrong with him?'

'I'd rather you found out for yourself, Prime Minister. I feel I should have sent him packing. Any approach from the FO should have come through Sir Arthur at the least, even granting one makes full allowance for the activities being unusual. But Smithfield said he knew the reason for this black-out . . .' Warwick ended apologetically.

'You did quite right, Pingo,' the Prime Minister nodded. 'We can't leave any stone unturned, even if it's only the millstone of the Foreign Office.'

Smithfield's appearance didn't improve the Prime Minister's opinion of the Foreign Office one jot. As usual, he was dressed in a suit half a size too big, which enhanced his washed-out appearance. He rose from the chair in which he'd been sprawled as the Prime Minister came in, half an inch of ash from the cigarette in the corner of his mouth spraying on to the carpeting.

'If there's one thing I dislike more than flies it's cigarette ash on the carpet, *my* carpet!' howled the Prime Minister.

'Oh that,' Smithfield acknowledged in some surprise, and then added, 'I thought you were interested in Russia, not in cigarette ash. But at least you haven't got a big fan growling away all day up there on the ceiling.'

'I *am* interested in Russia, but I'm also interested in cigarette ash on my carpet.'

'Funny priorities,' grunted Smithfield, flicking his cigarette into an empty fireplace with a snap of the fingers.

'Who might I ask has a fan growling all day on the ceiling?'

'Sir Arthur Nobody, the chump I work for at the FO.'

'You mean Sir Arthur Fotheringham, I take it?'

'That's right. Sir Arthur Fotheringham, like I said. Out of Oxford by Harrow. Ex-President of the Jockey Club of Ranjipur. He grows ferns in his office – if you're interested.'

'I'm *not* interested.'

'You would be if you had to face 'em every day of the week like I have. Worse than files, with fronds that might be concealing a boa constrictor.'

The Prime Minister had already decided that enough was enough. But before Smithfield was summarily ejected, one item of overwhelming curiosity demanded resolution.

'How did you secure employment at the FO?'

At this frequently asked question, Smithfield eased himself back into the chair, lit another cigarette, and said:

'Took the Civil Service Examination. You know the sort of stuff they ask. Translate:

Lugete, O Veneres Cupidinesque,
Et quantum est hominum Venustiorum.
Passer mortuus est meac puellae,
Passer, deliciae meae puellae.

Well, I translated. See? If you don't know Latin, Prime Minister, it means:

> Come, all ye loves and Cupids, haste
> To mourn, and all ye men of taste;
> My lady's sparrow, O, he's sped,
> The bird my lady loved is dead.

That's real Foreign Office stuff. Fits you for understanding the world.'

'Yes, but . . .' the Prime Minister interposed.

'Oh, you're wondering about the interview. Easy for somebody of my background. Not having the advantage of being the ex-President of the Jockey Club of Ranjipur, I hired an actor from one of the agencies – bloke with a straight nose and an accent like ripe plums in the autumn. Coached him for two weeks in the bull I knew the examiners would be wanting, and then sent him along in my place. Easy, like I said. Passed with flying colours, like they say in the Navy.'

'This actor?'

'Came to a bad end, the way most of 'em do.'

Smithfield coughed, blowing out a cloud of smoke, to the Prime Minister's continued annoyance. Yet there was an abominable fascination in the man. The way he was sitting there in the chair made the sleeves of his oversized coat cover most of his hands, so that only his fingertips showed; and the way he talked without making any effort to hold the cigarette in his mouth – it simply hung there in the left-hand corner, defying gravity.

'You were intending to tell me about the Russian black-out.'

'That's right, I was. But you're not going to believe me. I wouldn't believe it myself. Not from someone who simply walked in here like I did.'

'I'll know whether to believe your story when I hear it.'

'Well it's not a military exercise that's going on in Russia, I can tell you.'

'Then what is it?'

Smithfield took a pull on his cigarette and flicked it again through the air into the empty fireplace, exhaling the smoke through nostrils which he widened for the purpose. Then he said:

'It's the mad itch.'

'That doesn't sound a likely story, I'm afraid,' the Prime Minister replied in a soothing tone, convinced now that Smithfield really was a madman.

'The mad itch,' Smithfield repeated, in a doleful tone which didn't increase his credibility. The Prime Minister kept silent, so Smithfield continued in a despairing last attempt:

'It's a new disease which started in northern Russia, in a one-horse town called Onega. There have been a few outbreaks in other places, the Solomon Islands for one. It's got 'em all itching and there's no cure in sight.'

'Who exactly?'

'The Politburo. They're riddled with it. The black-out is to stop the news leaking. See?'

'We could consult the Medical Research Council,' the Prime Minister suggested, thinking to humour the man.

'Or you could consult Father Christmas,' Smithfield replied sarcastically. 'I came to tell you personally because it's important, and they'd have stopped my report from reaching you.' Rising quietly from the chair and hitching up the sleeves of his coat, he added:

'And now I'll be on my way.'

A minute or two after Smithfield had gone, Pingo Warwick brought an armful of papers into the Prime Minister's upstairs office.

'Did the man have anything worthwhile?' he asked.

'He said the Politburo is down with a new disease called the mad itch.'

Pingo Warwick let out a guffaw.

'I'll be able to dine out on that one for the rest of the week,' he chortled.

Smithfield made his way slowly to the end of Downing Street. When he reached Whitehall he lit another cigarette, coughed for a moment, and slouched off in the direction of the Cenotaph. He didn't mind people ignoring him or disbelieving him. It was the unspoken accusation all the time that he wasn't doing his job that was hard to take.

Chapter 56

─────◦◦◦◦◦◦─────

'What a soddening awful day,' said the Prime Minister, as Isaac Newton came in out of the heavy cold rain into the large entrance hall of the Prime Minister's country residence near Princes Risborough.

'Frances Haroldsen has arrived already,' the Prime Minister added, while guiding Isaac Newton along steps and corridors to the small library alongside the larger library at the end of one wing of the house. The Prime Minister stayed behind for a moment in the larger library, as Isaac Newton went through to greet Frances Margaret with kissings and huggings in a manner well-known to a wide section of the human race. Then the Prime Minister came through into the small library, and sitting down at a table came straight to the point:

'Well, how are things going in Swindon?'

'CERC will swallow it, as you guessed the Council would. We can go ahead the way you wanted, Prime Minister. Although I'd like to add that after a couple of weeks in Swindon I've no taste at all for trying to reform the Council itself. I'll see the telescope work through, but I'll leave the rest of it to go the way it was going before.'

'Which is the best way, I've learnt,' nodded the Prime Minister. 'Instead of making a brouhaha over stamping out the old, you start something new, and then let the new take over from the old. By the way, the French are making noises.'

'About telescopes or the butter mountain?'

'Both. What view d'you have?'

'The same as with the Germans. Let them get started. It would be an advantage if we all chose the same design.'

'This NASA thing?'

'Yes. Besides being a good design, it will avoid national rivalries between us and the Germans and the French – if, as you say, they really want to come in.'

'You're on your way to Germany now, the two of you, I understand.'

'Yes, I'm due for a meeting with Otto Gottlieb. He's my opposite number, as they say in Swindon. It was about the meeting with Gottlieb that I wanted to have a word with you, Prime Minister,' Isaac Newton said.

'About what exactly?'

'About the scale of our proposed project. The Germans have the idea we're only thinking in terms of a handful of instruments, and the French will obviously think the same. Do we disabuse them, or do we leave them to go for a handful themselves while we build hundreds?'

'That's a somewhat delicate matter, isn't it? And your instinct would be what?'

'My instinct is always to be frank – in this case, provided I have your assurance, Prime Minister, that the position is definite. There are still formalities at the Treasury.'

'I think you can take it the formalities will soon be behind us.'

'Really that's all I wanted to know.'

'You can count on the green light, say a month from now,' concluded the Prime Minister.

The journey from Princes Risborough to Heathrow Airport took Frances Haroldsen and Isaac Newton about forty minutes. They parked Isaac Newton's car and then made their way to Terminal 1, with an hour still to spare before their flight to Frankfurt, where they expected to be met by Otto Gottlieb, or by one or more members of Gottlieb's staff. Terminal 1 was crowded, as it almost always is, and it was about fifteen minutes before they had checked in their luggage and walked to the lounge area, where they took seats from which they could see a big indicator board. They'd been seated for about five minutes when there came an announcement over the airport intercom:

'Will Professor Newton, travelling on BA Flight ninety-two to Frankfurt, please report at the information desk. Professor Newton, please.'

'It must be an afterthought from the Prime Minister,' suggested Frances Margaret.

She then continued reading a magazine while Isaac Newton made his way to the information desk in the foyer near the entrance to the building.

Frances Margaret's mood changed suddenly from inconsequential contemplation to a sense of unease. Glancing towards the indicator board she saw that BA Flight 92 had moved up to a leading position; a boarding signal could be expected at any moment. She glanced at her watch and saw that Isaac Newton had been away for almost fifteen minutes. There was nothing to be done, of course, but wait, which she did, but standing now to get a better view of the concourse that ran towards the entrance. Occasionally she glanced back over her shoulder towards the indicator board.

The minutes passed by, and now the indicator board really was flashing a boarding signal for Flight 92. The situation was not yet pressing, however, because it always takes a while for the bulk of the passengers to pass through passport control and through the security check. Still, it was not like Isaac Newton to mess up the arrangements for boarding a 'plane. Then it struck Frances Margaret that perhaps the message had been from Otto Gottlieb, postponing the meeting in Germany. In that case there was no rush, and it was just a nuisance that they'd checked in their bags for the flight. Perhaps Isaac Newton was trying to get their bags released, which would explain the delay. This seemed the best explanation, and Frances Margaret reconciled herself simply to waiting there, telling herself that when two people become separated in a crowd, the one in a place known to both must stay put. Otherwise the two can never find each other.

Having thus convinced herself that there was nothing to worry about, and with no other course of action suggesting itself as sensible, Frances Haroldsen waited minute after minute until there was a sudden flurry on the big indicator board, with the sign for Flight 92 disappearing. So they'd missed the plane. So what? There would be others to Frankfurt, of course. Feeling free to move now, Frances Margaret walked rapidly to the information desk in the foyer, only to find it unattended. Swearing, more openly than under her breath, she looked towards the particular BA desk where they'd checked in their suitcases an hour before. But, just as before, there was still a long line of passengers waiting at the desk, and also at other nearby desks. With mounting frustration, Frances Haroldsen went to a policeman standing nearby and explained the situation. To her further irritation, the policeman showed no concern and simply directed her back to the BA desks. Likely enough it was a situation that arose ten times in an afternoon for a policeman on duty at Heathrow.

Realising she'd no change for the telephone, and making a mental note never to be caught in such a situation again, she marched to the bookstall where she'd bought the magazine. After queuing there for five minutes, the assistant demurred at changing a five pound note, whereon she grabbed a bag of sweets at random from a stand beside the cash register, and shoved them together with the five pound note at the assistant. Putting the change in her purse and leaving the sweets behind, she then looked around for the telephones, swearing to herself, 'Where the bloody hell are they?'

'Where the bloody hell are the telephones?' she stormed at a girl seated at one of the BA desks. The girl pointed down the foyer, and then shrugged at the line of passengers queuing at her desk, as if to say that she had one of them like this to deal with every minute.

The telephones were open and were all occupied, and Frances Margaret had to stand for another five minutes watching what seemed to her the vacant expressions and inane smiles of the people who were occupying them. At last a place was free. She dialled the Prime Minister's office and told the person answering the call that she had an important message and would be calling back in a moment with the charges reversed. Then she rang with the charges reversed and explained the course of events from the time she and Isaac Newton had left Princes Risborough. Before ringing off, she asked that she be contacted by the Airport Security Police and said she would be waiting beside the information desk in Terminal 1. 'Terminal 1,' she repeated, making another mental note never to visit the place again, as many passengers before her had done.

The information desk was still unattended.

'Why do they call it an information desk?' somebody asked.

'It's like all these places which are supposed to be run on behalf of the public,' somebody else replied.

At last two men in uniform with walkie-talkie sets arrived. Frances Haroldsen followed behind them as they led off through the crowd at a smart pace. But they took her only as far as the VIP lounge, apparently being under the impression that a comfortable seat and a cup of coffee would keep her mind occupied. At this, an icy fury descended on the girl.

'Take me to your communications centre. Not here,' she spat out, with an intensity that took the men aback.

'We were told to bring you here,' one of them replied.

'And I'm telling you to take me to your communications centre. Doesn't it occur to you that something serious has happened, and that I might have information worth listening to about it?'

So they took Frances Haroldsen outside the building to a Land Rover in which they drove around the apron of the airport to a moderately large, three-storey, hut-like building, which was supposed to be temporary but which never seemed to get replaced. From the third storey there was a good view over the apron generally. This was the monitoring centre for police activities over the whole airport, as could easily be seen from the amount of electronic equipment and from the number of personnel who were attending to it.

'The young lady insisted on being brought here.'

'Yes, well, we don't like members of the public being brought here,' began an older man in a uniform with more stripes than the others.

'Aren't you under instructions from the Prime Minister's office?' Frances Haroldsen snapped.

'We had an urgent call, but the Prime Minister's office seemed to have got lost in the system,' the man replied in some surprise. 'But I think we have some information, miss. It seems that at about two-forty-five p.m. – that would be the time wouldn't it? – a man collapsed, near the information desk in the foyer of Terminal 1. A tall man, apparently. He was taken away by ambulance and we're enquiring now around the hospitals. So I hope I'll have more news for you soon, and that it won't be bad news.'

'What do the first-aid people say about it?' Frances Margaret asked.

'It seems he was taken away by ambulance, on a stretcher. Our report was from a police officer who was on duty outside the building.'

'Not from the first-aid people?' Frances Haroldsen repeated.

'No, the first-aid unit would give place to an ambulance unit, obviously. We're making enquiries now through the Metropolitan police, enquiries around the London hospitals, I mean.'

'Hospitals be damned,' Frances Haroldsen now blazed out, her frustration boiling over completely. 'D'you mean to tell me that if someone is suddenly taken ill in one of the passenger buildings there would be an ambulance crew, stretcher and all, waiting to rush in? Rubbish! Somebody would call the airport first-aid unit, and a few minutes later a nurse would appear and possibly a doctor. If the situation were serious, then they'd call for an ambulance and it would be another ten minutes before it arrived. For heaven's sake man, start making sensible enquiries. Start with the first-aid unit.'

'We've done that already, miss, and they didn't have anything to report,' said one of the younger men who was manning an electronic switchboard. The remark was made with the intention of taking the girl down a peg, but its effect was the opposite; for as the implications of the situation dawned on the more senior officer, he realised on the instant that he was not dealing with the usual run-of-the-mill case of a passenger taken with a heart attack, such as occurred in an airport the size of Heathrow scores of times every month.

'Have you any reason to believe, miss... Well, that there might have been foul play?' the senior officer asked.

'Yes, there could have been a reason. There could have been quite a strong reason. In fact, we were remiss in not arranging to contact you in advance,' answered Frances Margaret, reverting to a calmer temper.

'A pity, miss. But what can we do? You know what the traffic is like into London. And an ambulance would have automatic priority. I don't like to say it's hopeless, but...' The senior officer's voice trailed away.

'Outside the airport is one thing. Inside it is another,' Frances Margaret returned immediately.

'Meaning what, miss?'

'Suppose the intention were to get somebody out of the country. How could it be done?'

'I'd do it through cargo,' somebody said.

'Then *find out* if an ambulance was seen at about two-forty-five in the cargo section,' Frances Margaret said urgently, raising her voice again.

They all stood around listening to the conversation on the airport intercom system as it flashed around between the passenger buildings, the cargo section and the traffic-control tower. The expression on the senior officer's face became more grave as the minutes passed by.

'So now we know,' he said at length, 'there *was* an ambulance in the cargo section, and five cargo planes have taken off since two-forty-five. We'll see no more of them get away without a thorough search for the missing man. Pity we didn't know about it before.'

Frances Haroldsen restrained herself with difficulty.

'If you do come up with anything, will you ring this number, please? And will you now get me a taxi.'

The taxi took Frances Margaret into central London, to Trafalgar Square and thence to Downing Street. The two policemen at Number 10 admitted her after a short enquiry. The Prime Minister had driven back to Downing Street from Princes Risborough, and was waiting there as the distraught girl was shown upstairs. She had kept herself reined in for overlong, but now, at the sight of the Prime Minister, she suddenly burst into floods of tears. It seemed such a short time ago that everything had been set fair, in spite of the unceasing rain which had fallen throughout the day.

Chapter 57

Isaac Newton returned to consciousness with a sharp headache, dreadfully enhanced by a sense of stifling confinement: his hands refused to move, and thick blackness smothered him. The thought of Boulton the Professor of Geostrophics swam into his consciousness and then drifted away. His hands must be tied, he decided through the headache, which was made even more unbearable by a perpetual vibration enveloped in a never-ending roar, as if he were strapped inside a crate that swirled in a fast-flowing river on its way to some huge waterfall.

The sight of Boulton should have warned him. The man had come towards him. Where had that been? Was it recently, or a long time ago? Isaac Newton tried to think his way through these questions. Recently, he eventually decided. Yes, now he had it in focus. In an airport. His head seemed to be clearing, except that there were lapses from time to time when he floated off into vagueness again. An airport? Was it Geneva? No, London was more likely if Boulton was there. He'd seen Boulton coming towards him with a signal of recognition, which he'd instantly known to be a warning. But of what? Before he could answer this question, there was a splintering noise, as if the crate in which he felt entombed had hit a rock in the bed of the fast-flowing river, with the waterfall ahead now appallingly close.

The splintering continued, a noise of tearing wood. To Isaac Newton it was a mystery why water from the river wasn't already pouring into the crate, and why, with the waterfall evidently so close, he wasn't over the lip of it by now, twirling and twisting through the air to crash violently on the rocks below, or to drown, choking for air in a furious maelstrom of thrashing water below the fall itself.

Three things then happened: there was a pulling force from the upper end of his body outwards, so that Isaac Newton decided he was being sucked from the crate; he was conscious of a dim light, which would be consistent with his being deep in a pool of water; and he felt a sudden, intense cold, also consistent with this thought. The cold, he realised with dulled perception, would kill him very soon.

Three more things happened. The pulling force resumed, so that Isaac Newton felt as if he were being dragged over the floor of the icy pool; then, as suddenly as he had been hit by the cold, there was an almost instantaneous jump in temperature to a stifling warmth; and in that moment he heard voices and could at last see his surroundings clearly.

Isaac Newton had been heavily blindfolded. He'd been right about the wooden crate in which he'd been imprisoned. Now he saw that the crate was in the unheated cargo section of a 'plane, and that it had been heavily insulated against the cold. It was the thick insulation which had dulled the roar of the 'plane's engines, making them sound like a waterfall in his imagination. The pulling force had been supplied by an enormous mountain of a man, accompanied by another who seemed dwarf-like in contrast. The small man had opened an airlock between the unheated cargo section and the warm passenger section and Isaac Newton had been dragged through by the big man, which explained the sudden surge in temperature. There was a conversation in a language he didn't understand, with a third voice now joining in, at the end of which Isaac Newton felt the straps that had hitherto bound him up like a Chinese doll suddenly released. Slowly and shakily he climbed to his feet, to find a second powerful-looking man standing there, a bald man of about fifty with very blue eyes and with a skull that flared out curiously above the temples.

'I hope Bolbochan did not handle you roughly, Professor Newton,' the man said in English, smiling broadly to display an even set of very large teeth. 'Permit me to introduce myself. The name is Kaufman St John. If you will be good enough to come this way you will soon see that you are among friends.'

Kaufman St John led the way to the front of the 'plane, which was furnished with armchairs in the style of the first-class section of a commercial aircraft. Seated in one of the armchairs, affecting to read a magazine, was the Professor of Geostrophics from Cambridge.

'Oh, they've let you out at last! I'm glad of that. I'd tell them what they want to know if I were you. No point in making a fuss about it. After all, you won't be losing anything personally,' said Boulton, causing Kaufman St John to smile again broadly and say:

'Doubtless you will be wondering, Professor Newton, how Boulton and I came to be acquainted. We met a couple of years ago in an attempt to corner the world's pepper market, in which enterprise I regret to say we were foiled by the CIA. But not before poor Boulton had quite lost his shirt.'

'I rather suspected as much.'

'Your business acumen does you credit, Professor Newton. Losses were sustained. Losses which now will be repaid, I am happy to think. Repaid with considerable interest, I am even happier to think.'

'By whom?'

'The Americans. It is the Americans always, isn't it?'

'I don't know. Is it?'

'They want the code to Comet Halley, you see,' broke in Boulton. 'All you have to do is to write it down, and to explain it so that the Americans will be able to understand how to use it to contact Comet Halley themselves.'

'For which they will pay?' Isaac Newton asked.

'Of course,' Kaufman St John answered tersely, 'they will pay.'

'Plenty?'

'Plenty.'

'Enough to corner the world's pepper market? It was the pepper market, wasn't it?'

'Let us not enter into what for the moment are irrelevancies, Professor Newton.'

'I'm curious, Mr St John. Curious to know how such payments are arranged. In what currency? And where? Or do you do it in the futures to which Boulton seems to be addicted?'

'I said to avoid irrelevancies, Professor Newton.'

'Would it be irrelevant for me to ask what happens when I have given you this code?'

'You will be landed at Stockholm Airport.'

'I am a little bit concerned at the prospect of overshooting Stockholm,' Isaac Newton persisted, 'in which case we would be in much less friendly territory from my point of view. Indeed, I would have thought we must almost have reached Stockholm already.'

'All this borders on irrelevancy, Professor Newton. It is as if for some useless reason you are trying to gain time. But to settle your curiosity I will tell you that we are close now to the North Pole, well away from normal flight paths. Our procedure will be to circle the Pole until our business is completed.'

'And if I refuse to complete it?'

'But you can't refuse, Newton! You can't refuse. Don't you realise this 'plane is a flying torture chamber!' whined Boulton nervously.

At this Isaac Newton became more keenly aware than before that the rear part of the 'plane was hidden by a curtain. Even as his eyes lifted towards it, the curtain parted and a figure appeared in the gap, a figure with a waxen face, straight white hair worn shoulder-length, and dressed all in white like a surgeon.

'It is a matter of arithmetic,' said Kaufman St John. 'Nobody refuses beyond the seventh injection. Already with the fifth comes some disordering of the brain. With the tenth comes death. The choice is yours, Professor Newton.'

Isaac Newton knew that he must refuse, but he did not yet know why it had to be so. Why it had to be done the hard way, when in the end his writing down of the code would have no importance. If that was the case, why not give it to these creatures immediately? Yet it shone crystal-clear in his mind that the time had not come for that. Before the time came, the hard way must be followed, as others throughout the long millennia of history had been compelled to take that road – Scrooge the humble storekeeper at the Laboratory among them.

Bolbochan lifted him as easily as a child out of his chair, out of the smooth luxury of the front of the 'plane, and into the very different world that lay beyond the curtain – a world of glaring light, furnished with the instruments of an operating theatre. Kaufman St John was shouting from behind:

'The injection only, this first time.'

With a speed which suggested routine, Isaac Newton was strapped on a narrow bed, his coat removed and his shirt pulled up towards the shoulder. There was an icy-cold dab on his arm. 'To prevent you sensing the needle,' said the white-coated waxen-faced man in a soft, cooing voice. Then came the prod of the needle, with the waxen-faced man continuing in the same soft but chilling voice, 'Just a little pressure, a *little* pressure '

The straps holding Isaac Newton's arms and legs must have been released automatically in some way, for he felt them come free just as a steel cage about two feet high was lowered over the bed from above.

The cramps came about thirty seconds later. Muscles contracted violently all over the body – muscles in the legs, the belly and back, the chest and throat – causing him to scream, to croak, to sob without remission. As unbearable pain eased in one place it began somewhere else. A breathless choking cut off the air to his lungs. The pain produced repeated spasms of unconsciousness, from which he was forever being spurred violently back by the same red, blaring, shrieking pain. At last there was a final period of unconsciousness, from which he eventually recovered to find himself back in the chair in the front section of the 'plane. As he opened his eyes, he heard a voice say:

'We will give him just a few moments to recover. Play the recording and keep playing it.'

There were times when Isaac Newton could just recognise the screaming voice played back over loudspeakers located on either side of the 'plane as his own, but for the most part the sounds that emerged from them were the unrecognisable ravings and gaspings of a creature *in extremis*, lacking any discernible human quality. As Isaac Newton recovered sufficiently to become aware that the shirt on his back had become soaking wet, he noticed the waxen-faced man standing slightly behind the half-open curtain, slowly combing his long straight hair. In the opposite direction, at the front end of the main cabin, was a firmly-shut door which must lead to the flight deck, where there would have to be an aircrew of some kind. Was the crew simply made up of several more or less normal airmen who followed a prescribed flight plan without worrying too much about what went on in the main cabin behind them? Whatever the answer to this question, Isaac Newton had a sudden conviction that his salvation would come, in some way, from that door to the flight deck. As his glance flickered towards it, he was reminded of the psalmist whose eyes were lifted towards the hills. But as to the why and wherefore of this conviction, he could make no rational sense of it.

Boulton's face was as white as that of the ghastly waxen-faced creature behind the curtain.

'I should tell them what they want to know. There's no point in torturing yourself like that!' Boulton gibbered, almost hysterical himself.

'The Professor is correct,' nodded Kaufman St John. 'The Professor of Geostrophics is correct. Geostrophics! Wind! I have had enough of this windbag of a man. Let me show you, Professor Newton, what happens when my patience is exhausted. Bolbochan! We will advance our plan for the windbag of a Professor.'

Step by step, slowly, on the balls of his feet, the giant Bolbochan advanced towards the chair where Boulton was sitting. Watching every step with an admiring expression on his face was Bolbochan's dwarf-like companion.

'Oh no, not *me* !' Boulton began, screaming now without restraint. '*I've* done nothing wrong.'

'Except to be yourself,' Kaufman St John scornfully replied.

'Oh *no!*' Boulton shrieked again, with Bolbochan now no more than two or three steps away. 'I'll pay you everything I owe,' yelled Boulton, 'every last kopek of it.'

'You will indeed,' returned Kaufman St John in his most suave manner. 'Your debt will be repaid in a valuable contribution to my archives. Away with him!'

Bolbochan seized the Professor of Geostrophics as an adult seizes a struggling child. Isaac Newton half-expected to see a brutal blow from Bolbochan break Boulton's neck instantly. But no, they marched the man away from the front of the cabin, leaving Isaac Newton with the momentary hope that this might provide him with an opportunity to settle his score with the waxen-faced creature behind the curtain. The trouble was, however, that he had no strength left anywhere in his body, as he realised with a sense of desperation when he tried to push himself up quickly from the chair in which he was sitting.

But Isaac Newton was not left sitting for long. Two or three minutes later Bolbochan was back. He seized Isaac Newton and partly marched and partly carried him down to the lowest deck of the 'plane, where Kaufman St John and Bolbochan's dwarf-like companion were staring through the translucent upper half of a broad door. On the other side of the door was Boulton the Professor of Geostrophics, of winds as Kaufman St John had correctly remarked. Bolbochan forced Isaac Newton's nose close up against the translucent material so that his face was only inches away from Boulton. Isaac Newton watched in horror as Boulton, his face contorted by panic and fear, shouted desperately for help; but not a word of what he was saying could be heard through the door.

Boulton was trapped in a small compartment with the broad door on the inside and the fuselage of the 'plane itself on the outside. To Isaac Newton's dawning horror, he realised that Boulton was trapped within the intermediate compartment of an airlock. Even as this comprehension struck him, the dwarf-like man arched up on his toes so as to reach a large push-button, which he proceeded to press with an exaggerated gesture, as if he were a conjuror's assistant on some kind of Mephistophelian stage. With seemingly infinite slowness, sliding doors on the outside of the compartment inched open. Isaac Newton could see Boulton trying to dig his fingernails into the hard translucent material. A fraction of a second later and the Professor of winds was gone, sucked away by the slipstream of the 'plane.

The dwarf-like man, repeating his performance of arching up on his toes, pressed another push-button, and Isaac Newton watched incredulously as the outer doors of the airlock slid back into their closed position. Then he noticed that Kaufman St John was speaking into an intercom microphone. Although the language used was unfamiliar, Kaufman St John was evidently giving instructions to the air crew, because the 'plane immediately went into a steep dive, twisting and turning as if the pilot were hell bent on crashing them into the ground below. At last the dive straightened out, with the 'plane coming first on to a level course and then going into a steady climb. After minutes spent bracing himself against the drastic and quickly varying accelerations, Isaac Newton was hustled by Bolbochan back to his chair in the front part of the main cabin.

Nothing happened thereafter for several minutes more. The waxen-faced man was still standing there, waiting immediately behind the curtain. The also ever-present Bolbochan stood close to Isaac Newton's chair. How much would one need to remove from the front of Bolbochan's face to make him indistinguishable from an ape? Not much, Isaac Newton decided. The dwarf-like man kept his eyes rivetted on the closed door that separated them from the flight deck. Meanwhile, Kaufman St John was writing animatedly in a large leather-bound book which he eventually closed with a snap, saying with his blandest smile,

'My archives!'

A red light went on above the door to the flight deck, whereon the dwarf-like man gave a passable imitation of a pirouette and made his way to the door and passed through it, thus proving it to be unlocked. This would have given Isaac Newton the opportunity he'd been seeking to satisfy his curiosity a little about the air crew, except that the bulk of Bolbochan happened to intervene between him and the door. He would have been in a better position to see through the door from any of the other chairs, he realised; but, for some reason he couldn't put words to, it seemed important for him to be placed just the way he was now.

The dwarf-like man reappeared, carrying what seemed to Isaac Newton to be a portable video camera. Once again, the door to the flight deck was snapped shut before he could gain anything of a view through it. But the sight of the video camera had gone a long way towards extinguishing any small hope Isaac Newton had entertained of obtaining assistance from the air crew. Evidently, thought Isaac Newton, they were not the uncommitted professionals they might have been, an opinion that was soon to be dramatically confirmed. Yet Isaac Newton still couldn't shut out the door from his mind; but as to why this should be so, he remained as uncertain as before.

The dwarf-like man placed the camera he'd brought from the flight deck into what was apparently a projection instrument hidden behind a partition. After pressing a number of switches, a beam of light emerged from the instrument, passing through a hole in the partition at a height of about five feet above the floor of the cabin. The dwarf-like man re-emerged from his fitting of the camera, gave another twirling pirouette, and then pulled down a viewing screen of the kind frequently used for the showing of in-flight movies.

'Quite the electronics expert, I see,' Isaac Newton found himself saying, to which Kaufman St John immediately replied:

'It is not wise to make fun of Margolis, as others have found to their cost, including our mutual friend the Professor of winds.'

Isaac Newton could see it was tape, not film, that had been used to follow Boulton falling through the air, arms and legs widely extended so that he rotated rather slowly like the sails of a windmill. The pilot of the plane had taped the fall cleverly, sometimes bringing the plane below the doomed man, so that Boulton appeared to fall towards the viewer. His arms and legs seemed so stiff that Isaac Newton wondered if Boulton had frozen rigid in this configuration, or if ice had condensed and become firmly fixed around him. The tape included views of the seemingly endless arctic mountains towards which the 'plane had dived. At first, the mountains seemed low and insubstantial, but as the altitude of the 'plane lessened they grew quickly in scale until the details of ridges and glaciers flashed in a rapidly-changing kaleidoscope of silver and white. And always there was Boulton, falling towards a snow-covered mountainside, half in sunlight half in shade. It was when the twirling figure crossed from the sunlight to the shade that the Professor of Geostrophics at last disappeared from view as he fell into the darkened abyss below.

The film had gone on for two minutes or thereabouts, but it seemed to Isaac Newton to have lasted much longer. He found himself trying to recall the terminal speed of a human body falling through air. Was it a hundred miles an hour? No, surely it must be faster than that! Which meant, Isaac Newton decided, that Boulton had fallen from a height of at least thirty thousand feet, from a height where the temperature was probably below $-30°C$. He remembered the bitter cold when he had himself been pulled out of the crate in the cargo bay of the 'plane.

They showed the film again and yet again, and each time Isaac Newton watched it with fascination, noticing more and more of the dynamical details with each showing, especially the way in which the axis of rotation of the falling figure changed in the manner of a falling leaf on a still day. Then he told himself that such curiosity was quite out of place – but his attempt at reaching a moralistic stance failed him. Whenever he tried to feel sorry for Boulton, he remembered the dead figure of Scrooge as they brought him on a stretcher from the Laboratory. With this memory, Isaac Newton was suffused by a consuming anger against the creatures around him, and with the anger came the strange conviction that the time was almost ripe... But ripe for what, he could not yet imagine.

'For my archives!' bellowed Kaufman St John in massive delight.

'No, not for your archives, for something far more dreadful than that,' Isaac Newton said absently, almost without noticing the others. Whatever it was about the door to the flight deck, it had nothing to do with the air crew, he now felt certain. It was a doorway to something quite different.

'I said for my archives,' Kaufman St John roared again. 'And now we come to your own case, Professor.'

'I think you also said it was the code you wanted. The Comet Halley code, wasn't it?' Isaac Newton asked in a distant voice he found difficult to recognise as his own.

'You have shown skill in delay, Professor. Irrelevant delay. But there will be no more delay. The code!'

'The code isn't simple. Otherwise those who wish to have it would have deciphered it long ago. Give me a pad and I will write it down. There will be a number of pages.'

The dwarf-like Margolis brought writing materials and Isaac Newton began to set down the code in a shaky hand. After a while, he realised the waxen-faced man had appeared and was standing behind his chair, watching, and constantly combing his shoulder-length hair.

'If you want this code,' Isaac Newton snarled at Kaufman St John in a voice that at last expressed the intensity of his anger, 'tell this abominable washed-out creature to stand away from me.'

But for the constant drumming of the engines of the 'plane, Isaac

Newton's last remark would have produced a long moment of silence, with shocked expressions on the faces of Bolbochan and the dwarf-like Margolis.

'Professor, does it not occur to you that a time may come soon when you will think with every screaming nerve in your body that the one-time Professor of Geostrophics was very lucky in the manner of his death? Impetronius is hurt, Professor,' Kaufman St John replied at last, in a tone which suggested that fur had grown suddenly in his throat.

'Then why should I bother to give you the code? Wasn't I to be landed at Stockholm Airport?'

'You will give me the code, Professor. You will give it to postpone the time. Simply to postpone the time. But if you are left there to write as you will, how am I to know you are not writing nonsense in order to postpone the time?'

'You can have the sheets as I write them,' Isaac Newton answered, tearing the first one off the pad and throwing it with a contemptuous gesture towards Kaufman St John, whereon the dwarf-like Margolis retrieved it with another of his ballet-style gestures.

'Then Impetronius will stand back. For a while.' Kaufman St John nodded as he took the sheet from Margolis.

The waxen-faced Impetronius moved back to the half-open curtain, standing in front of it, however, rather than behind, and perpetually combing his long, featureless, white hair.

Isaac Newton was acutely conscious of the noise of the engines. Which was peculiar, because for the past hour he'd managed to tune the noise of the engines out of his mind. His hand shook as he wrote. It shook more and more as the minutes passed. He forced himself to concentrate, otherwise he could have written nothing at all because of the fear which had replaced the anger – a fear that was sharp and diagnostic, a fear he'd experienced before, the night of the storm in the cottage on the Norfolk coast. Just as a nameless something had entered the cottage on that occasion, so it was in the 'plane now. Isaac Newton had the frenzied thought that the thing had somehow entered the 'plane in the moment when Boulton had been expelled from it, as the outer door in the fuselage had been opened.

Inch by inch as he wrote, Isaac Newton found himself shifting the position of the chair in which he was sitting. It was important that the chair wasn't fixed in its position, but could be moved on a guiding rail like a seat in a car. Moving the chair, bit by bit so that the others wouldn't notice, now seemed more important to him than the code itself, which he continued to write in a trembling and distorted hand, throwing a sheet down on to the cabin floor every few moments. He was aware of Margolis retrieving the sheets and handing them to Kaufman St John. This too seemed strangely important, and in spite of his constant trembling it puzzled him.

The throbbing noise of the engines died suddenly to a purring sound, and then even the purring was gone. Isaac Newton wondered for a brief second if he'd become mentally unhinged. Then he saw the others staring urgently towards the door which separated them from the flight deck. The door! The door to what? It was a metal door no longer. The door was wooden, and the wooden door had a stout bar fixed across it. Isaac Newton could see it was really a cottage door, not an aeroplane door, and, as suddenly as the engines had gone, there was now the sound in his mind of a howling wind and a crashing sea.

It was the cottage on the Norfolk coast the night of the great storm; and just as on that night there had been an apparition in the room, so there was now an apparition so brilliant that Isaac Newton instantly rolled himself away from it. But not before he'd seen the ghostly thing double itself into two, and the two double themselves into four – four towering glowing figures that stalked their way from the door and into the cabin. It seemed to Isaac Newton's frenzied imagination that a roaring sea poured in behind them.

Chapter 58

There were voices now in the 'plane. Isaac Newton listened carefully, half-expecting the language in which they were speaking to be unearthly. But the language had a Germanic ring, although it certainly wasn't German. He listened with his eyes shut, lying still like a wounded animal, trying not to be noticed; until somebody actually touched him and rolled him over. He opened his eyes to find two men and a woman standing there, all three in some kind of uniform, police by the look of it. After a startled expression from one of the men, Isaac Newton said:

'Where am I?'

'English,' the woman remarked to the two men, and then went on: 'You are at Stockholm Airport.'

Through the clouds of mist which filled his head, Isaac Newton remembered he'd been on his way somewhere with Frances Margaret. But that had been to Frankfurt, not Stockholm. So the 'plane had evidently gone off course and crash-landed. Then he suddenly remembered about Boulton being ejected from the plane, about Bolbochan and the waxen-faced man, and the insane creature with the flared-out skull. Kaufman St John, wasn't it? But all that must be a fantasy occasioned by the crash, he decided, a derangement in his own mind. So what had happened to Frances Margaret? With this thought he began struggling to his feet.

'No, no!' exclaimed one of the men. 'It is better for you to wait.'

'Until we have a stretcher to carry you,' the woman added.

They tried to restrain him, but this made Isaac Newton angry.

'Let me be,' he told them as loudly and firmly as he could. 'I must find out what happened to the other passengers.'

At this, he saw the policewoman and two policemen look closely at each other.

'It is better that you do not see,' the woman then told him, in a soothing but firm voice. The effect, however, was to increase Isaac Newton's determination.

'To hell with the stretcher,' he told them as he regained his feet.

With a better perspective now of the interior of the 'plane, he could tell from the absence of wreckage that there could have been no crash. A bumpy landing, perhaps, but no crash: even the lights in the 'plane were still on. Besides which, Isaac Newton recognised the half-open curtain. So his nightmare memories had been true after all. There really had been a waxen-faced man, and Boulton, and the others. He knew what had happened to Boulton, but where were the others?

The answer to this question was grisly. Not far from the chair where he'd been sitting, a number of dark objects like cylinders of the height of a man could be seen. There were four of them, and there had been four of the others, after Boulton was gone. Four stalagmite cylinders, not white like natural stalagmites, but black as jet. The cylinders stood there as a man might stand there. Isaac Newton moved towards the place where the waxen-faced man had been.

'Be careful!' the policewoman shouted.

Because Isaac Newton was unsteady on his feet, he had inadvertently touched the black stuff, which instantly crumbled as a charred newspaper crumbles. He looked then towards the door to the flight deck, the door that had seemed so important, the door which had taken on the appearance of the one in Howard Baker's cottage, the door which seemed to him to have mysterious access to some other dimension. Where did it lead? Deciding he would at last find out, Isaac Newton moved, still very unsteadily, to the door. One of the policemen took him by the arm in an attempt to dissuade him, but Isaac Newton shook his head and forced himself forward as best he could. The policeman kept step with Isaac Newton, and his companions followed immediately behind, so that Isaac Newton and the man who held his arm and the other two passed through the door almost together.

To Isaac Newton's surprise, if not his disappointment, the flight deck was normal, chock-a-block with instruments. But not quite normal, not really normal at all, for filling the limited vacant spaces were four more of the ghastly black cylinders.

'But how did the 'plane manage to land?' exclaimed Isaac Newton.

'That is the question,' replied the policeman at this side.

'One of the questions,' added the policewoman.

Before he would consent to leave the 'plane, Isaac Newton insisted on visiting the cargo bay, where it was apparent that the wooden crate of his memory had been thrown against the fuselage by the force of the landing. The sheer presence of the wooden crate demonstrated the absolute correctness of his memory. Then he insisted on making his own way down a flight of landing steps, brushing aside repeated offers of a stretcher and ignoring the policeman at his elbow who repeatedly told him:

'We cannot be responsible for your safety if you won't take our advice.'

'I'm not asking your advice,' Isaac Newton snapped in return. Now that the danger was past, all this solicitude irritated him. Nevertheless, he allowed himself to be whisked away in an ambulance after he'd verified from lights in the distance that the place was indeed Stockholm Airport. From his wristwatch he saw that the time was coming up to 10.00 p.m., about seven hours had passed since he had left London. In that time interval, the 'plane must have travelled a distance much greater than the direct route from London. Possibly it had actually been to the North Pole, as the now-incinerated Kaufman St John had claimed. In which case the last hours of the 'plane's navigation needed more than a little explanation. Isaac Newton thought there might have been some automatic pilot arrangement, although this would hardly be sufficient to fly a 'plane from the North Pole to Stockholm Airport. But his head ached too severely for his thinking to be worth much.

A captain of police and a man in a white coat together with two nurses were waiting in the lounge to which Isaac Newton was taken. Something was said in Swedish and immediately the man in the white coat shook his head disapprovingly, saying then in English, 'It is not wise to be so obstinate. I wish to examine please.'

'And I wish to use a telephone. And after that I wish to take the first flight back to London,' replied Isaac Newton.

'It is not wise...' the man in the white coat repeated.

'I am not consulting you doctor,' Isaac Newton returned. 'Get me to a telephone without any more of this nonsense,' he then said to the captain of police.

'Could I have your name please, sir?' the man asked.

'Newton. N-e-w-t-o-n.'

At this the captain nodded and said:

'Would you please excuse me, Mr Newton. I will return here in a moment.'

One of the nurses, a round cuddly-looking fair girl, brought him two white pills and a glass of water.

'What are these?' he asked.

'Aspirins. You are very suspicious. Please take them.'

As he swallowed the pills, the room swam momentarily and Isaac Newton was afraid he was going to fall. The trouble, he decided, was that the doctor's white coat reminded him of the waxen-faced man.

'Does your name happen to be Impetronius?' he asked the doctor, who shrugged and shook his head. 'No, I thought not,' Isaac Newton added in an acid tone.

'Professor Isaac Newton?' the captain of police asked on his return.

'Yes.'

'Then, Professor Newton, you are I think a responsible citizen. From this, you will understand,' the captain went on, 'that it is necessary for a statement to be made.'

'From me?'

'From you, of course.'

Isaac Newton thought for a moment and then replied:

'I understand, captain. But wouldn't it be possible for me to return here from London? You see, there must be anxiety in London. About my whereabouts, I mean.'

'It is easy to telephone.'

'I asked to telephone the moment I came in here. Perhaps you've forgotten?'

'It will be best, Professor Newton, for you to sleep the night here.'

'The telephone?'

'Yes, yes, that can be arranged. You see, there are no flights to London until tomorrow.'

'Then suppose we do the telephoning,' Isaac Newton insisted, getting up from the chair where he'd been sitting.

'It will be arranged, if you give me the number.'

The captain handed Isaac Newton a notebook in which he wrote the all-night number of the Prime Minister's office, saying, 'You seem to be making something of an opera of this, captain. I'd prefer to make the call myself.'

'It is not a very pleasant opera, the 'plane out there.'

'Let me ask you clearly, captain. Are you denying me the use of a telephone?'

'It is an order, Professor Newton. But your safety will be reported.'

'An order from whom?'

'I cannot say.'

The anger that now swept through Isaac Newton only made his headache worse, to a point where he decided to defer thoughts of retribution. Reflecting that Swedish law might well give the airport authorities the right to detain passengers for some limited length of time, as the laws of most countries probably did, and also reflecting that the circumstances of his arrival in Stockholm were certainly most peculiar, it would surely be best to sleep off the headache first, and then to raise the wind in the morning.

'Where then do I sleep?' he asked.

At this, the doctor moved towards him, whereon Isaac Newton lost control and shouted in German:

'Come a step nearer and I'll hammer you against the wall!'

At this, the captain of police signalled curtly to the doctor, who immediately left the lounge.

The second nurse, not the cuddly one but a platinum blonde with a haughty expression, led Isaac Newton silently through a small hallway and along empty corridors to a short flight of stairs at the top of which she unlocked a door, which proved to be the entrance to an apartment. After indicating the bed and taking from a locker a pair of pyjamas, which she threw on the bed, the haughty nurse left him.

The pyjamas were too small. Damnably too small. So he threw away the top, retaining the bottoms, which came six inches up his leg. To compound his irritation, just as he was on the point of getting into the bed there was a tap on the outer door. This time it was the cuddly nurse. Not that he had any cuddly thoughts. His head was too bad and the pyjamas, or the lack of them, made him feel ridiculous. The cuddly nurse was carrying a tray with another glass of water and more pills.

'They're for sleeping. But you don't need to take them if you're still suspicious,' the girl remarked, and in a moment was gone, apparently having no cuddly thoughts herself.

Isaac Newton decided that there wasn't any point in punishing himself further. So to avoid puzzling about the dark cylinders in the 'plane he swallowed the pills. The bed had a duvet, which normally he didn't like because the damned things made him too hot. But now he was glad to pull the duvet up around his shoulders. He was shivery. Shock probably. His last act before falling into an exhausted sleep was to bunch a pillow under his head, an act which always seemed to stop insoluble problems from churning endlessly in his mind.

Chapter 59

The moment he awoke Isaac Newton knew he'd slept for a very long time. From his watch he saw the time was almost 3.00 p.m. So much, then, for last night's talk of a morning flight to London. For a while, as the events of the previous day returned in his memory, he simply looked up at the ceiling. Then, all in a brief moment, he realised the room here was wrong. It was bigger and higher than it should have been, and the diffuse light coming through thick curtains was daylight. The apartment he'd been taken to at the airport had been enclosed, without any outside window.

A few quick strides brought him to the curtains. Partially drawing them, he looked out on rolling fields; there was no sign of an airport. A glance sideways showed a large country house built of a solid-looking yellow stone. Yet the bed in the room looked the same as he remembered it, and he was still wearing the same absurdly short pyjama bottoms.

The room was large and it took Isaac Newton a few moments to look carefully over it and to examine the contents of the various cupboards and wardrobes. He found a big warm dressing gown, but his own clothes were gone. The pyjama bottoms and the dressing gown hardly provided a sound basis for an attempted escape from the yellow stone house. Then he made a mental note never again to trust cuddly-looking girls, especially when they brought gifts. The second lot of pills, the ones he didn't need to take if he was suspicious, must have contained some powerful stuff.

It was easy to see what had happened. Once he was well under, they'd simply lifted the bed out of the apartment at the airport – what airport remained in doubt. Then they must have put the bed, with him still in it, into a van and simply driven to this place in the countryside. Where? That also remained in doubt.

There was a tap on a door, and a dark-haired girl came in with a tray. The tray carried a large teapot, tea service, and a plate of cakes.

'Ah, you are awake,' she said, adding, 'that is good.'

After setting down the tray on a low table near the windows, the girl went to the curtains and efficiently drew them back.

'It seemed you were going to sleep for an age. Like the American van Winkle.'

'Where are my clothes?' Isaac Newton asked.

'They are being cleaned.'

'Where are we? I mean, where is this house?' Isaac Newton asked again.

'I am afraid, sir, that I am not permitted to say.'

'But in Sweden?'

'Of course, but I cannot tell you more than that. There is a gentleman waiting to see you who will answer your questions.'

Isaac Newton noticed the tray was set with two cups and that the teapot was large.

'Has this gentleman been waiting long?'

'For several hours.'

'Then he can't be very important.'

'I think he is very important. I will tell him you are awake.'

When the girl had gone, Isaac Newton made a quick tour around the room to find the bug, but he didn't find it, although he felt certain there must be one. Otherwise they couldn't have known so promptly that he was awake and thus produced the tea so quickly.

Isaac Newton sat and poured the tea, not awaiting the arrival of his visitor for his mouth was dry. And not having eaten since lunchtime the previous day, he was hungry, so he bit into one of the cakes. And then, after the first mouthful, he stopped abruptly. It simply wasn't credible that he was in Russia, near Leningrad, as he'd suspected briefly. It simply wasn't credible because nowhere, throughout the length and breadth of the Soviet Union, did they have large cups of the quality of these cups, or the tea, or the cakes.

There was another tap on the door and a man as tall as Isaac Newton himself, with fair hair cut short, came in.

'Eriksson. Gustav Eriksson,' he said briskly, holding out a hand.

'I'll shake your hand, Mr Eriksson, if the 'phone call I asked you to make last night was in fact made,' Isaac Newton responded.

'Frankly, it wasn't,' Eriksson replied, withdrawing his hand.

'Isn't that rather peculiar?'

'Yes, it is peculiar. Like many other things in this case. D'you mind if I pour myself some tea?'

'Not at all. Especially since it's your own tea. To whom should I express my thanks for being entertained so warmly, Mr Eriksson?'

'The Swedish Army.'

'Then shouldn't I use your proper rank?'

'Colonel. Colonel Eriksson, if you want to be formal about it.'

'It seems to me, Colonel Eriksson, that you've a great deal of explaining to do.'

At this Eriksson laughed loudly and took a chair on the opposite side of the small table at which Isaac Newton was sitting, with the tea-tray now between them as if it symbolised a battlefield.

'*I* have a lot of explaining to do! You're evidently quite a humorist, Professor Newton. Still, I will tell you that transferring from the airport police to the Army gave a fine opportunity for the telephoning to become forgotten. But of course I have informed your British Embassy in Stockholm. I did so at five-thirty this morning. You see, I was on the case very early.'

'It would have been simpler to make the call to London.'

'It would have been foolish,' replied Eriksson, shaking his head. 'I discovered the number was that of your Prime Minister's office. So a call there would have started prompt action, probably directly from your Prime Minister to ours. Then my opportunity would have been gone.'

'Opportunity for what?'

'To find out what happened in the 'plane which brought you here, of course.'

'But you told the Embassy I was here?'

'Yes, very early, as I just said. If you arrive very early at an airport for a flight and check in your bags, what happens, Professor Newton?'

'What does?'

'When eventually you reach your destination, by some mysterious feature of the loading process your bags always come out last. Or perhaps you haven't noticed?' Eriksson said as he sipped the tea.

'I see. You calculated that by the time the senior staff at the Embassy came on duty the information would have been lying around for hours.'

'And very likely would go on lying around for a little while longer. Besides which, Professor Newton, your Foreign Office has something of a reputation for the tardiness with which it passes information to other branches of your Government. So I calculated on another delay. But, I confess, I began to fear you would sleep away all the time I had so carefully gained.'

'Gained for what, Colonel Eriksson?'

'Do you know what the flight plan of your 'plane was supposed to be? I mean where was the 'plane?'

'I was told far away to the north, towards the Pole. Which must have been true,' Isaac Newton replied. 'You know, Colonel Eriksson, there *is* something I must report to you straight away. On the flight a man was done to death. He was a colleague of mine at Cambridge.'

'I am not entirely surprised. How did it happen?'

'They threw him out of the plane.'

'Not nice people, I'm afraid. Not a nice situation. We found what lay behind the curtain. I hope they didn't take you there?'

Isaac Newton sat for a moment and then nodded, saying brusquely, 'Let's not talk about it. You'll find they had a video projector. They made a tape of the man falling through the air. His name was Boulton. He was Professor of Geostrophics, the Head of the Cambridge Meteorology Department. My point is that you'll find pictures of the terrain below the 'plane. It was arctic and mountainous.'

'The 'plane came into Swedish air space from the north, Professor Newton.'

'Which checks my impression.'

'What didn't check at all was the radar echo on our screens.'

'What about it?'

'It was enormously too strong. You see, this is rather my business. We know quite well the proper strengths of the radar echos produced by 'planes of various sizes. The echo for your 'plane was far too strong. Ten times too strong, I think. How might that have been done, do *you* think?'

'You said radar is your business.'

'Come now, Professor Newton, you are a physicist with an international reputation. How could such a very strong echo be produced?'

'By increasing the reflectivity of the 'plane, I suppose.'

'By some sort of an extended corona around the 'plane,' nodded Eriksson.

'Ionized gas, possibly,' Isaac Newton nodded in return, pouring himself another cup of the tea.

'Just the reverse of the American stealth bombers – where the reflectivity is reduced. You know, Professor Newton, it was almost as if the 'plane was deliberately trying to draw attention to itself – just the opposite from the stealth bombers.'

'Which leads you to what?'

'To the landing of the 'plane.'

'Do you have blind-landing facilities?' Isaac Newton asked.

'We do.'

'Then what's the problem?'

'The problem,' Eriksson grunted, 'is that while the 'plane certainly used our blind-landing facilities, it wasn't fitted with any blind-landing equipment.'

'That sounds rather contradictory.'

'It is also contradictory that eight men in a 'plane were incinerated...'

'Like scorched newspaper.'

'While a ninth man was left unscathed,' Eriksson continued, refusing to be deflected by scorched newspapers.

'Lightning does strange things.'

'Lightning would have passed through the outer metal skin of the 'plane. Of this too I have some experience. And even if an electrical current had been discharged inside the 'plane it would have fused inanimate objects as well as cauterising the eight men. Yet not a single such object seems to have been disturbed. It is all very strange, Professor Newton. I have been hoping you would help me to understand it.'

'Isn't it just too strange?'

'For what?'

'For me to give you help in understanding it.'

'You know more about comets than I do, especially about Comet Halley.'

'Your astronomers...'

'Our astronomers know nothing about the code to Comet Halley, Professor Newton. It was the code the eight men were seeking, wasn't it?' Eriksson persisted.

Something which had been ticking at the back of Isaac Newton's mind suddenly burst forth. The code! Of course, he'd been writing down the code, throwing the sheets one by one to Kaufman St John. Had those sheets been incinerated along with the man? From what Eriksson had just said, about inanimate objects remaining untouched, all the sheets might have survived and been recovered by the airport police.

'You must have recovered the pad, the one I was writing on when the lightning struck,' Issac Newton said, exposing himself as little as possible. Eriksson started to eat one of the cakes.

'Yes,' he nodded after a while. 'Bearing what I think is your hand-writing, Professor Newton.'

'Doubtless you found it interesting.'

'Up to a point. It will need more study of course.'

'What would you do with the code, Colonel Eriksson? If you could decipher it. Hand it to the Americans?'

'Good heavens, no! Sweden is a neutral country.'

'Or the Russians?'

'Your suggestion is ridiculous, Professor Newton.'

'Then what use would it be?'

'Glory, Professor Newton. It would be a passport to glory.'

'Rather an unusual concept, Colonel Eriksson.'

'Why so, Professor Newton? I can think of nothing more important. Perhaps it is because you come of a mongrel people yourself and so do not understand us Swedes.'

'It seems that I don't.'

Eriksson put down his teacup and then, with an animated expression in his blue eyes, made over to the window, where he turned, saying, 'I am something of a student of history and of prehistory. Ten thousand years ago what today we call the Germanic peoples must have been a rather small group with a distinctive language, living a hard life at the limits of survival, close to the edge of the northern glaciers of the last ice age. As the ice age came to an end, the glaciers retreated and the group expanded in easier conditions, covering an ever wider area. Do I make myself clear, Professor Newton?'

'Perfectly.'

'Tell me if I become boring, please. Well, the Germanic tribe expanded, the same way as other ice-age tribes expanded. Numbers increased and the language fragmented. The weaker ones, the ones without firm niches, were pressed outwards the most – into the Norwegian mountains and to the south, into what today we call the German plain. So it came about that the strongest stayed in the centre and to the north, the centre which had been their homeland for many thousands of years. This was the case with the Swedes. This little history, Professor Newton, explains why we Swedes still consider ourselves to be the aristocrats of the Germanic peoples – in spite of a strange inversion. The inversion came about because those who moved to the south chanced on wider and more productive lands, and so increased in number far more than those of us who stayed in the homeland. So it has been with you English and with your founding of the American colonies. To begin with it was the weaker ones, the ones without niches, the disaffected ones, who emigrated. But because North America chanced to be a naturally large and wealthy continent the numbers of the emigrants increased, until today you have the less successful pulling the noses of the more successful.'

'These are hardly populist sentiments, Colonel Eriksson. I'm surprised you're not a bit worried by the bug in this room,' Isaac Newton managed to interpose.

'Ah, the bug. You found it?'

'No, I didn't.'

At this, Eriksson went to the bed, saying, 'Excuse me.'

After rummaging for a while near the base of the bed he came back to Isaac Newton carrying a small portable microphone and transmitter with battery.

'You looked in the room because the room is permanent and, of course, the bed is temporary. But it was a rather elementary mistake,' Eriksson said in a disapproving voice. Then he went to the door and called out in Swedish. A moment or two later the same dark-haired girl appeared with a bottle of schnapps and two glasses. Eriksson slopped the fiery liquid into the glasses, but Isaac Newton raised a hand and said firmly:

'Not for me. I haven't really eaten since yesterday. Besides which, I don't have your Swedish aristocratic constitution.'

'Ah, of course,' nodded Eriksson, going to the outer door again. Returning shortly he picked up his glass.

'It was thoughtless of me. They will bring you some proper food shortly. Tea!' he added with a grimace, then, '*Skol!*' and drained his glass in the characteristic Swedish style.

Eriksson was just waiting while the warmth of the schnapps hit him, when the dark-haired girl came in once more with another tray on which there was a plateful of what clearly smelt like stew. Isaac Newton thought that when one is really hungry nothing smells more delicious than stew, but Eriksson recoiled with a thoroughly disgusted expression.

'Awful. My apologies for our cuisine, Professor Newton. Naturally you will be finding my point of view a little peculiar. For a mongrel of an Englishman like yourself it must be nearly impossible to understand my point of view.'

Eriksson waited for the girl to withdraw before pouring more of the schnapps.

'The girl is Calvinist you see, so I have to be just a little careful. You will forgive me I hope, but I am now coming to the matters which it would be impossible for me to discuss if I had not drunk.'

'Such as what?' Isaac Newton asked, taking a mouthful of the stew and still thinking it delicious.

Instead of actually drinking the schnapps, Eriksson looked Isaac Newton full in the face across the low table, the intensity of expression returning to his blue eyes.

'There is no way of incinerating eight men and leaving a ninth man unharmed except by deliberate choice, Professor Newton. No way at all. There is no way of bringing a pilotless 'plane into a safe landing except by deliberate and intelligent action. No way at all. Do not contradict me, Professor Newton. Because I am likely to become violent when contradicted. In fact I have a name for becoming violent when contradicted. That's why the girl disapproves of me. She doesn't want the house breaking up, like all the Calvinists.'

'I wasn't contradicting you, Colonel Eriksson,' Isaac Newton said amiably, taking another mouthful of the stew. Eriksson nodded his approval, but was still avoiding the schnapps, Isaac Newton noticed.

'From which I deduce,' Eriksson then proclaimed, holding up a hand in the dramatic style of an actor, 'that we are no longer living in a world of confrontation between two superpowers. I deduce that we are living in a world of three superpowers.'

'In the interest of not having the house broken up, I'm still not contradicting you,' Isaac Newton said again, taking a further mouthful of the stew.

Eriksson stared fixedly at the stew, and after a long moment said:

'Don't you find it tastes abominable?'

'Not at all. It tastes delicious. You were telling me about your deductions.'

'I have come to the conclusion that the time might have come for Sweden to abandon its neutrality.'

'Why would that be?'

'Because the overwhelming probability, it seems to me, Professor Newton, is that the other two superpowers are going to take a shellacking, as the Americans say, or are going to find themselves at the knout-end, as the Russians say.'

'I can't quarrel with your logic, Colonel,' Isaac Newton nodded with his mouth full.

'Of course you can't, Professor Newton, because what I'm saying is the truth. I will also tell you a little more of the truth.' Eriksson paused for a moment and then went on cryptically, 'You must be a very important person, I think.'

'Why would that be?'

'Because this third superpower must have known you were on the

'plane. How did the third superpower know you were on the 'plane?'
'I'd like to know the answer to that question as much as you would.'
'Because you're emitting some kind of a signal. Some kind of a blip.
There's no other way. What is this signal, Professor Newton?'
'Do you want to use it yourself?'
'You didn't answer my question.'
'Frankly, I wish I could, but I can't.'
'No? Then let me give you some advice. Three pieces of advice. My
first advice is a matter of form. Never again must you permit yourself
to be trepanned from the middle of a busy airport. That was very bad
form. Not decent social class at all. Second, when you are searching for
a bug always look in the bed. Third, do not leave vital papers behind in
a 'plane.'

Eriksson took an envelope from the inner pocket of his suit and
pushed it across the low table. A glance at the contents showed them to
be the sheets on which Isaac Newton had written instructions for
deciphering the code to Comet Halley. Forbearing to suggest that
Eriksson might have photocopied the sheets, Isaac Newton asked:

'So you are joining the third superpower?'

'It would seem so,' agreed Eriksson, pushing the still unconsumed
schnapps away as there came a further tap on the door.

'That damn girl fancies herself as an evangelical reformer,' he
explained to Isaac Newton.

But the girl who burst into the room was Frances Margaret. She
rushed forward and embraced Isaac Newton, with Eriksson standing
watching in amazement. When Isaac Newton eventually turned to
introduce Frances Margaret, Eriksson shook his head.

'It is hard to believe. I could take you to some villages and show you
twenty girls exactly like this one. So much the same that ten metres
away you could not tell the difference. What, I ask, does this mean? It
means that a thousand years ago a boatload of young people sailed
away from the shores of Sweden – never to return, but still to be the
same people. It is infinitely sad,' he said to Frances Margaret, 'that you
should return after a thousand years without knowing your home.'

Shaking his head at this supposed tragedy, Eriksson made his way
slowly from the room.

'Drunk?' asked Frances Magaret, noticing the schnapps bottle.

'Yes, but with his own ideas, not with alcohol. He's potentially a
great man.'

'Potentially?'

'If he could find a cause. Perhaps he may have found one,' Isaac
Newton said as he picked up the envelope and slipped it into a pocket.

Chapter 60

'Wowee!' exclaimed the Master as an immense squall hit the windows of the big upstairs room in the Lodge of Trinity College, a squall that was the beginning of a spring-time cloudburst destined to deposit two inches of rain on Great Square.

'Lucky the Easter Term hasn't started yet, otherwise we'd have had half our undergraduates washed away in the flooding,' the Master continued to the Chancellor of the Exchequer.

It was the occasion of a meeting of the Project Halley Board, and the long table normally used for private dinner parties was now set with writing materials, instead of with a multitude of wine glasses scattered among a brilliant display of the Master's much-beloved silver. The Board had formed the habit of seating itself in a particular arrangement, the Prime Minister at one end of the table, the Master of Trinity at the other, with Isaac Newton on the Prime Minister's right and Sir Harry Julian the Treasury mandarin on the left, with the Chancellor on the Master's right and Kurt Waldheim on the left. Frances Haroldsen, who kept the records of the meeting and who did her own typing and duplication of documents, thus preventing all risk of the Board's business springing any leaks, had her own smaller table, placed a little behind the Master and to his left.

For the first time since the Board was formed, Isaac Newton was absent as the meeting began. The clock on the Edward III Tower was striking 10.00 a.m. as the Prime Minister announced:

'I thought it advisable to ask Professor Newton to be absent during our morning session today. Otherwise it would have been difficult to discuss several of the documents before us without embarrassment. I'm referring, of course, to Professor Newton's own account of his recent experiences, to the communication from the Swedish Government, and to the report from Colonel Eriksson of the Swedish Army. Unless all of this is wide of the truth, which I can scarcely credit, the situation goes far outside my own experience.'

'Outside the experiences of all of us, I should think, Prime Minister,' interposed the Master.

'Except possibly for Dr Waldheim. Could you start things, Dr Waldheim, by giving us your thoughts. Let's take Colonel Eriksson's report first. On the condition of this 'plane as it landed at Stockholm Airport. How could eight individuals have been reduced to cylinders of carbon? Colonel Eriksson gives us their dimensions with a macabre precision, and a diagram of their positions, together with the position of Professor Newton at the time he was discovered unconscious. How could all this have been possible?'

Kurt Waldheim drew a hand through the quiff of hair which stood up from his broad forehead and, shaking his head deprecatingly, replied:

'You're not referring to the motivations of the people?'

'No, no, I'm referring to what happened.'

'And why,' added the Master, with a keen interest.

'It must have been some kind of discharge, an electrical discharge it is natural for me to assume, that boiled off water,' Kurt Waldheim suggested self-consciously. 'It is lucky Isaac is not here, otherwise I would not have dared to offer that opinion, because he would have laughed for a long time, I think.'

'I must confess, the thought of boiling off water had never occurred to me,' responded the Prime Minister, glancing towards Sir Harry Julian, whose Chestertonian bulk was sunk into an especially large chair which the Master had thoughtfully provided, and who appeared to oscillate rapidly between being asleep and glaring fiercely down the table through his pince nez.

'People who become much dehydrated suddenly look very old. I saw once a picture of a climber who had survived for several days at very high altitude in the Himalayan mountains without water,' Kurt Waldheim said in his slow quiet way. 'He was actually less than thirty years but when he came in a dehydrated condition into camp he looked as if he was eighty. There are pictures to prove it. Now,' Kurt Waldheim continued, lifting his right hand, 'the water which comes out when a person becomes dehydrated is only what biologists call free water. There is also bound water, and if that comes out the person chars. This is what happens when coal is formed from the remains of organic material.'

'Is it what happens when you draw up an open fire with a newspaper? I mean if the paper gets too hot,' asked the Chancellor.

'That is exactly correct,' nodded Kurt Waldheim. 'I did it many times. If the paper actually touches the fire it burns, of course, but if you keep it away from the flames it chars, because the bound water comes out of the paper.'

'I did it many times too,' nodded the Master, 'and the charring always starts as a brown spot which spreads. But why d'you think this happened in the 'plane?'

'There is no water in metal objects, and the Swedish Colonel says the other objects in the 'plane were unaffected. Most objects in a 'plane are of metal. So it seemed logical to think it might be the water.'

'So something acted like a fire which charred but didn't burn,' nodded the Prime Minister. 'How would *that* be possible?'

'I do not know everything,' Kurt Waldheim replied, repeating his slow smile.

'Lightning perhaps?'

'Perhaps, but the electric current in a lightning stroke would be expected to fuse the metal objects. Some people claim lightning can do very strange things, but none has ever been proved in the laboratory. Isaac would know more about that than I do. The biggest mystery for me is to understand why the stroke was so directive. Why it avoided Isaac and hit the others.'

'Colonel Eriksson says it was deliberate,' the Prime Minister reminded the meeting.

'Colonel Eriksson is probably right,' nodded the Master, adding, 'although it sounds a bit daft.'

'Yes, but saying it was deliberate doesn't solve anything,' Kurt Waldheim went on. 'How was it done, even if it *was* deliberate? That's what I keep asking myself.'

'The Comet,' grunted the Master. 'It's always the Comet, isn't it? I knew it from the moment I saw it shining in the sky, brighter than Venus. I knew we were in for it.'

'For what, Master?' the Prime Minister asked.

'Surprises. Trouble.'

'I'd rather have thought we'd have been in trouble *without* it,' the Prime Minister replied. 'What is it you find so hard to understand, Dr Waldheim?'

'The precision of the directivity, of course. There are important rules which govern such things – what in physics we call phase control. Control from a big distance requires very large equipment. Here we have control within the 'plane to within a distance of about one metre. To exercise deliberate control from the distance of Comet Halley, and to do it to the precision of one metre only, would require equipment at least as large as the whole Comet itself. It would mean the whole surface of the comet was being used to generate some kind of a directed ray.'

'Literally, a death ray,' the Master breathed. 'But how can you be sure about your rules? There can be things you know nothing about, surely, Dr Waldheim?'

'Yes, but the things I know nothing about cannot contradict what I already know to be true. Otherwise the world would be self-contradictory.'

'Are you absolutely certain about your rules?' the Chancellor intervened.

'Even if I am cautious, I would still say yes. The rules in this case are very fundamental. I can believe in wonders of technique I know nothing about, but I cannot believe the fundamentals can be changed. I have trouble even when I use the whole surface of the Comet, even when I place this death ray thing far out in the ultraviolet. So, you see, I am led by the fundamentals to a strange and disturbing conclusion.'

It was at this point, with everybody's attention on a knife edge, that the College Butler arrived with morning coffee. He was tall, slender and grey-haired, with so grave a manner that the Prime Minister felt unable to prevent him temporarily dominating the scene, as he served the coffee from place to place around the table with a seemingly infinite repertoire of *haute monde* gestures. Sir Harry Julian was fully awake now, watching the minutiae of it all, even down to the gloves which the Chancellor knew had more than symbolic significance since the Butler handled the huge silver coffee-pot with the greatest of confidence. The gloves, the Chancellor speculated, must have been manufactured, probably on special order from the Master, from some insulating material. He watched as Sir Harry kept adjusting his pince nez to keep tabs, as they say, on the situation – evidently with the thought of introducing the system in the Treasury offices in place of the inevitable morning coffee lady with her lacklustre trolley. 'But he'll never get away with it,' the Chancellor said to himself with a tinge of regret.

When the Butler had withdrawn, the Prime Minister instantly plunged ahead.

'You were on the verge of a profound observation, Dr Waldheim?'

'I hope it is a sensible observation,' Waldheim nodded, again running a hand through his hair. 'Deliberate action need not be direct, need not come straight from the Comet, was my thought.'

'I don't follow that, Waldheim. Can you explain more clearly?' the Master asked.

'It will be best if I give an example. Television companies don't necessarily send their programmes directly all the way from the transmitter to the viewer. They often transmit to a local booster, and it is from the local booster that viewers receive the programme.'

'How could there have been a booster in the 'plane?' the Chancellor asked.

'A booster would need to have been created, of course. But the accuracy needed to position some form of a purposive agent in the 'plane would have been – what? Ten, twenty metres perhaps. Not so difficult as the nearly pinpoint accuracy of only one metre. Or the purposive agent could even have been positioned outside the 'plane – so long as it moved along with the 'plane. Of course, it would then have needed to get inside the 'plane in some way.'

Because of her penchant for talking, Frances Margaret had made it a rule to be seen and not heard throughout the formal sessions of the Halley Board. But now she burst out:

'The apparition of course. The apparition in the cottage.'

After that it was necessary to tell the story of the events which had transpired the day of the storm on the Norfolk coast. France Haroldsen then ended her unaccustomed intervention by saying, 'Until now we had no idea what it was.'

'Good heavens, a light begins to dawn at last!' exclaimed the Master.

'It all sounds very strange,' nodded Kurt Waldheim, 'but if we are to understand the facts it has to be like that. Otherwise we would have contradictions.'

'Which you don't like?' grunted the Master.

'Which are impossible,' Kurt Waldheim replied decisively.

'This brings the Board to the larger question we haven't touched on yet,' the Prime Minister said, recovering control of the meeting.

'Which is?' the Master asked.

'Are we doing the right thing? Is our policy right? Or is it too little? Should we be doing more? Can we be doing more? Sir Harry, if I were to say double the programme, or triple the programme, or quadruple it, where would you tell me I must stop? For economic reasons, I mean,' the Prime Minister continued with great emphasis.

At this, Sir Harry Julian lifted himself with some effort about six inches into the air, and then relapsed back with an audible thump into the special chair which the Master had provided. Whereon he proceeded to adjust his pince nez, and looking up and down the table with a severe expression said:

'The best way to approach your questions, Prime Minister, would be to persuade the Chancellor to brief the meeting on what we at the Treasury call our eyewash seminars.'

'Eyewash seminars?'

'Our eyewash seminars, Prime Minister,' Godfrey Wendover the Chancellor began with a smile, 'are concerned with in-house discussions of a kind that we would normally prefer to keep in-house.'

'I can understand that, Godfrey, but why eyewash?'

'Because the seminars are predicated on the idea that all the usual economic theories are eyewash,' the Chancellor replied, still smiling.

'Common sense seminars would be more like it then,' grunted the

Master despondently, wondering if the cloudburst, which was still beating down outside, was washing away the foundations of the College. It would certainly be making the fountain in the middle of Great Square superfluous in the extreme, he decided.

'Yes, well, there are two ways in which you can look at economics, Master. You can start from the existing state of affairs and try to decide which adjustments would make things a little better, or prevent them from getting a little worse. This micro-economics, as you might call it, is the way we always proceed officially: nudging the economy one per cent up here, preventing it going one per cent down there — that sort of thing.

'But,' the Chancellor continued, 'there's another way, a wild-eyed way. You can forget all about the existing state of affairs. In its place you can try to plan a quite different economy, one that you hope would be much better than the present economy.'

'Utopia,' grunted the Master, unimpressed, wondering if the foundations of the Colleges fronting the river, Queen's and St John's especially, would really stand up to this cloudburst he could hear slashing away on the windows.

'I seem to be getting a long answer to a short question,' the Prime Minister observed.

'To push along with the answer, Prime Minister,' the Chancellor went on in a quiet, unperturbed voice, 'all the evidence is that people who look for Utopia never find it.'

'Then why bother?'

'We don't. Instead, we've tried the more modest approach of trying to understand the broad principles of what makes for a successful economy.'

'And what does?'

'Yes, what does?' asked the Master, echoing the Prime Minister.

'Obviously you have to grow things and to make things. The necessities of life.'

'Obviously,' the Prime Minister repeated somewhat tartly.

'The surprise is that the number of people working in this essential category is really quite small. When you separate the things which are truly necessary from those we pretend are necessary you still haven't accounted for more than one third of the work force. So what happens to the rest?' the Chancellor asked rhetorically.

'They sit around and talk the way we're doing, and get more highly paid for it than the people who make things and grow things,' the Master answered.

'Or cook food in restaurants when people could cook it at home,' nodded the Chancellor.

'Or build up a home computer industry,' Sir Harry Julian came in with his severest manner. Glaring up and down the table and fixing the pince nez securely as he did so, Sir Harry went on:

'A large computer industry with very high ratings on the stock market. For what? For playing video games. For playing an illusion.'

'Is all this very deep, Sir Harry?' the Prime Minister asked doubtfully.

'It is not deep, Prime Minister, to say that a large fraction of what we call the economy is based on illusions. Illusions of what are important,' Sir Harry Julian replied, repeating his trick of lifting himself six inches into the air and then plopping back into the chair.

'The depth comes,' he went on, removing the pince nez and twirling them by means of a black cord to which they were attached, 'the depth comes when one realises that illusions are not foibles but *necessities*, that it is successful illusions which make for a successful economy.'

'I've heard dafter things than that,' the Master acknowledged.

'It sounds a bit Keynesian to me, like digging holes and then filling them in again. Isn't that rather frowned on these days, Sir Harry?' commented the Prime Minister.

'Digging holes and filling them in again was always a bad idea, Prime Minister,' Sir Harry answered, still twirling the pince nez. 'It was a bad idea, not because it was an illusion, but because it was certain to be an *unsuccessful* illusion.'

'How can you have a *successful* illusion, Sir Harry?'

'A *successful* illusion is one that persists, Prime Minister. Digging and filling holes would not persist. People would soon find it ridiculous. The point *is*,' Sir Harry emphasised with a scowl and a twirl, 'the point *is* that when we are enthusiastic about an illusion the economy booms, when we abandon an illusion the economy is depressed, $\pi\acute{\alpha}\nu\ \alpha\ \acute{\varrho}\epsilon\hat{\iota}$, $o\dot{\upsilon}\delta\grave{\epsilon}\nu\ \mu\acute{\epsilon}\nu\epsilon\iota$. A wise saying indeed,' Sir Harry declared, glaring around the table and then burrowing himself deeply into his special chair.

'Am I expected, then, to draw the conclusion that what we need for sustained prosperity is an indefinitely sustainable illusion?'

'Exactly so, Prime Minister,' agreed Sir Harry. Whereas a moment ago he had seemed higher placed than anybody else at the table, now he seemed lower. 'A long-continuing illusion, such as your building of these telescopes. The illusion is interesting, very interesting,' he added, sinking ever deeper into the chair and staring up now at the ceiling. 'It will provide employment for a most diverse set of people. Construction workers, steel and metals, electronics, maintenance workers, operating staff, secretaries, groundsmen, a small restaurant in the environs of each telescope, employment even for civil servants. I can touch only the fringe of it. More important still, it has the look of an illusion that will persist. Therefore I say,' said Sir Harry, suddenly coming upright and scowling once more, 'that, subject to natural limitations and wastage, we should expand our activities without a defined limit. δό ζ μος που στῶ καὶ κινῶ τὴν γῆν. Give us a firm spot on which to stand and we will move the Earth.'

Isaac Newton joined the rest of the Halley Board for what the Master was pleased to call a working lunch, a lunch of four courses and as many wines. Almost inevitably, therefore, the clock on the Edward III Tower was striking 2.30 p.m. by the time the Board reconvened for its afternoon session, with the Prime Minister determined to press on at maximum speed in order to be in the House by early evening. The session had not been long started when the Prime Minister was called away to the telephone. The Master, accompanied by the Chancellor, stood by the windows looking down onto Great Square, which appeared more like a shallow muddy lake than its usual trim and dignified self. The storm had gone, for as the Master quoted to the Chancellor, repeating what John Jocelyn Scuby had said at an earlier stage:

'Small showers last long, but sudden storms are short.'

As if to emphasise the truth of this statement, a bright April sun now shone in a clear blue sky.

Then the Prime Minister was back with so pale and stricken an appearance that Godfrey Wendover, the Chancellor, instantly said:

'Is anything wrong, Prime Minister?'

The Prime Minister moved forward three or four steps with a dragging gait, saying with an aghast expression, 'Yes, Godfrey, something *is* wrong, terribly wrong. The Russians have launched a first-strike attack.'

'Could there be a mistake...'

'No, that was the American President. He said he was giving over an important forty seconds to tell me Cruise missiles are being launched.'

It was an occasion when Isaac Newton found himself speaking out without any sense of volition.

'Stop it!' he said in a commanding voice that rang through the room large as it was.

'I don't see how I can...'

'Then try. Move in whatever military force is needed,' Isaac Newton continued in the same voice.

'But the Russians...'

'The Russians will gain nothing because the fall-out from their weapons will blow back straight into their own faces – the winds blow from west to east. And there are submarines at sea with more than enough capability for the most dreadful response. Nuclear weapons aren't for use. They only exist to stop themselves from being used. And tell the Germans to stop the Pershings from being launched. Whatever has happened we must *not* add to it.'

'Newton is right, Prime Minister,' the Chancellor now said in a quiet voice, coming forward and taking the Prime Minister by the arm. 'Let's at least try.'

When the Prime Minister and Chancellor had gone to the telephone, Isaac Newton joined the Master as he looked down upon the muddy pool that was Great Square. Glancing towards the Edward III Tower, towards the clock which had sounded hours by quarters over so many centuries, the Master asked:

'How long do we have?'

'They'll be here before you next hear the clock,' Isaac Newton replied. 'If the clock ever strikes again.'

Chapter 61

By an odd chance, the group assembled in the Presidential Office with its well-known oval shape was the same as had been present there a few weeks earlier. And by another odd chance, it was now the Secretary of State who had the snuffling cold and not the female Secretary of Commerce, who on this occasion was blooming with health, her dark hair specially done for the occasion and dimples in her cheeks – dimples that went down exceedingly well on TV, making it difficult for the President to fire her no matter what she said. And she was likely to say something dreadful to the five-star General, who sat there blowing clouds of smoke in the direction of a clearly very much upset Secretary of State.

The white-haired Director of the CIA was turning over in his mind how much of what he knew on a clandestine basis he could reasonably tell the meeting, how much he could reasonably tell the President for that matter. Everybody around the table was aware, of course, of the sinister mobilisation of the Red Army, but none knew – the CIA Director told himself with a certain measure of satisfaction – of the strange disease which had recently attacked, with only a single known exception, the whole of the Soviet top echelon of political leaders. This was a tit-bit not to be dispensed lightly around the table, the Director of the CIA decided, even though the Secretary of State was evidently in need of some sort of dispensation.

The meeting began promptly at 9.00 a.m. Eastern Standard Time, or 2.00 p.m. London time, or 4.00 p.m. Moscow time. It was odd indeed, considering the immense number of crackpots distributed everywhere over the whole world, that nobody had ever put forward the notion that it was really differences in the time zones which fuelled the superpower confrontation. Because Americans and Soviets ate, slept and worked at such very different times of day it was only too natural for each to feel that the other belonged to a different sub-species of humanity. On a typical day there was scarcely any moment when the American President could communicate with the Soviet President without one or other of them being half asleep, or without their digestive and bodily processes generally being in wholly different phases of the twenty-four-hour cycle: one on full-belly, the other on empty-belly, as it were. For instance, at the time in question the American President, this being an election year, had made do for breakfast with a meagre bowl of crunchies and skimmed milk, whereas if it hadn't been for the mad itch the Soviet President would have been sleeping off a gargantuan late lunch in the fashion of a hibernating bear.

But the meeting in the Presidential Office had been called without reference to such matters. It had to do with the looming issue of the budget deficit, an issue of more than passing consequence in an election year. The five-star General was in watchful attendance to defend the numerous big-ticket items thought up by the Pentagon and its ingenious advisers. Properly speaking, the Secretary of the Treasury should have been present instead of the Secretary of State, but the Secretary of the Treasury was down with spring fever and had asked the Secretary of State to stand in for him, since the Secretary of State was the only man in Washington whom the Secretary of the Treasury approximately trusted. Both were in charge of traditional departments of Government that had served the Republic well over the quarter millennium of its existence, and for this service both were under perpetual attack from latterday committees, from Presidential aides, and indeed from every Johnny-come-lately which the prolific system managed to dredge up, for which reason it was natural for them to stand together as the guardians of one-time America. The Director of the CIA was present because he liked to be present whenever anything was going on.

'You'll be delighted to learn, Mr President, that the crunch – not the crunchies – is, conservatively speaking, one term away at least,' the Secretary of State snuffled.

'Meaning what?' the five-star General grunted as he blew a foot-wide smoke ring upward to the ceiling of the office.

'Meaning bankruptcy,' the Secretary of State replied sombrely as he watched the rising smoke ring. He wondered if the President would object if in future he defended himself by bringing along an artificial smoke-producing machine that consumed tobacco by the pound, a machine that would blow vile clouds of smoke in whatever direction he chose by some kind of powered exhaust device.

'We're up to twenty per cent now,' the Secretary of Commerce observed with a bright alert smile, her dimples showing as she widened her mouth to make them do so.

'Twenty per cent of what?' the President asked.

'Twenty per cent of budget, of course. Taken up by interest charges on the national debt, which stands now at one point four trillion dollars, you will recall, Mr President. Making allowance for increasing interest charges, and figuring for a continuing two-hundred-billion overspend, just to fund the General's absolutely essential big-ticket items, the meeting will discover that interest on the national debt will rise to consume the whole budget in about seven years' time – unless the Director of the CIA can somehow contrive to have the properties of the exponential function suspended,' the Secretary of Commerce continued, still more radiantly.

'Assuming no increase of taxes,' sneezed the Secretary of State. The President shook his head vigorously at the mention of increased taxes and said:

'Seven years is a long time away.'

'Then General,' dimpled the Secretary of Commerce, 'I'd advise you to seize the dollars coming to you as far ahead of time as you can and convert them immediately into Swiss francs.'

It was at this point that alarm buzzers rang out throughout the White House. The buzzers were of a droning kind the Secretary of Commerce hadn't heard before. She was wondering what they might signify when the five-star General shouted, 'To the bunker! It's a red alert,' at which the President took a small coded receiver from an inside pocket. Sure enough, a light bulb on it was glowing red.

'You're right, General,' he acknowledged. 'Hadn't we better get people out?'

'No time, Mr President. Seconds count now. To the bunker!'

The General and the President led the way out of the office at a smart dash, with the Director of the CIA not far behind, and with the Secretary of State and the Secretary of Commerce tagging along last. Indeed, the latter two members of the party would have been lost if it hadn't been that the President couldn't locate the key to a special elevator, the special key he was supposed to be carrying. The General knew, however, of a small panel let into the wall, which he opened to reveal a key hanging on the far side of a glass panel. Sheathing his hand in his tunic, which he removed for the purpose, the General shouted, 'Stand back!' and then drove his fist powerfully into the glass panel. The General retrieved the key and opened up the door to the special elevator, whereon the party piled into a small compartment with the President asking as the elevator door closed, 'Couldn't all this have been computerised?'

The elevator dropped like a stone, almost as if it had no restraining cable. Since it took fully forty seconds before slowing and oscillating for a while, the Secretary of State estimated they must have descended pretty deep. As they quitted the elevator the General shouted again:

'Into the tube!'

The tube was an opening covered by a stiff material with a slit across its diameter through which the General and the President inserted themselves in turn, then the Director of the CIA with some alacrity, followed, as before, by the Secretary of State and the laggard Secretary of Commerce.

When it came to the Secretary of Commerce's turn, she found herself sliding smoothly down a chute which narrowed quickly to about a three foot diameter. The chute went down at a gentle angle with the motion more in the horizontal than the vertical, so that they were evidently moving well outside the perimeter of the White House, and even outside the perimeter of the White House grounds. The underground route took her around corners and down what were clearly three distinct levels, always smoothly and with a degree of friction that kept closely in balance with gravity. Eventually the tube debouched into a large brightly-lit underground cavern. The Secretary of Commerce picked herself up from a sliding posture, automatically checking that her earrings with the blue sapphires, of which she was so very fond, hadn't been lost in the brouhaha, which evidently was some kind of a schoolboy exercise the Pentagon had dreamed up. She wondered, as she moved towards the centre of the cavern, or bunker as these schoolboys liked to call it, if the time might not have come for her to consume some new boyfriend, in keeping with *Time* magazine's persistent description of her as the 'Administration's most active member'.

The U.S. defensive warning system was consistent in its complexity with the importance of a superpower. The earliest warning came from satellite-borne systems, both radar and infra-red. Then came the over-the-horizon ionospheric backscatter detection of the trails of approaching enemy missiles, and thirdly and lastly there was the usual above-horizon radar. Each of these three stages fed data constantly, every second of every day, into computers which analysed the data for evidence of approaching missiles, especially with respect to the directions and speeds of motion of suspect echoes, the whole process being brought together for inspection at Air Force HQ near Omaha, Nebraska, whence identical information was instantly transmitted to the Presidential bunker in Washington D.C.

In spite of the response of the Presidential party being almost as fast as it was possible to be, much time had already been lost. Yet if the President had been in a press conference, or in an electoral confrontation on TV held under the auspices of the League of Women Voters, it is hard to see how any response at all within the flight time of missiles from the Soviet Union would have been possible. Or if the President, or his Soviet counterpart in a reversed situation, had even been occupied with the elementary necessities of life about which one does not normally speak, the situation would have been the same.

In view of the urgent need of a Presidential response, because of the dual key system used in the control of nuclear weapons, it defied logic that such simple domestic matters hadn't been subjected to big-ticket-item study. Of course, as everybody of importance knew quite well, the Presidential nuclear key was carried in person in a specially-sealed pocket, and could have been quickly activated in response to a telephone call, without the President even needing to stir an inch from the desk in his office. But the President would then in effect have been taking instructions on perhaps the most responsible aspect of his office, instructions from the person at the other end of the telephone. Only by seeing the evidence for himself could the President make the independent assessment of the gravity of the situation he was supposed to make. And how, without a descent to the bunker, was that to be done? All this only went to show how exceedingly unstable the whole system had become, viewed either from the West or the East. Which meant that sooner or later the balloon was going to go up, inevitably so.

The Secretary of Commerce watched in fascination as two military officers cut an inner pocket of the President's jacket open and took a small cassette therefrom, thinking that this was surely carrying a schoolboy exercise a little too far. The officers went quickly to an important-looking console and clipped the cassette into a vacant space, and then proceeded to type with fast-moving fingers at a large keyboard, whereon the five-star General shouted:

'And now we can go! Soviets here we come!'

At this outburst it at last dawned on the Secretary of Commerce that the brouhaha might be for real. With this sickening perception she went immediately to study a huge wall display in many colours. It was an enormous world map showing streaks of red light converging on the major cities of the United States, with the oceans across which the streaks were moving displayed in a light blue. According to the babble of conversation around the console, the red streaks were missile tracks.

Then, after studying the vast wall display for a while with mounting horror, the Secretary of Commerce saw with immense relief that it couldn't be for real.

'There's a missile track coming from Antarctica,' she said to the President and the five-star General, who were now standing close by, also studying the wall display.

'I always said those Soviet scientists down there in the Antarctic were a bunch of suspect bastards,' answered the General.

True, there was a big cluster of tracks emanating from the direction of northern Canada, which looked as if they might really have come from Siberia. But there were several others that seemed odd to the Secretary of Commerce, who by now had an eye sharply-tuned to the pattern of the red-coloured trails.

'Look,' she said, 'there's one from the Sahara.'

'It's the Libyan bastards in Chad.'

'And another from West Africa.'

'The Cubans,' roared the General. 'My God how we've been sold down the river,' he added in disgust.

'And another from the Indian Ocean.'

'Submarines!' the General instantly countered. 'This is a world-wide conspiracy. How is it we had no warning I'd like to know, sir?' he asked the Director of the CIA with fierce belligerency.

It was at this point that the President telephoned the British Prime Minister to say that Cruise missiles were being launched from British bases, a call that was followed after a forty-second interval by one of similar duration to the German Chancellor, to say that Pershing II missiles from German bases were being launched. Afterwards, the

President was able to point with pride to the fact that in a situation of extreme tension, where every single second counted, he'd nevertheless set aside nearly a minute and a half to inform his allies of the desperate nature of the situation.

'There's one coming straight from the Himalayas,' the Secretary of Commerce squeaked.

'Now we know why the Soviets invaded Afghanistan, Goddam it!' the five-star General thundered in reply.

'And another from Australia,' the Secretary of Commerce squeaked again.

'It's not from Australia. It's from a submarine in Australian waters,' one of the military officers remarked, taking the load off the five-star General.

'You said that right,' nodded the General.

'Wouldn't it have been more sensible for the Soviets to have submarines in Californian waters?' the Secretary of Commerce persisted.

'It would be more sensible if you kept quiet, miss,' another military officer remarked in a sharp voice.

'You said that *damn* right,' agreed the General.

All eyes were suddenly turned on another large wall display which had just been illuminated. The second display showed the United States invaded by a multitude of broad streaks of red. It was the same as the first display but on a much bigger scale, so that the advance of the broad streaks on American cities could be observed from one second to another. The streak headed for Washington D.C. could be seen to be ahead of the others.

'My God, we're going to take it,' the President observed as the distance of the head of the streak from the city shrank swiftly to nothing at all.

Everybody in the bunker ducked involuntarily as the streak reached them. The Secretary of Commerce was at first surprised that there was no audible explosion, but then she realised that none of the explosive features of a missile would show themselves so far underground, which, of course, was exactly the way the bunker had been planned. Yet it still seemed a bit odd that nothing at all in the bunker was affected.

'The electric supply is still OK,' she said to the Director of the CIA.

'We're on a separate circuit, generating our own current. Otherwise there'd be no point in it,' the Director of the CIA answered.

'What *is* the point in it?'

'The point in it, ma'am,' the five-star General, who was standing close to the Director of the CIA, said in a raised voice which rang throughout the bunker, 'is that we must now begin planning for World War Four – once we've got our own silos functioning. Lucky we had them fully hardened,' the General added to the President.

'Yes, now, how are things going, General?' the President asked, looking from one wall display to another.

'New York goes,' someone sang out as if in reply to the President, and indeed one of the several broad streaks moving inexorably towards New York reached it at just that moment.

A dozen or so points in amber light, mostly located in the mountain states along the chain of the Rockies, were now winking on the large-scale wall display.

'Silos that are operative,' the General explained.

'But I thought we had many more than that,' the President remarked in a puzzled voice.

'The others are having problems, Mr President,' a military officer explained.

'There are no problems with the Pershings and Cruises, I hope?' the President enquired anxiously.

'Some are operative already, Mr President,' another officer at the console informed him.

'Los Angeles goes,' a voice rang out.

'That means the end of the Getty Museum, I'm afraid,' the Secretary of State thought to himself, sneezing violently without bothering with his handkerchief, which by now was sopping wet anyway and therefore uncomfortable to use.

'There's one coming at Boston right from the middle of the Greenland ice-cap,' the Secretary of Commerce observed in a high treble.

'Get that woman out of here,' the General ordered, his patience with the Secretary of Commerce exhausted. There wasn't going to be much commerce for a long time to come, he thought to himself with satisfaction, as two orderlies bundled the woman away. The Secretary of Commerce was hustled from the region of the bunker with the console and wall displays, along corridors and through triple doors, hustled at such a pace that it wasn't until the familiar sight of an elevator jerked her back into a normal state of mind that she found the voice to ask:

'What's that?'

'An elevator, miss,' was the uninformative reply.

'I mean where does it go?'

'To the surface, miss.'

'Then why aren't people coming down it?'

'It has three stages, miss,' said the other orderly.

'And the power supply will be off at the top,' the first orderly added.

'Even so, I think I'll make the trip,' the Secretary of Commerce said, widening her mouth to show the dimples and adding, 'Would you boys care to come along for the ride?'

'Don't you understand, miss? The city up there is horrible,' one of the young fellows said.

'It's gone completely,' said the other.

'Then how are you expecting to survive down here?'

'We have food and fuel for months. We'll survive until the Fourth Army is organised.'

'I see,' nodded the Secretary of Commerce, 'but I don't think I'll be staying for the party.'

When she stepped towards the elevator the orderlies tried to restrain her, whereon the Secretary of Commerce produced her official high-toned papers of Government rank, which left the young fellows with little option but to stand back and let her proceed on her mad enterprise.

'She'll be back soon enough,' said one of the orderlies to the other as the elevator door closed behind the Secretary of Commerce.

'Not a bad bit of cheesecake,' the second orderly acknowledged. 'Pity she's going to be contaminated.'

The elevator went up a long way before stopping. The door slid open and the Secretary of Commerce stepped out on to a spacious area, which was one of the stages mentioned by the orderly. The door slid closed again and a light indicated that the elevator cage was on its way down again. With the momentary fear that she'd somehow stranded herself, the Secretary of Commerce touched the button of a second elevator which evidently led upwards towards the surface. After an agonising few moments of waiting and repeatedly stabbing the button there was a faint noise from within the shaft of the staged elevator. This told the Secretary of Commerce that, thankfully, the cables were working on the second leg of her journey.

The second elevator deposited her on a second landing, and now everything became suddenly much more critical: stabbing the button of a third elevator, the one that was supposed to lead up to the surface, produced no response, just as the orderly had warned her would be the case. Yet surely there had to be stairs somewhere, she decided. Eventually, on the far side of a metal door, she found stairs which ascended very steeply as if they were in a naval ship. At the top another metal door took her back towards the upper elevator shaft, a door that shut itself on a powerful spring with a loud click, and which, from the elevator side, she found to be locked. So here she was, close to the surface now, with her retreat back into the bunker below entirely blocked. There was, of course, an elevator button here at the top of the third stage which she tried. But, as before, the electric power was off.

A faint light from the surface could be seen coming down two short further flights of stairs, much less steep than before. The Secretary of Commerce ascended them slowly, listening for sounds from the world outside – but listening in vain. Everything outside was silent. Should it have been silent if raging fires were consuming the remnants of the city, she asked herself?

At the top of the stairs there was an odd kind of exit which reminded her of the entrance to the tube that had taken the Presidential party down into the bunker. The tube had been covered by a stiff material with a slit across it and here the exit was similar but with several layers of the stiff material. The Secretary of Commerce wriggled her way through the layers like a mole coming plop to the surface of a grassy field. And indeed it was onto a wide area of grass that the Secretary of Commerce emerged. After a first moment of intense surprise she realised that she was close to the centre of the Ellipse. Now she knew what all the months of mysterious construction work inside the Ellipse, construction work fenced off by high barricades from the public, had been about.

The scene that met her eyes was astonishing beyond belief. Not a person was in sight. Not a sound from traffic. Yet every building was intact, exactly as it always had been. Thinking that her instinctive feeling of something most peculiar having happened was dead right, the Secretary of Commerce set off across the grass towards the south-east corner of the Ellipse. For want of anything more obvious to do, she then decided to walk along Constitution Avenue to the Trade and Commerce Building with the modest thought that once she reached her own office she could always brew up a pot of coffee.

She'd reached the intersection of Constitution and 14th when there was a muffled shout from behind. Turning, the Secretary of Commerce let out a shriek, for lumbering towards her were two goon-like gesticulating figures. They had big metal helmets festooned in gauze with huge piped gas-masks, and they lumbered like persons in ski boots because they were wearing heavily-leaded contamination-proof boots. The Secretary of Commerce observed that they also wore boiler-suits festooned with various gadgets and instruments. And, for some reason best known to itself, the leading figure was waving something which looked like a French policeman's baton. Her curiosity not being up to an investigation of the situation, which she thought had probably more to do with civil defence than with a landing from a flying saucer, the Secretary of Commerce took to her heels, crossing deserted Constitution Avenue at a run and making rapidly towards the Mall, which leads in an unbroken sweep to Capitol Hill.

She was quite out of breath by the time she reached a wooden bench close to the Smithsonian Institute. From the bench she could examine Government buildings both north and south of the Mall. They all seemed to be OK. Whatever the red streak had done that hit Washington, it certainly hadn't damaged the buildings. The Secretary of Commerce was trying to make sense of this undoubted fact when a hoarse voice declared:

'Repent! The end of the world is at hand.'

The hoarse voice belonged to a tattered figure who now sat down beside her.

'Has there been a big explosion?' she asked.

'We are the only people left in the whole world. God has struck with heavy hand on Sodom and Gomorrah,' was the unpromising reply.

'Did you see it happen?'

'The world is a brief illusion. Prepare yourself for the Kingdom of Saints.'

'Which is at hand?'

The question seemed to put the tattered tramp-like figure out of his stride, for now he said in a puzzled tone:

'The ungodly have withered like a green bay tree.'

'*Why* have the ungodly withered?'

'Because the Lord cometh to rid the world of those who sin against Him.'

Seeing that the conversation was leading nowhere, the Secretary of Commerce took out a ten-dollar bill from a small purse which she always carried on her person. Handing the bill to the tattered man, she rose from the bench. As she walked away the hoarse voice repeated:

'Repent! The end of the world is at hand.'

The Secretary of Commerce suddenly remembered the winking lights of the hardened silos, and the Cruise and Pershing missiles which had actually been launched. With this terrifying thought she concluded that the tattered man was only too likely to be prophetically correct.

Chapter 62

Isaac Newton had been wrong. The clock on the Edward III Tower moved slowly, infinitely slowly, towards 3.00 p.m. As it struck the hour again the Master grunted:

'It's lucky you're sometimes wrong. Let's hope we can see it through to three-fifteen.'

So, quarter-by-quarter, they waited in the long upstairs room of the Trinity Lodge, until eventually the Chancellor returned with really bad news.

'Several of the Cruises have been launched. We were too late to stop them all,' he told Isaac Newton.

'Even if the fat wasn't in the fire before, it is now,' the Master said with resignation.

As if mention of fire had triggered some in-built response, the Master led the party into his private snug, where an open wood fire had been laid. When the others moved to help as the Master got down on his knees to light it he waved them back, nodding slowly as if to himself.

'No, I can manage. I used to catch trout when I was a boy and then cook 'em on a camp fire. This may be the last time I'll light one. Pity there's no trout.'

When the fire began to crackle, the wood being dry, Sir Harry Julian settled himself into a big chair at the Master's direction, and then, to everybody's amazement, fell asleep.

'That's the spirit that made the British Empire what it used to be. You young people won't remember, of course,' the Master said quizzically. 'The trouble nowadays is that it's all discos, always on the go, in time and out of time. No rest. No peace. No snoring,' he went on as Sir Harry's breathing became audible. '*Fin de siècle. Fin de* everything.'

'I'm not so sure,' Frances Haroldsen remarked.

'Why aren't you so sure?'

'Because I've a feeling it's all to do with the Comet.'

'How could that be, Frances Margaret?' Kurt Waldheim came in, breaking a long silence during which he had been wondering about his wife Rosie in Geneva.

'I was thinking of your purposive agents.'

'What purposive agents?' asked Isaac Newton.

Kurt Waldheim shook his head in embarrassment and tried to avoid the question.

'It was only a speculation.'

'The speculation was that Comet Halley can generate purposive agents,' Frances Margaret began, 'capable of doing very remarkable things. Otherwise we couldn't understand what happened in the 'plane which landed you in Stockholm. Couldn't it be something like that? Apparitions in the air?'

'If nothing happens in the next hour, it has to be something like that,' agreed Isaac Newton.

So they waited, minute by minute by minute, until eventually the Prime Minister joined them with more depressing news.

'Pershing IIs have been launched. I've tried to raise both Washington and Moscow – the lines don't seem to be dead so I went on and on trying. But I can't get any sense. Either way, East or West. We've stopped the Cruises, but I don't suppose that's really going to help.'

'You've done what you could,' nodded the Chancellor. 'There's a slightly hopeful suggestion here.'

'What?'

'That it might be a sort of decoy by the Comet.'

'Heaven pray it is.'

The Master padded forward.

'You know, I'm going to assume it's the Comet. That can't do any harm, can it?'

'I suppose not,' agreed the Prime Minister.

'Then I'm going to prepare to celebrate. I've got a few bottles of a very nice champagne.'

'I couldn't face it.'

'I don't see that, Prime Minister. If we're going to be blown to perdition I don't see why we shouldn't be blown there with champagne glasses in our hands,' grunted the Master as he padded out of the snug.

'What does the FO say?' asked the Chancellor.

'They say they've detected no change from Moscow. There was a black-out before, and there's a black-out now.'

'Not very informative.'

'You know,' went on the Prime Minister, 'about a week ago I had a visit from a funny little man at the FO. A sort of dissident there. He came with a ridiculous story of the reason for the black-out. He said the Politburo is incapacitated.'

'Incapacitated?' Isaac Newton asked with sudden interest.

'Incapacitated by a new disease, which goes in Moscow under the name of the mad itch.'

'Is this information important, Isaac?' Kurt Waldheim exclaimed in surprise, noticing the animated expression on Isaac Newton's face.

'I wish I'd known it before.'

'Why?' asked the Prime Minister.

'Because it make sense of some of the recent coded messages.'

'From Comet Halley?'

'Yes.'

'Can you explain in plain language?'

'ἄριστον μὲν ὔ'δωρ,' growled Sir Harry, opening a stormy eye and surveying the company.

'And what might that mean, Sir Harry?'

'It means "Water is best", Prime Minister.'

'Even so, I think I'll go along and help the Master with the champagne.'

'In plain language, Prime Minister, I'm almost certain now that we've experienced a decoy.'

'The missiles, the Cruises and Pershings, weren't decoys. They were the real thing. And they were really launched.'

'Then it seems they got nowhere,' Isaac Newton concluded.

Chapter 63

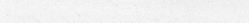

Isaac Newton listened in amazement.

'We've been thinking,' the Chancellor said, 'that it would be better for you to move back to Cambridge.'

The meeting in Isaac Newton's office at CERC in Swindon had been arranged at short notice by the Chancellor, who had just driven from London via the M4.

'Why the sudden change of mind?' Isaac Newton asked. 'I'm not at all sure the Cavendish Chair is still warm.'

'It is. The Prime Minister has been in touch. The point is this: while we were in a static phase, I mean with telescope-building as our main priority, it made sense for you to be here, where you could have most influence on the building programme. But now...'

'But now...?' Isaac Newton repeated ironically.

'Now the Comet has become distinctly active, the situation is

different. The building programme has become long-term and
therefore somewhat moot. The communication problem, the code and
so forth, is now the really important thing. And of course the code
connections are better done from Cambridge. Didn't you say the other
day that you'd missed something?'

'Which really was quite important, I suppose.'

'You're surely not going to quarrel?'

'No. Provided we understand that this is to be the last *volte face*,'
answered Isaac Newton. 'It's odd the way I always hate beginnings,'
he went on. 'I get to know people and I get nostalgic when I have to
leave them.'

'I've always found it so whenever I've had to change ministerial
responsibilities. But now I want to come to a matter of blazing
urgency,' the Chancellor continued in an anxious voice.

'We seem to move from one crisis to the next. What is it this time?'

'There's the devil to pay, Newton. Can't you imagine the reaction
at the Pentagon? Their defensive dispositions *and* their ideas on what I
think is called "launch under attack", both ending up in confusion.'

'I can't say I'm particularly surprised,' Isaac Newton replied,
without any of the Chancellor's emotion. 'You see, experience shows
that systems which become over-complex are only too likely to end
that way. Especially when an over-complex system is called on to
operate in a once-off situation.'

'I'm not arguing technicalities,' the Chancellor went on, with a
shake of his head. 'I'm saying the situation was just about ideally suited
to produce red faces everywhere in Washington. I'm also saying that,
human nature being the way it is, red faces in high places inevitably
look for scapegoats.'

'I can accept the truth of that proposition without any difficulty,'
Isaac Newton nodded calmly.

'And I suppose you can accept that Comet Halley is the designated
scapegoat?'

'Isn't that a bit like crying for the Moon?'

'Except in the case of Comet Halley it isn't difficult to find a
surrogate scapegoat.'

'Good heavens! What *is* a surrogate scapegoat? A scapegoat for a
scapegoat?' Isaac Newton asked with more animation.

'The surrogate scapegoat in this case is *us*.'

'Why *us*?'

'Because we are, *you* are, the channel of intelligible communication
with Comet Halley.'

'Is Washington trying to say we put the Comet up to it?'

'In effect, yes.'

'But that's ridiculous.'

'Is it? How should they know we didn't? For that matter, how am *I* to know that *you* didn't?'

'For better or for worse, we're not quite as advanced as that.'

'How far advanced are you, in fact?'

'Numeric and scientific, fairly good. Semantic, a little. Politic, not at all.'

'Then why did it happen? My God, just think of it, Newton! The chaos of it! All like the real thing. Infra-red detection from satellites and radar echoes – just like real missiles, triggering the entire U.S. warning system, civilian as well as military. A warning in every American town and city. People plunging into shelters to escape the gamma rays, which they were told on TV and radio were only minutes, or seconds, away. People hearing it on the freeways and either driving into monstrous pile-ups or quitting their cars and choking the whole road system. In cities with subways, like Washington, people rushing into the stations in such numbers that the power supplies had to be cut off to avoid thousands of electrocutions on the live rails. Long after the missiles were supposed to have struck, the civilian warnings went on and on. The chaos took hours to unsnarl itself.'

'The stress was much the same for us, Chancellor.'

'Yes, but the Americans believe more than we do in their inalienable right to be compensated for stress.'

'How's that?'

'Reckon it out – the stress bill, I mean. Set the stress for spending several hours thinking you're under nuclear attack at a thousand dollars, which most would claim to be derisory. Yet a thousand dollars for every American man, woman and child amounts to a total bill of two hundred and fifty billion dollars. It needs a pretty substantial scapegoat to foot a bill like that. Besides which, according to our Embassy in Washington, the strikes weren't altogether an electronic illusion. Anybody who happened to be near the surface was hit by a definite form of temporary insanity. I've got a report from one of the attachés at our Washington Embassy, a young fellow called Tim Bassett. I'll read you the relevant passage,' the Chancellor replied, taking a slim file from his briefcase.

' "I was on duty," ' the Chancellor quoted, ' "when warning of imminent attack was received. I immediately sought to shred certain documents, instead of making my way to the basement where the Embassy's shelter is located. It was while I was thus engaged that a strange and hitherto unexperienced state of mind overtook me. In the briefest moment, I had the sensation of having become a hibernating animal, and that my duty was not to shred documents but to hunker down for a long sleep." '

The Chancellor stopped abruptly and shut the file with a decisive snap.

'That's quite enough of that. Insane it may sound, but it fits the undoubted facts.'

'What facts?'

'That Washington became entirely deserted of people. First, the air raid warning sent most to ground. Then whatever it was that struck caused the streets to be swept clean of the remaining few.'

'Entertaining as this might be, Chancellor, I can't quite see how we are involved ourselves.'

'We're under pressure, big pressure from both sides. To a point,' concluded the Chancellor, 'where we may be forced into a retreat.'

'A retreat?'

'Abandonment of the whole programme.'

'You know, Chancellor,' Isaac Newton said in a puzzled tone, 'I'm always reading about pressure. The EEC putting pressure on Morocco, the U.S. putting pressure on Brazil, the U.S.S.R. putting pressure on Syria – commentators are full of it. But unless there's a hostile army at your gate, or somebody is in a position to take the food out of your mouth, it doesn't seem to me to be anything more than an illusion, like thinking yourself to be a hibernating animal.'

'Political leaders form a kind of club,' the Chancellor began by way of explanation.

'I can believe that.'

'By which I mean we've a sort of code that normally we don't break. Even the Russians don't break it too outrageously. I mean we don't interfere with the political balances within other nations. Frankly, I hardly know which party is which, or what they're all supposed to stand for, even in nations as close to us as the Germans. I simply deal with whoever comes out on top, in elections or whatever.'

'I thought the CIA did nothing else except interfere with elections, everywhere up and down the world.'

'I should have said interference among the developed countries. The CIA breaks the rules among under-developed countries, I'll admit. But that's basically why the CIA is always in trouble with the U.S. Congress.'

'Are you trying to say, Chancellor, that you're afraid of outside interference in British politics? That your friends in the club are going to break the rules and upset the Westminster apple-cart?'

'That's correct, Newton. You see, there are scores of ways in which extremely powerful nations can interfere so as to favour the Opposition party. Economic reasons for instance.'

'But you have a substantial majority in Parliament, Chancellor. Obtained in part, I should perhaps mention, due to our first communication with Comet Halley. So I'm at a loss to see what any outside nation can do to harm you.'

The Chancellor began to march up and down the office, making no sound in the thick carpeting, a fact of which he suddenly became aware. Stopping, he pawed the carpet with his foot.

'You know,' he exclaimed, 'I wouldn't mind having a carpet like this in my own office.'

Then he continued marching and at last, in a voice rising high with anger, burst out:

'You've forgotten what the newspapers call the backbench revolt. I suppose you've seen the newspapers? Doesn't it look pretty threatening?'

'I saw the Opposition is bringing a vote of no confidence. But not for the first time. Surely your own party won't support it?'

'Look, once you start getting defections it quickly becomes serious. Each abstention removes one from your majority. Each defection to the Opposition removes two. So it doesn't need many defections for a quite substantial majority to melt away completely.'

'What would be the motivation? It would mean another election. Your defectors might lose their seats.'

'Not if the seats are safe ones.'

'But your party might lose power.'

'Giving other factions the opportunity they're looking for to gain an ascendancy in the party. That's what the game is all about. You've got to realise, Newton, that the Americans are telegraphing the end of the special relationship, which must have a big effect anyway – quite apart from the effect of the Comet, which can then be represented as a serious threat to world peace. With some justification, even *reasonable* people might think. Because Cruises and Pershings really *were* launched. You know, I still can't quite understand what happened to them.'

'The internal guidance systems are sensitive at certain moments to external radiations, Chancellor. Rendering an enemy missile inoperative is already a major part of military strategy, so I don't think it would have been at all difficult for the Comet.'

'With the incessant howling going on in Parliament all the time, it isn't easy to explain things like that to Members.'

'Well, Chancellor, I suppose I can always teach physics in a small school tucked away somewhere in the leafy lanes of Devon,' Isaac Newton said with dull resignation. 'But not for long,' he then added. 'Nor can you expect to garner many more crops on your farm, I'm afraid.'

'I don't understand. Why?'

'Because we can't simply go back to the situation as it existed before the Comet. We wouldn't be allowed to do so, you see. Suppose you try looking at things from the point of view of the Comet itself for a moment. After thousands of millions of years an important communication with Earth has at last been established. But it's a fragile communication. The Comet must understand the communication to be fragile, otherwise it would respond freely to everybody, instead of only through the code to us. From the military transmissions that stream out all the time into space the Comet may perhaps understand something of our human superpower confrontation. Recent events pretty well imply that this is so. The Comet might well understand that everything here is very much touch and go. If the situation deteriorates, with the only connection to humanity it appears to trust going dead, likely enough there will be a violent reaction.'

'Exactly what d'you mean by that?'

'The Comet has already shown us enough, hasn't it, to make it clear that wiping out the human species wouldn't be at all difficult? The whole lot of us converted into cylinders of carbon perhaps? Remember Eriksson? Remember he said there was now a third superpower in the field?'

'Why shouldn't it simply leave us alone?'

'It might well wipe us out to give another species a chance. There would be another dominant species you know, in five million years' time or in ten million years' time. This might seem remote to us, but to creatures that have already waited thousands of millions of years it wouldn't be much more than a few ticks of the clock. When you come to think about it, Chancellor, wouldn't wiping out the human species be pretty sensible anyway?'

Isaac Newton walked over to the big window that looked out over Swindon towards the south, and then continued:

'Often enough when I was a boy I watched wild animals trying to survive through a cold winter. I've watched hares on a moonlit night nibbling at one or two shoots of plants that stuck up through thick snow – just humbly trying to survive through the few weeks until the spring, not greedily trying to pile up a fortune in the bank, not spending untold billions of dollars piling up missile systems to blast the whole Earth away. You know, Chancellor, if I were the Comet, and if I saw all this nonsense going on, I might very well think it would be as well to be rid of such an arrogant, greedy, and generally unpleasant creature as man.'

The Chancellor sat down with a thump, as if trying to emulate his colleague Sir Harry Julian. With a weary gesture he drew a hand across his forehead.

'I'd some such perception myself, of course. Which was why I came here in a kind of panic. What would you advise, Newton?'

'If the press were to come out strongly on the side of the Government, would that help? Say on the morning of the vote of confidence.'

'Of course. It would be decisive. But the press is strongly *not* on the Government side.'

'Could you arrange for the Prime Minister to set up a press conference? Could it be done at 10 Downing Street? The day *before* the vote of confidence?'

'Who is to give it? The Halley Board?'

'Frankly, Chancellor, I'd like as few from our side as possible. I shall have to let loose, you see,' Isaac Newton said in a firm voice. 'Keep it to the Prime Minister, yourself and myself, please.'

'I think you and the Prime Minister would be best. Frankly, I'm not at *my* best in such situations,' acknowledged the Chancellor.

Chapter 64

The Prime Minister had decided to give maximum weight to Isaac Newton's suggestion of a press conference by holding it in the Cabinet Room at 10 Downing Street. Isaac Newton glanced around the long table for familiar faces as he and the Prime Minister took the two remaining chairs, which were placed half-way along the table, facing towards Downing Street. Not that familiar faces meant friendly faces, Isaac Newton reflected, as he recalled his somewhat disastrous meeting with the press on a former occasion. He recognised Alan Bristow, the editor of *Nature*. He also recognised Tom Taylor from the *Observer*. Or, more precisely, he recognised the astrakhan hat which Taylor was insisting on wearing even in the Cabinet Room. Also noticing the hat, the Prime Minister began:

'Would the gentleman wearing the hat please remove it. Or remove himself.'

To Isaac Newton's mind this wasn't exactly the most tactful way to begin a most critical encounter, as the dead silence that instantly descended on the room confirmed. After perhaps twenty seconds of dead silence, Taylor got to his feet and staggered from the room, still wearing the astrakhan hat.

'Nobody has worn a hat in here since Disraeli,' the Prime Minister observed in a brisk tone, adding, 'I have an especial dislike for astrakhan hats, as well as for flies, and for cigarette ash upon the carpet. And now Professor Newton is going to make a statement.'

'Two years ago the Prime Minister asked me to comment on disarmament talks which were then taking place in Geneva,' Isaac Newton began. 'My brief was to consider the status of the British nuclear deterrent, together with matters related to intermediate range missiles, explicitly the SS20 and SS21 on the Soviet side, and to Cruises and Pershing IIs on the NATO side.'

'Is it true that Cruises and Pershing IIs were actually launched? Fenwick of the *Mirror*,' a voice asked.

'We'll come to a full discussion of that question eventually, Mr Fenwick,' the Prime Minister replied calmly. Reflecting that the Prime Minister was well used to never-ending interruptions in the House, Isaac Newton went on, picking up the thread of what he'd been saying:

'My thinking about the British deterrent and about NATO didn't fit me very well, I'm afraid, for understanding the bigger issues of the superpower confrontation. Only gradually over the past two years have the appalling strategic changes which have taken place since 1970 become clear. To me, I mean,' Isaac Newton admitted in a quiet voice.

'Hardy of the *Mail*. Can you extend that please. By explaining exactly what you mean by *appalling*.'

'If you go back to the 1960s, Mr Hardy, there was a widespread comforting belief that nuclear war would be so great a disaster to everybody that no Government, of whatever political colour, could possibly contemplate it. This comforting belief was held by Governments, by the public, *and* by military planners.'

'And you say it has changed?' another voice asked.

'Unfortunately, yes. It changed decisively with the invention of the multiple warhead. Although in the early 1970s, when this happened, most of us didn't realise it,' the Prime Minister intervened.

'I'd like to hear your views on that, Professor Newton. As you probably know, we've had views of our own at *Nature*. For longer than two years I might add,' remarked Alan Bristow.

'With multiple warheads,' Isaac Newton replied, 'it became possible to conceive of a first strike so powerful as to be capable of entirely disabling the strategic weapons of the other side. At first it was only a conception. Now, you might say, the conception has become a reality. A first strike by the Soviet Union could quite probably destroy the capability of the U.S. to launch its Minuteman missiles.'

'Aren't they hardening up their silos to deal with that kind of a threat? Alan Cross of *The Times*.'

'All the indications are, Mr Cross, that protection of hardware is the lesser half of the problem. The real weak spot is the command structure. Timing sequences for the side under attack are becoming almost impossibly tight,' Isaac Newton explained.

'Cutting away the time available for political consultation,' interposed the Prime Minister again.

'And squeezing the time available for essential fail-safe procedures,' added Isaac Newton.

'I thought this was the whole point of having a large submarine fleet. Even if a treacherous first strike attack were launched, the other side would still have plenty of time to reply with a powerful second strike from submarines,' said Hardy of the *Daily Mail*.

'Because the locations of submarines are hidden, of course,' added Alan Cross of *The Times*.

'The trouble came with improving technology and increasing accuracy. Look, Mr Cross, suppose I knock out your main first strike weapons, and with such a measure of accuracy that your cities aren't greatly damaged. True, you could come back at me with your submarines. But do you? Knowing your cities remain at the mercy of my more powerful first strike weapons. Likely enough you don't. To preserve your cities you knuckle under. That's where the problem for military planners now lies,' Isaac Newton emphasised.

'I happen to agree with Newton on this, if not on everything,' Alan Bristow nodded. 'You see,' he went on, 'the temptation to mount a treacherous first strike is increasing all the time. If you don't, the other fellow might. The advantages of the first strike...'

'...are getting bigger,' Hardy of the *Daily Mail* nodded in turn.

'So where does that leave us?' asked Fenwick of the *Daily Mirror*.

'Pritchard of the *Guardian*,' said a new voice. 'It leaves us with an ever-dwindling margin of safety. The question I'd like to ask, Professor

Newton, is this: how much further does the world have to go, in your judgement, before nuclear war becomes inevitable?'

'The end of the century. If we're lucky,' replied Isaac Newton.

'*If* it hadn't been for the *Comet*,' the Prime Minister came in, judging the moment for discussing recent events was now ripe.

'Yes, Prime Minister, that's of course what we all want to know about. How was it done, to put it bluntly?' Alan Bristow asked immediately.

'If we knew the answer to that question, Dr Bristow, we would be the third superpower, wouldn't we?' the Prime Minister replied, obeying a natural instinct to evade the question.

'I appreciate that point, Prime Minister. But inevitably you must know more about the situation than we do,' Bristow persisted.

'What happened,' Isaac Newton continued firmly, 'was a war games exercise, grim in purpose but carried out somewhat ludicrously – perhaps to show us the absurdity of it all. First, the Russian leaders were immobilised, presumably to simplify a situation that became complex enough as it went on. A first strike on the U.S. was then simulated with a precision which, frankly speaking, I still find astonishing.'

'What would you say has been the result?' asked Hardy of the *Daily Mail*.

'That a hugely complex military network was seen to be vulnerable.'

'In the West you mean? Axeford of the *Morning Star*.'

'By implication also in the East, I think, Mr Axeford. The other very obvious implication, of course, is that of the *three* superpowers, the *third* is much the most powerful,' Isaac Newton replied.

'Which is why we've been allied with the third all along,' came in the Prime Minister, instantly seizing the opportunity.

'Which brings us to a rather sensitive point, Prime Minister,' Alan Bristow said, leaning forward in his chair and tracing a pattern in the air with his left hand.

'Which is?'

'Did the Halley Board have anything to do with recent events?'

'Would you prefer me to say yes, or to say no, Dr Bristow?'

'Whichever *you* prefer, Prime Minister.'

'I'm going to refer the question to Professor Newton, because frankly I don't know the best answer to it.'

'The answer is both yes and no,' Isaac Newton told the meeting, well aware that he was verging on making sensational headlines. '*Yes*, in the sense that we almost certainly supplied the Comet with information that enabled it to understand the human situation. *No*, in the sense that we had nothing at all to do with overtly planning the operation.'

'Are you disappointed, Dr Bristow?' asked the Prime Minister.

'Frankly, I don't quite know. But can we come now to the launchings of Cruise missiles? This seems to have been doubly serious, in that they were both launched and incapacitated. What happened to them?'

'They were disabled, along with Pershing IIs and Minuteman Is. It isn't too hard to disable missiles. X-rays will do it,' Isaac Newton answered.

'If you know how,' agreed Bristow. 'The other serious point is that, after the first few launchings, others were stopped – on your orders, I believe, Prime Minister. I'm not quarrelling with your decision...'

'Thank you.'

'I'm wondering what this is going to mean,' Bristow persisted, 'for the position of this country. Where exactly do we stand?'

'We seem, perhaps more by accident than design, to have become allied with the *third* superpower. Like it or not, that appears to be the situation,' the Prime Minister replied, fully aware that here was the crucial point.

'Whether the position is advantageous or not seems to me to depend on whether the alliance continues. Is there any danger of it becoming unstuck? Of our being left in the lurch?' asked Alan Cross of *The Times*.

'Some of you have kept a close watch on Project Halley from its inception,' began Isaac Newton in answer, glancing towards the editor of *Nature*, 'and I think you will agree with me that the trend has been quite otherwise. We've become more and more involved, mostly without expecting to be, I'll admit. But by now one can see that the potential of Earth as the solar-system centre of an information network is almost unlimited. What is obviously holding us back from realising this potential...'

'...is the superpower confrontation. Don't recent events make a great deal of sense in that light?' concluded the Prime Minister.

'Pritchard of the *Guardian* again. The strike on American cities doesn't appear to have been entirely harmless. We've had a report from our New York correspondent. He says that, at the very moment the strike occurred, everybody anywhere near ground level was hit by a strange miasma. Do you have any comments, Professor Newton?'

'Well, I understand that in military exercises people who are judged to have been hit are supposed to retire from the battle. This miasma of yours, Mr Pritchard, would have had that effect, I suppose. Have you any idea of what form it took?' Isaac Newton asked by way of reply.

'Our correspondent says it hit him as an intense desire to hibernate for the winter like a bear. But I find that a bit difficult to believe. He's really quite a hard-headed character.'

'I see, he can hold his liquor,' the Prime Minister smiled, sensing that an opportune moment for terminating the meeting had arrived. 'If you gentlemen would like to move upstairs, we'll see if *our* refreshments can transform you all miraculously into hibernating bears – like Circe in the *Odyssey*.'

Leading the way upstairs, the Prime Minister whispered to Isaac Newton:

'I was beginning to think we'd have to send for Harry Julian and his Greek. But it went well. I've got a pretty good instinct in these things.'

Ten minutes later, with drinks and refreshments served by a posse of waiters, Isaac Newton was surrounded by reporters with one insistent question:

'What's next, Professor?'

Noticing that the Prime Minister was suddenly absent from the throng, he decided to throw caution to the winds.

'The obvious next step is to get the European nations behind us.'

By the time Isaac Newton had spent another ten minutes expounding as best he could on this topic, the Prime Minister was back, brandishing what appeared to be a telegram. The babble died away to a silence in which, Isaac Newton thought, you could have heard a mouse crunching celery.

'Listen to this,' the Prime Minister cried. 'It's from the French President. It says: "All our support, guaranteed." '

After a further round of drinks had been dispatched, the reporters made their way noisily downstairs and out into Downing Street. As he passed Isaac Newton, Alan Bristow asked:

'Exactly what support is guaranteed?'

'I haven't any idea,' Isaac Newton replied. Then, when the others were gone, he asked the Prime Minister:

'Exactly what support are the French guaranteeing?'

'I haven't any idea,' the Prime Minister replied, 'but the French do this sending of encouraging messages extremely well, don't you think?'

Chapter 65

The morning press the day after the seemingly triumphant conference at 10 Downing Street was not as positive as Isaac Newton had hoped or expected. There was too much questioning of the wisdom of the contact with Comet Halley for his liking, too much fear of the unknown showing itself. Frances Margaret came up from Cambridge and in the late afternoon she and Isaac Newton made their way to the Houses of Parliament, knowing the coming vote of confidence would decide the shape of the future. On explaining their business to a policeman at the gate they were allowed into the entrance hall of the Commons where they were told to wait.

A slim young man with straight fair hair, half a head shorter than Isaac Newton, eventually appeared.

'I'm Pingo Warwick, you remember, the Prime Minister's PPS,' he said, holding out a hand. 'There are one or two things the PM wants to check with you,' Warwick went on, 'and we've just nice time before the balloon goes up. If you'll follow me I'll lead the way.'

Pingo Warwick set off at a good pace along corridors with many twists and turns, and with Frances Margaret's shoes tapping out loudly whenever they came to an uncarpeted section. Before the Prime Minister's office was reached all sense of direction had been lost.

The Prime Minister was seated at a desk strewn with papers, wearing reading glasses which Isaac Newton did not recall seeing before.

'Before these shows I like to think up the worst questions I might be asked. Then I write out replies and do my best to memorise them,' the Prime Minister explained, pointing to sheets which littered the desk. 'I find the homework pays off.'

'Was there anything . . .?' Isaac Newton began.

'Just questions of timing. What time was it, would you say, when I was called away from the Halley Board meeting? To answer the President's call about the launching of Cruises, I mean?'

Isaac Newton thought for a moment and then replied:

'Well, the Master walked over to the window looking down onto Great Square, and I went over to join him. We had a clear view of the clock on the Edward III Tower. By that clock it was about two forty-six, I'd say.'

'And the time when I came back? Not from that call – from the one you sent me off to make, the call about stopping the Cruises from being launched?'

Isaac Newton thought again, longer than before, and eventually said with a shake of his head:

'I can't be so sure about that one. We were all in a pretty disturbed state of mind. But the Master went on and on watching the clock and I was with him for much of the time. So I'd say it must have been somewhere around three-twenty.'

'Thank you. I'm sorry to fuss about such details, and they probably won't be important. But you know it's amazing how often Ministers get themselves into trouble over mistakes of detail which don't seem important when they're made, but which get blown up out of all proportion later on. Now if you'll excuse me, I'll have a last minute glance through all this stuff. The trouble is I have to prepare for everything which might be asked, and that's a lot of preparation. Pingo will look after you.'

As Pingo Warwick led off once more along the corridors, he said:

'The PM's in a fighting mood.'

'So I could see. How did you assess the morning papers?' Isaac Newton asked.

'Made to order.'

'Oh, I was a bit disappointed. I hoped we would score rather more heavily . . .'

Pingo Warwick waved a hand in the air as they mounted a short flight of stairs and said:

'Some reporters may have had second thoughts. Editors may have toned down some aspects and toned up others. Each paper has its own special class of readers to which it must tailor things. The great thing is we scored a solid fifty to sixty. When you start ahead with a good majority you don't really need to score more than a solid fifty, you see. It's only when everything goes against you, one trouble after another, that it becomes worrisome.'

Their journey ended in the Visitors' Gallery of the Commons Chamber, an ornate place strung somewhat incongruously with many microphones, and of about the length of a cricket pitch. The Gallery was already almost full. Three places had been reserved, however, to which they were directed by an attendant.

'I'm looking forward to a good slanging match. It raises the body temperature,' observed Pingo, adjusting the tip of the handkerchief in the breast pocket of his suit.

The Speaker announced that the Prime Minister would make a statement to the House, and the Prime Minister began.

'Mr Speaker, Honourable Members, I wish to report to the House the circumstances surrounding events of the eleventh April of this year. At two forty-six p.m. on that day I received a personal telephone message from the President of the United States informing me that he had ordered the launching of Cruise missiles in response to a first strike Soviet attack.'

There was an indefinite growling from members.

'No polarisation yet,' whispered Pingo.

'As members will know already, the signals which had been received by American warning systems turned out to be a decoy, an exceedingly realistic decoy, instigated, the Government believes, by electronic interference from Comet Halley. The Government, as members will also know, has for some time been in electronic communication with the Comet. As a consequence of our experience in this respect, it was apparent to us at a somewhat earlier moment than it was to others that the supposed Soviet first strike was in fact a decoy. With this understanding it became important for the launching of Cruise missiles to be countermanded. This was done at about three-twenty p.m., through consultations between British Army commanders and the American Commander on the spot.'

The Prime Minister now sat down amid more indefinite growling, and the Speaker called on the Leader of the Opposition.

'That was just setting out the stall for them to shy at,' Pingo explained.

'With the obfuscation which the House has come to expect from the Prime Minister . . .' the Leader of the Opposition began, and then paused as opposition cheers rang out behind him.

'With the obfuscation, the obfuscation, I say . . .' The Leader of the Opposition paused again as the Government benches shouted, 'Rubbish, man!' giving the Speaker little option but himself to shout: 'Order! Order.'

' . . . with the *obfuscation* which the House has come to expect from the Prime Minister,' the Leader of the Opposition ploughed on like a warship through heavy seas, 'we have heard a statement replete with half-truths. It is a half-truth that the launching of Cruise missiles was stopped by *consultations*. What happened to the missiles that were *actually* launched before the supposed "consultation"? The House deserves a full answer to that question, and the British people deserves a full answer to it. Will the Prime Minister not come straight out with the whole truth, that an insane military system was set in motion by what turned out to be a mere *decoy*? A *de-coy*. Think of that now. A *de-coy* set off missiles which could have terminated the lives of hundreds of millions of people.'

Cheers and counter-cheers echoed through the Chamber, with Pingo Warwick now hard put to it to hold himself down to the comment:

'There was a lot of wind in that one.'

Isaac Newton forbore to reply that he thought there was a lot of sense in it too.

'Will the Prime Minister consider the urgent need, in the light of these unhappy events, to reconsider the whole policy on which British security has been based?' the Leader of the Opposition asked.

The Prime Minister stood and simply said, 'Yes, sir,' at which Members on both sides of the House jumped up to face each other, it being easier to shout standing up.

'I think I'll go and do some baying myself, if you'll excuse me,' Pingo Warwick said, apologetic at abandoning his assignment but unable any longer to resist the compulsion to be in the fray – shouting from the Visitors' Galley being rigorously forbidden, not that the most determined shouting from visitors would have added much to the uproar on this occasion, Isaac Newton thought.

The Prime Minister was still standing. After waiting for the storm to die down, the Prime Minister then added:

'The Government has the security of the nation under review at *all* times, and the present occasion is no exception to that basic rule.' Then the Prime Minister sat down with a smile, as if to say, 'I got you there.'

A backbencher from the Government side was now called by the Speaker.

'Would the Prime Minister clarify the nature of the consultations that took place between ourselves and the United States, consultations both political and military?' the backbencher asked.

'That's a hotter one,' whispered Frances Margaret. The Prime Minister replied in an easy confident manner, however.

'The consultations on a political level consisted of the telephone call of which I have just informed the House. On a military level it consisted of a request from the British area commander that the launchings of Cruises be stopped. This, I must emphasise, was *after* we had become convinced the situation was really caused by a decoy which, as the House has also been informed, was apparent to us somewhat earlier than it was to others.'

'Will the Prime Minister assure the House that relationships with the Government of the United States have not been impaired by these events?' the backbencher then continued with a planned follow-up question.

'On our side there has certainly been no cause for any change of relationship with the Government of the United States,' the Prime Minister answered, again in the same confident manner.

'Then there should have been,' someone shouted from the Opposition benches, to which there were added cries of, 'Answer the question!'

'Now it's between Scylla and Charybdis,' said Frances Margaret.

'That's only too right. Between the devil and the deep,' agreed a voice beside them. 'Ferguson of the *Telegraph*,' said the man, reaching over to shake hands.

'It was a very stressful time for everybody concerned, especially for the Government of the United States. I would hope that as a more normal situation prevails it will be seen that our actions were in the cause of peace, and that it would not have been to anybody's advantage if more missiles had been launched from British territory,' the Prime Minister replied.

'Answer the question!' the Opposition benches continued to bellow, to which there were now even louder jeers from the Government benches, whereon the Prime Minister immediately sat down with the air of a mission accomplished.

Thereupon the Speaker called on the *éminence grise* of the House, a member of very many years' seniority who had managed to fashion a cross-bench role solely for himself, and whose speciality lay in making himself widely unpopular by speaking the plain truth in situations where nobody else would recognise it.

'Will the Prime Minister not admit what has long been clear to thinking people, that the British strategic alignments have become without any conceivable basis in logic or even in expediency in recent days? Does this decoy, brought about apparently by Comet Halley, not make a pointless *embroglio* into a farce from which the British people should be summarily delivered? *Atque omne ignotum pro magnifico; sed nunc terminus Brittanniae patet.*'

'There he goes again! I wonder what that means?' whispered Ferguson.

'If I'm not mistaken it means: Speculation grows when knowledge fails, and now the very extremities of Britain are laid bare,' Frances Margaret whispered in reply.

'If you don't mind I'll use that. I write the funny column, you see. On the back page of the *Telegraph*,' Ferguson nodded.

'The Honourable Member will be aware,' replied the Prime Minister suavely, 'that the Government has been in the vanguard of research into, and communication with, Comet Halley. A policy for extending this position will shortly be laid before the House. Let me simply say now that it is our intention to press this extension to the maximum extent that is consistent with our commitments elsewhere.'

'It's becoming a foregone conclusion,' said the talkative Ferguson, adding, 'I'd been hoping for a tighter run race.'

Another Government backbencher was called. 'Rebel,' Ferguson told them, 'let's see if he's got any steam in him.'

'The House has been told that Cruise missiles were launched. Will the Prime Minister explain the circumstances in which they came to be aborted?' the rebel asked.

'They came to be aborted when it was known that we were in a decoy situation. The whole experience demonstrated that the positive control procedures worked satisfactorily at launch, and that negative control procedures worked satisfactorily at abortion. As the Honourable Member will appreciate, the Government is well satisfied with this combination of procedures,' the Prime Minister answered, to cheers generally from the Government benches and to half-hearted shouts of, 'Resign!', from the Opposition.

'Beaten dogs,' said Ferguson scornfully. 'But if the PM had put a foot wrong it would have been different,' he added. 'You'd be surprised what one unguarded reply can do. All hell would have been let loose. Pity in a way. Makes life dull.'

Isaac Newton and Frances Margaret were glad to escape when the vote of confidence was taken at long last. An attendant directed them to an exit.

'Really you should have been guided out. Will you report to the officer on the door, in case there are enquiries.'

After explaining to a policeman at the door that their guide, the Prime Minister's PPS, was in the lobbies, Isaac Newton and Frances Margaret walked out into Parliament Square and hailed a taxi.

'11 Downing Street,' Isaac Newton told the driver.

'That's the most unknown residence in London,' the driver remarked. 'I'm not asked for it more than twice in a year.'

Rather to their surprise, the Chancellor had already returned by the time the taxi reached 11 Downing Street.

'First into the lobby, first out, and my driver knows the route home by now,' he explained, and then went on, 'I thought it would be better for you to stay the night here, rather than next door. After these sessions the Prime Minister is apt to be a bit violent.'

'I thought it went easily,' Frances Margaret remarked.

'Every debate is like walking a tightrope, especially a vote of confidence. Fine as long as you stay on, but once you're off you're off. There's no getting back,' the Chancellor smiled. 'The trick is never to give anything away, not even straw to make bricks from. I'm not good at it myself, but I only get it thrown at me two or three times a year, and even then the pattern is set. In budget debates you know in advance by experience what you're going to get. The PM has it all the time, from all directions. I'd feel like breaking the furniture myself, if I had to do it. But then I couldn't,' the Chancellor went on, bringing drinks and adding, 'There'll be dinner soon and then you can sleep until midday. I must apologise, Newton, for being a bit windy the other day.'

'All's well that ends well. Cheers!' Isaac Newton replied.

'Yes, the press conference worked out very nicely.'

'I'm glad you think so.'

'Do you remember, by any chance, the walk we did nearly two years ago? The Aldbury round. We've come an amazing way since then. At first rather clandestinely, then more openly, but still a bit under the table. Now it's wide open with a big vote of confidence behind us,' the Chancellor declared expansively.

'Comet Halley wasn't mentioned much tonight.'

'No, but everybody knew what lay behind it all. They know about the third superpower, even if it wasn't put that way. You know, Newton, I'm reminded again of those shipwrights of old Bayonne – in the fifteenth century, you remember? They built a carrack that could ride out the big Atlantic storms. They conceived of it only for coastal traffic at first, but it opened the way to crossing the Atlantic itself, to the discovery of America. That's the position we've just about reached,' the Chancellor concluded as an attendant indicated that a late dinner was ready. 'We've built our carrack, and now it only remains for us to make our voyage of discovery.'

Chapter 66

It was astonishing what the combination of itching skin and of the world's most repressive bureaucracy managed to achieve in the Soviet Union; and it would have been quite beyond human capacity to predict the eventual outcome.

With the sole exception of the air-gulping Number Eleven, recently demoted to Number Fourteen via Number Twelve, the mad itch had by now disabled the entire Politburo. In a democracy such an eventuality would have had instant and widespread repercussions, but in the Soviet Union the eventuality counted in public for almost nothing, since the ever-pervasive bureaucracy simply carried on as usual. But if a strange disease had chanced to hit trees instead of the political front rank, the situation would have been very different. The whole political and economic order would indeed have collapsed in a turmoil of unparalleled proportions had a devastation of Soviet forests destroyed the supply of paper to the bureaucracy, since a resort to the ancient system of town criers would not have been effective in a land so far-flung as the modern Soviet state.

The political and economic order demanded that the bureaucratic machine be fed by suitably processed paper as well as disgorge it. When properly conceived of, the machine was, in effect, an enormous amplifier of paper, with a small input streaked in crucial places by carbon, and with a huge output having great blocks of carbon stamped upon it. In plain language, the input consisted of documents written, as one might expect, by the bureaucrats themselves, to which the signatures of the political big-wigs were appended. The amazing aspect of it all was that without the few streaks of carbon representing the signatures of the big-wigs nothing of the vast complex machinery of the Soviet Union would function, so that an impartial person with a grain of common sense could have guessed that the machine would collapse eventually under the weight of its own absurdity, just as it was now threatening to collapse because obtaining signatures from the front row of the Politburo had become dead impossible.

How, one may wonder, had the Russian people become saddled with such a system? The answer lay in the fact that the bureaucracy was the only aspect of Soviet life having continuity with the past, essentially because the bureaucracy was a vast conglomerate of long-established family businesses. In no other aspect of Soviet life was nepotism so readily possible, and without nepotism continuity is impossible. A son following the father at high political level was unheard of; nor was nepotism workable in the arts and sciences. But child followed parent in the bureaucracy with easy success, continuing in precisely the same way as before, with every instinct closely tuned to the system. Until the advent of the mad itch, that is to say. The mad itch separated the bureaucratic sheep from the bureaucratic goats by creating an environment which placed a large premium on sly ingenuity.

Despite constant attention from leading members of the medical profession, sufferers from the mad itch became incapable of either reading or signing documents. Even verbal communication with them became difficult. Nevertheless, the slyest of the bureaucrats discovered a neat trick. It was found that if a suffering Politburo member were asked a question in a negative form, such as, 'We shouldn't permit the wearing of dissident-style caps by workers in the bakeries of Chelyabinsk, should we?', then the answer was invariably a yell of, 'No!', followed instantly by an angry cry of, 'Get out of here!' Whereas if a question were asked in positive form, such as, 'We should close the Mausoleum in Red Square for a month to give the Lenin Waxwork a touch-up, shouldn't we?', the answer was invariably a yell of, 'Yes!', again followed by an enraged, 'Get out of here!'

It was seen that this odd situation provided an opportunity for what the bureaucratic mind saw as the ideal method of governing the country. Simply by asking questions in positive or negative form to suit itself, bureaucracy could obtain the answers it wanted to every issue under the Sun – but unfortunately without the signatures, the streaks of carbon around which the whole system revolved. Nevertheless, by a clever use of tape-recorders to obtain undeniable permanent evidence of the cries of 'Yes!' or 'No!' from Politburo members, the situation had been ingeniously adapted to the exigencies of the moment. Besides which, the hale and hearty new Number Fourteen could be prevailed upon to supply his signature, always provided he were supplied with copies of the tape recordings as an assurance that he was keeping himself in line with majority opinion. Indeed, much of Number Fourteen's time these days was occupied with signing documents and cannily classifying his mounting stock of recordings.

Because signatures had, by constitutional requirement, to come from full members of the Politburo, the number of full members had, of necessity, been increased to fourteen, a detail much commented on by Kremlin-watchers in the West, who nevertheless quite failed to understand the reason for the sudden change which had removed Number Fourteen from the dreaded candidate status.

Only the problem of the infrequent public appearances of leading Politburo members remained in need of urgent solution. Occasions like Kremlin meetings, to which members were driven through Moscow streets and avenues in large black limousines, could readily be dealt with by the crude use of dummies. Regretfully, however, the bureaucracy decided that dummies simply weren't a satisfactory answer to the absolute need for members to be on public show at the traditional May Day Parade through Red Square. Despite the attendant awkward details, it was decided that for the May Day Parade lookalikes were essential.

So remarkable an instrument is the human eye that every individual can be distinguished from every other individual, except in rare cases of identical twins. Perforce, a perfect lookalike for a typical individual is an impossibility. Compromises had therefore to be struck. If the need had been for close-up appearances on television, the facial features rather than the bodily proportions of lookalikes would obviously have been of prime importance. But for display at the May Day Parade, it was the bodily proportions, especially the manner of walking, which really mattered. Provided the movement was right, moderate inaccuracies in other respects could be attended to by the padding of garments, by the wearing of spectacles, and by the use of oddly-shaped hats.

Security was, of course, the most worrisome headache. The typical Soviet citizen pressed into service as a lookalike would almost inevitably start leaks concerning his principal that would run their way with surprising speed through the whole population, on the principle that each person-in-the-know tells two others and the leak soon grows into an unquenchable torrent. The lookalike breathes in the strictest confidence only to his wife, the wife breathes in the strictest confidence only to her closest and dearest friends. One makes two, two make four, four make eight, and so on through only twenty-seven steps, by which time all but the most innocent folk would know the awful truth, without anything but the strictest confidence being involved at any of the twenty-seven steps.

After much agonised discussion of this dilemma, the bureaucracy decided to search for lookalikes not among ordinary citizens, but among the numerous persons incarcerated in jails and labour camps. Under the threat of their sentences being tripled in the event of any leak occurring, such persons had a vastly greater incentive to maintain rigorous silence than ordinary citizens, or so it was agreed and decided.

The tactic was acknowledged to be somewhat chancy, but it worked. Just as members of the vast crowd that thronged Red Square for the May Day Parade, happy to be given a holiday for the occasion and to be awarded a plus mark on their *nomenklatura* charts, were unaware that it was a waxwork that lay close by in the Lenin Mausoleum, so they were unaware that the nation's leaders were being represented on the specially constructed balcony by convicted criminals. The exception, of course, was Number Fourteen, who for the first time in many months was enjoying himself, as, together with those around him, he took the salute to the future glory of the Motherland. Number Fourteen was indeed particularly pleased that the lookalike for the up-

and-coming Number Eleven had been equipped with a hat so large in its cranial capacity that it sat down fairly and squarely on his ears, so proving, if proof were needed, that despite the most meticulous planning bungling still went relentlessly on.

Chapter 67

Intelligence had done its work well. The scale of the proposed British programme of telescope-construction, and the quantity of space stations and ancilliaries of all kinds which the French and Germans were intending to add as an outcome of very recent discussions, were known to the meeting which met in the Presidential Office in late August.

'There's no way a programme of that magnitude could be funded by the Europeans themselves,' said the Secretary of the Treasury, a solidly-built man of middle height and middle age, dressed in a linen suit and with a thin-stemmed pipe clenched between his teeth.

'There's no way they're getting any of our money, unless it's for an attack on this comet monster,' stated the five-star General, tapping ash from his cigar into a tray with an inner reluctance. The General was finding himself spending too much of his time nowadays at meetings in the Oval Office, but his presence there – in order to veto the spending of money on harum-scarum projects like this one – had become regarded as essential by his colleagues at the Pentagon.

'The Europeans are thinking of their programme as a roll-up. It generates its own momentum as it goes,' the Secretary of Commerce told the meeting.

'It would surely spark up their economies,' agreed the Chairman of the Council of Economic Advisers.

'Better to spark up this comet monster. Better to spark up all comet monsters,' grunted the General, putting on an expansive, smoke-generating display with a widening of his chest.

'What we don't want,' continued the Chairman of the CEA, a well-known gnome-like figure of uncertain age, 'is for the Europeans to be carrying a begging bowl through the streets of Washington.'

'Yes, well, they've arranged a Summit, three weeks from now,' the President remarked.

'In fact, the French have offered the Palace of Versailles for it,' the Secretary of State informed the meeting, glad that on this occasion he was sitting at the opposite end of the table from the smoke-producing General.

'I rather fancy myself as a courtesan in the Palace of the Sun King,' remarked the Secretary of Commerce, smiling widely, as she was given to doing in order to bring out the dimples in her cheeks. 'Are we accepting the French proposal, Mr President?'

'I figure that in three weeks' time it will be September. Another two months and it will be November, and in November we've got the not-so-small matter of an election on our hands,' answered the President.

'With computerised opposition tactics to be studied, TV rehearsals, performances, you name it,' interposed an aide.

'Critics answered, especially the *New York Times*,' another aide added.

'That's *right*,' agreed the President. 'Make a note to do something mean about that paper.'

'Which adds up to the proposition that we can't be away sum-mitising in some European dump or other,' the first aide attempted to decide.

'The problem, Mr President, is that the Soviets have also been invited. If they go, can we afford not to go?' the Secretary of State countered.

'Will they go?' the second aide asked.

'They'll go. Especially if we don't,' the Secretary of State replied crisply.

'They'll go,' agreed the Director of the CIA.

'A slippery situation,' the President admitted in a reflective voice.

'When it's slippery, sir, the best policy is to slide,' proposed the Press Secretary.

'Meaning what?'

'Meaning it has angles we can use.'

'How big can you inflate it?'

'We can surely inflate it big. Summits are always good for two or three days of media time, regardless of whether anything happens. Besides which, we have both the Soviets and the Comet to whip up into a razzle dazzle.'

'A big scare like the last one,' nodded the Secretary of Commerce, repeating her disarming smile and adding, 'Twenty-four hours in the bunker. Or was it thirty-six, General?'

'In my reckoning we have to take serious steps about that comet monster,' the General repeated doggedly.

'With the Soviets going, we can't not,' the Secretary of State observed firmly, taking a sip of medicated water from a glass.

'Agreed,' the Secretary of Commerce instantly said, holding up her right hand as if casting a vote.

'Agreed, we can't not,' the Director of the CIA nodded.

'Maybe we could work on the speeches during the trip. Maybe we could transfer the computer and all tapes into Air Force One,' the first aide suggested.

'Better security that way, Mr President,' the second aide immediately added, not wishing to be outdone. 'I mean Air Force One isn't Watergate.'

'Now that's a great idea. We can convert Air Force One into a TV studio. Why didn't somebody think of that before?' agreed the President.

'But don't spend any *money*,' groaned the Secretary of the Treasury. 'That's what the Europeans want. Money, not kisses.'

'That's *damn* right,' nodded the General.

'How foolish of them,' the Secretary of Commerce managed to slip in.

'I thought we still had plenty of deficit left,' interposed the President.

'If it wasn't for international capital inflows we'd be busted, Mr President – busted with big-ticket items.' The Secretary of the Treasury gritted on the stem of his pipe, glowering towards the five-star General.

'As the President says, there's plenty of deficit available,' the General replied, leaning back in his chair and blowing his largest smoke ring to date up towards the ceiling where it hovered over the table like a bird of prey.

The Secretary of the Treasury now clamped his teeth so tightly on the slender stem of his pipe that it broke with a sharply audible crack. He held up the two parts of the broken pipe for everybody to see.

'There,' he said, 'busted!'

It was at this point that buzzers droned everywhere throughout the White House, giving most of those present at the meeting a sense of *déjà vu*. The General, however, automatically shouted:

'It's a red alert. To the bunker!'

'This will be the fourth Soviet strike in as many months that turns out to be a decoy,' the Secretary of Commerce remarked in a calm voice. 'I suggest, Mr President, that you put a call through to Moscow on the hot-line.'

The President had taken the special warning receiver from his pocket and, sure enough, a bulb on it was showing a red light. Then, picking up a specially-marked phone, he said with a nod:

'It can't do any harm. What shall I ask them?'

'Ask if they've launched any missiles.'

'It's a trick. Using the decoys as a screen!' exploded the General.

'Well, we'll find out, won't we?' the President just had time to remark before he began speaking into the telephone. The monosyllables that followed his queries were difficult for the meeting to interpret, especially as the General suddenly erupted from the Office shouting, 'Wolf! Wolf!'

He was followed by the Director of the CIA, who said as he left:

'I think I'll go along. Just as insurance.'

'I wonder how far they'll get this time, preparing for World War Four . . .' the Secretary of Commerce began, only to be cautioned to keep silent by the President.

Eventually the President put down the telephone.

'They appear to be in one helluva mess over there in Moscow. I couldn't locate the Soviet Number One. But one of the Politburo guys says no missiles have been launched, either now or at any time. Funny guy. Seems to have the gulps. He kept on saying that so far as he was concerned a bed of wood was better than a coffin of gold. He also said the responsibility was weighing on him and that he was getting lonely. Sounded screwy, the way they do in old Russian novels.'

'Say, I've got a great idea, Mr President,' interrupted the first aide.

The aide's great idea manifested itself three hours later when the President appeared on nationwide TV with a special announcement to make.

'I thought you'd all like to know about a little experience I had this afternoon,' the President began. 'At about four-fifteen we had another of those missile decoy affairs which have caused so much trouble and worry to all of us over the past few months, especially to senior citizens and children. What I thought you'd all like to hear is that this time around we managed to identify the decoy so as to avoid troubling people in their homes and on the highways driving home from the office. We used the special line to Moscow which is always open night and day. The Soviets, we discovered, have been having the same trouble with decoys. So we were able to assure Moscow that no U.S. missiles had been launched, and they were able to assure us that no Soviet missiles had been launched. Well, I thought you'd all like to know about it, this stride forward in the cause of peace . . .'

The Secretary of Commerce, who was busy cooking a meal in her apartment, switched the TV off at this point. Over recent months she'd found herself looking more and more nostalgically back to the days when she taught classes at Mt Holyoke College. Did she really want a second term of it, she asked herself, pounding two steaks vigorously in anticipation of a visit from her latest boyfriend.

Chapter 68

The French Government had announced that plenary sessions of the Summit were to be held in the Theatre of the Palace of Versailles. Since Isaac Newton had been asked by organisers of the Summit programme to make a 'presentation' at the opening session, he and Frances Margaret flew two days before the opening from London to Orly Airport, where they hired a car. Reconnaissance of the region to the south-west of Paris secured them a room at a pleasant old inn. This was in the small town of Dampierre, whence it was an easy drive to Versailles.

The day before the Summit they explored the Palace itself, with a view to checking that all arrangements were in order. So far as the seating arrangements were concerned they'd no complaints, as they discovered that they had been placed a mere five paces to the right of the spot where Queen Victoria had sat on the evening of 25 August 1855, on the occasion of a supper party given in her honour by Napoleon III. But on all other matters there seemed ample cause for disquiet, for the overwhelming reason that the Theatre of the Palace of Versailles was just about the most awkward place in which to hold a summit meeting of modern proportions. This was amply demonstrated by the army of technicians now struggling with the acoustics of the place. Wires trailed everywhere, and threading their way among them were men with cigarettes hanging from their lips, moving backwards and forwards without discernible purpose.

Similar scenes are being enacted throughout the world, going on and on without remission in a so-called technological age. Scenes reminiscent of *L'Apprenti Sorcier*, except that this was worse than anything Isaac Newton had seen before, essentially because the technicians, being French and therefore honest men, knew from the beginning that their case was hopeless. Wherever they put the microphones, wherever the loudspeakers, all that emerged were barks and roars imposed on a hissing background.

'I might as well gargle as talk into that thing,' observed Isaac Newton after examining the microphone on the speaker's podium.

'You might get liquid down the windpipe. Much better to hum,' advised Frances Margaret.

'How the devil am I supposed to convince anybody of anything? That's what I'd like to know.'

'Not by talking and arguing. Just bark and hum. Or hiss if you prefer it. Only keep the thing within bounds, especially the gestures...'

Frances Margaret was interrupted by a scream from one of the technicians, and then somebody shouted, '*Frelon!*' Others took up the shout and in a matter of seconds a wild cry of '*Frelon!*' rang through the Theatre of the Palace.

'I think it means hornet,' said Frances Margaret.

'It *does* mean hornet. Look out!' shouted Isaac Newton himself, taking a vigorous swipe at the air, just as technicians everywhere throughout the Theatre were doing. 'They're all over the place! There must be a nest. Let's get out of here. Fast!'

'Not a nest, in fact,' breathed Frances Margaret when their dash had taken them into the open air, 'but a wine-cask. A wine-cask with a fine bouquet to it, full of hornets.'

Then, as they drove into the woods of Fontainebleau, Isaac Newton said briefly:

'Hoopla.'

'What's wrong with hoopla?' Frances Margaret, who was driving, wanted to know.

'It's symptomatic of the whole situation. We have people and Governments taking notice, but not seriously enough.'

'I thought we were doing rather well. A really big programme on the verge of getting international funding.'

'Yes and no.'

'What d'you mean yes and no?'

'I'm reminded of an incoming tide.'

'Why?'

'For a while it seems as if an incoming tide must go on and on rising, carrying everything with it. But eventually there's a turn and down it goes.'

'The tide hasn't turned yet.'

'No, the tide hasn't turned yet. But I'm only too afraid it will. Because Governments only think short-term, only as far as the next election. It's hard to run a very big long-term programme like this on short-term psychology. Finding all their expensive weapons were no good at all has certainly drawn them up pretty smartly, but the trouble is that once they've got used to the shock . . .'

'. . . they'll relapse,' concluded Frances Margaret, navigating the car around a snarl-up on the road.

'That's right, they'll relapse. What we need is some kind of a shock they can't forget.'

'I wish you wouldn't say that!' the girl exclaimed severely.

'Why?'

'Because what you think seems to have a habit of happening. It's all those blips you said you felt you were emitting. I think you're being tagged,' Frances Margaret added, negotiating more traffic.

'Nonsense.'

'Well, don't start sending out blips advertising that it all seems hopeless. Makes me jumpy.'

'Superstitious more like.'

'Sensible more like.'

'OK then, sensible. I think we turn off this road fairly soon,' said Isaac Newton, who was studying a map.

Chapter 69

━━━◦⋙⋘◦━━━

The Theatre of the Palace was a species of opera house, in which capacity at least it was well suited to the occasion, Isaac Newton thought when he and Frances Margaret arrived the following morning for the opening session of the Summit. There was a base-floor, where in days gone by the lesser mortals had sat, with two levels above it, each having a dozen or so boxes in a circular arc around the outer wall, the uppermost set of boxes being arranged between big vertical columns built in imitation of a Grecian temple.

The official delegates of the various nations occupied the two tiers of boxes, while back-up staff and media personnel had been assigned chairs and tables on the main floor. The British delegation had the box immediately to the right of the central box, which had been given over more than a century before to the supper table of Queen Victoria. On the present occasion, the French, in their capacity as hosts, occupied this central box. The Germans had the box to the right of the British and the Americans had the one to the left of the French. The Russians had the first three rows on the floor below, built up into a dais, which was intended to remind them of the balcony at their May Day Parade. Some were dressed in medal-bedecked uniforms, others in dark suits, white shirts, ties and platform shoes that winked in the spotlights as they mounted the steps leading to their seats.

Isaac Newton and Frances Margaret had come early to make sure their presentation would be transmitted in English on one of the channels of the headphone set issued to every seat in the Theatre, thereby avoiding the barks and hissings of the loudspeakers. Assured, eventually, on this point, they sat watching the delegations arrive, and after studying the Russians for a while Isaac Newton decided:

'The head of the Russians looks ill. He's fighting for air.'

'Looks more like the hiccoughs to me. Too much breakfast, I suppose, at their luxury-loving Embassy. Not that continuing hiccoughs can't be dangerous when they get up to a rate of about three a minute, I believe, and go on for hours and hours. Hiccoughing is one of my specialities, you see,' Frances Margaret replied. If she hadn't already been in an uppity frame of mind, a woman staring across at them from the American box would certainly have given her cause to do battle. The woman had dark hair, a wide smile and dimples, Frances Margaret noticed keenly from a distance of fifteen yards.

'According to our briefings the head of the Russian delegation is Politburo Number Eleven,' continued Isaac Newton obsessively.

'Actually, that's not quite correct, Professor Newton,' a voice beside them said. A man with a face which an unkind person would have described as looking like a ripe tomato was standing there.

'Jamesborough. John Jamesborough. Foreign Office. You remember me from the old Geneva days?' he enquired by way of introduction.

'Of course,' nodded Isaac Newton. 'What isn't correct?'

'The Russian. He's been demoted to Number Fourteen.'

'It doesn't look as if the Russians are taking things very seriously then,' Isaac Newton concluded.

'Which is where you could be wrong, Professor,' a new voice cut in. It belonged to a washed-out looking man with a cigarette in the corner of his mouth whom Isaac Newton had at first taken for a technician struggling in desperation with the sound system.

'Smithfield,' the man said, hitching up his arms inside overlong coat sleeves. 'It's really the military types on the right you have to watch – the ones connected with weapons procurement. Among the Borises that's where the real power lies. Looks as though it's going to be a bit of a circus, doesn't it? Watch out for surprises, Professor. The French have something going. I had a tip-off from a pal at the Quai d'Orsay. *Le nez de Cléopâtre; s'il eût été plus court, toute la face de la terre aurait changé*, as they say down the road.' Smithfield concluded with a nod and a pull on his cigarette.

The British delegation arrived – by Rolls Royce from central Paris – in a group with the Prime Minister at its centre. The box where Isaac Newton and Frances Margaret had been sitting almost alone was now suddenly full to bursting. And so were the other boxes in the arcs around the Theatre.

The session came to order with the French Prime Minister bashing a massive two-kilogramme gavel that made the far-flung loudspeaker system thunder like a tempest through the hall. Then the French Prime Minister gave a speech of welcome, delivered in carefully-chosen mellifluent language. Several screens had been placed at strategic places around the Theatre, and the French Prime Minister's face, head and shoulders could be seen on them in close-up. Since the cameras were mobile, Isaac Newton realised that when his turn came it would be unnecessary to force his way to the podium. He could simply give the presentation directly from his seat.

A note was passed to him by hand. He wrote a reply and dispatched it back by hand. Frances Margaret watched the note travelling until eventually it reached the Prime Minister, who opened and read it. This, together with Smithfield's remark about the French having something going, gave her an idea. She wrote a note of her own and folded it. She would have liked to send it to the woman in the American box, the woman with the dangerous-looking smile, but not knowing her name she addressed it to the American President. Then she caught the dangerous-looking woman's eye and lifted the note to mark its place of origin. After launching it, Frances Margaret watched in fascination as it went, hand-by-hand, first through the British box, then through the adjacent French box and so into the American box. At last it reached the American President who immediately opened it and read:

TO ALL COLONISTS

The English have a wine cask full of hornets which they intend to release at a strategic moment. Advise taking evasive action.

Lafayette

As the time for his presentation approached remorselessly, Isaac Newton found himself more and more aware of how tired he'd become over recent months. Somewhat grimly, he remembered the advice Frances Margaret had given him over breakfast that morning.

'The last thing to worry about is what you actually *say*,' she'd told him. 'What you *say* is instantly damped away to nothing in the air, by viscosity, by the carpet, by people's clothing and by their hair, especially by women with long hair. All that remains then are the notions you've managed to instill into people's heads, and it is here, or there as the case may be, that grim reality rears its ugly head. For in the circumstances all you can hope to convey is an image, not an argument. It is not what you *say* which counts in producing an image,' Frances Margaret had repeated, 'it is *how* you say it. If you develop a tic of the lip, *everybody* will remember it. Years later, whenever your name is mentioned, they'll say: "Ah, yes. That's the man with the tic of the lip. I once heard him give a talk on land reform in Central Africa." Actually,' Frances Margaret had concluded, 'I wouldn't recommend a tic of the lip, but loud clicks with the tongue wouldn't be a bad idea.'

Actually, feeling a supreme effort was required of him, Isaac Newton took up the first fifteen minutes of his time explaining how it had been discovered that comets were alive. He went on to describe how communication with Halley's Comet had been established, and how telescopes had been adapted to serve as the eyes and ears of the Comet itself. There were thousands of other comets within range of the telescopes for which the same had to be done. Eventually indeed, as the years passed by, there would be millions, if not billions of them, at still greater distances from the Sun. It would be a project of staggering magnitude, the farthest-reaching and most adventurous the human species had ever attempted.

The reward would be a sudden access to technology that, in the ordinary course of events, might not have been discovered for a thousand years. It was a reward that would come just at the moment when the human species was at a crossroads – a desperate crossroads – of inter-species confrontation between the developed nations, and of poverty and overpopulation among the underdeveloped nations. These were problems for which no other solutions were in sight. They were problems that otherwise, Isaac Newton concluded, did not promise a favourable future for the world.

When the applause had died away, written questions were handed in. They were first read out by the French Prime Minister and then answered as briefly and forcefully as Isaac Newton could manage. To the inevitable question of what the cost of such a project would be, he came out with a forthright answer. The cost would be closely comparable with the present military budgets of the developed nations. At this reply a deep silence filled the Theatre of the Palace, a silence made memorable in the minds of all present by the manner in which it was broken. It was broken by a piercing yell from a journalist employed by the *New York Times*. Almost immediately there were further yells and shrieks, yells and shrieks rapidly translated into bedlam as they were picked up by microphones and amplified to monstrous proportions through the many loudspeakers placed throughout the Theatre.

'Hornets,' said Frances Margaret with a wide smile of satisfaction. 'I knew they'd never track them all down. Not without fumigating the whole Palace.'

Chapter 70

The morning session thus unceremoniously ended, the participants emerged from the Theatre into the spacious grounds of the Palace, where – the day being warm and fine – an outdoor buffet was served.

'I wonder where they get them at this time of the year,' observed Frances Margaret, taking a bowl of strawberries and cream from a passing waiter.

'Scotland, I expect. You see now what I meant yesterday?' Isaac Newton replied, taking a bowl of the strawberries himself.

'I thought it went as well as could be expected.'

'That's just the point, isn't it – as well as could be expected.'

'Then the time is ripe for an assessment,' Frances Margaret decided, broaching a particularly large and very red strawberry.

'The assessment is clear. With a deal of argument we'll eventually get some sort of an international project going, on about the same scale as we've got back at home already. Only with much more bureaucracy and paperwork,' Isaac Newton argued grumpily.

'I couldn't avoid hearing you say that,' a familiar voice said. It was Alan Bristow, the editor of *Nature*. 'At least an international project has more stability. Once it's started it can't be stopped. By a change of any particular Government, I mean,' he went on.

'That's true, of course,' Isaac Newton acknowledged, but still much out of countenance.

'But why d'you want things to go at such a tearing pace? That's what I can never understand about your point of view, Newton. You're fond of saying that a stalemate which has lasted for billions of years has now been broken. Why, if you're dealing in billions, should a few years more or a few years less matter at all? Why not let events follow their own course?'

'Because we're really deciding between alternatives.'

'Which are?'

'Military budgets for one; or a big programme of the kind I talked about this morning for the other.'

'Why should they be exclusive?'

'Because if the military budgets go on we'll be annihilated, quite probably before the end of the century. Frankly, I want the second alternative to present itself so forcefully and fast that there's nothing left for people to blow themselves to pieces with. The choice is really very clear, and there isn't any convenient middle way.'

'And you think everybody here, the Governments I mean, are looking for a convenient middle way?'

'Of course. Don't you? Then back to business as usual.'

'Well, I wish you luck. You'll need it,' Bristow said, just as the Prime Minister came up with the admonition:

'Come now, break it up. We're here to talk to people. Let me introduce you to the American President.'

Frances Margaret moved away on her own, thinking her message about the hornets might conceivably introduce a discordant note into a conversation with the American President. In the instant she saw Isaac Newton disappear a shock hit her, a shock so obvious and perceptible that she wondered for a while if it could be a heart attack. Then, after satisfying herself that it wasn't, she wondered if the sudden shadow, a shadow like the Sun passing all in a moment behind a cloud, could be due to poison in the strawberries. Whatever it was, she had an intense conviction of something exceedingly peculiar, a conviction that changed her previously exuberant state of mind into a dreamy condition, as if the entire scene around her had become quite unreal.

There in front of her now was the American woman with the dark hair, the dangerous-looking woman with the dimples, who said:

'I've been looking at the Russians. It's all very curious.'

'Because they're like the pack of cards in *Alice in Wonderland?*' Frances Margaret replied.

'Funny you should say that,' nodded the American Secretary of Commerce.

'Why is it funny?'

'Well, take a look at Russian footballers, ice-skaters and musicians. What d'you see? You see normal people with normal faces and normal bodies. But these politicians and generals are quite different. They're all chunky and square and heavy and beetle-browed. How come? I ask myself.'

'It's because they *are* a pack of cards,' Frances Margaret replied, thinking this firming up of her previous remark trivially obvious.

'I kept on wondering myself if they might be sort of cartoon characters. You know, characters with three fingers instead of five.'

'Did you ask them?'

'Of course not,' the Secretary of Commerce laughed.

'Then let's go and ask them,' Frances Margaret said with decision, leading the way towards the group of Russians. The woman with the dimples was dead right, she decided. To a man, the whole group *was* heavy and chunky. Although not every one was beetle-browed, some certainly were.

There was a compelling certainty about the manner in which Frances Margaret, followed by the American Secretary of Commerce, approached them which caught the immediate attention of the Russian interpreters.

'You're surely not going to?' giggled the Secretary of Commerce.

'I certainly *am*,' Frances Margaret replied without a trace of a smile, adding, 'I'm not going to be put down by a pack of cards.'

The Russian interpreters moved forward with ingratiating smiles, and the senior group behind them, conscious now of the approach of two very good-looking women, also shuffled a step or two forward. Frances Margaret's voice was loud and clear, as she could make it very loud and clear when the occasion warranted.

'We would like to know,' she asked, 'whether you all have three fingers like cartoon characters, or five fingers like normal people?'

One would have needed to study a filmed record of the situation with something of the care that a football team devotes to filmed records of the tactics of a rival team to say precisely how the group around Frances Margaret dissolved away. It was a phenomenon she'd experienced before many times in her life, people simply dissolving at something she said. It was, in fact, a little exceptional that the dark-haired woman with the dimples still remained standing there, her shoulders heaving with helpless laughter.

'I never thought you'd do it,' gurgled the Secretary of Commerce. 'I just couldn't and I'm fairly tough.'

'There was nothing in it at all. Didn't I tell you they were only a pack of cards.'

This sent the Secretary of Commerce off again. 'Stop it, you're killing me,' she gasped. 'What's your name, if I might ask?'

'Frances Margaret.'

'There isn't too much wrong with that. It's inside the head where the trouble seems to be. Were you the one who sent the note about the hornets?'

'Of course.'

'How did you know about them?'

'Don't you sometimes know what's going to happen in a dream?' Frances Margaret answered, congratulating herself on the subtlety of her reply.

Because, of course, that was what it was all about. Not cards but a dream, a dream right from the beginning, from the moment Isaac Newton had arrived at the Cavendish Laboratory. Because, of course, there was no Isaac Newton. How could there be with a name like that? When she woke she would be dressed in jeans and an old shirt, not in her present court dress and shoes. She wouldn't be Cinderella at the ball, she'd be Cinderella lighting the fire on a cold winter morning, with Mike Howarth moaning away in the corner about his crazy ideas. Frances Margaret again congratulated herself on the exquisite subtlety of being able to reason so correctly even from within a dream as wild as this one.

Another thing she reasoned: it was always the case in a dream that characters mysteriously come and go. They pop off, saying they'll be back again in a minute. But they don't come back. Then you start searching for them, but try as you might you can never find them again. This would be so with Isaac Newton. Frances Margaret had keen eyesight, and she could see the American President clearly in the distance, but of Isaac Newton – nothing. With some care she now scanned the whole assembly: of Isaac Newton – still nothing. Frances

Margaret fought down a sense of desperation, telling herself that she could always put an end to it simply by waking up to the jeans and old shirt, and to Mike Howarth moaning about his comets.

'What's all this agitation? You sure must be in a funny state,' the woman with the dimples said.

'And it sure must be funny for you to be only a character in my dream,' Frances Margaret replied, sending the woman into more helpless laughter. 'The amazing thing,' Frances Margaret continued, 'is how I managed to conceive of you.'

The woman now staggered so badly that Frances Margaret grabbed hold of her.

'Hey, you're strong! Not so hard,' the Secretary of Commerce cried out.

'Don't think you're going to trick me by dissolving away,' Frances Margaret replied, sending the woman into what seemed like a real fit.

'Ah! Haven't I seen you before, young lady?' the American President asked, as the uncertain course pursued by Frances Margaret and the Secretary of Commerce brought them eventually in his direction.

'Varenna,' Frances Margaret immediately answered, pleased again that she could remember even the smallest details of her dream.

'That's *right*. Varenna! Now I've been puzzling my mind, young lady, about those hornets of yours.'

'That's past, Mr President. And what's past is prologue.'

'Now why would that be?'

'I've often asked myself the same question, Mr President,' replied Frances Margaret, noticing that the woman with the dimples had slipped away. Just as it always is, she thought. You make a vow somebody isn't going to dissolve, but they always do, often in the most ingenious fashion. Now she vowed that the President wasn't going to dissolve away, come what may.

'Have you noticed, Mr President, how all the people are disappearing?'

'As a matter of fact I had, young lady. There appears to have been some kind of an emergency.'

'I'll bet there has. It always happens that way,' Frances Margaret nodded, wondering why she bothered to humour a character in her dream. 'Remember this, Mr President,' she went on, 'if you hang on to me, you'll survive.'

'I'm sure glad of that,' the President responded. 'We should be moving back to the Theatre. People really are disappearing.'

'Into nothingness,' Frances Margaret agreed.

Eventually they reached a point where the path forked. Frances Margaret knew perfectly well the way she'd come, so when the President took the other fork, she said:

'I wouldn't go that way if I were you.'

'Why not, this is the way I came?' the President stated in surprise. Of course, in a real situation there could indeed be a number of routes back to the Theatre, but in this situation Frances Haroldsen knew that any deviation at all from the one route could lead almost anywhere, into the middle of London or Cambridge or New York, or anywhere. Determined she wasn't going to be tricked again, she kept to the path by which she'd walked with the imaginary Isaac Newton, calling out to the President:

'Go your own way, Mr President, by all means. But once you round that next corner over there, you'll be done for.'

Determinedly now, Frances Margaret kept to the remembered path, expecting it would only too likely lead her to Timbuktu – but not through any carelessness on her part. Nobody was around now. Of all the previous crowd – nobody, just the way it always was in a dream. Her court shoes rang out on flagstones, which at least was consistent and logical. She tried to guess where she might be going, to anticipate the next big surprise, only to find, to her disappointment, as she rounded a corner that what lay ahead seemed, on the face of it, to indeed be the Palace of Versailles.

Then the obvious hit her. It wasn't that she was walking into some other place like Timbuktu or onto the top of Mount Everest. She was walking into another time, probably the seventeenth century, when thousands of people thronged the Palace here. Pulsating scenes, pulsating bedrooms, pulsating kitchens. Come to think of it, why was the present moment of time any more real than the seventeenth century? No reason she could think of consistent with the laws of physics. So the seventeenth century it must be, she decided. She'd wondered how so much that was illicit had managed to go on at Versailles, because the layout of the Palace didn't seem to favour privacy. Maybe in the seventeenth century they just didn't bother about privacy. Maybe they just stood around and watched it all.

The Theatre of the Palace came into sight. At once she realised the dream had tricked her yet again, but that thankfully she was too clever for it. The dream was storing up its big moment, a big moment of horror. When she went into the Theatre of the Palace she would find what? Cobwebs. Empty, except for cobwebs.

There were attendants on the door of the Theatre of the Palace – examining the tickets of day visitors no doubt. They accepted the badge pinned to her coat without comment, and in a moment she was inside the Theatre. Immediately there was the same queer shock she'd experienced an hour before. With it, the strange state of mind was gone, and she could see the Theatre really was full of people, not cobwebs. She could also see Isaac Newton among the delegates in the British box. It was an instantaneous jerk back to normality. Apparently so. Yet her entrance into the Theatre coincided exactly, as if in simultaneous response to the pressing of a switch, with a devastating interruption in the proceedings.

The interruption came from the French President, whose face in large close-up suddenly appeared on the screens throughout the hall, displacing the speaker at the podium, and whose voice suddenly boomed out over the erratic loudspeaker system:

'Pardon this interruption, please, but I have an unwelcome announcement to make. News has been received from the Observatory at Meudon informing the French Government that an object with a diameter of nearly two kilometres will hit the Earth tomorrow morning between two a.m. and four a.m. Greenwich Mean Time. Unfortunately the damage will be extensive. The point of impact of the object is said to be uncertain, so it is unknown which places will be safe and which places will be unsafe. It is clearly understood that many people will wish to return immediately to their countries, and I wish to tell you that the French Government will take all steps to arrange such matters smoothly.'

Chapter 71

Frances Haroldsen pushed her way through the severely shocked crowd towards the British box. Isaac Newton said as she approached:

'I was wondering where you'd gone. Have you the car keys? Yes, good. Then I'll join you at the car in a few minutes. I just want to make one or two enquiries about this information from Meudon.'

It was more than a few minutes, perhaps twenty, before Isaac Newton appeared at the car to find Frances Margaret in the passenger seat. 'Will you drive?' he asked.

'I'd rather not. I came over with a turn.'

As Isaac Newton manoeuvred the car out of the parking lot and into the long avenue which led towards the town of Versailles, Frances Margaret described the peculiar hallucinations she'd experienced.

'So you didn't escape after all,' Isaac Newton then remarked.

'Escape what?'

'Remember the cottage on the Norfolk coast? Something was there that night.'

'I didn't see anything.'

'You mean you don't remember seeing anything, which isn't the same thing. I don't remember seeing much myself, but I've had these turns twice now. You were lucky you could still keep walking around. I was knocked right out.'

'What does it mean?'

'Well, coming just before this announcement from Meudon it obviously means something. As if you were emitting blips as well.'

'I can't understand why this object, or whatever it is,' Frances Margaret said with a puzzled expression, 'wasn't known before. You'd think astronomers could easily have seen an object as big as they say it is.'

'They did see it. The object has been known for about a year.'

'Then why spring the news on us now?'

'Because the thing has changed its course suddenly. Otherwise it would have passed by the Earth quite safely, the way small asteroids do.

'Was it like a missile then, making a mid-course correction? To hit a target, I mean,' Frances Margaret asked in a more reflective voice.

'Seems like it.'

'How could it have been done?'

'Nobody really knows, of course. Probably a sudden evaporation process – like a rocket firing off a jet.'

'It must be deliberate, surely?'

'Deliberate yes, like your turn, and like a feeling I've had all through this morning. Especially when I'd finished my talk.'

'What sort of a feeling?'

'That I'd done my job. That I'd had enough of trying to persuade people. It would fit with your queer impression of talking to a pack of cards. You could say my feeling was really the same.'

Isaac Newton pulled the car into a vacant space near the centre of the town of Versailles, saying as he switched off the ignition, 'I just want to see if I can buy one or two special items.' Then, handing his briefcase to Frances Margaret, he added: 'Why don't you read the data file from Meudon. I neither asked for it nor begged for it. I stole it fair and square from under their noses, with the thought that the French Government can get another copy – whereas we can't.'

A while later, Isaac Newton returned with two packages. As he pushed them over into the rear of the car and squared himself up again in the driver's seat, he explained:

'Sleeping bags and a thermos flask. If the night is fine we might want to go out to some place where we can get a view of the sky. I thought we might search for a suitable spot on the way back to the inn.'

'But what is everybody doing?' asked Frances Margaret.

'There's ferocious chaos back there. We were well out of it.'

'Chaos? I thought the French President said they'd be glad to make *smooth* arrangements.'

'They'd be glad to be *able* to make smooth arrangements – which is different.'

'Did you discover anything definite?'

'The French are trying to persuade heads of Governments to assemble at some château near Fontainebleau, not far from where we were touring yesterday. But mostly there's been a demand to rush back to their own home grounds. The Americans will probably fight it through in Air Force One, but the Russians won't make it so they'd do better to stay. The French say they'll bring in military helicopters to ferry people the shorter distances. The Prime Minister wanted us to go along, but it seemed rather pointless, because there isn't anything we could do. I felt we'd just be reduced to standing around.'

'But there's still twelve hours before this thing strikes. That's a lot of time.'

'Not when airports snarl up, not when transport facilities are paralysed. And I'm not thinking about outright panic as the news spreads.'

'Then what are you thinking about?'

'The irresistible impulses of an enormous number of people.'

'To do what?'

'To move, simply to move. It will be Christmas Eve chaos multiplied a hundred times over. You know, when the French President made his announcement, I immediately thought of rushing back to Devon, back home – something I haven't done on impulse in years. Then I thought about rushing back to Cambridge. Then I thought about Kurt and Rosie Waldheim, about their chalet in Wengen and how it would be the ideal place to spend the next twelve hours. We could sleep out there on the balcony, I thought, looking towards the mountains and looking up at the sky – the object will be very bright when it comes in. Then I realised we just couldn't make it to Wengen. We would end up in a huge crowd milling around some appalling airport. So I decided the simplest and best thing was for us to stay exactly where we are.'

'Well, thanks for deciding for me. How did you know *I* didn't want to go back home?' Frances Margaret asked.

'Frankly, I took it for granted. You've always spoken as if your home were off-limits. Where is it, by the way?'

'North of Morecambe Bay, where valleys like the Duddon run up into the high hills behind. There's limestone near the coast, with good grass for stock, and a fantastic Silurian landscape before you come to the hills. My people came in there a thousand years ago – exactly as that mad Swede, Eriksson, said – round the coast of Scotland in longboats. After a wild journey they must have thought they'd found heaven. At least my family have been there, tucked away in their private little valley, for a thousand years. Property stayed with the eldest son, and the younger sons went off into the army or navy. Or into piracy, I suppose, in the good old days.'

'So you're descended from a line of eldest sons? Until this last generation?'

'That's right. Twenty or thirty generations, all gone now. Shadows marching farther and farther back into the past.'

'Why didn't you mention it before?'

'Oh, it's an embarrassment to our sort of family. To have a child, especially a female child, who solves quadratic equations – like being born with one eye or twelve toes. So you go out into the world and join other people who've been born with twelve toes.'

'I find my twelve toes very useful. Did you manage to look at that data file?' Isaac Newton asked.

'It's not encouraging, is it? The sheer speed of the thing is so high. Like the one that hit at the Tunguska River in 1908.'

'The Siberian meteorite?' Isaac Newton asked as he turned the car into a smaller road leading to the country town of Dampierre where they were staying.

'Yes, and although the Tunguska meteorite was a lot smaller than this one, it still felled trees for a hundred kilometres around. The blast wave is going to be absolutely terrible.'

'I've been trying to think about the physics. Starting with the speed, fifty-one kilometres a second – the astronomers claim to have measured it,' Isaac Newton began. 'That's much faster than the speed of sound in any solid or liquid. Inevitably there must be gasification on an enormous scale. It will become a huge hot bubble of gas that blasts its way outwards in every direction.'

'Lifting the atmosphere right out,' agreed Frances Margaret bleakly. 'Over the region of impact, I mean. Then the surrounding air will try to rush in to fill the hole. Which will end up as the most appalling cyclonic storm in a million years.'

'How big is the area devastated by the blast-wave going to be?'

'At the back of my mind, I've been thinking of little else since that announcement back there in the Theatre,' Frances Margaret answered in the same bleak voice.

'With what conclusion?'

'Well, if you say as big as the black patches on the Moon you won't be too far wrong.'

'A thousand kilometres?'

'Yes, about a thousand kilometres.'

'What fraction of the whole area of the Earth do you make that?'

'A percent or so. Not overwhelmingly large, luckily. Except the data file says the thing is likely to land in the northern hemisphere, where most people live.'

'Suppose people to be living scattered at random over the northern hemisphere. That means at least eighty millions are going to die. It's like a world war; worse than either one, actually.'

'And all in a single night,' Frances Margaret nodded mechanically. 'Besides which,' she went on, 'our own chances are two times worse than random.'

'Why?' Isaac Newton asked once more.

'Because the object is moving *towards* the Sun, meaning it must strike the Earth on the dark side; and since it happens that we'll be on the night side at the time it arrives, between two and four a.m., our chance is doubled above random.'

They left the main road several times in the neighbourhood of Dampierre, exploring side tracks until they came on an open stretch of grass with a clear view of the sky in all directions. Then they continued, reaching the inn at about four o'clock. The inn was situated beside a stream which, in times gone, had driven a watermill. The proprietor was standing at his desk when Isaac Newton asked for the room key. As he handed over the key, the man said:

'You have heard the news, m'sieur?'

Isaac Newton acknowledged that he had and the proprietor continued:

'I was in the Second World War, m'sieur, and my father was in the First World War. People are saying this will be as bad.'

Then the man simply shrugged expressively, leaving Isaac Newton to marvel, as they went up to their room, at the unerring ability of ordinary folk to arrive at the truth of a situation.

Instinctively, Isaac Newton locked the door to the bedroom. Seconds later, it seemed, they were in bed and he was listening to Frances Margaret whispering urgently and hoarsely:

'It may be the last time.'

Chapter 72

'It's lucky we thought to bring the pillows,' said Frances Haroldsen, forcing herself to make trivial conversation as she slid into one of the sleeping bags which Isaac Newton had bought in Versailles that afternoon. The time was 11.45 p.m.

The proprietor of the inn had taken some pride in refusing to be budged an inch from his normal routine. Dinner had been served exactly as usual. Isaac Newton and Frances Margaret lingered over it until after 10.00 p.m. A look outside the inn had then shown a broken sky, with some brighter stars showing through gaps in the clouds. On the strength of this observation they'd decided to drive to the spot they'd chosen in the afternoon. Saying they were going 'outside for a while', a key to the outer door of the inn had been obtained, without any mention of events to come, so as not to disturb the *sang froid* of the proprietor.

They had carefully arranged their sleeping bags to align them from head-to-foot pointing north towards the Pole Star.

'It must still be as far away as the Moon,' Frances Margaret went on. 'If it reflects sunlight like the Moon it'll be about three million times fainter – about fourth magnitude.'

'You'd need to be an amateur astronomer to notice an interloper as faint as that. I'll bet the professionals couldn't. Besides, it's too cloudy,' grunted Isaac Newton.

'If it's coming straight towards the Sun, it must be practically on the northern meridian at midnight, which is more or less now, at an elevation of about fifty degrees – up there in Cygnus, not far from Deneb. That's the brightest star, the one you can see at the head of a sort of cross. I suppose the cross was taken in ancient days to be a swan in flight. You see, I once took a course on astronomy. When I was at school. I'm just telling you all this so you know where to look,' Frances Margaret continued, with the words flowing on as they sometimes did. 'It's amazing when you come to think about it.'

'What's amazing?' Isaac Newton grunted.

'That it can make the distance from as far away as the Moon in only two or three hours.'

'If it gets here at three a.m., which seems to be the most likely time, it must still be one and a half times as far away as the Moon.'

'I suppose so. Which makes it a magnitude fainter than I said. A fifth magnitude star, and that's about the limit you can see in this sort of a sky. You want to either be out in a desert or on a cold frosty night to see fainter stars. Funny that destruction should be coming from Cygnus the Swan, isn't it – like Swan Lake. Only Tchaikovsky was just pretending. Funny how people can write such impressive music when they're only pretending. I suppose they must somehow convince themselves that it's really real. Funny how. . . '

Frances Margaret continued like a child until she realised she'd talked Isaac Newton to sleep. Then she stopped and began to examine the stars more carefully, watching as the clear gaps between the clouds widened to reveal the whole of the sky.

Isaac Newton awoke suddenly. With Frances Margaret almost shouting in his ear he could hardly have done otherwise.

'I think I've got it.'

'What's the time?'

'About two-twenty.'

'Good gracious, was I asleep as long as that?'

'Never mind now. Start up there with the head of the Swan – Deneb. Go up from Deneb a degree or so, and then about four or five degrees eastward. It's the brightest star in that area.'

'But good heavens, it's quite bright. Are you sure?'

'Yes, I've been watching. I didn't want to wake you until I was sure it had moved.'

'You mean in relation to the other stars?'

'Yes. That's good, isn't it?' replied Frances Margaret, trying to keep hysteria out of her voice. 'I mean if it was coming dead at us it wouldn't move at all, would it?'

'No, it wouldn't. What do astronomers call this sort of changing position?'

'Parallax. The parallax is changing as it comes nearer the Earth. Which makes it seem to move with respect to the true stars.'

'Let me see if I can detect any shift.'

Isaac Newton watched steadily for a while and then said:

'You know it *is* brightening. And I think it's moving downwards and towards the east. About equally, I'd say.'

'That's right. It means we're safe, doesn't it? I mean, there must be a sideways motion, which means it can't hit us.'

Frances Margaret's hair was suddenly in his eyes and Isaac Newton realised that she had burst into a flood of silent tears. Unwinding himself from the sleeping bag, he ran his hands through her hair and said:

'It's lucky you were able to solve those quadratic equations.'

After she had recovered and blown her nose and said, 'You must have nerves like an ox,' they lay back to watch, with their heads together on one of the pillows.

'Where d'you think it's going to land?' Frances Margaret asked.

'My geometry really isn't up to it, but I'd say to the north of us, somewhere. If it had moved upwards, I think it would have gone over our heads and landed to the south.'

'Home is to the north.'

'Almost directly to the north. The thing is still thirty degrees or so to the west of the meridian.'

'Yes, but it's moving towards the meridian all the time.'

'We can't tell yet,' said Isaac Newton, trying to keep his voice as calm as possible, conscious that the incoming missile was now brightening still more alarmingly. 'What we *can* say,' he went on, 'is that it's going to go below the horizon somewhere to the north. My feeling is that if it crosses the meridian before it sets, the impact will be in northern Scandinavia.'

'Poor Eriksson, the mad Swede,' Frances Margaret whispered, 'and if it sets to the west it's going to land in Iceland or Greenland or somewhere like that.'

'That's right. We can only watch and wait.'

The wait was not long delayed. After brightening slowly and almost imperceptibly over the hours, half-hours and quarter-hours, changes could now be seen by the minute. The incoming missile became quickly as luminous as the star Sirius. Within twenty seconds more it was as luminous as the planet Venus, and still the brilliant white point of light had not moved in position by more than a few degrees.

'My God, where is it going to end?' exclaimed Frances Margaret.

Ever more frighteningly luminous, the incoming missile soon shone as brightly as a thousand stars of the first magnitude. Then, like Lucifer falling from the heavens, it came down smoothly, deliberately, and almost languidly, to disappear below the northern horizon.

'It fell *exactly* to the north!' shouted Frances Margaret, and then she relapsed immediately into unrestrained sobs. Isaac Newton took her in his arms and said loudly and as steadily as he could:

'It doesn't necessarily mean Britain has been hit; it could be anywhere from Britain right up to the Arctic. We shall know in a minute or two.'

'How?' Frances Margaret asked in a choking voice.

'If it really is home that has been hit, the blast-wave will be here in only a minute or two. If it's farther to the north, the wave will take longer to get here. Really we must get ourselves into the car now, for protection. There's no sense in remaining exposed out here.'

At first deliberately, and then with increasing haste, they wriggled out of the sleeping bags and moved quickly to the car. When they were safely inside, Isaac Newton said:

'I should have thought of it before, but if the impact was as close as Britain we'd surely have had an immediate flash from the blaze of light generated by the impact – through atmospheric scattering, I mean.'

They waited in silence, timing the silence, feeling that as each few seconds passed by without the arrival of any blast-wave they were themselves pushing the region of impact farther and farther to the north. After fifteen minutes had gone, Frances Margaret said:

'Could it have been a miss after all? Perhaps the astronomers had their observations wrong.'

'Or there may have been another change in its path.'

'Done deliberately, perhaps, as a warning.'

'It rather looks like it,' agreed Isaac Newton.

With this thought there was a relaxation of tension which brought them both to the verge of hysteria. The euphoria lasted for several minutes until Frances Margaret said:

'The sky is clouding over.'

They quitted the car again and looked towards the north, where the stars were blotted out in a broad horizontal band. Even as they watched, the broad band became still broader – broader and ever broader until it was no longer a band but a whole hemisphere. All the sky to the north of them was blacked out, while the stars to the south were still shining.

'Good God, it's explosion debris. It must be very high.'

'How d'you know?'

'Because it's soundless. Anything spreading like that in the lower atmosphere would generate a terrific hurricane.'

They continued to watch, now in great awe, as the blackness swept inexorably into the southern sky, until the remaining visible stars shrank to a band in the south, a band that became smaller second by second. As the last patch of sky became covered, total blackness enveloped them. Even though the car was only ten yards away, their blind instinctive search for it quickly became hopeless, until they hit on the idea of clapping with their hands. Using this primitive form of sonar, they at last stumbled onto it.

A rumbling with a sound like distant gunfire started during the drive back to Dampierre. There was no need for them to slip clandestinely into the inn, for the whole town was afoot, out in the lit streets, listening to the rumbling thunder from the north, which continued long after Isaac Newton and Frances Margaret had once again reached the bedroom in the inn.

Chapter 73

There was no dawn the following morning. It wasn't until clocks showed three hours after what should have been dawn that at last a faint ominous light percolated through to ground level. And by mid-afternoon even this faint light was gone again, so that if it hadn't been for artificial lighting the heavily populated regions of Europe, North America and the Soviet Union would, by 3.30 p.m., have been plunged into total darkness, a situation familiar to people who spend the winter months in Arctic regions. For all practical purposes the Sun had gone as it does throughout an Arctic winter.

Most people began the new phase of their lives with the belief that it was Comet Halley itself which had crashed its way into the Earth. Repeated statements to the contrary on television and radio eventually corrected this mistake, however, so permitting a new and more likely belief to emerge: namely, that the missile which hit the Earth had been guided by Comet Halley. Isaac Newton refused to comment on this matter, although he was repeatedly asked about it. He simply said that people must draw their own conclusions. This saved him a lot of trouble because, of course, people draw their own conclusions anyway.

Conclusions were actually not particularly difficult to draw, if one took into account the place where the missile actually landed. The

Arctic basin is itself shaped like a very large crater, with its main exit channel between Greenland and Norway, the other much smaller exit being through the Bering Straits between Siberia and Alaska. As craters often do, the Arctic basin had filled with water which had become frozen to a depth of about a hundred metres: not a smooth level plain of ice like a frozen lake, but an abominable jumble of icebergs which stuck together in winter and came apart in summer, an entirely impossible region in which to live, even for the hardiest eskimo. It was into this hell of ice that the incoming missile had fallen. As reports from seismographs throughout the world were given a preliminary analysis on the day following the impact, it quickly became apparent that the missile must have hit close to the North Pole. Then, as records were analysed with greater and greater precision, the amazing fact emerged that the missile had hit exactly at the North Pole. Incredible shooting, as people said.

This fantastic accuracy would surely have been impressive enough as a demonstration of the strength of what had become widely known as the third superpower. Yet in addition there was the remarkable fact to be noticed that the missile had hit the Earth at a place where the impact resulted in not a single death. No infrequent explorer happened to be abroad in the wilderness of polar ice at the time; nor had there been military submarines in the clear water below the ice – or at least nothing was ever admitted if there were.

Military nations had from time immemorial sought to demonstrate their power by killing people. The irony of the present situation was that the world turned out to be much more impressed by the opposite – by the third superpower having contrived to provide such a remarkable demonstration of strength without killing anybody. This was far more impressive than if the expected eighty millions had been destroyed. It was as if a grandmaster at chess had brought off a subtly conceived checkmate instead of butchering every piece on the board.

Vast quantities of water had been thrown out in all directions from the whole surface of the Arctic Ocean, especially from regions close to the North Pole. The latter had no angular momentum, as scientists said, and because of this the water, spreading itself out in the high atmosphere at heights above a hundred kilometres, did not experience what scientists call the Coriolis force. In plain language, this meant that the water, which soon condensed back from vapour into ice crystals, was shot out from the Pole along lines of longitude, rather like the rays which spread out from well-known craters on the Moon. It was this process which Isaac Newton and Frances Haroldsen had seen blot out the stars. And it was this process that was responsible for the inability of sunlight to penetrate more than fractionally to ground level.

There was another lucky aspect to the situation. Unlike volcanic dust, which does not evaporate and may take years to settle out of the high atmosphere, the crystals of ice could evaporate. Indeed, as they fell back to the top of the stratosphere in ensuing days there was sufficient evaporation for enough sunlight to penetrate to the ground for people to get around generally, although through the winter to come the days were to be lit no more strongly than on a dark and lowering landscape. It would not be until the late months of the following spring that the people in northern latitudes would again see the Sun itself.

The energy dumped instantly into the Arctic Ocean was enormous by human standards. It exceeded the energy consumed by the human species throughout the whole of history. It even came close to melting the oceanic ice, the whole of the monstrous conglomerate of icebergs covering an area of a million square miles. Not quite, however; circumstances had another trick to play besides a direct melting of the ice. The energy was more than sufficient to generate immense currents into and out of the Arctic Ocean, currents which swept the iceberg conglomerate southward, mostly through the channel between Greenland and Scandinavia. Such an effect occurs normally throughout the northern summer, but on a comparatively tiny scale. Now it occurred on a huge scale. Icebergs with a combined area of a million square miles poured southward into the Atlantic Ocean, where they encountered water that had just been heated to a maximum throughout the northern summer. All these southward-moving bergs were doomed to melt gradually away. The bigger ones would survive through the coming northern winter and penetrate extensively to the south of Britain, threatening shipping even as far as the tropics. Nevertheless, it was only a question of time – months, in fact – before every berg would be denuded, inch by inch, until only liquid water remained.

As the surface layer of ice was thus skimmed away from the Arctic Ocean, as a person might skim a layer of algae from the surface of a green pond, liquid water welled up from below, and a transformation of enormous and long-lasting significance for the whole Earth had been achieved. It was the opinion of scientists that the Arctic Ocean became frozen over about a million and a half years ago, after which the blocking effect on the free movement of surface water exercised a trigger effect on climate throughout the whole northern hemisphere, and, to an extent, throughout the whole world.

With the surface ice now in the process of disappearing, in only a few years the Mediterranean climate of southern France would move northward to southern England. The wheat-growing prairies of Canada would extend much further to the north, and Siberia would at last become a viable agricultural prospect.

On a time-scale of centuries, the vast icecap of Greenland would gradually melt away, revealing a new continent shaped rather like a saucer, with high mountains around the rim and a habitable bowl in its interior. There would also be some shrinkage of the still vaster ice-fields and glaciers of Antarctica, which together with the melting of the Greenland ice would raise sea-level everywhere by about a hundred feet. This further melting would force people to move many of the largest cities throughout the world to higher ground, or to build dykes to protect them. This would happen over the centuries, however, not all in a moment. In sum then, no generation down the centuries could avoid a keen awareness of what happened during the approach of Comet Halley in 1986, because the consequences of it would be ever-present with each generation. Indeed, the details of what happened during the approach of Comet Halley would be remembered long after the word superpower had ceased to have any current meaning. Such was to be the long-term historic outcome of all these events.

Chapter 74

It seemed a simple and harmless decision at the time they made it, and they could hardly have foreseen the events that were to follow. In keeping with the bride's family tradition, Frances Margaret and Isaac Newton decided to marry in the church at Outerthwaite, the little town nearest to the small valley where the bride's family had lived for so long, close by the better-known valley of the Duddon. They did not marry immediately, but waited until the Sun shone brightly again. Kurt Waldheim, who was to be best man, set himself to determine the precise date of the wedding by means of extensive computer calculations of considerable difficulty – calculations of the time required for the cloud of ice crystals in the high atmosphere to evaporate away. Then three weeks were added to permit the short-stemmed wild daffodils which bloom in immense profusion throughout the whole Broughton district to push their way in triumph through the snowdrifts of a dark and formidable winter. This put the date of the wedding in late May. There it was fixed for sure.

The first move towards stirring up what was supposed to be a family gathering came from Frances Margaret's two brothers, both officers in the Royal Navy. They decided to grace the event with a contingent of their messmates, which in view of the exalted one-time naval status of their father, Vice-Admiral Sir James Haroldsen, was seen officially as appropriate. It was expected there would also be a small number of political dignitaries, but in a strictly private capacity which it was hoped would escape the attention of the media. To no avail, however, for in mid-January the Russians suddenly announced that they would be sending a delegation, so highly was the matter rated in the Soviet Union, where Politburo members had staged a seemingly miraculous recovery from the mad itch, dating, it was noticed, from the moment of Isaac Newton's presentation to the international assembly in Versailles.

The Russian intervention put the occasion immediately into a very different light, for if the Soviets were to be represented, so must other nations, especially nations in Europe and North America. In effect, events concerning Comet Halley were beginning already to assume a legendary quality. From a small family event, the wedding had thus escalated almost into a state occasion, with the concept of the naval guard now being changed from a boisterous contribution to a stiff formality in which higher-ranking officers became involved.

The day of the wedding dawned soft and misty with, it seemed, rainbows everywhere. Arriving early at the church, Isaac Newton and his best man found it to have been decorated with birch boughs, and of course with large bouquets of the short-stemmed daffodils.

Kurt Waldheim's memories rushed back to his own marriage, not so long ago. This church at Outerthwaite had been standing just the way it was now for many years. Generation after generation of the local population had been christened here, had been married and had died, accompanied by ceremonies of very different kinds, generation after generation going back in time more than half-way to the days when his own people had emigrated from the German plain and its northerly borders. The way the media viewed time – down to the last minute and second – that was ages distant, but viewed in comparison to the years themselves, measured by the movement of the Earth around the Sun, it was really very recent.

Isaac Newton's thoughts were on his parents, sitting immediately behind him in the front row of the assembled congregation. It was a different world for them, this green Lakeland valley, rising in its length from pastures to rocky, snow-covered heights. Yet it was not so difficult to exchange the tilled red soil of Devon for the stockman's grassy hillsides as it would have been to transport themselves into city life. They were work-worn now, as all farming people become in their sixties, but with the quiet triumph over life of those who live close to planet Earth itself. Isaac Newton had often wondered why his parents had chosen to christen him the way they did. Probably it was to do with something they had seen or read. For really, you couldn't christen a child Isaac Newton any more than you could christen a child William Shakespeare.

The bride arrived on her father's arm. As they walked up the aisle, Frances Margaret wondered why the ceremony had come to seem important to her, when to be frank about it she'd already been living as married for the past two years. It had to do with being born with twelve toes, she decided, with solving quadratic equations or whatever at the age of ten or eleven. People who were born with twelve toes were forced out into the world to join other people with twelve toes. They formed a community which overcame local prejudices, that crossed races and creeds, a powerful community which had ultimately accumulated sufficient knowledge to flash out from the Earth itself to join a still larger universe. Yet it wasn't a community that was properly self-maintaining. It did not reproduce itself from generation to generation. Without its roots in the green valleys and the red soils it would soon decay and be gone. It was because of those roots that the ceremony was important.

The ceremony itself was brief. As Frances Margaret and Isaac Newton walked the short distance from the altar to the church door they were at last aware of the congregation itself. Besides their respective families there was the Project Halley Board and members of the Cavendish Laboratory staff. But there were others they had not expected. Frances Margaret could see the dark American woman with the dimples who could never refrain from laughing whenever Frances Margaret appeared. There was Dave Eckstein, who had played a significant role at a critical juncture, and his wife. There was the same Russian who had headed the Soviet delegation at the Palace of Versailles, a man with an enormous bellow of a laugh who had apparently been moved up in the Politburo ranking to the position of Number Seven.

Isaac Newton picked out John Jocelyn Scuby. Another surprise was Alan Bristow from *Nature*. Eriksson was also there. Because of his

height he could hardly have been missed the way John Jocelyn Scuby
might have been missed. Isaac Newton caught Eriksson's eye as he
passed him in the aisle, and the memory of how Eriksson had returned
the code flooded back to him.

As they came out of the church there was a formal naval guard,
sharp and precise to the last detail. Isaac Newton remembered how at
one stage a guard had been greatly needed at the Lab, only it had been
provided by the army on that occasion not the navy. So long as there
was *esprit de corps* it really was the same thing, he decided.

After the long days in which time had dragged, it now raced.
Suddenly Isaac Newton found himself speaking at the end of the
wedding breakfast. It was a duty he had half-dreaded, but somehow it
passed almost effortlessly. The Prime Minister replied for the guests, as
usual without a word out of place.

A large barn had been cleared for dancing in the evening. Eriksson
had brought a small party from Sweden, the girls remarkably like
Frances Margaret in appearance, just as Eriksson had said. The party
were experts in barn dancing, the men of the up-to-the-rafters variety.
This was the cue for the Russian *trepak* dancers who had been sent to
show their strength of leg – but by going down to the floor instead of
up to the rafters. It was also the cue for Russian bureaucracy to show
its chronic inability to manage anything properly. Musicians to
accompany the *trepak* dancers had been inadvertently omitted in the
preparation of travel papers. It was, in this impasse, no surprise that
the Master of Trinity proved himself an expert with the accordian. Just
one of the useful little things he'd learnt in his old theatre days, he told
the mob once the *trepak* dancers were fully exhausted, for unlike the
usual self-effacing musicians who stand in the background, the Master
of Trinity stood out in front of the dancers, roaring them on to
destruction in his big voice. In fact, he roared everybody on to
destruction, a process in which the Royal Navy was not to be outdone.

Chapter 75

As the 'plane lifted out of Manchester Airport and headed south to Greece, Frances Margaret and Isaac Newton both lay back in their seats with eyes closed, at first thankful that it was all over. Vivid in their minds were the faces of those who had waved them off – the Waldheims, Mrs Gunter from Cambridge, the Master, the Chancellor, the foreign dignitaries, their own families. After living on his nerves over the past few days, days in which he almost counted off every hour that must elapse before the moment of release, Isaac Newton suddenly felt a deep sadness. Now it was indeed all over, he realised belatedly that no power on Earth could bring these last days back again. Although events were still close and vivid, only a few hours, or even minutes away from the last farewells, as each further day passed by the distance in time would increase, memories would gradually become less distinct, and in the end there would only be the memories of a few old folk, a grey finish to what had been so vibrantly full-blooded in the brief span of its existence.

The events of the past two years would likewise march away in time, eventually to become a fable as the Earth emerged from obscurity to become the communication centre of the solar system. After the particularly dramatic events which followed Isaac Newton's presentation at the Versailles Summit, there could now be no question that his vision of the vast Cometary Network would indeed come to pass. Not that its doing so would put an end to human rivalries. There would be rivalries over electronic systems, over the siting of equipment, over manufacturing contracts. The pushing and shoving would go on just as endlessly as before, but in a new direction.

'When I was a boy,' Isaac Newton said to Frances Margaret, 'I used to go on holiday to a place in Cornwall. There's a spot where you can get down cliffs to within about fifty feet of the sea. As long as you arrive when the tide is at the right level, you'll find a couple of oyster catchers always perched on the same rock, because with the tide at that level there's a pool among the rocks where crustaceans, or whatever they eat, tend to be washed up. I was able to make a lot of interesting deductions from that spot.'

'Such as what?'

'Well, since my observations extended over an interval much longer than the life of an individual bird, I decided that particular spot on that particular rock must be handed down from generation to generation, just as a human business is passed from father to son.'

'Very interesting I'm sure.'

'Perhaps it was the great-great-great-grandfather of the present generation of oyster catchers who first found it. A business of well-established antiquity, as one might say.'

'As one might say,' Frances Margaret echoed.

'Well, when I watched the foaming pools among the tangle of rocks, I used to think to myself how very like human life it all was – so much rushing back and forth, so much seething activity, with every little splash among the rocks competing for your notice. Yet nothing ever came to anything, except of course for the oyster catchers. Every now and then an unusually high wave came roaring in. I used to say to myself, "Here comes a real whopper." But it simply dashed itself to smithereens on the rocks. There was a huge splash for a few seconds, but in a minute it was all gone. Without any trace remaining, just like the world of men. Just like Alexander. Just like Napoleon.'

It was at this point in its journey south that the 'plane came into clear sunlight, making them both realise that the Sun which had shone over Morecambe Bay was still partially obscured by high cloud in the stratosphere. It had been but a ghost of the true Sun, which appeared at last as they crossed the Carpathian Mountains.

'Really, we've been fantastically lucky to have taken a step which isn't going to be forgotten, even if it eventually becomes legend, and ultimately myth.'

'We should feel pretty good,' Frances Margaret agreed.

'To be members of a species which has made it,' Isaac Newton continued in the same quiet voice. 'You know, I don't think there was much time left for us. The window of opportunity was very narrow. A century ago our technology wouldn't have been capable of even understanding the opportunity. A century from now it would all have been over. If we hadn't seized the chance we'd have been headed for self-destruction. It's almost as if we're pre-programmed either to succeed quickly or to self-destruct. The dawn must come swiftly. That seems to be the law.'